RAINN ON FIRE

RAINN ON FIRE

An Enchanted Wood Novel

Book One

Jason Stempin

Cover design: Todd Stempin
Editor: Bruce Shuman

ISBN: 979-8-9896103-1-0

Nostalgica Books

First Edition

Sometimes I yearn for access to a life in, say, the nineteenth century. My parents are my closest connection to previous lifetimes, and I am eternally grateful for all their love, guidance, and support in this lifetime. Thus, this book is dedicated to my mom and dad.

Prior to the publication of this novel, my dad passed away, moved on to another sphere of existence; he had seen enough of Earth. But I know he's currently watching, listening, and smiling. My mom, with unwavering love and support, has been rooting me on, for eons, to get this book finished.

My son, too, has been instrumental in filling me with unconditional love and encouragement to keep going.

Special thanks go out to my brother for his dedicated creativity in crafting the book cover design, and he knows how to me laugh.

Kudos to my sister for gracing my life with her progressive-California vibe. And a unique shout-out to my elder brother, who passed away in 2014. He was an active, positive role model and peace-bringing giver of laughter and love. He once said, "Happiness is a choice. Choose to be happy!"

With happiness comes love. LOVE IS what brings out the creative fire within each of them.

Zane first discovered he talked in his sleep in algebra class. Solving linear equations, according to Zane, should be listed as a narcotic. Downright dangerous to his health.

Sleep-talking, however, was livelier than math. Hell, cleaning cat litter was more interesting than balancing mathematical equations.

"I'm an avid sleep-talker. Probably the best in town," he offered to his math teacher when he was caught doing it the previous week. He claimed to have trophies at home and would love to show them to his teacher sometime.

His math teacher gave him a slate-flattened stare, arched an eyebrow, as if not impressed by his monkey-boy mockery.

Today, during another sleep-talking episode in class, Zane stood up, stabbed a finger at a metal filing cabinet and blurted out, "Who's that? Look. There she goes. Someone stop 'er!"

A soft-haired, golden lady drew a bolt of lightning into her woolen cloak, turned, and stared at him with bright eyes. Even with her hood drawn up, her eyes flashed at him. Gemstone-blue twin flames. Then she darted out of the classroom, disappearing down the corridor of Math Path, the hallway for math courses at Anklesteam High School.

"She's running away!" Zane hollered. "Someone stop 'er."

Zane thought of rushing into the hall and pulling the fire alarm. But he just stood next to his chair, mouth hanging open. What was he supposed to do if no one else could see her?

"Unbelievable," he muttered. "You people are un-flipping believable."

Why didn't anyone see her? She was in the classroom, in full blooming color. It made no sense to Zane. Neither did algebra.

"Yes, you are. You're an unbelievable idiot," uttered a student with a silver hooped snake piercing her nose. Or was it a barbed fishhook?

Students snickered; others grumbled. Two teens in the back row pulled up the collars of bleached sleeveless jean jackets and whispered, "Hallucinatory Hall Monitor's at it again."

One thing was certain: when Zane performed, people responded.

Zane never liked his nickname: Hallucinatory Hall Monitor. It was like a bad tattoo on his neck: always there, always within reach, but just out of sight. Students and staff were just jealous because the voices talked to him. Was it his fault he could see things that others couldn't?

Get some glasses, people, he thought. *Open your eyes. Open your true self. Get past the mindless drivel keeping you from what's really out there.* Oh, if only someone would listen to him!

Something about that gold woman had his undivided attention, which was saying something since he was ADHD. Yep, being distracted was a skill he had mastered. But this hooded woman in his math class piqued his curiosity. Imposing, elusive, striking.

Whenever she appeared, his mind became a brushfire of hot slippery images. Then 'POOF' she would vanish. He tried to recall her beautiful features: the line of her face, the brightness of her eyes half hidden in that cloak, but the more he thought of her, the less he recalled. It was as if his own mind was frantically drawing a pencil sketch of her, and then it came in with a fat pink eraser, leaving dark eraser dribbles on the now-gray canvas of his mind.

Trying to recall a sleep-talking episode was like trying to remember the details of a dream.

Zane stirred from his stupor, but only because his teacher, in a thunderous tone, had called out his name, and for an old lady, she could really howl. He sighed and returned to his seat. His hands felt warm and tingly. He turned them over and stared at them as if he had stolen them and was trying them out for the first time.

It seemed so real. That vision. That woman. Was it another full-blown daydreaming episode or another encounter from a visitor from an alternate reality? Seemed like the latter. Again.

Uh, oh. Here she comes.

A student leaned over and whispered to Zane, "It's chilly outside. Don't forget your jacket—your strait-jacket."

Zane sank in his seat. His algebra teacher, Old Lady Camelback, glared at him. She was a lanky, hunchbacked woman who was getting on in years. Sarcastic teens were something she'd rather see on a skewer. She was a woman who loved numbers, loved them to death. Zane had a few fateful wishes of his own for numbers and equations.

"Please, Zane," she said, "if you're done with your staged theatrics, tell us the significance of our current math postulate. From Chapter Twelve. It'll be on the final."

Postulate? How 'bout your posture, your bumpy old leather bag?

Old Lady Camelback, as she was referred to by the student body, earned her nickname by posture alone. No one called her that to her face, but it was a name that stuck. Like a dark spell. Long silver hair spun into a tall bun with one of those funny-looking chopsticks stabbed through its heart. The stick gleamed in the overhead lights. Her hunched shoulders were almost too painful to watch.

She smoothed out her plaid skirt, clasped with an oversized gold safety pin, with the sweep of a wrinkled hand. A gray

V-neck sweater fit tight around her frame. Pantyhose and black buckle-strap ankle boots completed her outfit. She flared her nostrils, allowing a miscreant nose hair to curl around it, like a spider planning its exit. Camelback tapped her foot insistently on the floor. Zane watched that shoe in action, refusing to make eye contact because her coffee breath was clouding his vision.

"Well?" she asked hoarsely, pursing thin lips.

Zane leaned back to distance himself, just enough to breathe without gagging. *You have no idea what's keeping me up at night, Camelback. I've got an imaginary voice speaking in my head. Her name's Esmeralda. You know her? Didn't think so. I'm a bit sidetracked. Math is the last thing I'm thinking about.*

"Like I said…I talk in my sleep. Uh, sorry." Although he wasn't.

He started to doodle nervously on his paper, drawing a picture of a pair of Egyptian eyes, a clone of Cleopatra's.

Old Lady Camelback cleared her throat and did her best to stand upright, which looked about as easy as straightening the curves in a rollercoaster.

"I hope you all understand how easy you've got it," she professed in a raspy tone, as if a handful of pebbles rattled around in her throat. Her eyes drummed across the front row of laptops, a mixed look of distaste and envy filling her frumpy face. She folded her arms across her chest and scanned the class, making sure all eyes were on her.

"Slackers," she went on to say," bog down the learning process. Goes against *my* code of conduct. We must keep pace with the curriculum. Sleeping in class and causing disruptions results in repercussions. Simple-minded actions deserve simpleminded consequences." She twirled around. "And what would that be?"

Silence from the gallery.

"Detention," Camelback spiked gravely and slid a pencil behind her ear. "I remember teaching before the advent of computers. Yes." She raised her finger as if signaling 'Eureka!' "A time when the Dewey Decimal system and library card catalogs were the only search engines out there. No such thing as Facebooking or Googling Gaggling. Such mindless drivel," she scoffed.

Most students just stared at her as she regurgitated her take on detention. They had heard this speech before.

"Detention's nothing more than a slap in the face, but an effective slap in the face. Students, if you truly call yourself students, should spend more time in the library where it's quiet and one can concentrate."

Zane wondered if this guy called Dewey was responsible for inventing the decimal point in mathematics. Never heard of the scoundrel.

Zane didn't want another detention, but it was too late. Old Lady Camelback was already filling out a detention slip.

His mind began to wander, thinking of summer. Summer meant hanging out with friends, swimming in the local lagoon, diving off rocky cliffs, and plunging into river-fed tide pools. College was next fall, and he hoped for one last summer in the wilderness. But the voice of that girl who talked to him in his thoughts—that was his number one priority. He had no one to talk to about it. They would just think he was nuts and send him to a therapist for some 'talk' therapy. Talk therapy was a waste of time. He had more than enough conversations with this Esmeralda chick to fill him with conversations. Why share it with a therapist who would not believe him?

Zane rifled his eyes across his open textbook, hoping to appear to be paying attention. He could feel the teacher's eyes boring a hole into his skull. He peered up through curly bangs falling over his eyes as Camelback scrawled an equation on the board. She underscored it twice.

"This is review," she reminded the class, speaking as if she had something else on her mind. She trolled up the aisle, horseshoed her way around Zane, and returned to the digital projector.

Zane sighed, feeling his nerves stiffen. "By the might of Zeus, give me some energy. I'm so damn tired," he said, not caring if anyone heard him. Senioritis had set in sometime back in February. "Esmeralda, why don't you make yourself visible? School is boring."

"Who're you talking to?" asked a classmate, brushing back blonde bangs covering half her face. "Who's Esmeralda?"

Suddenly, he felt a twittering sensation in his head. Sound intensified. Everything around him, every action, every noise in the classroom was an exact replica of events that had transpired just seconds ago, and it was happening all over again. Déjà vu. The way the rain pelted off the window and streaked the glass pane, the underwater sound of the marker clanging in the gutter beneath the whiteboard. This had just happened seconds ago and was happening all over again. Right now.

No one else seemed to notice the amplified sounds in the air. Even the crinkle of someone's loose-leaf paper was magnified, echoing in Zane's ear. He stared off, fumbled a hand into his backpack, and pulled out a pencil before realizing he already had one in his hand.

He then seemed to snap out of it. This mysterious sensation that washed over him faded away. Gone. Dirtied his mind with sticky images of darkness and the unknown.

He sank his chin back onto his sleepy arm. Why was it so easy to drift off at school? Yet late at night, at home, under a bright-eyed starry sky, he seemed to be jacked up on some new bio-fueled save-the-earth blend of honey, electricity, and corn. Revved up and ready to go.

He didn't care much about saving Mother Earth. He closed his eyes. Nap time…

An obnoxious yet familiar buzzing sound woke him—the school bell. He sat bolt upright and sent a calculator spinning off his desk and across the tile floor, an imprint of his beaded amber bracelet tattooed to his forehead. Two girls dressed in tight denim jeans torn along the pant leg—as if they were attacked by a dragon on the way to school—staggered past him, carefully stepping over his fallen calculator. No one thought to pick it up.

Zane sat on a blue-stitched Afghan at the foot of his bed, opened his Algebra book, and smoothed out his wrinkled note sheet. Oddly, the book felt warm, as if baked in an oven. He ran his fingers along the spine. It hummed under the pads of his fingertips. He smiled, enjoying this sensation. Until he heard a voice call out to him. He looked up. No one else was in his room. Then, from inside his closet, the voice said, "Ready to climb a tree and reconnect with the real you?"

A silvery sensation rolled through his shoulders, and he studied the closet, narrowing his vision to the accordion doors. A knocking came from inside it. Zane, then, figured his sister was hiding inside, playing a joke on him, or maybe his laptop was logged onto a website playing a looped pop-up ad. His eyes spotted his computer sitting quietly on his cluttered desk, buried beneath a stack of comic books.

The voice spoke again. "I said, time to climb a tree. You do love trees, yes?"

"Yes," Zane found himself saying to the closet.

The voice was scratchy. Ancient. Sounded like an old man.

Zane cringed, thinking back to Esmerelda's whispering voices. But this was far from a woman's voice, and it wasn't speaking in his head.

Please tell me this is my imagination.

Box springs under his mattress creaked as he stood up. He tiptoed to the closet and slid the wood-paneled door open. He sucked in a breath of air and froze.

An old man was standing there. Glowing. Silvery-blue. Zane stumbled backward and fell onto his bed.

This closet intruder folded his arms across his chest and stepped into a square of sunlight that bled right through him.
The man was less than paper thin. Didn't even leave a shadow.

He spoke in a calm tone, "Lad, I'll ask you one more time: ready to climb a tree?"

Zane's heart raced; he fumbled with his thoughts, uncertain what to do.

"What—who are you? What're you talking about?" Zane stifled a frown and gazed into the man's dark eyes. "How'd you get in here?"

"The front door," he said in a mild, good-natured tone. He spun on his heels and turned his back to Zane, twirling with the fluidity of the wind changing direction. A remarkable maneuver for someone so old. He splayed his fingers and inspected his fingernails. "Don't be frightened. I've been watching you." Gee— that made Zane feel so much better. Was this guy stalking him? Zane placed a hand over his mouth. A staring contest ensued.

He had been hoping for a normal day. Nothing normal about this. Zane began spitting tiny half-moon fingernail bits onto the carpet. Was he going to be mugged in his own bedroom?

"Allow me to introduce myself. Name's Stanley. I'm your great uncle. Great Uncle Stanley." He strode across the bedroom, pausing to dust the stiff shoulder pads of his brown tweed blazer. "Hope I didn't spook you. Boo." He smiled, revealing nice white teeth.

A warm buzz cycled through the air; Zane, for a moment, was able to swallow and breathe again.

Great Uncle Stanley had snow-white hair. Thick and wavy. Pencil-thin peppered mustache. He moved across the shag rug with purpose. Seemed to hover inches above the carpet. He was all aglow—literally. He smoothed out a few wrinkles in the sleeve of his finely stitched jacket.

"You heard me, lad.," he croaked. "Time to leave this joint."

Zane said nothing.

The man called Stanley chuckled. "We've been watching you. Pay attention. It may be a real lifesaver for you one day soon."

"Who are you? You're…oh shit, I can see right through you." The intruder wavered and solidified again. "The hell's going' on? You were transparent as all get-out for a second. You a ghost or something? An angel?"

Zane was intrigued by the notion of ghosts and haunted basements, but it did not mean he wanted one haunting his bedroom.

The old man laughed. "Not an angel. Nope."

Zane did not have a violent streak in him. Hated guns, but now would be a good time to have a crossbow and bolt stowed under the bed.

A silvery-blue sepia tint outlined Stanley's head and hands. Navy-green slacks and a pair of thick-soled Doc Martins complemented his outfit. For a second, Stanley looked transparent.

Zane could see right through him. But then he would solidify. Glowing.

Great Uncle Stanley claimed: "I'm a ghost. Can't you tell?" He spun on one heel and wiggled his hips with as much spunk as a senior citizen after one too many vodka-and-tonics. Stanley looked at his reflection in the bedroom window, adjusted his yellow bow tie, and patted his chin with the backside of his hand, ironing out the flabby flesh that hung there. "I hope you've been in contact with Esmeralda. She's been on your case."

On my case? What did that mean? How did he know Esmeralda?

Zane's eyes widened like twin cannonballs, and it felt as if he'd been hit with a bomb. He had not shared any of his personal, seemingly telepathic conversations between him and Esmeralda.

"You know her? Wait. Who the hell are you?" This had to be some sort of trick.

"Esmeralda and I are on the same team. Takes a village to run an operation." He wagged his eyebrows and his hands disappeared into his blazer pockets.

The front door clicked open and closed. A moment later, his sister, Rainn, strolled down the hall, passing his room. Zane's eyes volleyed from Stanley to the hallway and back to Stanley. He remained seated on the edge of his bed and called out, "Hey Rainn…what's up?"

"Uh. A few clouds. Some birds. Dust mites," Rainn said from down the hall, lacking any semblance of enthusiasm. "Come in here a minute, will ya?" "Why? I'm busy," she grumbled.

The sound of her backpack thumped onto the floor. Zane could hear his sister's TV monitor click on and the sound of *Resident Evil Village* cueing up on her Xbox.

"Rainn? Please." He looked at Stanley. "It's an emergency," he begged.

Rainn muttered something incomprehensible and poked her head into Zane's room. "What?" she said flatly, her long bangs hanging over half of her face.

Zane darted his eyes in Stanley's direction, then pointed with his chin at the ghost.

Rainn stared at her brother. "What? What is it?" she asked, sounding thoroughly bothered.

"Don't you see 'im?"

Rainn looked around. "See who?"

Stanley shrugged, placing his hands on hips. "You didn't let me finish. No one else can see or hear me. At least not here. Consider yourself lucky, Zane."

"Can't—don't you hear that?" Zane pleaded to his sister, all the while thinking: *How does this old man know my name?*

"Don't hear a thing. Having a coronary about finals, are you?" Rainn waved a hand at him and rolled her eyes. "When the next emergency happens," she stared at him, "text me."

Zane tried to get his mind off seeing Great Uncle Stanley, but that was not going to happen. A ghost? Really? Well, he didn't really have another choice but to believe. He knew what he saw, and what he heard. But what really bothered him was this: the old ghost knew about him and Esmeralda? *I guess that means Esmeralda was not my imagination creating theatre.*

He went for a bike ride in the woods. This quiet, unblemished wilderness borough, better known as his hideaway, was a great place to release tension mounting in his mind.

Zane leaned his bike against a wide-bellied oak tree.

Roots snaked around tall ferns and wildflowers and fuzzy weeds.

He started his ascent, monkeying his way up the trunk with the grace of Tarzan's unknown brother, digging his boots into notches in the trunk, grabbing branches that seemed to take him by the hand and hoist him higher into the canopy. Ground zero disappeared below him as he traversed into the crown. Up here, a good fifty feet off the ground, he sat on a branch and stared up at the slippery expanse of green leafy sky, legs dangling.

"Love it up here," he said, inhaling that tall-treed aroma.

A large shadow loomed overhead. He knew what it was: his destination, the underbelly of his handcrafted treehouse.

His secret entrance, fit with a porthole doorway, creaked open on rusty hinges; the door happened to be his idea. He was proud of his novice attempts at carpentry. Just like his dad, Zane enjoyed messing about with wood projects. This treehouse was his ultimate creation, shaping something out of scraps in the garage.

Zane pulled himself in through the narrow, round doorway. Wiped dirt from his hands onto his T-shirt and gazed into the narrow-peaked ceiling, home to a few spiders who had taken up residency in corner penthouse estates. A small oak desk and highbacked bamboo chair fitted with a faded yellow pillow decorated in dragonflies lay in one corner: his favorite—and only—seat of reflection. Several dirty dishes and a fork lay in a bowl where flies lazily buzzed.

Before he could think another thought, something new in the room captured his attention: a dollhouse with a drawbridge carved of creamy mahogany sat on top of a red velvet cloth, sunlight from the window massaging its tiny silver-buckled drawbridge.

Where did that come from? No one else had ever been up here, not that he knew.

A rumbling sound got his attention. He made his way to the window with one eye on that mahogany structure. The clip-clop of hooves echoed through the woods, a wooden coach led by a two-horse team of Percherons flitting in and out of sight through the mass of trees. They were black muscular steeds dusted in powdery white with vanilla manes.

Zane loved horses but was really wowed by the sight of this antique coach constructed of dark teakwood. It looked to have come straight out of a museum.

The coach rolled to a halt, and the driver lifted his floppy leather hat and let it hang off his back on a drawstring. He ran a hand over his bald head and made his way to the rear of the coach, where he opened a canvas flap and began rummaging through a wooden chest studded in brass. He pulled out a scroll and unrolled it. Zane squinted but was too far away to make out what the writing said.

The man spun round, quickly as a whip, and glanced skyward. Zane ducked, but figured there was no way the man could see him up here with the treehouse hidden amid a maze of leafy branches. Zane peeked over the windowsill, doing his best to play sniper, sans rifle.

The man rolled up the scroll and shouted, "Hey, tree man. Got a sec?"

Zane cringed. *Tree man?*

No way. He sees me? Who is that? Didn't look or sound like his dead Great Uncle Stanley.

Zane slid under the windowsill with his back to the wall, heart pounding.

Horses whinnied. A moment of silence sighed in his ear.

Another moment went TICK and then TOCK.

A gentle tapping came to his porthole door. Zane's eyes got big, and he held his breath, as if that would scare off this strange treehouse visitor.

A voice called out, "Hello. Anyone home?" Sounded like the man from down below, voice raspy as rust.

Zane took a slow breath.

The hinge slid open.

The porthole lifted.

"Hello?" called out the voice again.

Then, a ringed hand poked through the hole and waved at Zane.

Zane said to the hand: "Can I…help you?"

A hairless head poked up through the opening. He grinned at Zane, revealing a gold eyetooth, and lifted his eyebrows. "Hope I'm not intruding."

What a stupid question. Course you're intruding, you weird old freak. You're an idiot! You need to leave. Now!

But he said none of this; Zane decided now was not the time to retaliate with rude comments, but this fool might be a thief. Shit, he might be a murderer.

Zane gave the thin old man another glance; if push came to shove, he could take him down.

Take me down where, chimed a slick old voice in his thoughts, speaking right between his ears.

The hell?

Zane shook this comment off. He was stressed. Just a trick of the mind.

He could rush at him, tackle him to the ground. But then what? If he had reacted quicker, he could have slammed the porthole door on his hand. Game over.

He chose a more assertive and less aggressive tactic. This would come in handy, seeing as he failed to slam the porthole on his invasive hand.

"Can I help you?" Zane repeated, doing his best to hide his shock. "Why're you here? I've got nothing to sell." What a dumb thing to say.

Zane opened his mouth as if to speak.

The man's eyes sparkled.

"Help? Not me. Nothing could be further from the truth, my boy. I'm here to help *you*," he finished with a twinkle in his voice.

No reply from Zane.

"Might I come in, then?" he asked, his head and shoulders now sticking through the opening.

"Uh, you already are in." *What planet did this guy fall off?*

Zane continued to eye the stranger with caution. "Not much room up here." *In other words: you're not invited. Get the hell out.* "Join me down on the forest floor then, just for a moment. Don't think of me as a stranger. I'm here with a gift."

Zane made a funny face, twisting up his lower lip. This guy was up to something, and Zane was not liking the vibe in his normally peaceful treehouse.

Esmeralda's voice called out in his head. *Gee, Einstein, whatever gave you that idea?*

Esmeralda? Do you know this guy? Zane found himself responding with psychic clarity. *Who climbs up an old tree and knocks on my tree house door?*

No reply from the phantom voice of Esmeralda.

"Don't be alarmed," the man continued. Just his head was sticking through the opening of the floor. Then he began drumming his fingers on a creaky floorboard and giving Zane's secret hideaway the once-over. "I know what you're thinking."

This guy did not have a clue. "I'm thinking you're starting to freak me out. All I can see is your head, but that's far enough, thank you very much. Dude, what do you want?"

The man set his chin on the floor. "I can sense things." He sighed. "I sense I'm frightening you…dude." That was the first sensible thing he had said.

"I'm not frightened," Zane lied.

The intruder pressed his hands on the floor and pushed himself up, now standing in the tree house. Exceedingly tall. Lanky frame. Wide-shelved shoulders. Head nearly touched the ceiling. He hadn't looked so tall when all Zane could see was his head.

Zane's fear grew as this man dusted off his long, lean frame. But it was not the man's grin that startled him. The man's red vest sparkled hypnotically. The fabric glowed for a few seconds. Zane's eyes were transfixed on his bright buttoned vest.

Zane blinked.

"Tell you what," the bald man said, "I'll leave you to toy with your thoughts." He gave him a wink. "I'll head back to my coach." He glanced at the bamboo chair. "Nice place you got here. Give you a moment to gather your thoughts. Then you can join me for a little tea. It'll calm your racing rabid thoughts. I know I'm a lot to take in."

"I don't drink much tea."

"Just a little simple conversation, then. In my coach. I've come a long way to see you. My gifts are simply divine. What I have'll make you rich beyond your wildest imaginings."

"A coach?" What was he talking about? Zane's confusion continued to mount.

"My horse-drawn carriage, my lad. Surely you understand."

Uh. I suppose, thought Zane. Where did this guy come from: the Wild West circa 1876?

If that old man thought Zane was gullible enough to get into a coach with a stranger, he was mistaken. Not going to happen. If he had the gumption, he might have just said, "Get the hell out." None of those words came out of his mouth.

"Hey, you happen to know a man named Stanley? Great Uncle Stanley?" Zane inquired hopefully.

"He's a snake, that one. Steer clear of his venomous fangs."

Folding arms across his chest, the tall intruder hopped through the porthole opening and disappeared. Before Zane could move, the sound of branches crackled. Zane peered through the opening in the floor.

"No flipping way," Zane whispered. The intruder was gone.

There was no THUMP. No screams.

The man was now standing on the forest floor. He hollered: "By the way, my gifts have to do with dead dudes, my little dude. And I left something for you. Hope you like it."

Zane had no idea what he was talking about as he peered down the hatch, wondering how he hopped through the opening without falling to his death.

Seconds later, horses were whinnying. Zane scrambled over to the window.

How did he do that? thought Zane.

Zane was done assuming that all these events were simple everyday encounters. But even if the old man were an experienced tree climber, even if he had carabiner clips and ropes to navigate down the tree—which he didn't—there was no way he could have scaled down the tree in a matter of seconds.

He capped his bald head with his floppy hat and began stroking a horse with a large brush.

The man pulled a fur-collared coat snug around his frame, tipped his hat to the sky, and led his coach down the trail, disappearing into the green.

Zane felt relieved that the man was gone, yet at the same time, curiosity curled its fingers through his thoughts.

He told me he was going to wait for me, Zane mused. *What gives? How can he just leave like that? And he knows about Great Uncle Stanley? Or does he?*

Zane spotted an ornate wooden dollhouse on the floor. Was that the gift? The old man had come in with nothing in his hands.

Zane got on bended knee to get a better look at the dollhouse. Red-velvet interior walls. Tiny paintings on the walls. Figurines of two women dressed in 19th-century attire: floor-length gowns, long gloves. Over a dozen miniature elaborately carved models were in various rooms in the dollhouse. One man of pewter was midway up a rope attached to a balcony with a lady on the balcony giving an 'Oh my. A handsome thief has arrived to steal my virginity. Hope he hurries.'

This was no simple dollhouse. More of a castle. It reminded him of a dollhouse his sister Rainn might have once played with. A miniature four-poster bed with twin sewing-thread spool end-tables. A tea tray with a kettle and four tiny teacups.

"Hey thief. Stand back," called out a tiny voice from inside the dollhouse. "Get away from my house. Go on! Move it, ya land-loving idiot."

Zane, startled, thought one of the pewter dolls had spoken.

A buzzing noise sounded over his head.

Zane looked up to see a tiny, winged creature hovering over him. Dozens of them appeared at the window. This tiny hive of long-legged fireflies in one big mash of electric-blue light were all staring at him. Upon closer inspection, these were not insects at all. They were faeries. Dressed garishly in purple gowns, yellow bonnets, bright lizard-green miniskirts. Men dressed in tweed knickers, bright gold sneakers, black leather vests. Lightning bolts stitched along pant legs and the hems of dresses. "Oh, it's just a human," said one of them.

"He best be leaving my treasure alone!"

"Smells like a thief."

"Don't trust humans as far as I can throw 'em."

Zane, to his happy surprise, was pleased to see them.

"Whoa! Way cool! Who're you?" he asked.

"He's the one."

"Nah! Too big. Smelly."

"Like rancid meat."

"Nope. That's him all right. Matches the picture," a redhaired fae said, holding a crinkled sheet of parchment in her hand. She waved it at Zane.

Zane leaned in to get a closer look: a Wanted poster with Zane's face on it.

"Get your fat paws off me property, boy," barked a doll from inside the dollhouse.

Zane stepped away from the dollhouse. More fae zigged and zagged around him. He swatted at the air, and they all darted off.

A pewter doll fell to the ground, hit a rock, and went CLANG!

Something landed on Zane's wavy locks. He ran a hand through his hair. Something was crawling around on his head.

"You sir, you are indeed the one." "Hey, what're you doing?" Zane asked.

Tiny feet scurried atop his head.

"It's all right, or as you humans like to say, 'it's all good.'"

Zane recognized that voice and started to relax, just a bit, mind you, but the voice offered a smidgen of calm. Better than a sharp stick up his nose.

"I can hear you," Zane began, staring at the dollhouse. A bunch of faeries waltzed through the treehouse's rooms, hallways, and balconies.

"And I see you," a familiar voice said.

Her voice was so familiar. It was the voice he had been hearing in his head for years.

"Esmeralda?"

"What's your name?" spat a hairy-faced fae, now hovering at Zane's nose.

Zane leaned back in surprise. "Uh, Zane."

"Last name, you bloody human. What is it?"

"Moss. Zane Moss."

"Yep, he's the one," sang that familiar feminine voice of Esmeralda. She swung on a strand of his curly bangs and smiled at him, swinging back and forth from his left eye to his right. "I'm right here, Zane. It's me, Esmeralda." "I knew it." Zane's eyes lit up.

"In the flesh." She somersaulted through the air and then stood up and curtsied, hovering in front of his face.

She had long dark hair, wavy like silky river water. Ropy dreadlocks snaked around on her head. Was she Medusa's pretty fae sister?

To say Zane was a wee bit crestfallen was the understatement of the century. He had fallen head over heels for a tiny faerie?

"There you are," Zane said. "In the flesh. You know, you've been living in my head, rambling around in my thoughts for years. All those psychic calls. All that telepath-time. I had no idea you were so small. I think you owe me some rent or something."

"Can't help you there. We don't deal with money. We're faeries. Your thoughts are worth more than all the gold in California."

My thoughts? Really? Zane wondered.

Slowly, dozens of fae became hundreds: from under floorboards, behind table legs, from under boxes, from a stack of comic books, from the dollhouse.

A hairy-faced fae dressed in a striped shirt and three-cornered pirate hat landed on a balcony of the dollhouse. He stroked a long, forked purple goatee fringed in gray as he twirled brass knuckles in one hand and stared at Zane with accusing beady eyes.

"So, you be the disabled witch, then, eh?" said Purple Goatee. "Bah! Show me something. Something worthwhile, you big old bugger."

Disabled witch? The hell did that mean?

Zane reached into his pocket and pulled out his Aventurine crystal, a nickel, and a dime. Gave the crystal a rub for good luck. Esmeralda now hovered in front of him. Lavender pleated skirt. Snowy white blouse. Yellow plaid scarf. Leather boots. Tiny lightning bolts etched along a black belt.

"So, Zane, you ready?" Esmeralda smiled.

"Ready? For what?"

"To work with the fae."

"He doesn't have a choice," said Purple Goatee. "He's in trouble, as it is."

Zane was utterly amazed and showed this by revealing an honest grin. "What have I done? Why am I in trouble? And you're all so tiny. But very cool. Hip little creatures."

Purple Goatee spat. "This one's as bright as an eclipse. He never showed us nothing. I want some proof." He punched his brass-knuckled fist into his palm. "You best respect Queen Esmeralda Robbinstone."

"Queen?" Zane found himself bowing to her. "Did any of you see a very tall man? Even taller than me. He was just here."

"Didn't see anyone. Just you, human," said a lady fae with rainbow-colored overalls and long white hair.

A faerie in yellow overalls said. "See. We got proof of our Queen. Where's yours?" She waved a card in front of Zane.

It read:

Queen Esmeralda Robbinstone
Ruler of the Canopy
Eastern Rim, Enchanted Wood

Zane didn't know much about queens and whatnot, but what sort of queen carried business cards?

"And here's mine," rumbled a fae with tattoos covering her arms, her neck, and her legs.

Claudia Curtain
Master Thief
Robbing Since I Could Walk
Better Check Your Pockets

Zane opened his mouth but said nothing.

"No time for small talk," cut in Esmeralda. "This is the one we've been waiting for. I've been prepping him for years. We've got big things in front of us." She gave Zane a wink.

All the fae stared off, avoiding eye contact with Zane.

"We have to get going, Zane," Esmeralda said. "Time to connect with Great Uncle Stanley. I suggest you head home and pack your bags."

"Oh, we've got that covered, Queen E," said Purple Goatee.

Zane, pleased Esmeralda knew Great Uncle Stanley, turned to the sound of something being dragged across the floor. "Hey, that's my duffle bag," Zane said. "How'd you…" A dozen fae dropped his bulging bag at his feet.

"Oh, but he'll need to stop by his house before we leave," ordered Esmeralda. "Don't worry, he's got a portal."

Zane had always been the sole occupant of his treehouse. No visitors. None. All that changed in one day. His mind was spinning.

First, he met a ghost named Great Uncle Stanley, then some strange old bald dude invaded his private aerial bungalow, then a hive of faeries. Hundreds of them. All this excitement had his brain on slow boil, crackling with uncertainty and eagerness.

"A land beyond imagination—that's what I've unearthed. And those faeries. Just too cool," he muttered, staring at his reflection in his bathroom mirror.

Zane had always been a loner, so talking to himself was as natural as breathing. He had to be his own best friend, since others accused him of being an alien from a distant planet. He didn't fit in here. Earth. Bah, what a strange planet!

He pushed a wheelbarrow with the dollhouse in it across the front yard.

The front door swung open. "What've you got? Wow!" Rainn exclaimed as she marched up to it, blocking his path to the barn. "A dollhouse. Who gave you that?"

Zane, startled, having been drifting in his own inner thoughts, looked up.

"Oh, it's you. What're you—I thought you were out with your girlfriends or something. It's Saturday." He hoped she would ignore him. Zane was not ready to share any information, but he didn't have anyone else to tell.

"I'm always one step ahead of you, brother. You've known that since the day we were born. So, tell me: what's going on?"

He tilted his head, studying the dollhouse. "I thought you were always one step ahead of me." He thought of Esmeralda. Yes, he was smitten by the little lady faerie, but there wasn't a snowstorm's chance in Costa Rica Rainn could know this. "Well, I'm several minutes older than you. I'm your big sister." He shrugged, having heard that about a thousand times.

"What do you care?" he asked defensively. "I've been building barbwire fences and dollhouses. The fences are to keep you out of my space."

"Meet any cool people lately?" she replied, ignoring his little jab. "Gonna have a tea party with your dollhouse?" Her smiling green eyes stymied him into submission. She had a way about her. Somehow, she could get into his head.

"Nope. Just hanging out in the woods." He suppressed a sigh, wanting some alone time to digest his recent encounters.

She gave her brother a shove in the arm. "Just wondering. Someone at school told me you met someone new."

What? Surely that was just girl gossip, he presumed, or maybe she was lying. Zane considered himself mildly attractive, but he was no smooth talker with the chicks. Gossip. Had to be idle gossip. Just a bunch of girls who loved to talk about other people.

"Right," he replied and rolled his eyes. "I've been hanging out at the bus station. Looking for prospective girls to date. Thought I could tell her I build dollhouses. See if she'll show any interest in me."

"Is she cute? Heard she's a cute little thing, sharp as a pinhead. Tiny." She winked.

What was that supposed to mean? He just stared at her with blank eyes. *She's not going to rattle me, not this time,* he thought.

"So, about this dollhouse? Is it a gift for your 'girlfriend'?" She offered air quotes. "Come on, tell me about her."

"About who?"

"Esmeralda."

Zane's eyes got big again. How the hell did she know? His stomach gurgled like yogurt warming in the hot sun. He tried to play it cool. Rainn had one-upped him again. Should he be surprised? Well, he was.

"What're you talking about?"

"Esmeralda, the queen." She blinked like a sleepy cat.

Zane could not hold up his nonchalant shield.

The hell? "How do you know about her?" Zane asked.

"We've been friends since I was in Kindergarten."

"Shut up! No way!"

Her eyes lit up. "Yep."

"And you never told me? This is—what the hell!" Zane tossed his hands in the air.

Rainn's bright eyes mirrored the glow of a mid-morning blue sky. "Probably the same reason you've kept quiet about your psychic conversations." She shrugged and grinned. "It just never came up."

Zane opened his mouth, closed it, opened it. "How do you…you're a blabbermouth. You talk so much you disrupt radio frequencies?" How did she know about his little psychic conversations?

"Just one of my specialties. But thanks for the compliment, brother." She smiled as if she had just won an award.

Zane wondered what else she was keeping from him when a creak from the wheelbarrow interrupted his thoughts.

There, standing on a balcony on the dollhouse, was Esmeralda, brushing a hand through her hair, silver bracelets jangling. She sat on the railing and crossed one leg over the other. Her hair hung all the way to her feet and brushed against the rusty wheelbarrow.

"I've got important matters to discuss," Esmeralda began. "With both of you. First, Zane."

"So, you *do* know my sister?" He tried to act and sound cool, but he could feel his sister laughing in his head. Or was that Esmeralda?

"Let's start at the beginning, shall we," Esmeralda continued. "With your name?"

She already knew his name. Why ask? "I'm Zane," Zane said. Just what did Rainn know about Esmeralda, and vice versa?

"Indeed," Esmeralda replied. "I mean: your destined name."

"Pardon?" he asked, staring at Rainn, who was all smiles, sitting on the front step. Again, Zane was feeling a little behind the two ball here. A phrase he and Rainn, twins, used instead of the clichéd colloquialism: behind the eight ball.

"Oh, right. I mean your magical disability. Sometimes I forget I'm talking to a simpleton. No offense, but earthlings are…simpletons."

Even though Esmeralda's words came out like warm honey, it still was a bit off-putting.

"Isn't she great?" Rainn clapped her hands together.

Air-thickening silence followed.

"I mean, since you're only a human, Zane," purred Esmeralda. "Tell me you know your true calling"

Was she trying to make him feel better by claiming he knew about a supposed *Calling*?

Another sideways glance from Esmeralda. Both Esmeralda and Zane appeared befuddled as two bees in a snowstorm.

"Let me back up a bit, shall I? Something's amiss here," the fae thought out loud.

Zane and Rainn waited in silence, watching her. The gentle hum of her blurred wings filled the silence.

"I need you to understand what's happening here," she said while coiling her hair up into a massive bun. She took a tiny step back, then another, walking on air. "We travel together, you see."

No, he didn't see. We? What was that supposed to mean? That was a big part of the problem. He didn't know what she was talking about.

"You, referring to your swarm of traveling fae I met in the tree? Where'd they all go?" He darted a glance at the dollhouse on the wagon. No faeries in sight.

She smiled. "Yes, they are my Tribe. We've been telepathing for years."

"Really?" Zane asked with interest.

"Psychic telecasting is what we do," Esmeralda claimed. "You and your sister can telepath, too, but this is only one of your gifts."

"I didn't know Rainn could do that," Zane said. "Hey, what was that you said earlier? Something about a magical disability?" He then looked to Rainn, seeking some sort of confirmation.

This time, she shrugged. "You got one and don't even know it," Rainn said.

Zane muttered to his sister, "You know something. I can feel it." Rainn shrugged again.

"Seems like that's how you like it," Zane added.

"You understand now, Zane?" the fae said.

"Just a little confused, is all." Zane sighed. Again, he looked to Rainn, hoping for a little positive support, but that was about as hopeful as a positive Covid-19 test result.

"I always thought you had a few missing screws in your head," was all Rainn offered. "Time to find those screws, brother."

In the backyard, Esmeralda chirped, "You've got a disability. A lacy one, indeed. Too much of this lacy energy is like a spiderweb hiding your true gift. But it is a magical disability."

Zane shook his head. "Oh, thanks for clearing up absolutely nothing." Another sigh. "What the hell are you talking about?"

"She's here to help, Zane."

"Really?" Zane looked down at his shoes. "You're both just messing with me."

"You've got a seizure disorder," purred Esmeralda. She buzzed near a barn window.

With that said, she pirouetted and then raised her hands over her head. "Ta-da!"

What? No way. Seizure disorder? That was not possible. He'd never had a seizure. He did know a girl back in elementary school who was epileptic, a rather roundish girl, about as wide as she was tall. She rarely spoke. She had seizures often in school.

"Yes, you do," said Esmeralda while, at the same time, humming. She could hum and speak at the same time. Zane liked that about her. It calmed him. And right now, he needed to remain unruffled by all this information.

"Your magical disability just hasn't shown its face yet," Esmeralda continued, as if reading his thoughts. "Sort a like an electric grave waiting to jumpstart a corpse back to life. Exciting, huh?"

The air around Zane went still. He remained confused. "If you really knew me, you'd know I've never had a seizure. Don't you think I'd know if I had one?"

"You ever experienced déjà vu?"

He gave this some thought. He did recall numerous occasions where he felt déjà vu, the eerie feeling of falsely reliving an event that just happened seconds ago.

One day, about a month ago, he had sat in the barn, barefoot, atop bailed hay. The sound of a butterfly flapping its wings, with his feet itching in the hay, a bead of sweat dripping down his brow, the way the sun cast a long shadow from a crossbeam across his face—all of it had happened seconds ago and was happening again right now: déjà vu. And he just sat there, stone-still. Time seemed to slow during this replayed life experience. And then it was gone. Poof! He returned to the here and now.

"Déjà vu's a precursor to unleashing your magical talent," Esmeralda added. "You just haven't had a full-blown epileptic convulsion. But fret not. It's coming. And the electric fire in your mind is an iron-red furnace. For both of you." Zane stared at her in disbelief. "You know what, lady? You're crazy. You're both crazy." He fired a glance at Rainn. "Rainn's nuts, I've known that, but why didn't you say anything to me, Rainn? This is nuts."

"I was instructed not to."

"And you, too. A faerie queen?" If any of this was true, Zane felt dishonored. "It's like you're keeping things from me. Important life-altering information. If you know all about me. Prove it." He jabbed a finger at Esmeralda.

"My all-seeing crystal globe is in my sanctuary," said Esmeralda with a snap. "I think you need a good lie-down. I've shared a lot with you, but it's time you know: I have keys to the Akashic Records, a place where your life is cataloged. And this magical disability is something you were born with. You are smart, Zane. For a simpleton. You lucky cat, you."

Rainn stepped closer to Zane and gave him a hug. A rare display of affection.

"Oh, check that. I mean, lucky dog." Esmeralda clapped her hands. "Glad we got that all straightened out. Where'd you put your portal? You need to get home." She winked.

"Portals?" Zane said in dismay. Right now, she was making as much sense as seeing a gorilla shaving. "I am home. This *is* home." He stabbed a finger at the ground as if staking a claim to this barn. "I don't know a thing about portals."

She floated in front of him, shaking her hips and waving her hands in the air.

"Why're you dancing?"

"Not dancing. I'm entrancing."

"Oh." And although he was unaware of it, Zane was staring at her in a hypnotic, far-off Romanian trance.

BEEP! BEEP! BEEP!

Zane peered out the window. A pickup truck, hauling a tall wooden crate half-covered in a plaid tarp, stopped in front of the barn.

"Who're those guys?" Zane said, not expecting an answer.

"Made a few calls," Esmeralda said. "Seems as though someone messed up the order."

The driver called out, "Where do you want the delivery?"

Esmeralda nodded to Rainn.

Rainn stepped up the driver.

The driver looked past Rainn.

"You. Fae Lady. "I need a signature."

"Can't trust anyone, especially interdimensional moving men," Esmeralda whispered to Zane.

"This portal was to be delivered weeks ago."

"Lady, do you want the package or not?" he grumbled.

Another funny look from Zane. Rainn appeared non-plussed by any of this.

Two men dressed in flannel shirts and blue jeans got to work, unloading the crate on a hand-truck and into the old red barn.

They drove off. No paperwork given to them. No tablet pen seeking an electronic signature. Nothing.

Rainn stared into the bathroom mirror, clippers on the counter, electric shaver in hand. Tilted her head and went for it.

BZZZZZZ! BZZZT! BZZZZZZZT!

She started to shave her hair, going in a slow, sweeping motion around the side of her skull. Clumps of hair clung to her purple tank top and the rest clouded the floor. She grinned an evil grin and continued with the clippers. She buzzed around certain areas of her skull, allowing a dozen long dreadlocks to remain. The long dreads brushed her teacup-bumped chest.

She pulled her purple-dyed locks into a ponytail, leaving several thick tentacles dangling over her face.

"What's going on in there?" she heard Zane say from down the hallway.

He poked his head in. "Oh…whoa! Big time buzz. What's next: a tattoo and a leather collar?" He smiled. "And all this time I thought I was the one trapped outside the box. Nice costume. Hanging with a new band of Menace these days, are ya?"

Rainn cocked her head. "You just be ready. We need to open that crate. Before someone discovers it."

"Already tried. Thing's locked. And who's gonna come and look in our barn? Mom and Dad are in Europe for two more months.

And those crazy movers didn't even leave a key. No directions. No receipt. Nothing. And Esmeralda just disappeared on us." He gave her a good long study. "Shave it all off."

"Once again, I see you're behind the two ball." She set down the clippers and picked up a broom to sweep up the hair. "She didn't tell you?"

"Tell me what? What else do you know? Why're you smiling like that?"

Now Rainn had a decision to make. Tell her brother now, or just lead the way? Being an Alpha, Rainn feasted on these leadership opportunities; for her, leading the sheep to the shearing was always better than getting buzz-sawed by someone else's decision-making.

A clicking sound echoed in her head. She recognized that psychic ringtone and pressed a finger to her temple.

"Hang on a sec. Be right back, brother." She closed her bedroom door in his face, clicked off the light, plopped onto her bed, and stared at the ceiling littered with celestial, glow-in-the-dark star stickers. She blinked three times, channeling her energy to the psychic messaging queue in her mind.

Over the years, she had learned to organize her Psychic Messaging System, making storing and retrieving calls easier. Now, when she closed her eyes, she could see a sheet of paper with names and dates of recent psychic messages.

An image appeared, hovering at the periphery of her third eye—knowledge provided by an invisible eye located on the forehead that offers discernment beyond ordinary sight. Or, in this case, a tiny floating notebook opened and displayed handwritten messages on a sheet of crisp white parchment in her mind. Red roses were stamped in each corner of the page. The Elizabethan cursive came into full focus when she closed her eyes: 6 NEW PMS MESSAGES.

Whoa! How did she miss those? All six messages were from one caller.

Might be SPAM.

She did not recognize the caller ID: DAG

Curiosity got the best of her, and she psychically tapped the first missed PMS call:

Greetings, Rainn. I come with clear intentions. I'm here to inform you of a private meeting set aside just for you. We must meet in person. We'll meet three Wednesdays from today at my camp in Graveyard Gardens, a suburb of Enchanted Wood.

Your Endless Leader,

Doyle Alfred Grimes

Rainn had never heard of anyone by that name. She needed to scroll through her remaining messages.

Welcome. You have five new messages, said her own voice in her thoughts, her personalized psychic voice stamp.

She blinked, cueing up a message from Esmeralda.

Rainn. Esmeralda here. Change in plans. You and Zane are needed at the Eastern Rim. Portal that was delivered is ready, but it needs Zane's epileptic boost to engage transit. Toll due when destination reached. Check the dollhouse for a portal key. And please be on time.

Rainn enjoyed Esmeralda's soothing, honeyed voice, probably because the fae hummed while talking. But this time, her tone spoke of urgency.

She gazed up at Orion's Belt in her galaxy of star stickers. "When? Now? Next week?" she said aloud.

KNOCK! KNOCK!

"Yes?" she said, eyes fixedly honed in on Orion's Belt. "What is it, Zane?"

"Can I come in?"

Zane opened the door without awaiting a response. "I feel a little strange. Dizzy."

He sat on the edge of her bed.

She leaned up on an elbow. "All this information too much for you?"

Her smirk flattened as she sensed he was struggling with something. Was it a virus, a cold, or just some sick thoughts trapped in his mind? He did tend to get lost in all his ADHDness.

"You sick?"

He stared out the dark window. "No. Just feel weird. I don't know, but…I'll be fine." He started to stand, and his butt plopped back on the bed. "Whoa. Dizzy. Kind of feel like I'm in a dream or something."

A figure was now standing in the doorway. A tall, dark shape dressed in a silver pin-striped black suit and a black fedora with a white feather in it.

"Good evening, my teenage beauties."

They spun their attention to the stranger at the door.

"Who—who're you?"

"How'd you get in here?"

"Thought of using the window," the stranger replied, "but that might freak you out. Used the front door."

"This is private property," Rainn claimed. Certain she had locked the front door, she grabbed her phone off the end-table. "I'll dial 911."

"Oh, puhleeze! Calm down. I'm not a burglar or a thief. There's nothing in your little home of any value to me. It's you I want." He looked at Rainn long enough to unsettle her normally stoic semblance of calm. "And you, young lady," he tsked while spinning a ring on his finger. "I just sent you a PMS. You need to stay on top of your psychic messages."

The intruder reached out a long, bony hand in a hand-shaking gesture. Zane stared at the hand as if it were infected.

"My name's Doyle. Doyle Alfred Grimes. And you two are Zane and Rainn. The lovely and ever-enchanting Moss twins." He tipped his fedora and bowed.

The twins glanced at each other and said nothing.

"Tell you what. I won't stay long. Just checking in. I'll be seeing you in an alternate forest one day soon. You see. I'm dead. A ghost. A famous ghost. Popular with the living and dead. And I want you two to join my team." He handed Zane a business card.

DOYLE AL GRIMES
ENCHANTED WOOD HAUNT
THRILLING SOULS FOR LIFETIMES

Zane stared off. His head wobbled, and then his arms and shoulders began to quiver.

"Zane! You…" Rainn began with concern in her voice.

Zane said nothing. His mouth clamped shut as he suffered a petit mal seizure: just staring off, his mind blank, his body remaining still.

"What? You don't remember me?" Doyle smirked a crooked grin; his wrinkled baked-apple flesh had enough lines for a Google Earth roadmap.

Doyle took a step back, waved from the hallway, and disappeared into a cloud of mist. Gone.

Rainn hopped off the bed and peered down the hallway. She clicked on the porch light but didn't see him anywhere.

Zane snapped out of his petit mal seizure and slowly followed Rainn down the hallway.

Rainn clicked on the floodlights. All was quiet. That stranger was nowhere in sight.

Rainn could sense Zane was a little more confused than her. She was familiar with Enchanted Wood from her conversations with Esmeralda. She knew of Doyle, but this was her first encounter with the ghost.

She returned to her bedroom with Zane and explained everything she knew about Doyle and Enchanted Wood. Which wasn't much.

"Brother, I should tell you: that guy's a bad man. He's, you know, dead."

"What?" Zane replied with squinting eyes.

"He's undead. Lives in Enchanted Wood. That forest is filled with fae and ghosts and other weird beasts. Paranormal activity is common there. Doyle's a Being with dark powers. He's been known to kill people."

"Really? A murdering ghost? he asked in an unemotional tone. Zane said nothing else, showing little reaction to all this news about psychic energy and ghosts and faeries. "You're taking all this pretty well, Zane." He stared off.

"Well, since all this has come about, I need to talk to you about some other stuff." She went on to say, "Important stuff." She half-expected him to turn to face her; the other half demanded it.

"Zane? You listening?"

He slumped forward and then fell onto the floor.

Rainn flew off the bed and was at Zane's side. He started to convulse, mouth clamped shut, body exploding in a fizzing convulsive outburst. Zane's rumbling epileptic earthquake lasted ten seconds and then his convulsive fit expired.

She placed a hand on his forehead. Although his spasms had stopped, his jaw remained locked. Blood dribbled from his clenched lips.

A chiming sounded in her inner ear, notifying Rainn of an incoming PMS caller. "Now? Really?"

She chose to ignore the clairvoyant PMS and focused on Zane.

She blinked twice, engaging her automated PMS message: *Hi. You've reached Rainn. I'm not able to take your call. Leave a message. If you're dying to hear from me, you'll have to wait. Die for me next week instead. Ta ta.*

She stared at Zane, half wondering if she should give her Uncle Bob a call. She dismissed that idea. Most adults were clueless when it came to ordinary emergencies, and having to explain to her uncle that Zane had had a seizure was not how she wanted to spend her morning.

Then, as if on cue, Esmeralda appeared, hovering over an unlit squashed candle.

Esmeralda tsked and spoke evenly, "The lad needs to manage his energies. I see he's doing fine this morning. He's picked a rather untimely moment to erupt."

"He's seizing!" How could Esmeralda say that? Rainn wanted to tell Esmeralda to chill, but all her attention remained on her brother. "Zane. Zane. C'mon, wake up!" She sat back on her heels.

"He'll be alright. Gonna need to learn to manage his energies. Just blowing off a little steam," Esmeralda said while humming.

That's enough steam to make a spa full of Jenny Craig Weight Watchers shed twenty pounds, thought Rainn.

The following morning, Rainn decided it was time to ditch school. After a brief discussion with Esmeralda, Rainn agreed not to take Zane to the doctor. No doctor could help him today anyway.

Even though they were living alone, Uncle Bob came by twice a week, just to check on them. But lately, it was mostly just text messages.

She texted her brother, even though his bedroom was just down the hall.

LET ME DRIVE US TO SCHOOL TODAY. IT'S AN EMERGENCY. EXPLAIN LATER.

Zane woke to the PING notification and, after wiping the sleep out of his eyes, fired back a reply: SURE. I DON'T WANT TO HANG AROUND IN THIS HAUNTED HOME, ANYWAY.

Zane poured himself a bowl of *Boo Berry* cereal, milk turning a sugary ghoulish gray. Zane accepted that he had a seizure, and the gash on his inner cheek confirmed that he had some sort of involuntary muscle spasm.

They parked outside Perry Drug's parking lot and waited about ten minutes, long enough for Zane to ask: "What're we doing here? Why're we skipping school? What's the big secret? Better be important. We've got finals in two weeks. And I had a seizure. I remember feeling dizzy and then, well, I didn't."

Rainn said, "Uncle Bob mentioned that he might swing by this morning. I texted him back to say we had to be at school early. Just wanted to be gone, in case he popped in."

Zane shrugged. "Hardly checked in on us lately."

She drove back home, steered around back, and parked near the barn. All was quiet, except for a dim flickering light from under the barn door.

"Is this about that ghoul Doyle Albert Grimace? Did that even happen?"

"Zane, that shit was real. It's Doyle Alfred Grimes."

"Whatever."

She hopped out of the Ford Bronco and ran a hand along a dent in the rear quarter panel. Two weeks ago, she took a corner too closely in a crowded 7-11 parking lot and hit a mailbox. She fled the scene, escaping an accident report and afraid of potentially losing her driver's license.

The barn interior was dark, save for sunlight streaming through a small hole in the wall near an empty horse stall. Along with the bits of sunlight poking holes in the walls, something more interesting pulled at her attention: a long trail of bluish-colored water streamed from the Porta Potty all the way across the barn, near the horse stalls.

They stared at the strange, glowing little river of water.

"Must have a leak," she said.

"A leak?"

It was the color of blue watery electricity. Ripples glistening in the light spilling from under the portal door. Was there a light ON inside the portal potty?

"What is it?" Zane said while crouching next to Rainn as she dipped a finger into the growing puddle; her fingertip tingled, and she pulled it away. What she thought was water clung to her finger like a spiderweb of energy. And this webbing crawled up her finger. She shook out her hand, and the webbing disappeared.

"Zane, I need to tell you something. That seizure you had—it's a good thing."

"Huh?"

"It's your magical disability."

He sighed. "As much as that sounds crazy, I think I'm starting to believe you. I mean It'd be cool if I could use my epilepsy as a tool instead of a scary crutch. And you know what? Every now and then I feel a buzzing in my temples. Sometimes my fingers. I tried to move this fizzy energy in my fingers. I got it to move to my thumb."

She gave him a quizzical look. She was impressed. "That's great, Zane. Thought you wouldn't believe me. Keep up that attitude. Now, I need you to use your epileptic energy to open the crate."

"Already tried. It's locked."

"Esmeralda told me there's a key in the dollhouse."

Zane retrieved a key from his pocket. "Esmeralda told me, too." He grinned. "I was about to try to take an axe to it, too, but then she told me the key was in one of the tiny rooms, on a bed, in the many-roomed dollhouse."

He tried the key in the portal. Jiggled it.

"It won't open. The hell? Maybe just take an axe to it?"

"Nope. Can't damage the portal. Use your epileptic energy. Use your mind-energy. Funnel your epileptic vibrations to the key in the lock. Your mind is tuned to the lock."

"Sounds straight-up crazy, but I'll try."

"Just believe in your epileptic energies. Breathe."

"Just move, okay?" He forced a dramatic exhale through his nose. "How's that for breathing, sister? Let me do it. Move!"

Zane put his hand on the lock, calmed his racing mind, and then focused on his breathing.

CLICK. The lock opened. Zane displayed all his shiny teeth with a grin.

Inside was a portal potty with green fiberglass corrugated walls.

"So, this is our portal potty. Cool."

Rainn noticed a leak in the portal wall. Neon-green liquid dripped from a portal vent, trickling down the wall.

Zane dipped a finger in the small puddle. It was not water.

"It's pooled light energy. Be careful what you touch."

"That's why it zapped my finger," Zane replied, wiping it on his shorts.

His fingertips tingled, and he stared further into the barn. "Look."

There, standing behind Rainn, a familiar ghost appeared.

Great Uncle Stanley, dressed in his tweed blazer and yellow bow tie, waved at Zane.

"You see him?" Zane nudged Rainn.

"See who?" Rainn appeared mesmerized by this odd pool. The puddle swaying like a hammock, a few inches off the ground. She kept her attention on the liquid.

Great Uncle Stanley disappeared into the portal.

CLICK went a bolt, fastening the door locked again.

"Did you hear that?" Rainn asked and tried the door. "Shit. It's locked again."

The voice of Stanley spoke from inside the portal: "Zane, she can't see or hear me. I'm contracted to work solely with you. We discussed this already."

"Rainn, there's a ghost in the portal. The barn's haunted, too.

Maybe we need to hire an exterminator."

"Stop screwing around, Zane! Come check this out. We need to figure out what's wrong with the portal. If you psychically locked the door, unlock it." She had little time for his wandering thoughts and games. "Unlock the door. I know you locked it," Rainn said in a faraway tone, devoid of emotion.

"I didn't. He did."

She stood up from her crouch, and sniffed the air. "Maybe Esmeralda's here."

Zane shook his head. "Rainn, it was a ghost."

Someone was whistling inside the portal potty.

"There. You hear that?"

"Hear what?" Rainn said.

"The whistling."

A small sign hung off the door handle. In lightning-blue letters on a blackened sign, it read: Portal Potty. Just a flush away. UNDER REPAIR.

Two flashing neon-red lightning bolts were etched around the door handle.

Zane knocked on the door. "Great Uncle Stanley?"

"Just a minute."

Zane looked at Rainn. "Tell me you hear that."

Just then, the walls of the portal potty started to shake, followed by what sounded like an old pickup truck cranking but unable to turn over.

"Needs to be recharged, is all," Zane heard Great Uncle Stanley say.

The door swung outward; Stanley stepped out and made his way to the workbench, opened an amethyst-purple toolbox, and rummaged around. Warm yellow light poured out of the open toolbox filled with crystals, each in the shape of various tools: screwdrivers, wrenches, pliers, nail clippers, tack hammers. He pulled out a pair of garnet needle-nose pliers and tugged at a strand of wire near the leaky vent.

Rainn noticed the open toolbox—a toolbox she had never seen before. It wasn't Dad's. She did, however, see wires being tugged from the vent.

"Okay, what's going on, little brother?"

"I'll tell you as soon as I know."

She did not like the idea of her brother seeing anything from the ethereal plane that she could not. "Is it Doyle?" "Nope." Zane grinned.

Up until last night, she figured she was the only person in town with such a paranormal gift.

"Who're you talking to?"

"Great Uncle Stanley. He's standing right here. Hey, Stanley. Say something to Rainn."

With his back to Zane, Stanley raised a string of coiled-up diodes. "This ought to do the trick."

"Rainn, tell me you see him," Zane said again.

"Did you open the door?" Rainn asked.

The portal potty door slammed shut.

"*He* did." Zane slinged a pointed finger at Stanley, who was now approaching.

"You'll need to charge this old portal up, lad," Stanley said, tossing the needle-nose plyers into the toolbox.

"I saw that!" Rainn said. "Who's here tossing tools around?"

"Just a sec," Zane told Rainn and made his way behind the portal, where Stanley lifted open a small metal grate in the fiberglass wall, pulled out a small beaker, and handed it to Zane. "You'll need to fill that with a little bit of…you." He arched his eyebrow.

Zane held the beaker in the palm of his hand. It was made of Pyrex, a tree stump with rings circling its base, and a long, narrow neck with a rubber stopper.

"A bit of me, eh? What do you mean? Like a stool sample?" His expression was weighed down in question marks.

Rainn poked her head around the back of the portal. "What're you doing?"

"He's helping me. You can't hear him." He returned his attention to Stanley.

"Your core energy is rooted to your base chakra near the old belly." Stanley rubbed his stomach. "You've got to harness your magical disability. Your epi energy will get this old heap up and running again."

"Believe me, I would, but I don't know how to access my epi energy. Although, I did have a seizure last night if that's any consolation. I just…" He looked at Rainn after realizing she was staring at him. "Last night, when I blacked out. I was—"

"Zane, this ghost, or whoever you're talking to, how do you know you can trust him?" Rainn countered. "Ghosts are known to spin tales and twist tales."

Zane's eyes moved from Stanley to Rainn and back again. "He says he's our Great Uncle Stanley. Mom's uncle. He kind of looks like Uncle Bob would look if he was a very old man."

Something about his nose and hair growing out of his ears, thought Zane. The resemblance was striking.

"Tell Rainn I'll send her a PMS."

"PMS?" Zane furrowed his brow. "Premenstrual syndrome? She's…"

Rainn squinted in the direction Zane was looking and crossed her arms in defiance, but she did not see a ghost or its aural glow. But her instinct told her: Zane's not bright enough to scheme something like this. Must be talking to a ghost or a ghoul or a demon. She was not amused by any of this. She should be the one leading the conversations, or at least privy to what was being said.

"He's talking about sending me a psychic message, Zane. Okay, Stanley. Dude," Rainn said with arms crossed. "Send me the PMS."

"Tell your kindhearted sister: I'll need her encryption code to unblock her supernatural pathway. Most humans are born without any blocks, and babies can freely commune with ethereal beings, but a subconscious block is formed by the age of six months or so. Human nature pulls the plug on your innate ability to commune with us dead folk. Without help from us, you humans are good at one thing: making a royal mess of situations."

Stanley reached a hand inside his blazer and pulled out a small book bound with soft blueish leather. It was held together with a rubber band, corners curling. The cover etched in crafted gold stenciling read: *Akashic Records Warehouse Volume 17*.

Beneath the title, inlaid in vibrant electric-blue ink, sat a dragon on a tree limb smoking a doobie of roses.

Stanley licked his fingertip and flipped to a page, running his finger halfway down. "Here it is: Moss Family Lineage:

"Rainn Moss: pathway blocked, six weeks of age. Block removed at the age of six (faerie realm only).

"Tell her Queen Esmeralda and the fae in her colony are the only clan with a claim to her access code. She's blocked all other callers from her PMS."

Zane watched Stanley work on the leaky portal using the crystal wrench and screwdriver.

"Stanley," he said. "I know you're buy, but can you say something to help me encourage Rainn? I don't think she trusts you."

Rainn spoke up: "He's a ghost. Ghosts shouldn't be trusted."

"Come on, man," Zane pleaded to Stanley. "She's getting anxious. What should I tell her?"

Stanley was busy with the crystal tools, fixing the leak. He raised a sheaf of coiled diodes with his back to Zane.

"Rainn," Zane said. "He's busy."

She nodded. "Yeah, I can see those diodes floating. Does he know what he's doing?"

"Oh, I know," Stanley affirmed, sticking out his tongue and tightening a screw onto a circuit board.

"Chill, Rainn. He's almost done. Right, Stanley?"

"Stanley, sir, do you know where Esmeralda went?" Rainn finally asked, walking up to the portal.

"She had some business to take care of. Go on, tell her, Zane." Zane told Rainn.

"Okay, if you're seeing a ghost, why can't I see him? I've just as many extra-sensory abilities—no, check that. I'm more attuned than you'll ever be, little brother." Her tone slithered along the floor like a pregnant snake, bumping with self-assurance.

"Zane. Hop to it," said Stanley as he pointed to the portal door. "It's time. Needs a bit of your energy."

Zane held the tree-stump beaker and closed his eyes. His hands started to gather heat, and then a river of energy flowed from his heart to his fingertips into the vial.

Stanley raised a silver key on a chain fit with a miniature decorative, hand-carved toilet. "Allow me. I've got a duplicate."

Rain asked, "Where is he?"

Stanley jiggled the key in the lock and put a little *English* on it to *pop* the lock.

The portal door swung open.

"Okay," Rainn said, "I guess this ghost opened it. Tell me what's going on, brother."

"Tell you as soon as I know."

Zane, pleased that he had one-upped his sister in seeing the unseen, added, "You just think you're the only person in town with such a paranormal gift."

Rainn seemed to cave just a little: "All right, I know you've got potential, but I've never witnessed you do anything extraordinary."

The following morning, brother and sister discussed, in detail, all of Zane's conversations with Stanley.

"Apparently that portal was delivered for us," Rainn said after listening, in earnest, to her brother. "And this phantom, who claims to be our great uncle, plays a part in what I, er, I mean what *we* must do."

"That's right. This is a group effort. You are not the lead alpha here, dear sister. Just lay off with your 'I am greater than thou' tone, would you?"

"But you had a seizure, and that's something you need to work out. It's all connected to your; oh, how shall I put it? Your mashed-up use of energy," Rainn said.

Zane took a bite of toast and boysenberry jam.

The way she said it so casually, as if reminding him it was his turn to wash the dishes, hit him like a punch in the gut. Then he remembered how he had used his epi energy to fill the beaker.

"It's a magical disability, sister. I just need to learn how to funnel all that energy before I black out and convulse."

He followed Rainn's gaze to crisscrossed swords on the wall: armaments his Uncle Bob had brought back from serving in the war in Afghanistan, each mounted in a bamboo scabbard painted black with a strip of faded silk hanging off the hilt. The silk danced and snapped like a flag on a windy day. What was making the silk swirl about?

Great Uncle Stanley appeared at the far end of the kitchen table. How long had he been sitting there?

"Oh. Hey. Good to see you?" Zane spoke up, as if broken from the spell of staring at the silk.

"Is he here? Great Uncle Stanley?" Rainn chimed in hopefully.

"He's sitting at the table,"

She stared right through him. "Wish I could see him." "He's here," Zane said again.

"Can you ask him if he knows how to channel your seizure energy? Esmeralda told me about your…. magical disability. I just wasn't sure if it was true." She looked down at her sneakers.

"And?" Zane said, a bit agitated, "I do, in fact, have a magical ability. I just don't know how to use it. But I'm worthy of a little respect here."

Great Uncle Stanley chimed in. "She's right, lad. You've got an overload of electricity buzzing through you. Your neuropathways are a charred treasure map." He shrugged. "The Portal Potty will flush you to other lands, faraway lands, all with the aid of your magical seizure energy."

Zane found this both remarkable and unbelievable. "Really? No way. Now that is some cool shit."

"What's he saying?" Rainn said. Zane

put up a hand to shush her.

He asked Stanley, "Where will the portal take me?"

"Enchanted Wood."

He thought for a second. That was the name on that faerie's business card he spotted in his treehouse.

"I know about Enchanted Wood. I mean, I saw a card from a faerie with that name on it."

"There you go, lad." Stanley tugged on the lapels of his tweed blazer. "But, I gotta fly."

Stanley was gone, leaving a blurry, haloed outline of his frame, as if an electric shadow hung there. But that, too, faded away.

Zane turned to look at his sister. "I can feel your eyes boring into the back of my skull. What?"

"Well? Spill it, brother? What'd he say?"

"Just take it easy. Give me a second."

He took a few small breaths, figuring she owed him this much. He had learned a lot over the past several days. Here again, what about her? She was the one keeping this secret since she was six years old. If anyone needed a little time, it was him. He waited all of ten seconds. Okay, that was enough. He was good to go.

When she opened her mouth, Zane figured she was going to make her own demands. But she spoke in a welcoming tone. "So, is he still here? Great Uncle Stanley?"

Zane reached into his pocket and dangled the keychain charm: a wood carving of Buddha sitting on a toilet with his robe hiked up around his knees.

"You know what *this* unlocks?" he asked with a wry grin.

They stepped into the barn. He fondled the portal keychain charm.

Zane unlocked the portal potty door. Inside: twin toilets with a pair of matching oval vanity mirrors in the shape of handprints. A large roll of toilet paper spooled between them. The toilet paper was filled with text written in beautiful calligraphy.

Zane flipped up the toilet seat lid with the tip of his sneaker. His eyes got as big as goose eggs as they took in a most unexpected sight.

"Hey," he shouted, "you better check this out."

Rainn glanced over his shoulder. "What is it? Oh, two crappers? Big deal. Must be for a hippie commune."

"No. Look." He pointed to one of the twin toilet bowls. Instead of looking down into a disgusting hole where human refuse gathered, they stared at something unexpected: a midnight sky of constellations. There seemed to be two hundred Milky Way galaxies swirling about in the bowl. Millions of stars. The stars moved in some sort of strange circular motion, like alphabet soup on a slow boil.

She smiled. "It's beautiful."

"Yeah," said Zane as he continued to stare at the swirling stars, unable to remove his gaze. "I feel kind of dizzy."

She put a hand on his arm. "Maybe you should sit down."

One of the vanity mirrors had lettering scrawled across it, red lipstick: Just a flush away."

Rainn sat on the twin toilet next to Zane, who had hands on his knees, staring between his legs.

"How're you doing?"

"I feel like we've done this before," Zane replied. "We need to flush. At the same time."

"What? Flush now? You sure about this? Do you even have coordinates for where we're going? This is a portal potty, you know? You might end up in—"

He didn't even give her a chance to finish.

"Ready? One, two, *tree* ball in the corner pocket." He stole that comment from his grandfather, who loved playing pool. His grandfather jokingly said 'tree' in place of 'three.' They had a pool table in the basement, and whenever family gathered for birthdays, holidays, and other occasions, he recalled hearing Grandpa sing out after taking a shot with his cue stick: "Tree ball in the corner pocket." And the cherry-red ball would bank off the felt wall and disappear into the pocket.

He gripped a handle over the toilet and pulled the flusher cord, and Rainn did the same. Zane, unsure of what to expect, trusted his gut instinct on this one.

His hand clenched the flusher cord handle as an oncoming seizure engulfed him.

The walls of the portal started to shake. Zane blacked out...

The portal walls shivered and quaked, as did her brother. Who was erupting more violently? She had no idea, because she was busy being tossed around inside the portal, shoulders, knees, and elbows absorbing the impact of rubber-padded walling.

A resounding THUD was followed by silence. She lay in a heap next to Zane. He was no longer seizing. Not even moving. Was he breathing?

She had gotten turned upside down and was staring at the floor. She slid down the wall and took stock of the situation: the portal potty was leaning heavily to one side.

"Zane? You okay?" Her words came out slow and quiet.

Zane remained motionless. Was this a good thing? At least he wasn't convulsing.

She tried to open the door. Locked. She reached into Zane's pocket and grabbed and inserted the key. A clicking sound was followed by the sound of bolts scraping. She tried to open the door, but it only moved about an inch. She rammed her shoulder into the door, and it rubbed against the grassy turf. She shoved again, putting her shoulder into it one more time, and the door pushed open enough for her to squeeze out.

The portal sat in a small crater of earth edged in burnt sand and stone, resting crookedly. She was in the greenest, darkest, tallest forest she had ever seen in this lifetime.

Trees, trees, trees. Everywhere she looked: trees with boughs that bent in the breezes. Evergreens, eucalyptus, oak, pine, misshapen alders, and standing as Giants above everything else: redwoods. Even the sky took on a new shade: green.

Canopied by a grove of redwoods.

This thick, vibrant crown was unlike anything she'd ever seen. So lush, so fragrant: she felt as if she were witnessing a living, breathing paradise. Unique and colorful, yet the longer she stared at this alien landscape, the more she began feeling welcome here. As she stared at the forest, her memory of a long-forgotten past began to surface. This great Wood was familiar.

Was it something in the air? She wasn't sure, but as she took a deep lungful of air, her mind drifted off.

Someone coughed.

Her brother.

"Ooohhh. What happened?" she heard Zane say after spitting.

She helped him squeeze out the portal door. He sat in the grass, arms wrapped around knees, looking out with a dazed expression coloring his features. His eyes, usually a vibrant periwinkle blue, were glassy and the color of smoke retreating from a flame.

She helped him to his feet.

"Where are we?" He turned his head slowly, as if making sure it was still attached. "Where's the barn. Weren't we just…"

"The portal, Zane. Somehow, we portaled here in that thing. This place is amazing, but—you okay?"

"Where is here?" He looked at all the trees, wearing a forced, unassuming expression as if one of the trees were tempting him and calling him closer.

A gentle rumbling sound came from inside the portal. The fiberglass walls started pulsating, and a bright orangish-red glow spilled out from the partially opened door.

BOOM!

The portal exploded, sending an eruption of black smoke. The roiling smoke was littered with silvery-white stars. Everything, to Rainn, seemed to move in slow motion: shards of fiberglass, bits of porcelain, cloudy stars of bright white light blurred past her. She and Zane tumbled to the ground, covering their heads.

Zane looked up to see his sister, a good twenty yards away, lying on the ground. Motionless. The portal potty, now charred black and gray littered the forest floor with bits of jagged fiberglass. This wooded area, an immense collection of Herculean redwoods, included flowering plants of the brightest shades of reds, golds, blues, and purples—a psychedelic carpet. Zane likened it to a penthouse Garden of Eden. Although his splitting headache of the century didn't feel very Eden-like.

He eventually pushed himself up onto his hands and knees. "Rainn? Rainn?"

A crackle of branches.

Three massive black birds flew off a branch, wings in the shape of lethargic windsails. Twigs and bits of bark fell toward the ground; Zane spotted something else amid the candy-coated forest floor. A figure was lying on the grass. A definite someone under the awning of an evergreen tree dwarfed by all the redwoods. He squinted, hoping to focus on the body, but squinting only made his head ache more.

Who was that on the ground? Then he spotted Rainn, also lying on the forest floor. His mind spun in neutral. What had happened here? And where was *here*? That was question number one.

Rainn appeared unconscious. He bent down to inspect her and looked out to the stranger a short distance away.

Someone moaned.

He then realized it was not Rainn moaning.

The moaning came from the stranger—the figure pillowed in the dirt about ten yards away from Rainn.

"Be right back, sister. Don't go running off on me."

The other apparent victim-in-training was a young guy, about his age. Upon closer inspection, Zane cringed. It was the most familiar person in his life. This was the last thing he expected to see: himself.

Now, this was too weird, even for Zane. Impossible as it seemed, the person lying on the ground was Zane. There were, in fact, two Zanes.

Not only was this forest new to him, but now there was this strange new guy. The twin Zane continued to moan; so, he wasn't dead.

Was that a good thing?

Zane tried to make a mental checklist of what needed to be done. Maybe if he took notes on what had happened, it would make sense.

He listed the things he remembered:

Standing in the barn at home with Rainn. Check.

Chatting with Great Uncle Stanley, his dead ghost of an uncle. Check.

Climbing into the portal potty with his sister. Check.

After that, he could not remember a thing.

"Rainn?" he called out to her as he heard twigs and grasses rustling.

Rainn was stirring in the tall heather. She slowly sat up. They stared at each other from across the grass; Zane had no recollection of being tossed around in the rocketing portal potty like a fresh salad.

He took one look at the portal, or what remained of it: two bent walls remained standing but were torn into crumbling bits; smoke billowed from the vents in one wall; fragmented bits of the porcelain toilets and fiberglass lay strewn about the forest.

"What a mess," Zane said.

One large segment of paneling had plunged into a tree like an arrow strike.

Fueled by the utter disbelief of seeing his twin lying in the grass, he pinched himself on the arm. Nope. Not dreaming. Gingerly, he stepped through tall straw-yellow grasses, looking from Rainn to this strange lookalike and back again. The Zane lying in the grass was dressed just like him. Olive-green fleece pullovers, khaki shorts, hiking boots. Even his socks had matching grass stains.

"Hey you," Zane called out to the other Zane. "You don't look so good." His left eye was blackened and swollen.

No response.

Rainn spoke while slowly standing up and battling her swirly equilibrium. Her eyes moved to the body lying in the grass near Zane.

"Whoa! That—who is that…? Oh. My. God!"

"Hello?" Zane called out a second time, voice cracking under the heat of this pressurized situation. "Man, he's a mess. Looks like he got into a fistfight with King Kong. Do you know how we got here? Last thing I remember is…" He could feel his sister staring at him.

"What?"

"Zane, your face…what happened?"

He touched his cheek gently and exhaled a sigh of pain. "My head hurts. How do I look?" He wished, just this once, that his sister had a mirror, but she was not the type to worry over her appearance and carry around a compact. She was a natural beauty.

She pointed to the body in the grass.

"What?"

"Your face…it's bruised just like his."

The combined weight of curiosity and distress was almost unbearable. Just then, a rumbling sound off in the distance gobbled up his attention. He fired a glance over his shoulder. A pair of headlights came into view. The vehicle, rumbling closer, sped toward them, bouncing along the bumpy mountain trail. It swerved around a redwood and darted between two boulders, coming right at him. He looked back to the Zane lying on the ground.

"You're on your own, dude."

Zane had more important things to worry about, like avoiding a pedestrian homicide. He and Rainn bolted toward a redwood tree, hurdled a large rock, and hid behind it. Brakes locked up. Car skidded to a halt, missing a tree by inches. Clouds of dust surrounded the taxicab. A shiny red checkered Studebaker. Quietly, it hummed. Looked like it came out of a storefront window display at a high-end dealership. A fat elbow hung out the open window, advertising a bazooka tattoo on the driver's hairy forearm. He flicked a cigar butt into a mound of dirt and snarled, "Get in."

Click. The doors unlocked, and the rear passenger-side door slid open like a car that magically opened with the click of a remote. The side panel was stamped in large block letters: Epi Taxi, Serving Seizure Minds.

Zane peered at the driver but couldn't make out his features in the mash of shadows. Tiny flashing lights framed the rear license plate: 12SEIZE.

The engine revved. White smoke laced in purple mist coughed out the exhaust pipe. In seconds, the air was filled with hazy smoke. Zane started coughing and looked at Rainn. He decided to jump in the cab before he gagged.

The door closed behind him. Click went the lock.

"Might want to buckle up," said the driver. "Seizure travel can be a bumpy ride."

Seizure travel? "Wait. My sister."

"Move over," hissed Rainn as the door opened on its own and she slid in next to him. "You mind telling us what's going on? We're not from around here."

The driver glanced at an iClipboard sitting on the passenger seat.

"Zane. I've been expecting you."

Zane's eyes widened curiously. *How does he know my name?*

Rainn remained calm. "Don't know anyone by that name," Rainn lied. "Sorry. We're in a bit of a mix-up and maybe you could take us somewhere where there's better cell reception. My phone's not working. We're lost." She shrugged. "How much is the fare?"

The driver gave her a long, steely stare. "You must be the second Moss twin, yes?"

He lifted the iClipboard; its digital screen, encased in tree bark, displayed two portraits, one of Zane, a senior picture from High School, and one of Rainn, a photo taken at a family vacation last summer.

Zane leaned forward to get a closer look at the screen. "That's from our trip to San Francisco." He pointed out the cable car rails on Market Street.

"So, you *do* have WIFI connectivity?" Rainn gave the driver a look of distaste. "Sir, can I borrow your hotspot. You know, just tether to your device for a minute?"

"I suggest you buckle up. Zane, you're gonna need to spool out a spindle of your epi energy. Consider it payment. It's not a free ride to Enchanted Wood. But you, lady, you're not on my queue."

"Enchanted Wood?" Zane and Rainn chorused, now staring at the back of the driver's head.

The driver tugged on his dirty baseball cap.

"That's right, kids."

The driver looked at Zane through the rearview mirror, pinpoint pupils swimming in hazel-gold-rimmed eyes. They seemed to glow, casting shadows on the bags under his eyes and across his plump, unshaven cheeks.

"Transport epileptic riders. That's my job. The name's Caesar. Enjoy your trip here, didja? Looks like you took one for the team, kid."

Zane remained quiet.

"Well, hello, Caesar," Rainn said, "I'd like to know why we're going to Enchanted Wood. I do have an appointment in the coming weeks with a faerie in the canopy, but our early arrival was unplanned." Her gaze moved to Zane.

Zane looked at her with as much shock as seeing his twin lying in the grass. Thoughts of doppelgangers from his youthful D&D role-playing experiences came to life.

"Look, lady, nothing is unplanned when it comes to arriving in Enchanted Wood. And, if you want me to transport you to another part of the forest, that'll cost extra. I'm scheduled to transport Zane. And unless you're a newly added fare…hang on a sec." He pulled out an eyepatch from his shirt pocket and placed it on the middle of his forehead, over his Third Eye, and looked at Rainn, his hairy elbow resting on the seatback.

"Please confirm your destination."

"Me? I told you I wasn't expected to arrive today."

"Yeah. Tell me that location."

"Eastern Rim. That's all I know. In the canopy." She went on to say: "How much for a lift?" She reached into a pocket and pulled out a hemp-stitched zippered pouch. "Two gold pieces, enough?"

Caesar grinned and scratched his beard. "That'll do."

"What's going on?" Zane demanded, looking at the ancient-looking gold coins now sitting in a cup holder. "You know this guy? Where'd you get those?"

"I know *of* him," she said. "He's the local cabbie for Enchanted Wood. A commodity in these parts among epi riders. Don't worry, brother, we can trust him."

"I'm not worried," Zane said. Zane was worried.

Something smelled rank. Either Caesar needed a bath, or the floor of this taxi stank. Decomposing food wrappers, hardened bread sticks, and blackened banana peels soiled the floor. Finally, his curiosity inflated larger than his dread.

Zane asked, "So…did I have a seizure in that portal?" His head was aching.

The driver's snake eyes stared at him through the rearview mirror, appearing displeased with such a question. "As I said, looks like you've been in a bit of a scuffle and on the losing end of that one, champ." He grinned.

Zane dared another question: "You said I was on your schedule or something? But I didn't schedule anything. Just like Rainn said."

Caesar leaned over and tapped the dashboard with his meaty fist. The glove compartment popped open. He pulled out a small disk about the size of a silver dollar, circa 1976, not one of those 21st-century quarter-sized coins. He stuck it into a slot on the dash near keys jangling in the steering column. Zane half-expected a jukebox to start playing music. Instead, a sultry feminine voice spoke through the rear and front speakers: "Zane Moss. Powered by convulsive energy. Destination: five miles southwest of Enchanted Wood proper. Home of Ick and Madge."

Who is this guy? Zane wondered. *A GPS hacker with djinni skills?*

Caesar put the taxi into gear and sped over a hill. Rounded a bend in the trail, tossing Zane across the backseat, slamming him into the door. Both teens buckled in just as they were approaching a wooden bridge.

The bridge spanned a quarter-mile-wide river, tires vibrating violently over wooden planks. The taxi caught air upon exiting the bridge, sailing over a ditch in the path. Sparks flew out from the rear bumper hitting rocks in the dirt path. Caesar careened through a dense redwood grove, increasing his speed as they got deeper into the Wood. The Studebaker swerved, the tail of the cab bumping into a jagged boulder, dinging the rear quarter panel.

He just kept driving.

All Zane could think was: this guy's crazy. Maybe he's bipolar riding out his mania.

"We trying to break a land-speed record or something?"

"You're the energy guy who oozed epileptic voltage all over my cab in one big psychotic burst, you crazed epileptic! Fool!"

Zane, a bit shaken, said nothing in reply. Caesar was a wee bit overconfident.

Tall trees and massive bushes and blooming flowers tall as a TRex blurring by. The cab was going too fast for him to focus.

"Why are we in such a hurry?" Zane muttered in a gritty tone, "Whose funeral are we late for? Mine?"

Rainn put a hand on his arm, as if trying to reassure him that everything was okay. It wasn't helping matters at all.

They swerved around another massive boulder and skidded to a halt.

"Here's your stop," Caesar said mildly, pulling a fresh cigar from a cigar box in the glove compartment. He gave each twin an impatient glance. "Well? Enjoy your.... lives."

"What's going on?"

The driver sighed and killed the motor. He spun around, resting his chin on his meaty forearm hanging off the leather seat. "Trippin' for the first time, are you? Newbie to your epileptic gift?"

There's that term again: Epileptic gift.

Zane sighed as the cabbie was busy chewing on his unlit cigar, saliva silvering his bewhiskered chin.

"You had a seizure back there. Somewhere. I'm just the messenger."

Messenger?

Caesar continued: "That's my job. Taxiing people from here and there. Better to have someone guide you along the way, especially someone with your kind of problem."

"What problem is that?"

He exchanged a glance with Rainn.

"You're green around the edges, kid. You seizure riders blackout and wander around aimlessly. But, on a positive vein, it's more of you to transport, which means more job security for me." He drew on his cigar, furrowing his brow.

Zane, already confused, was even further at a loss. More importantly, who gave this guy his driver's license?

"Man…I mean, sir, you're a reckless driver."

Caesar grinned, revealing nice teeth, which surprised Zane. "Only drive as reckless as a convulsing body. Your seizing body." He winked.

"Wait a sec. If I had a seizure in your cab, why didn't I black out, huh? Explain that."

"Really? You paying attention, kid? Is this your first epileptic trip?"

Zane's forehead screwed up into a wave of wrinkles. "My first trip in this cab. Help me out, Rainn."

"Maybe it'll be your last." Caesar tapped his fingers on the steering wheel. "You youngsters have a thing with short attention spans."

"So."

"So… I'm just reminding you, again, for the umpteenth time: I'm just the driver."

"A rather reckless driver."

"Consider me your guardian gatekeeper at the wheel." He turned his baseball cap around and pointed at it with a greasy, fat finger. A patch on his baseball cap read: Epi T.

"That's T…for taxi. I transport seizure-bound souls. Epileptics. That'd be you, kid." His eyes studied Zane for a moment. "From one place to the next. Speaking of next," he looked at Rainn, then back to Zane. "Didn't you need a ride somewhere, missy?"

Zane couldn't stop staring at this man's grizzled face. Caesar's small eyes were hypnotic, like a cat's gaze. Curly hair snaked out from under his hat, and looked like his hair was wet from just jumping out of the shower, but the stench made Zane think otherwise.

"I'll just stick with Zane."

"So…this is my stop, then?" Zane asked.

"Enchanted Wood central. Redwood forest. Look around. Soak it all in." The cabbie sounded thoroughly bored with the conversation. "*The* redwood forest. For telepaths, treezers, spellfarmers, and other Electric Energy enthusiasts. Yes, this is your stop, kid."

"What? What am I supposed to do?" Zane asked in exasperation.

"Not my job to know. I'm just the messenger. Remember? Deliver people from point A to point B…. Oh, but there is another option." He glanced down to a clipboard in his lap housing a digital screen, then peered thoughtfully into woods, as if searching for something recently misplaced. "Looks as though you didn't choose *that* option."

"What option? What plan you talking about? Rainn?" "Portal potty travel," Rainn said calmly.

Zane's forehead wrinkled. "Our portal potty blew up or something." Zane stretched out his arms in exclamation. "Intense situation. Good thing you weren't there to see it."

"Sucks to be an earthling," Caesar said dully, his eyes returning to the clipboard. "Looks as though you arrived with a little extra bang for your buck. But you may owe for damages to the portal."

"Huh?"

"You're energy's all wiggly. You need to learn to tame your electrical outbursts. Before you really cause some harm. The damaged portal may come back to haunt you." He winked.

The hell? No flipping way. "I didn't do anything," said Zane. "The portal crash-landed."

"I'm no lawyer, but you wouldn't want to wander around blowing anything else up, now, would you?" He waggled his bushy eyebrows. "Don't answer that. But I should warn you: your teenage electrical energies have become quite the commodity around here."

Zane fidgeted his hands in his lap.

"Too bad you blew up that portal. They don't come cheap." Caesar exhaled smoke out the window. "If convicted, how're you going to pay for it?"

Zane wore an expression of shocked disapproval. "I didn't blow it up, dude. A dead guy did."

Caesar didn't even bat an eye. Instead, rather calmly, he went on: "Most epi riders, if they crash, do disappear if a portal goes boom. Why'd you leave the scene? They could hit you with accessory to vandalism. And you, lady, you may be charged with breaking and entering. That portal is for epileptics."

"I need to speak to my Great Uncle Stanley," Zane claimed. "My Great Uncle Stanley's a ghost. If anyone caused the explosion, it was him—I think. In fact, the portal was broken or under repair when we were transported. Remember the sign on the portal, sis?"

She frowned.

As soon as the words came out of his mouth, he felt guilty for blaming his uncle.

"I didn't vandalize anything. I swear."

"Really?" Caesar said to the clipboard. "But if you left any trace of being at the scene, they'll find you. You're the young epi. Anyone else see you at the scene?"

"Just me and Rainn."

"No one? What about this dead guy you keep referring to? Better get your story straight."

"Uncle Stanley? He disappeared before it blew up. I think. And no. No one else saw us," Zane said in his own defense. "All I did was step into the portal and find a note in lipstick on the mirror. My dead Great Uncle must've written it." Zane met the driver's gaze. "Oh, there was something else. There was another guy outside the portal potty, lying on the ground. He looked like me. Exactly like me. Not sure if he was hurt. There was no time to check on him."

Caesar yawned and went back to chewing on his cigar as if this conversation was becoming a bit stale. "Don't know anything about three Moss siblings. Just you two."

"But I saw him." Zane added in exasperation. "And he was wearing the same clothes as me."

"You done with your tale? I've got other appointments. I'm taking your sister to her destination. Now begone. Get out!"

"But I want to stay with Zane!"

The door opened, and Caesar scowled, "Get out. Now!" Zane saw Caesar about to elbow him in the jaw. His face was full of enough bruises. He slid out of the cab. The door slammed shut. Rainn tried to open her door. Locked.

The Studebaker sped off with Rainn in the back seat.

The taxi skidded to a halt; the door opened.

"You forgot something'," Caesar shouted.

Good, thought Zane, *he's going to let Rainn out.*

Instead, the hairy mitt tossed something out the cab window.

He sped off, fishtailing up the path.

"The hell?" Zane tossed his hands in the air.

He turned his attention to the object in the trail. He picked up a wooden doll, dressed in a silk robe with a long single braid. It was a flaxen-haired puppet.

Rainn, suddenly fearful for her own safety, thought for a moment, wondering why her brother was kicked out of the cab. She went ahead and asked Caesar. "So, how long will it be?"

"Just answer my questions about this dead uncle," Caesar repeated.

Rainn took a slow breath and stared out the window. They were traveling along at a good clip, and she was trapped in the back seat.

"Don't know him. My brother claimed he could see him trying to fix the portal potty." Her sweaty legs stuck to the car seat, squeaked as she swayed back and forth.

"But this Great Uncle Stanley is not something your brother fabricated?"

"Nope. I believe my brother and I do know Stanley died years ago. When we were babies. So, no, he's not like me, I mean, yeah, we're related by blood, but I'm not dead," she said in an elevated tone. "Great Uncle Stanley's a ghost."

"Thought you said he wasn't like you?" Caesar retorted, dry as a stalk of wheat.

"He's not. And don't put words in my mouth. According to my little brother, Great Uncle Stanley was trying to help him. Dude's dead. A ghost. Zane's the only one who can see him. He did say

Stanley was always dressed in the same clothes: a tweed blazer and yellow bow tie.”

“Ghosts are spiritualistic gymnasts, but choosing a new wardrobe isn’t exactly a priority for them. They can change clothes, just like the rest of us. Although ghosts shop for special ethereal fabric.”

“I kind of figured that much,” Rainn said. “I have been to Enchanted Wood before. I know it’s got lots of haunts, but last time I was here, oh, it had to be when I was ten. Why can’t we go get Zane?”

“How old are you?”

She told him.

“Just making sure. Got to keep your story straight, for the authorities. You better practice your speech and keep all your facts, if they are facts, straight. Nothing wiggly. The authorities will not believe you.” He stared at her through the rearview mirror. She met his gaze. He winked.

“The authorities?” Rainn’s tone wavered. “I’m here to discuss personal matters with a fae.”

“So, you keep saying.” He tapped his cigar in an ashtray. “Zane needed to be separated from you. You’re both considered felons around here. I’m just trying to protect you both. Divide and conquer.”

Felons? They were not felons. She gulped and refrained from getting emotional.

“But Zane is not familiar with this place,” she said. “And neither am I. We’ve done nothing wrong.”

“Illicit energy travel is, to use your phrase, wrong. You’re both listed as felons. You arrived on a portal potty, yes?” She nodded.

“Without proper authorization, you’re here illegally, but I won’t turn you in. That’s not my department. I’m here to support all epis who are upstanding Epi innovators. Like the two of you.”

The cabbie was confusing her. One minute, he was pressing her with word of being wanted felons; the next he was calling both of them Epi innovators.

"That won't fly if you're arrested, though," he added.

Ah, there he goes again, Rainn thought, *filling me with worry.*

"Now that I've got your brother off my queue, where is it you'd like to go? I've got enough epi fuel for local-area destinations."

She gave this some thought. The only person she could think of was Great Uncle Stanley.

"So, are you familiar with the undead contingents and ghosts in the community?" she asked.

He scratched his hairy chin. "Sure. Anyone in particular?"

"Great Uncle Stanley—the one my brother kept talking about." "Not sure about that one."

Rainn decided she was going to have to figure out her next move on her own. She was still uncertain how much she could trust this hairy cabbie.

"Where do ghosts like to hang out?"

"You mean his haunt. His hangout. His place of residence. His domicile. His den. Or social situations?"

"Well, if you don't have a location on my dead great uncle, how many ghosts live here? I really need to find him. Maybe he's hanging out of with, you know, the undead." Of course, finding Zane would be even better.

"Lots of ghosts live here—if you call that living. More and more transient beings are taking up residency here. Lots of underground hangouts for ghosts. Tens of thousands of undead beings call Enchanted Wood home. Many of them have connections to cemetery property managers. Not my cup of tea."

"Is there any way you can take me to some of the popular ghost joints for elderly spirits?" Rainn asked. "Great Uncle Stanley was old when he died. Maybe he's spending time with the senior side of ghost life, yes?"

Rainn had formulated a plan; if she could find her ghost uncle, then he, Great Uncle Stanley, might have a location for Zane. He was supposed to be her brother's guide here.

"Hey, you think Uncle Stanley might have information on us being fugitives?" she asked.

"You're wanted fugitives. How many times do I need to tell you? Not sure where your Uncle lives. That's not my department, and I also already told you. I don't know much about this Great Uncle Stanley. But I can tell you this: the real estate market for dead residents is a booming industry in Enchanted Wood, and your uncle could be living anywhere. Be straight with me; are you worried about this ghost of an uncle having a criminal record, or something? So, you can pin this exploding portal and illicit energy travel on him?"

"What? Nononono! Nothing like that. Just curious about his…"

"Integrity?"

"Yeah," Rainn lied. "I just wish I could contact him."

The cabbie pulled the cab to the shoulder and parked. He scrolled through his iClipboard.

"Nope. No ghost by the name of Great Uncle Stanley on the digital press's list of fugitives. Does your Uncle Stanley have a last name?"

"Uh…Moss. I think. Not sure exactly."

Without using a mouse, he moved the cursor on the screen by staring at the cursor, then he blinked, the cursor lit up, and he dragged it across the screen by moving his chin; the cursor blinked on an ACTIVE FUGITIVE list.

"Nope. No Stanley Moss on the fugitive list. Just you two. Oh, for the love of dead dudes, I can sense a little anxiety flowing from the back seat. Don't worry, I'm not haunted. Just the forest is." He glanced back at her and smirked.

"You've got access to that kind of information?" Rainn was beginning to wonder about the authenticity of this cabbie.

"Course I do. It's public record."

He drove onward, crossing a bridge, headed into a small town, and stopped in front of *Freddy's Food.*

His pinpoint pupils read his digital clipboard from under the brim of his dusty cap.

"But epileptic emergencies go straight to the top of my queue…oh, your stop is just a few blocks away."

Rainn was known for her ability to remain unflappable during distressing situations, but Caesar was rattling her; there was something else here, something was amiss. The longer she sat there, the more she felt strained, as if someone was breathing down her neck and tinkering around with her thoughts.

Rainn leaned back, resting her head on the seatback, and, from her diaphragm, sighed. Then, just as her heart rate was beginning to level off, a thin, vaporous voice entered her thoughts.

The voice in her mind sounded as if spoken through a long metal pipe. She couldn't put a name to the speaker.

Don't mind me, said the voice. *Relax. I'm just here to make sure your brain-map matches the data in my queue. My little truth serum, if you will. You know teens are apt to lie. Not that you would ever lie, but, well, I'm just covering my* bases. *Common practice with all my clientele. Yes ma'am, things are checking out nicely. Good show.*

It wasn't a normal psychic call. There was something more to this voice, but Rainn couldn't place it.

Who's this? she inquired with PMS kindness.

CLICK.

Her psychic call lost connectivity. Dead on the digital rails.

Rainn snapped out of her PMS trance but was now staring, with hypnotic horror, at Caesar's index finger, his long pointy nail rapping away at the seatback.

Rainn, in a very soft voice, said, "Feel kind of…off. Strange. Odd. Did you just call me?"

"Not sure why you feel strange. You've been telling the truth."
Silence.

"Now's no time to be shy, kid," he said.

"Did you just PMS me?"

He said nothing.

Rainn began staring at her knees, "Just not feeling well. A little dizzy. Thought I got a psychic call, but the reception was lost."
"What, you afraid someone's window-shopping in your thoughts? This is Enchanted Wood, a forest filled with memory thieves."

"Memory thieves?"

"Rest easy, girl. That was me in your brain. Just checking under the hood, if you know what I mean. I'm no thief. It's my job to review portal rider memories."

She wasn't bothered too much by Caesar wandering into her thoughts, but the more she thought about it, the more invasive it felt. She decided to steer clear of making abrasive comments to Caesar because she wanted to keep their relationship as friendly as possible.

"It was just a little surprising, is all. Didn't sound like you." He shrugged.

"It'd be nice if you asked," she stated.

"I needed a clean look at your thoughts. Didn't want you hiding any memories."

People can do that? Hide memories? she wondered.

"Just verifying that you are who you claim to be. Yes, you're related to this dead uncle you keep mentioning, and you are Zane's sister. Your Great Uncle's new to his deadness. But that's not my department. No details on him. I tend to stick with tangible affairs. Much more fun than tracking down ghosts. How long ago did this uncle of yours die?"

She stared off a moment. "Bout fifteen years. I think. Something like that."

"This dead guy mean anything to you? I mean, why's he on contract with your brother?"

Now it was her turn to shrug.

"You didn't answer my question: does your dead uncle mean anything to you?"

"Don't know anything else about 'im. Zane told me he just showed up in his closet. Freaked him out. Our uncle died when we were toddlers. So, I don't remember him."

Caesar grinned, eyeing his iClipboard. "Good for you. You're telling the truth. It's the only way to stay on the straight and narrow in this land of magical intrigue."

Rainn decided that if she wanted to stay on Caesar's good side, she should play it casual. She shared some details about meeting Esmeralda and a few other faeries. And that she was scheduled to meet some of the fae in Enchanted Wood.

The end of Caesar's cigar glowed red as he drew on it and exhaled smoke out the side of his mouth. "If you think about it, you're right where you need to be, kid."

Rainn wanted to tell him she was hardly a kid anymore. She was a mature eighteen-year-old; her knowledge and core strength gave her the resources of a wise elder.

"I do have another question, though," she added. "I don't think we should've left Zane alone back there. Why'd you kick him out? It'd be better if he stayed with me. We can manage things here and camp out together. There's got to be a campground around here, yes?"

"What kind of campground? One for lost eighteen-year-olds?"

How did he know her age? She must look about eighteen. Yeah, that was it, or did he read into her age while peeking at her thoughts? She wasn't liking Caesar's ability to do this. Left her feeling naked.

"If you could get me and my brother together again, well, that'd be a start."

"Listen, missy, you are eighteen. *And* you're lost. And I've dropped your brother off where he needs to go. You told me you needed to meet some fae." Silence.

"Got something to say, kid? Am I not following through with your request?"

"How'd you know my age?" she asked in a rush and then bit on her lower lip and looked away.

"If that'll set your electric mind at ease—sure, you look like a teenager and I can see your age in your mind. But you look like a rather *befuddled* teenager." Caesar paused. "Now, it looks as though my job as your cabbie's about over." He put the car in gear, drove another half mile, and pulled the cab to a stop under a willow tree.

Rainn put her hand on the door handle. "Is this where Esmeralda is?" She stared out the window. "Wait. It'd be cool if you could drive me back and pick up Zane. I know your job is to drive epis around, right? We're twins. Virtually inseparable," she lied. "We do better teaming up." Another lie.

"I've got other appointments. I've already extended myself beyond my contractual obligation. Your brother must figure things out on his own. It's part of his soul contract. Your brother exited at his scheduled destination. And if I said I could take you back to him, well, I'd be lying. Lying is for dark magic entrepreneurs. You dabble in the dark side of enchantment, do ya?"

Was this cabbie more psychic than she gave him credit? She didn't meddle in the Dark Arts. So, he had to be misreading her.

"Nope. I'm a good queen." Another lie.

"And your brother? What sort of Dark Arts does he tool around with? Did he learn from you?"

Zane wasn't even capable of a good card trick. Rainn wasn't sure where Caesar was going with this conversation, but she was feeling even more invaded by his questioning than by having him search through her memories.

Caesar's clipboard started to beep with excitement. He tapped the brim of his baseball cap with a dirt-encrusted finger; an earpiece dropped into place over his ear.

"Caesar's E.T. here."

Caesar, since he was able move a cursor on the screen by staring at it, could also transfer his thoughts, psychically, onto his iClipboard; his iClipboard was linked to his brainprint, recognizing his brain with the ease of a forensic expert dusting for fingerprints at a crime scene.

"That works for me," he said. "Next Tuesday. Noon. North Ridge. Four Three Nine One. Yep. Seers Street. Got it."

His yellow gaze moved to Rainn, and his pupils tugged at her, inching her shoulders forward; some sort of magnetic energy pulling her.

"You got plans next Tuesday, Rainn?"

"Tuesday?" Rainn straightened her shoulders. "Look, dude, uh, sir, I need to check in with Esmeralda and my brother. And I presume this willow we're parked under is where I'll find her. I haven't thought ahead to Tuesday." Now that she thought of it: she didn't know what day it was.

He drew on his cigar and nodded.

"Now you're thinking. Whether you realize it or not, you've come here because of your capabilities."

"My capabilities?"

"Specifically, those revolving around energy work," Ceasar said. "This is a great time to make plans. Your brother wouldn't be called if he wasn't ready. What's the worst thing that might happen? Even if he dies, he'll just move in with some haunts. Make new friends."

"I'm not worried," she lied.

"I sense otherwise." He tapped his cigar out the window. "Listen, your brother's been chosen, too. Don't you get it? Stick with the plan, kid. Make it easier on yourself. Slow down. Breathe.

Go find that faerie."

"Here's a plan," Rainn offered. "Put this car into gear and drive me back to Zane. I'm sure I can scrounge up a tip for you. Then I'll find Esmeralda."

"If you're in such a hurry to find your brother, why not send yourself back to him? Use your energy."

"Me?" She wasn't an epi. "I'm here to see Esmeralda. With Zane."

"Rainn, this is a very safe forest to be lost in. You'll like it here. Safer than Earth."

"No way."

"Earth's a near-dead planet."

She ignored his comment, "If you won't take me to Zane, can you tell me why he's here?"

Caesar's eyes returned to his iClipboard. "Your psychic channels are open. You're a born leader. There's a fire in you. You and your brother are scheduled to meet up with a spellfarmer and a treezer. Beyond that, well, that's all I can share right now. I'm not a clairvoyant. Just reading the plan in front of me, kid," Caesar added dryly. "Shall I float back into your thoughts, scavenge my way around a little bit.
See if I can get you recalibrated."

"You'll be doing no such thing, sir." Rainn's eyes got as big as flying saucers.

"Trust your first plan: Find your fae."

"You're a cabbie. Surely you know these roads. Just drive me back to where we were." Her eyes studied the lush forest.

"No roads lead back to wherever it is you're so stuck on returning to," said the driver. "Zane's moved on by now. You need to stiffen the old backbone. Stop worrying about your brother." Caesar smirked. "Figured you'd be somewhat in tune with your electric potential."

A beeping sound came from his clipboard.

"Your brother's not the only epileptic I service. And I happen to be busy navigating this epileptic chariot."

"Chariot?"

"Indeed. My cab's pollution-free. Runs on epi energy. And your brother recycled his energy into my cab. We all must share our gifts. It's the only way to live."

"Unless you're a ghost."

"Ghosts are not my department."

Rainn shook his head and pursed her lips; portal lag was wearing her out. "But my intuition's telling me that Zane's lost, sir."

"Here's a tip. Stop thinking about being lost; instead, allow positivity to marinate; slow roast 'em like your favorite stew braised in honey and teriyaki sauce." He licked his salivating lips. "When you have faith, you'll tap into a new compartment of consciousness."

Caesar glanced at the sun. "Oh my, I've overstayed my welcome. Got plenty of others to assist. Consider yourself lucky, kid. I don't usually chat so much. Now, if you'd be so kind." Caesar paused and opened his mouth wide, like a dragon ready to breathe fire. His face reddened, and he shouted, "Get out of my cab!"

Rainn couldn't reach for the door handle quickly enough.

Outside, Rainn stared at the idling cab, shiny chrome fenders mirroring her reflection.

Caesar, in a sudden calmer tone, with bipolar intense tonal shift, purred, "Do a few good deeds for Enchanted Wood, unless you die first."

"Look," Caesar continued and pointed across a narrow stream. See all those trees?"

Youthful hundred-year-old redwoods with bands of ropy vines hanging down like Rapunzel's hair sparkled in the sunshine

"Redwoods believe in longevity, like no other living creation in the Wood. Slow your thoughts, rejuvenate, restore your electricity. Then step into the light. Glow. Like the trees. Remain steadfast and true. Patient and empowered."

The driver then started to growl through a cloud of cigar smoke.

Caesar sped off, tires kicking up rocks, brake lights flashing as the cab disappeared into the woods, leaving Rainn alone. In the woods.

Tiny stars twinkled in the graying sky like a scared little dog peeing on a moonlit black napkin. Critters and woodland birds chirped and made tick-tock sounds; a far-off humming noise came above this layered musical vibrancy. The crescent moon and stars offered enough light for him to see.

Zane, uncertain what else to do, gripped the puppet by its braided hair as the wilderness continued with its animalistic conversations.

Why would that crazy driver toss him out? And what about this puppet? Something inside told him to keep it with him.

Puddles in the path glittered silvery blue in the starlight. He listened, hoping to hear the Studebaker's engine approaching. No such luck.

Zane had to find a way out to reconnect with Rainn. He tried calling, but there was no cell reception in this forest. His iPhone was useless.

Zane lifted the puppet's face to his and then gazed at its halter top, spaghetti strap hanging off one shoulder. The wooden limbs warmed his hand as if this puppet had been heating in a kiln.

He tossed the puppet into a mound of heather. No time for dolls and puppets. His sister remained a priority.

"What do you think you're doing?" said a spry little voice from the scrub brush, sounding unnerved.

Zane stood over the puppet, its head buried in the heather, feet sticking up in the air.

"Pick me up, fool," it demanded.

He lifted it up, studying the puppet's amber eyes glowing like some possessed little creature.

"Your name wouldn't happen to be Chucky, would it?" Zane asked and gave her a gentle squeeze, as if to rouse this wooden puppet, all the while checking for a hatch that might house batteries and explain the voice. The puppet's eyes remained open and glassy. It glared at Zane, boring a hole through his skull.

"Did you just say something?" Zane asked.

Why was he talking to a puppet?

"Figures. You can't talk. You're just a toy, a kid's plaything."

She blinked.

Zane blinked.

The puppet worked its jaw up and down and furrowed its brow.

"Oh, bother. You need help. Another human." She rolled her eyes. "You're just a kid. Why do I always get the green ones? This one's going to be work."

Her mouth lost its clammy rigidity and her voice was more human than robotic.

What? She talks?

"You got a name?" the puppet asked. "Speak!" Zane, puzzled, said nothing.

"Humanoid. Silly creampuff cretin. Frog-brained freak. Hey! I'm talkin' to you."

Was this really happening? Zane had had his share of strange moments in his life, but suffering auditory and visual hallucinations simultaneously—that was new.

Back in elementary school, a classmate named Jericho, an undiagnosed schizophrenic, had common outbursts in class that soon became hazardous to his peers; he'd flip out and brandish weapons fashioned out of common classroom inventory; one day, he threw a chair at the teacher, and the metal leg struck her in head, knocking her unconscious; Jericho hovered over her, raised his chin and howled at the ceiling tiles before slicing her throat with the bladed edge of a ruler which sent the teacher to the ER with a concussion and throat lacerations. The teacher disappeared from school; Jericho's explosive tendencies continued, and the guy never made it to middle school. He went into phantom mode, and one day, POOF, he, too, disappeared from the public sector; school gossip claimed this schizoid, along with the many-hatted minds living in his head, were all shipped off to some mental institution.

The running joke: Jericho was housed in Alcatraz, where he lived in a locked one-room classroom where he studied from inside the coffin confines of a closet.

"I'm Zane," Zane found himself saying. "You look like something from a half-price sale rack at Toy Town."

She wiggled her way out of his grasp and landed on the ground with aerobatic accuracy. Standing with fists on hips, she demanded: "I'm here to help you get your act together. You're a mess, human." She stretched her arms, yawned. "Think about this: imagine you're a dead guy leaning against a tree, its bough swaying this way and that. You are mute, like a tree, but trees communicate without verbal language, and this tree is the only thing keeping you upright and away from the worms on the ground waiting to eat your flesh. You want to call out for help, but you're dead. You need to discover your true voice."

What the hell was this puppet talking about?

"Think, human! Think. You're connected to the woodlands. Yes, being woody, like me, is a thing of beauty. I am immortal. And you, most definitely, are not." She blew on her fingernails.

Zane squinted at her. "What are you, some kind of nut that fell from a dead tree? I've got things to do, girlie."

"You even listening?"

Night breezes mowed through his untamed curly locks and ruffled his shirt.

"Somehow, I think you're not very good at paying attention," said the puppet.

"I don't like paying for things," Zane fired back. *Especially to a puppet.*

A moment of silence hazed the air between them.

"Focus, you bloody human! Focus! Remember, you're nothing but a dead guy leaning against a tree."

"So, you said. Big deal. I'm not dead."

Zane looked to the darkening sky, moving his lips, as if trying to solve an algebra equation. "But here I am talking to you. If I'm dead and leaning against a tree, well, I don't think I'd be doing much of anything."

"Like right now. You're just as useful as if you were dead."

He still did not understand what she was getting at—other than getting on his nerves.

She whistled; a bird landed on her arm. A small black bird with oil-colored eyes.

Zane was about to ask: how can a puppet whistle? But he said nothing.

"And that's where you're wrong, human. Dead wrong."

"It's Zane."

"Sure, kid, fine, whatever. Now, back to my question. Just think to yourself: 'So this is it, then. I'm dead and leaning against a living, breathing tree. Hell, I feel okay. Maybe it's better this way. You know, being dead and all. Being dead opens doors you didn't know existed."

She climbed out of the heather and hopped onto a tree stump. Straightened out the wrinkles in her ruffled skirt. Her face twisted out a sinister scowl, crows' feet wrinkles and all.

"You know what you need? Some scissors to trim those nose hairs. And a little soap. Hygiene! Hygiene! Hygiene!" "Hi, name's Zane, not Gene." She scowled.

"Hang on a sec," said Zane. "What was all that talk about

'imagine being dead?'"

"Just something to think about. It'll bring you home. But it's time to go."

Go? Go where? "Not even sure where we are? I need to find my sister."

"I'll need a little pick-me-up, if you know what I mean."

He picked her up, turned her around, and lifted her skirt, searching again for batteries or a charging port, or maybe a sound device buried in her clothing.

The puppet swatted at him. "Hey, knock it off!" She slapped his arm. "How'd you like it if I started fondling *your* panties?"

"I'm not fondling anything." Another staring contest. "And I don't wear panties."

"Well, I should hope not."

"I'm just…looking."

"Stop it, perv. There're laws against such acts." She whisked a hand through a lock of hair hanging over one eye. "Okay, if you must know."

"Yes?"

"I'm a channel."

"Like YouTube? Tic Tok. Instagram. I knew it."

"No, you oaf! You know nothing." She arched an eyebrow, a snake readying to strike. "Did you dress yourself this morning, or did your mother help you?"

Zane's face reddened. "Listen, doll-face, I'll just toss you into a brush fire if you don't show a little respect."

"A little respect comes with a little knowledge. Bow to your queen."

Why was he even having the conversation?

"I'm extraordinary," she went on to say. "A legendary carving."

"Yeah. So's a turkey breast on Thanksgiving."

She raised both eyebrows haughtily. "I'm a channel, a connecting rod to the spirit realm."

That got Zane's attention. "Oh."

"'Oh' is right. I'm channeling a spirit as we speak. Channel lots of 'em. But it's best to only entertain one spirit at a time. It can be a challenge to placate the notion of schizophrenic energy. My mood changes, too. All dependent on who's lucky enough to enter the sphere of my wooden charm."

Wooden charm? She was a charmer, alright. Her eyes, once again, lost their woodenness. She had bona fide eye sockets and corneas and pupils. Somewhat avian, like an owl: gold and green, flecked in black. Yet she was most definitely wooden everywhere else. Or so he presumed.

"So…you tune into dead people?"

"Something like that. But I don't hunt down spirits and specters and ghosts. They come looking for me. I'm a hot commodity. Everyone wants to be in my wooden heart and soul."

"My Great Uncle Stanley. Does that count for anything?"

"You can be one too."

"Me?"

"Sure. Die, then reap the rewards of Death."

"Nonono! That's not what I meant." Zane did not want to die. "I spoke with a ghost." Zane put a finger to his chin. "My uncle's a ghost."

"Talking to ghosts? Big deal. Lots of people can. That's not even in the same ballpark, kid. But if you're good, like me, you can channel the energy of other Beings. Loads of fun. My spiritual prowess is like no other. I'm highly reputable. Loved by many. I can take you places. And, according to my contract, we need to go. Come on, shall we go, you and I?"

"So… you need *me*?" He squeezed her knee. That was the first time this alpha puppet relinquished any of her controlling personality.

"Knock that off. I'm not that kind of girl."

"But you're just a pup—"

"Don't say it, or I'll have my minions hunt you down. I'll have ghosts haunting you day and night. You'd be easy prey for the dead. Got some real nasty ones on my list, just looking to spook people like you. You'll think you've got a borderline personality disorder."

Minions? Zane stared into his hands, not wanting to stare at the puppet.

The puppet sighed. "You really are a dunderhead. I was carved from ancient redwood. By a specialist. The redwood tree was spelled before birth. When it was nothing but a seedling, a clan of spellfarming witches had gathered and spooled up a batch of spells. They cast these psychic spells onto the redwood seedlings. Or so the storytelling tales go."

"Who made you?"

"That's private information, but the one who made me…well, I no longer need him. He's a bit of a bother, if you ask me. Likes to order everyone around. My strings are simply there to add camouflage. I run the show around here."

"I see. Even though you are a moody little puppet, I find you fascinating," Zane said honestly.

Her redwood face curled into a grin, and, for a flash instant, she appeared human. But then her woodenness returned.

"Spirits use me as a voice of reason. But I'm in control of who I am. And that is something you need to work on, kid."

"Whatever you say, miss," he volleyed back absently.

"Don't call me miss. The name's Trixie."

Trixie. Zane liked how that sounded. It had a nice metallic ping to it.

"Many spirits from Enchanted Wood roam through me."

Zane leaned back, thinking about what it would be like to have spirits entering his body. Would he have to entertain them, like guests in his home? He said the first thing that came to mind:

"What do you do when you go, you know, into schizophrenic ghost-mode?"

She waved him off. "I'm in complete control of who enters me, for the most part anyway. My magical allowances don't come cheap."

"You don't say." Zane wasn't sure how much of this, if any, was true.

"I most certainly do."

"What spirit's rummaging around inside your woodenness now?"

She just stared at him with slow determination, like water dripping down an ice cube.

"I take that as: you're not telling me," Zane said. "So, where do we go from here? You said we had somewhere important to go. I hope it has to do with finding my sister." Zane glanced up the road, now thick with night.

"Follow the path west."

"Care to be a little less specific?"

"Let the stars guide you, Magellan. You're as green as mashed peas."

Zane sighed.

"See that clump of stars up the sky?" Trixie pointed. "No, over there. See it? Soon, there'll be a whole lot more. Just follow that clump. See 'em. They form a nice bright line—Orion's belt. It'll take you into town."

Zane did a little stargazing, trying to spot the triangle of stars, thinking of Rainn's constellation map on her bedroom ceiling.

With his gaze hooked on the starry sky, he said, "Okay. Now what?"

When he looked down, Trixie was gone.

Enchanted Wood is a lush redwood forest, which Reese was proud to call home. Reese, a thin, muscular man, was climbing a redwood, a youthful six-hundred-year-old tree from an established grove, practicing his Treezing skills at night. Treezing, likened to tree-climbing for Greek God gymnasts, was something he'd been practicing since he was a ten-year-old novice tree barker. By all appearances, he fit the mold of a Tarzan hippie.

Rainn, in the coming days, would begin to remember Reese, but now, her memory of a past life here in Enchanted Wood remained lost to her.

A branch crackled high overhead. She gazed upward, but could not see a thing in the darkening night sky. Was something up in the trees?

She sensed it and strained her eyes to no avail, but when she used her ears to listen, her eyesight adjusted to night, offering her an advantage. Somehow, she could see in the dark. Where was this coming from? The moon and stars cast light to help, but she felt as if she had catlike vision. A little voice in between her thoughts told her: *elfin eyesight.*

Deep in the thick canopy overhead, she spotted something moving, but it was well over sixty feet up the tree. Birds and other woodland critters squawked back and forth, deep in conversation.

High in the canopy, a figure navigated the tree limbs through fractured moonlight.

Rainn took a step along the forest floor. A branch snapped. The creature in the canopy paused. Did it see her? A staring contest ensued, but Rainn could only make out its shadowy outline a good fifty feet overhead. Was it a wild cat or ape-like mammal?

This Thing, whatever it was, appeared to be studying her. She took a few more steps, crunchily, through the underbrush of sticks and weeds. The creature had arms and legs and was now moving along a limb and into a clearing, the branch bowing under its weight.

The figure stepped further out on a rubbery branch, bending at the knee, getting the branch to flex.

The figure spoke: "Hello," it yelled, its mop of dreadlocks clinging silently. Brushing back a clump of long dreadlocked hair, it cupped a hand to its mouth and said, "Hello," again.

She scanned the treetops, and could see a figure up there attached to a man's voice. Yes, it was a man. She wanted to get something to defend herself, so she stopped walking, hop-scotched back a pace, and spun around, looking for a rock or some other weapon.

"No," shouted Reese. "I'm up here. In the tree."

She looked skyward but didn't say anything. *Yeah, man, I know you're up there.*

"Can you see me? Up here. I'm Reese," the man named Reese called out, waving his arm excitedly. "I won't hurt you."

Rainn, dressed in big-pocketed khakis and a neoprene top around her slim, curved frame, paused. Thinking. What should she do? She sensed he might be aware of her psychic energy somehow. What a strange thing to think at a moment like this! The man named Reese was now crouching high in the canopy.

"I can see you clearly, miss. I've got night vision. You're not from around here, are you?"

Reese spoke again, "Awfully late for an evening stroll? Doing research or something?"

"Research…? Uh, don't know how I got here," Rainn called out through cupped hands. She could see him clearly, too, but decided not to give away too much information. "I'm lost. Hope I'm not trespassing on private property. Just need a little direction, is all, then I'll be out of your way."

Reese said something, but Rainn couldn't hear him.

Reese, standing in the nucleus of thick leafy branches and flowering plants growing off limbs, nodded to a tree as if it had just spoken to him, barehanded a branch, and swung his legs outward, using momentum to propel him airborne where he clasped another branch, strands of ivy smacking against his sinewy muscled chest. He scaled down the mighty redwood with the athleticism of a professional gymnast. Wiry arms, spotted with freckles, stretched upward to grasp a corduroy-threaded vine. He swung out on the vine in a big sweeping arch, landed on another branch, spun 'round, and hung upside-down where he shook hands with another friendly vine.

He kept moving, skating along a rubbery redwood limb, knees flexed as if he had wheels on his bare feet.

He skidded to slow his blurry momentum as a trunk was fast approaching, pressed his palms off the thick, oily bark, performed a standing push-up, and paused.

From here to the forest floor, six stories, the redwood was bare of branches. Reese pulled rappelling equipment from a pack, an octopus of ropes and lines, clipped a pulley line to a carabiner, roped it off to a limb, and began his descent. With the zip line releasing under his weight, he pushed off the trunk with his feet, sprang outward, and dropped down in ten-foot increments. Reese repeated this motion all the way to the earthen floor, moving with ease, as fluid as water. He landed in a large bed of evergreen sword ferns, somersaulted, and came to a rolling stop, landing upright in a squatting, defensive posture.

He gave Rainn a quick smile while studying her. He wasn't even huffing for breath.

"Hello there! You a Treezing?" he asked, his tone riddled with doubt.

What? Rainn wondered.

"Years of practice have honed my acrobatic Treezing abilities. I liken it to skateboarding the sky. What brings you here?"

He didn't appear to be wielding any weapons, so Rainn relaxed, but kept her distance.

He reached out a hand in greeting. "Hi. I'm Reese."

Rainn paused for a moment and then sputtered out her name. "Rainn. Nice to meet you." A smile carved along her lips as they shook hands. "Sorry if I'm on your property or invading your personal space. I'm normally a great traveler, always up for an adventure. I love to roam at night."

Reese shrugged. "Not to worry. This isn't my property. It's free land for as far as you can see. Nobody owns the wilderness." He chuckled and looked at her clothing. "Strange outfit. Not from around here, are you?"

"Don't *you* know it?" Rainn muttered, continuing to stare at Reese. "I'm lost. Can you help me, uh, get unlost?"

Reese batted a thick dreadlock from his face. "Not good to be lost at this hour, but don't worry, I know this place like I know my hands." He showed off big, callused palms, hands that looked to be the perfect size for opening pickle jars.

"Yeah. Could use some help." Rainn held her stance, legs spread wide, hands at hips, as if she were ready to wield a sword, but she had no weapons, nor did he, not that she could see. She retreated a few paces, leaned into a tall, prickly bush, and then hopped forward as if she'd been stabbed by the brush.

"Don't worry." Reese smiled. "I'm a canopy collegiate. Treezing student. Trees are my specialty. Love 'em. Love the canopy, simply love it here!" he finished in a singsong tone.

"Well," Rainn said, staring back at the prickly bush. "Some guy dropped me off, not too far from here…in a car. A taxi. Bright red Studebaker. Seemed a little crazy. The driver, that is. Drove me all over the woods, then he kicked me out of his cab." She left out the detail of her brother, unsure how much she could trust Reese. "I've been walking around the woods for over an hour. Yep, I'm lost. And this is a first. I'm usually good with directions. Think I must have been an explorer in a past life. But I didn't get any directions. Not from the cabbie. No GPS out here."

Reese gave her a funny look.

She went on, hoping to inflate her wilderness know-how: "I've got years of experience as a tour guide in the woodlands; used to lead expeditions through our oak and elm forests," she lied. "But that's far from here; this forest is new to me. Won't bore you with too much of my drama. Columbus thought he was a seasoned explorer, too. Wound up discovering the wrong continent."

Reese paused, stared off thoughtfully, reached into his backpack and, retrieved a small strand of ivy, tied his dreadlocks into a thick ponytail with the ivy rope. "Taxi, huh. Epi driver?"

Rainn nodded, surprised. "You—you know about him? He'd be tough to forget. Big beard. Tall and wide. Possibly a little unstable if you know what I mean." Pointed to her temple. "Sinister down to the core. Guy called himself Caesar."

Reese nodded. "There aren't many cars around here. Caesar runs a business. If you got a ride with him, well, then, what's your specialty?"

"My specialty?"

"You know, your connection to universal energy. Eternal flow. Psychic hookups." He took a slow breath of forest air and smiled. "Telepaths come from all over the place just to check out Enchanted Wood. And that cab ride you took—that was no fluke. Caesar isn't exactly a tour guide. So…you an epi?"

"He sure doesn't look like a tour guide," she said, avoiding his other question. "He'd probably scare off tourists. But the thing is…" She paused and dragged the toe of her shoe through the dirt. She made a face that said she was still very confused, and decided to be honest: "I rode with my brother, portaled here, but we got separated. I'm just trying to find him."

Reese began speaking with confidence: "It's natural to be a little frightened. I can smell the fear in you, but just remain calm. You'll be safe with me."

"I'm not afraid, just a little confused, is all. This forest is a lot to digest in the dead of night."

He waved her off. "If you want to feel safe, your best spot to be is up there." He pointed a dirty finger at the treetops. "The canopy's where it's at. Most alluring place. Filled with exotic flora. Treezing is the best. Like surfing the clouds." His eyes studied her slim figure in the dark. "Oh, to be so high in the sky," he continued dazedly. "It's my life. An experience like no other."

"So is wrestling alligators," remarked Rainn. "Doesn't mean I want to get in the ring and go fifteen rounds with one of those prehistoric predators."

"What, you don't believe in Tree Energy?" He reached into his backpack. "Maybe this'll help."

He pulled out a clear grapefruit-sized crystal ball. Reese had huge hands—banana-bunched hands that swallowed up the orb as it shimmered with full-moon intensity. Looked like something you'd see in a gypsy's front office.

"Watch this." Reese studied the ball intently for a moment, as if attempting to solve a glowing orb discovered on a distant moon. He tossed it back and forth from left hand to right. "Remember, I'm kind of new at this."

He flung the ball high up into the air and blinked several times. The ball reached its apex and, instead of gravity getting *down* to business, paused in midair and hung there, five feet off the ground.

Hovering in front of Reese. It started to pulsate and glow. Lit up like a lantern mantle, casting grooved shadow and light on Reese's face, half-hidden in his forest of hair.

"Well? What do you think?"

"Cool, dude. Cool. Can I touch it?"

As she did, the peach fuzz on her arms and cheek stood up.

"You feel that?" asked Reese.

She smiled, and her eyes met his. "I do. It's so…. lovely. Feels like warm river water is coursing through my blood." She stumbled back a pace. "Whoa!" "What?" Reece grinned.

"Just got a shock." A crooked smile righted her sideways glance. "Feels like I just downed two Red Bulls." "Red Bulls?" His eyes smiled at her.

"It's a high-energy caffeine drink. Way better than espresso."

Zane gripped a long, thick tree root growing out of the earth and tugged at it. With a pocketknife, he sliced off a curly strand and tied the puppet's arms behind her back with it.

"Just what do you think you're doing?' Trixie spat on Zane's shirt, her eyes going black as pitted olives.

"Keep it up, you beastly little curmudgeon," he grumbled. "I'll gag your wooden mouth with barbwire."

"Not Barb! She's a friend of mine."

"Oh, do shut up, you chatty hunk of kindling. You know what? I'm done with you!" He shoved her in his backpack, listening to her mutter obscenities in what sounded like a variety of languages. Her kicking feet smacked the interior canvas of the backpack.

"The more you struggle, the longer I'll keep you in there," Zane demanded.

A branch fell from the canopy and landed in front of him. He glanced at the ground. It wasn't a branch; it was a snake, now slithering away, and tunneling through a small round hole in the turf.

Zane walked for close to an hour and then paused as he reached the peak of a bald hill overlooking a large lake. He sat cross-legged on a mound of grass to rest and slow his thumping heart rate; he tuned in meditatively, deciding now was as good a time as any to PMS Rainn.

Zane tapped his temple three times.

Unsuccessful.

He heaved out a sigh.

Rain started to fall, soaking the forest in a quickfire fashion. After thirty minutes of his hiking through muddy terrain, slipping several times on a steep hill, the rain finally subsided. Drenched, Zane looked into the night sky. Yes indeed: he was lost again.

He squeezed out rainwater from his shirt and shook out his wet hair, a waste of time. He was soaked. Trees. Trees. Trees. He was surrounded by pines and redwoods drippy with stormwater. The sloping wet terrain added to his challenges. Unsure which way to travel, he spotted something. There, just on the other side of a tall grassy bunker, a flickering light revealed a chimney releasing plumes of smoke.

Under the dark stormy sky, Zane plodded toward the chimney smoke. Quivering ferns and other strange flowering plants dotted the path in front of him. He was pleased to see a small home off in the distance.

"Hope someone's home, and they're not some undead haunt," he muttered quietly while ascending another hill. Finally, he approached the limestone cottage, taking cautious steps down the trail, wondering if he was trespassing on private property. Didn't see a mailbox or any *No Trespassing* signs. Smoke curled from a tall stone chimney decorated in sea-green mosaics. He wiped his dirty hands on his clothing, wondering what to do next.

Rain started to fall again in sheets. Should he take his chances and see if anyone's home? Get out of the rain, at least. Maybe the owners were friendly. He really wanted to get inside where it was dry.

The cottage appeared dark, save for a dim, wavering light pouring out the window from the hearth.

The storm muffled any sounds his invasive steps might create, so he wasn't worried about making noise. He made his way down a narrow path dotted with petrified tree stumps leading to the front door and walked across the grassy yard. He leaned over unmanicured shrubbery, peeked through the window, his breath fogging the glass. The room appeared vacant; he continued along the window wall, stepping around colorful azaleas.

A light went on in the house. Zane froze, staring at the pool of light reflecting off sparkly puddles. Something else caught his attention. It was the most immense wall of darkness he had ever seen. On the other side of a bluff, maybe a quarter mile away, stood a gigantic tree. Had to be a redwood. Something about it looked familiar.

He shuddered; déjà vu tumbled into his thoughts, bringing him to a standstill. A handful of seconds later, his stiff frame relaxed as the strange déjà vu feeling evaporated, like a ghost passing by him. His temples pulsated and his head cleared, as if waking from a dream.

He stepped around the house to get a better look at this monster of a tree off in the distance. Thick, dark air and the rain made it difficult to see. Even though this mammoth redwood was far away, its immensity held him at bay; the tree pulled at his thoughts, urging him closer. He was about to head toward the redwood when a metal bolt slid at the front door. It swung inward, sending Zane back on his heels.

"What're you doing out in the rain, boy?" grumbled a raspy voice. "Only fools stand out in the dark rains of nighttime." Was this an invitation?

"Come into the light, thief. I've nothing of value to pilfer."

"I'm no thief," Zane said. "I'm—I mean, I mean, I'm lost."

"Lost? That'll happen to a soul wandering around in the dark."

The man stabbed a crooked cane at the floor and held up a lantern with his other hand. He stepped outside. His posture was arrow-straight, which was surprising because he had a pouch of a belly.

"Can't see you in the dark. Come. Out of the rain, boy!"

Zane stepped into the path of light, doing his best to hide the stunned feeling of being caught on this man's property. He approached the man, stepping on a path of stone slabs. The man was small, about three feet tall. And green. A troll.

His wrinkly skin was speckled with moles. Long, flowing white hair hung off his back. Tufts of silver hair grew from his beak of a nose. He stepped into the rain. The old man remained dry; an umbrella of dry space followed him as he walked off the front step. He squinted at Zane, his lantern swinging in the wind in a pendular motion.

"Well? Gonna just stand there?" He waved his cane at the sky. "Come in, come in. You appear harmless enough. Lost fool!" He grumbled something else that was incomprehensible and spun into his house.

Zane moved from one petrified slab to the next and stopped at the front door. The warmth of the cottage spilled toward him, welcoming him in. He stepped inside, and the interior lights revealed a companion: a long-tailed, jade-green lizard darted across the floor and climbed the sofa, stopping midway, defying gravity. Tail twitching.

The old man chuckled. "Lumpy. Off the sofa!"

The lizard's eyes flashed at Zane and then to the man, talons clinging to the cushion. This troll of a man swatted at the couch cushion with his cane. Lumpy's forked tongue windshield-wiped its eyeball, and then it disappeared over the couch and scurried into the shadows. The lizard came to a rest on a wood pile near logs burning in the fireplace. Lumpy raised its chin skyward, eyes closed, basking in the crackling heat.

"What brings you here?" He pointed his cane to a chair in the kitchen. Zane's wet shoes sloshed across the wood floor. He took a seat on a tree-stump chair, puddled water pooling around his feet. "You hungry?" He waved Zane to the kitchen table.

The kitchen was neat and tidy; shelves filled with bottled herbs and spice, a bowl of fruit, and a row of tomatoes under a window.

"Feel free. Name's Longstump. Edge Longstump. You got a name, youngster?" He pushed a bowl of tangerines and cherries at Zane and took a seat across from him.

"I'm Zane. Sorry about the wet floor." Zane studied the man again. The tiny old man was bone-dry. His skin, more scaly than fleshy, looked more like lime pulp.

Zane grabbed a handful of cherries, eating them and spitting the pits into his hand. Edge grinned, showing a gap in his front teeth.

The silence bothered Zane, so he spoke: "Thanks for the fruit. How'd you do that?"

"Do what?"

"Stay dry out there. You a—"

"Been spelling for over, oh—seventy-five years now."

Edge stood up, which didn't add much to his seated height. "Come over to the fire. Looks like you need to dry off." Zane
followed him to the fireplace.

Lumpy zoomed off the woodpile and onto a scrambled assortment of redwood branches cemented in a clay pot.

"Zane, is it?"

Zane nodded, spitting another cherry pit into his hand.

"Toss those seeds in the fire."

Zane did so, pleased to be out of the rain and inside the fire-warmed cottage. He sat on the sofa, one eye on the lookout for Lumpy. "Thanks for the cherries."

"Anytime." He twirled a silver ring on his thumb. "Lost, are you? Where you headed?"

"Well, I think I'm close."

"Close to what? Being lost?"

"Close to what? Being lost?"

"No." His lips curled at the corners. "Looking for…" He caught himself and was not sure how to respond. Even in the comfort of this warm cottage with a friendly old troll, Zane's mind drifted to the giant redwood. But why?

"I was looking for my family, I mean, my sister and I, we…I mean I, that is to say, we got separated." He started to peel a tangerine. "Actually, my sister's looking for a fae." He paused, awaiting a reaction. Zane wondered why he revealed that tidbit of information. Something in the air, maybe, freed him up.

"Fae? I know many fae and witches in Beaver River. Which fae you talking about?"

"Esmeralda."

"That old queen. Bah, she's a hoot, but not to be trusted. I recommend you see a friend of mine instead. Once the storm passes."

Zane nodded. Sounded like a great idea. He wasn't sure how much he trusted the Esmeralda. "You know Esmeralda?"

"Indeed!" He twirled the cane. "You're in the vicinity of those fae, but what're you doing out in the middle of this rainstorm?"

"Long story."

"Trolls love good tales. Please. Elaborate. Spin a yarn." He tossed his cane across the kitchen; it hit the wall and stuck onto an open loop of three metal hooks.

"Impressive." Zane's jaw dropped in astonishment.

"That was nothing."

"I'm sure you can...so you're a…troll?"

"Yes, sir."

Zane bit into the tangerine. "Sorry to make another request, and I do appreciate you getting me out of the rain, but do you think you can take me to find my sister, er, I mean Esmeralda?"

"Don't get out much, anymore. Kind of set in my ways, here in this slice of the forest."

He stepped up to Zane, seated on the sofa, now at eye level. As he waved his bony arm over Zane's head, a trail of silver sparkles released from his fingertip, landing in his hair. Zane's hair dried in a snap, but the rest of him remained sopping wet.

"Think you can teach me how to do that?" asked Zane.

Edge reached into a small leather sack attached to his belt loop. Zane thought he was going to pull out a magic wand or maybe a blue bird. Instead, the tiny man fingered a gleaming red cube and flung it into his mouth.

"Cough drops," he said, "for my scratchy throat. Redwood canopy remedies keep me young."

Young? This clump of a troll looked as old as the hills.

"Think I'm an old man, do ya?" Edge smirked.

Zane shot a quick glance at him. "You reading my thoughts or something? Don't mean to be rude. I'm sorry. No disrespect. My mind's a mess. Tired."

"No need to apologize, Edge said." He raised a hand and patted Zane on the shoulder. "Haven't seen you in these parts."

"Not from around here. Think you can take me to Esmeralda? She might know how to find my sister. Big bummer that we got separated."

"Point you in the right direction."

"That'd be great." Zane's stomach gurgled.

"How 'bout some more food? Bet you could use a hot meal. Put some meat on your young bones."

"Actually, I'd love some food."

"You on the run? A bandit? You can trust me. Don't you worry, I work with all sorts of travelers."

Zane grinned. He was feeling a little more relaxed around this odd man. "Like I said, trying to find my way home…I mean find my sister."

Edge turned toward the kitchen, then spun back to face Zane. Waved his hands in tiny, rapid circles and then splayed his fingers out. Silver dust shot out from his fingertips—its flakes falling all over Zane. Zane's clothing dried before he could stand up.

"Thanks. That was amazing. I could use a friend like you."

"Here's a tip: don't *use* friends. They won't be friends for long."

Zane smiled.

"Let's eat," Edge said.

Zane glanced into the kitchen but didn't see an oven or stovetop. "What do you cook on? A microwave?"

"The fire. A good, smoked meal is the only way to go."

Zane smiled again, feeling famished with all this talk about food.

"Bet you'd like to see my laboratory?" said Edge.

"Laboratory?" Images of Edge dressed in a white gown mixing potions filled his imagination. "Sure. Where is it?"

"My cave."

"Right. Where else would a scientist have a lab?"

"I'm no scientist. It's all about White Energy here in the Forest."

Zane was liking and trusting this troll more and more.

"But let's cook some grub first."

Zane carried a cast-iron skillet to the fire filled with several ears of corn and sliced ham, given to him by Edge.

"Wait." Edge put up a hand. "Let me add a few spices."

They retreated to the kitchen. Edge stood on a step stool, reaching his long, bony arm toward the top shelf. Zane stared, amazed. He could have sworn Edge's feet floated about six inches off the step stool to reach the spice rack on the middle shelf.

They cooked the meat and then sat at the table to enjoy the smoked ham and rice, along with a glass of plum juice. Both were silent, focused on the hot food.

After eating, Edge led Zane outside. The rain continued. Edge created an invisible umbrella that kept them dry as they stepped through his backyard toward a narrow door built into the side of a hill. Zane followed Edge into the mouth of a cold, damp cave.

"Careful! Watch your step." Edge grabbed what looked like a barbequed baseball bat from a wire-mesh basket hanging on the craggy wall. He blinked twice, and the bat ignited into a burning torch. "Here. Hold this."

He passed the torch to Zane.

They ventured deeper into the murky cave. Walls glowed, reflecting torchlight off the deep-blue and amber crystalline craggy walls.

Edge took the torch and made his way through a narrow gap, pacing ahead of Zane. He disappeared into the dark and darted around a corner. Zane tried to keep pace, but because the dark tunnel seemed best designed for egg-shaped trolls, he was forced to squat to squeeze through the passageway.

Zane grunted as he banged his head on a stalactite, now crawling on hands and knees beneath the low-hanging ceiling.

"Edge! Slow down! Can hardly see where I'm going."

His voice echoed off the walls. No one responded. He stopped and listened. All he could hear was his own shallow breathing. His hands were wet and clammy, his mouth dry.

"Edge?" he repeated. He held the torch up, moving shadows along the glittery cave wall. He suddenly felt alone. The cave forked in three directions.

Where'd the old troll go? he thought. This was no time for games. *Why didn't I just head out on my own? I bet I could find Rainn and Esmeralda.* Zane was surprised to think such a thought. He didn't know the first thing about this wooded ecosystem.

He trekked on, scraping his arms and legs against the jagged walls. Then, a sound blasted through the darkness: a high-pitched laugh followed by what sounded like tires screeching.

Zane stopped. Everything went silent again. All he heard was water dripping off the walls: plink, plop, plip.

Zane cringed. He could not help but think this would be a prime location for a murder. He tried to think of something positive and bright, but butterflies and rainbows were not coming to mind, not here deep in this cave. If he fell, who would find him? Where had Edge gone? He'd had more than enough excitement for one day.

Zane studied the three passageways. Something inside him said, "Take the middle fork."

He decided to go with his instinct and listen to this little voice.

He wove his way through the narrow, middle path; a gust of air sent his dry shirt flapping. He rounded a corner and stopped atop an open, spiral stone staircase leading down two flights. The ledge revealed a large room filled with bookshelves, tables and chairs, and a couch. A small nook was filled with pots and utensils hanging off the stone wall; an assortment of wooden cutting boards, more herbs, and strange, colorful plants were scattered on tables. Some of the plants were attached to a line of string, drying out.

Edge stood on a small purple shag rug, working at a wooden table built for his dwarfish height. He held a large bone knife, dicing up something green and yellow on a cutting board. Edge had changed clothes and was dressed in a pair of yellow shorts, showing off skinny, hairless legs. He now wore a white shirt with dozens of lightning bolts stitched along the shirt sleeve.

The wall nearest to Edge was lined with torches, offering a ring of light. Zane started down the steps and then stopped; a metal cage off in the corner captured his attention. A dark shape was inside it. Zane gripped the iron handrail as the voice spoke in his head.

Glad you took the middle fork now, are you? You fool!

The voice sounded familiar. Was it Edge? Was Edge psychic, too? Zane narrowed his eyes and shrugged it off.

He was half-relieved when he heard Edge say aloud, "That's because it *is* me, you oaf."

Edge stood with both fists on his hips, one hand still gripping the knife. "Just testing our telepathic connectivity."

"Our connectivity? Oh, you mean the PMS," said Zane. "Right. Right. I'm sort of new to all this."

"That's right, my boy! You've got the gift. I could sense it. Just verifying my innate senses." He rubbed his round belly.

Zane scoped out the area. "So, you *can* talk to me in my thoughts? I'm not too surprised. What is this place?"

"My lab. Don't share it with too many people."

Not the kind of place I'd take a girl on a date."

"Oh, this would be a fine place to impress a lovely young lady! The energy in here could paint a room any color you choose. Impress the girls with your telepathing, my boy." Edge began chopping up some green onions on a wooden cutting board.

Zane glanced over to the cage. A long, black tail swished back and forth, hanging out of the cage.

"What's that?" Zane asked pointedly.

"Cookie."

"Oh, what is it?"

"My pet, a black panther."

"Panther? Panthers live here?"

"He's one of my creations."

"Really, Dr. Doolittle Troll. Is it friendly?"

"Cookie's smart and protective of me. Doesn't get out too much. It's a she. You want to see her? Up close?"

Zane made his way to the cage. Cookie looked threatening, even behind bars.

She growled and snapped her tail. She stood on all fours and stretched, lifting her backside in the air, front legs extended, sharp claws poking out.

"Don't call 'er an it. She's a girl cat." He waddled over to the cage. "Easy girl," Edge sang softly. "Want to pet her?"

"I'll just follow your lead," Zane replied, stepping behind the troll.

Edge retrieved a ring of keys from a hook on the wall and unlocked the cage door.

Zane retreated a few paces. Cookie remained in the cage, sitting upright, tail wrapped around her thick paws. She flicked her ears, which touched the top of the cage. She gazed between Zane and Edge, her green eyes glowing. She licked her furry shoulder, wiggled her whiskers, and jumped out of the enclosure. She shrank to the size of a black, long-haired house cat and started purring, rubbing in and out of Edge's stick-thin lime-green legs.

"That was cool," Zane said. "What sort of trick is that?"

"Illusion, my friend. The mind," he pointed his finger to his temple, "the mind is a powerful weapon…when managed properly, you can alter reality."

"So, why keep her in a cage? Just a cat, right?"

"All part of the façade. Trickery keeps the audience guessing."

"Wouldn't it be even more shocking if I walked down those stairs and saw that mammoth cat lounging on that rug or something?" Zane offered.

"Theatrics, my boy. Theatrics. A caged beast can appear threatening, especially if the panther escapes the unlocked cage." Zane wondered if Edge was going to share the secret recipe behind this illusion.

"Not today, my friend. There's much to do."

Zane made a face. *He's reading my mind again. Gosh, I never felt so naked in my life.*

Edge grinned and whistled through the gap in his teeth.

Cookie jumped up on the table and pawed at a clump of red flower petals in a wicker basket.

"So, you think you can show me some more of your magic, Mr. Edge?"

"Edge is fine. Just call me Edge. Thought you wanted to connect with your sister and that faerie."

"Uh…I do."

Zane took a seat inside Edge's cottage. Cookie, now the size of a house cat, stared at him unblinkingly. Gold eyes flecked with green flickered, as did her furry ear. Cookie wrapped her tail around her paws and then shapeshifted into a panther again, consuming the length of the sofa.

Zane's nerves stiffened, as did his body. Déjà vu funneled through him. Every image, every sound, every movement around him was an exact replica of events that had just transpired seconds ago: The way Cookie shapeshifted, Edge waddling into the kitchen humming a tune, flickering torchlight reflecting off the crystallized walls, all of it had happened seconds ago and was happening again. Right now. Déjà vu.

Poof! Zane disappeared.

Rainn slept.

Dishes clattered, waking her. She stirred and sat up in a bed, in a spare room in Reese's cabin.

The scent of fried eggs and the sizzle of a griddle grabbed her, as did hunger pangs.

Reese appeared, chatting about his travels to Enchanted Wood while they ate at a small wooden table in a rustic cabin. Rainn shared details about her ability to telepath, something she did not, under any circumstance, reveal to strangers, but Reese made her feel welcome. Trusting.

She sipped coffee, the morning sun brightening the kitchen and warming her face.

"Seems like weeks since I've had a full eight hours of sleep. Can't thank you enough for giving me a place to stay," she said.

"Portal lag'll take a lot out of you. Plus, you've got family matters to deal with. If there's anything else I can do, just let me know. I do need to get into town in a few hours, but my morning's free."

A framed photograph hung on the wall. A beautiful woman. Slender chin and pointy ears. Thick bobbed red hair, long bangs. Rainn stepped away from the table and inspected it.

"Who's this?"

"Lovely, huh. Her name's Belle. Belle—

"Gaia," Rainn finished for him. "She an elf. She's…oh, my. I just got the chills." She continued to study the image. "Something about her is striking. Radiant."

"You know her?"

"I'm…not sure, but her last name just popped into my head. Tell me more about her?"

According to Reese, Belle Gaia was an elusive elfin witch. Spellfarmer by trade. Lived near the canopy. He discussed her healing capabilities and her many gardens.

"Yes, she's known for her garden magic," Reese finished. "Popular in these parts."

Rainn smiled big and bright.

"Do you think you can take me to her place? Or give me directions? I need to talk to her."

She helped Reese clean up the kitchen and wash the dishes. Then they walked a few miles through the forest and came to a redwood grove. The canopy filling up the sky.

Reese opened his mouth, as if to speak, but Rainn interrupted:

"Is this it? Oh, this is where I need to be. Thank you, thank you, thank you!" She clapped her hands, beaming with excitement. "It feels so good here. The organic vibe is, oh, this is like home!" She hugged herself, breathing in tangy, sweet wilderness air. "It's so quiet. Does Belle live here?" She looked around at the tall trees. "Don't see any homes or camps."

"We're close, but I am running short on time. I must be off."

Rainn stared into the heavenly green-furred sky. She was getting the sense that everything was as it should be right now.

I'm going to connect with her," Rainn offered. "I can feel it. You'll see. I'll be fine here." She clapped her hands together and twirled on a toe.

"Before I go, let me fill you in on a little of Belle's history."

Reese shared these details: Being over 200 years old was easy for Belle, even if it meant outliving anyone who wasn't of elfin descent. The only forest creation to outlive forest elves were, of course, the redwoods. Redwoods were as near to immortal as the stars. Of course, ghosts and gypsy spirits and zombies were another wisp of energy to consider, but that fit into the Dead/Undead category. Then there were graveyard communities home to ghosts and the undead.

To deal with her longevity, Belle had gathered a lot of information; she learned to compartmentalize many of her memories, hang them on mind hangers in the closet of her mind, ironed, pressed, and safely stowed away. Occasionally, Belle, according to Reese, would let these memories and spellfarming know-how air out, like freshly harvested basil drying on a line. Belle Gaia, according to lore, had mastered the art of 'letting go': she learned to stow away unneeded emotions in a locked iron chest in the basement of her mind.

Rainn sat in the grass listening to all this from Reese. Excitement flooded through her as Reese finished his factual yarn and their hike.

Reese stood, hugged Rainn, and departed, disappearing back down the sloping, rugged trail.

Rainn kept hearing the name 'Belle' whispered in her thoughts. She needed a quiet spot to focus. She made her way to an umbrella shade under a youthful hundred-foot-tall redwood near a line of elms. She sat in a meditative pretzel shape and cued into her psychic Rolodex. She scrolled through her mental telepathic phonebook, thick as a brick, and located a new name on her contact list: Belle Gaia.

Time to PMS.

"Belle, Belle, Belle," she whispered as a meditative mantra.

Within minutes, she mentally tapped into the name: Belle Gaia, cued into her telepath channel and PMSed her.

Unbeknownst to Rainn, she was about to rekindle an old forgotten life: a memory of a past life, one she had forgotten.

Rainn's temples started to pulsate.

Oh, my dear sweet child, responded a voice in Rainn's mind. *You've reached out to me. Please tell me who you are! Is this Rainn Gaia?*

Uh, no. This is Rainn Moss. Rainn recognized the voice. *Do we know each other?*

I've missed you so much!

Rainn nodded. *You did? To be honest, I'm not sure I do understand, but I want to see you.*

They PMSed for a few minutes and then Belle told her: *I'm releasing a cord for you to climb. I'm living in the canopy. I see you down on the forest floor. Oh, we've so much to catch up on!*

Rainn wanted to believe what this woman was saying.

Those old memories will greet you soon enough, dear heart! sang Belle.

A long, thick, twisted ivy cord came swinging down from the green-canopied sky. Attached to the ivy cord was a large, clumpy bag.

Rainn opened the sack, revealing an assortment of tree-climbing gear: carabiners, grappling hooks arranged by size, harnesses, and coiled ropes.

Rainn, to her amazement, knew how to link all this gear, as if she had done it hundreds of times. And she had, but these memories were all but lost to her—until today.

She stared up the length of this tall, imposing redwood, its trunk wide enough to drive a steamship through, with one goal in mind: find Belle.

The redwood trunk, bare of branches for the first eighty feet, was her only way to ascend. She released any notion of fear and started to climb.

After scaling the tree with the aid of ropes and carabiners, finding foot and handholds in the knotted trunk, she reached the underbelly of the thick green canopy. She wiped her sweaty brow after swinging herself up onto a limb. "Well, now, that was a first," she muttered to the tree. She was amazed with herself and looked down. An eighty-foot descent to the forest floor.

She hummed quietly and began to hook a carabiner in place, and brushed back a thick branch with a strange yellow flower growing out of the trunk, and notched the cable to the limb.

She continued to scale the tree, using the pulley system with ease.

Thirty minutes later, another hundred feet up the tree, she spotted a treehouse in the sky.

A voice from a balcony hollered, "Oh, sweet child, I see you!" and a woman waved, grinning from ear to ear.

Rainn recognized her face, a smile she had known for a thousand years.

Inside, Belle embraced her. Memories flowered in Rainn's mind. Another life that Rainn had lived surfaced in her thoughts. A life with Belle. A past life.

"Do you realize how long it's been, Rainn?"

"Too long!" Rainn told her. "Too long!"

They sat at a table in her immaculate treehouse, drinking cucumber water and snacking on raisin peanut butter croissants.

"You remember this place?" asked Belle.

"It's coming back to me." Rainn allowed her eyes to sponge up the details of this aerial tree house. "I feel so alive here."

"Seeing you is a blessing, and today's doubly important," Belle said to Rainn. 'This home is your home. Think. Think back. Restore those memories, dear heart. I'd like to hear what you recall." Belle's eyes beamed with delight.

Rainn looked at a cushioned chair made of bamboo, a glass table with crystals piled in a seashell dish.

"Vague memories are starting to come to me. Did I…wait. Did I live here? I did, didn't I?"

"'Course, you did. Welcome home. Our cottage in the clouds.

You know what else is special about today?"

"It's my lucky day," Rainn said, her face all aglow. "The energy up here has me feeling glittery inside. I just love it."

"Luck has nothing to do with this day. Today is your birthday. And we're going to celebrate. Looks like you could use a bath."

"It has been a wild couple of days," Rainn replied. "But it's not my birthday."

"Oh, but it is. I'll get to more of that soon. To start things off, how 'bout an energy bath. I'm going to fill your birthday celebration with all sorts of entertainment."

Belle went on to say, "After your energy bath, we can go on a rope-ladder expedition, have a Treezing event, or go tree-hole diving. What do you think?"

"Sounds perfect, but I need to clear my head first. Some of what you just said sounds familiar, in a vague 'I don't know what you're talking about' way."

What was an energy bath?

"Energy bathing brings the past into the forefront of your imaginings. We can treeze barefoot to the bathing site. Living in the canopy is the only way to fly. Cloud canopy living keeps me young, and it's going to restore you."

"Can I take my bath now, Mom?" Rainn asked with a genuine glow filling her cheeks. She looked down, embarrassed. "Sorry I just called you 'mom.' It just slipped out. I *am* tired, but very happy to be here." She went on to explain meeting Reese. "When I saw your photograph in his cabin," Rainn continued, "my mind and heart opened. Like a flower eating up the sunshine. "I remembered you…you *are* my mom," she dared.

She hadn't called her 'mom' in close to two decades. More details of Rainn's past life as the daughter of Belle Gaia began to surface in her mind.

They hugged.

"It's all coming back to me. My past life here. I feel like a new person," Rainn exclaimed.

"Well, you are more than new, daughter. I need to tell you something. This is good news: you are living two lives simultaneously. This past life with me as your elfin mother, and your current thread of existence in your Earth life have collided. And I couldn't be happier."

"I love this house in the clouds!"

Belle had a home in the valley, too. "I purchased it after you…left Enchanted Wood in that previous life. Your soul began a new life on Earth. You have missions to complete on Earth, and you have unfinished business to attend to here in Enchanted Wood." Her smiling eyes warmed Rainn's heart.

"I left this place?" Rainn's smiling eyes dimmed. "Why would I do that?"

"Oh, let's not talk about that now." Belle put her hands on Rainn's shoulders, "And, now you've returned, and I love you."

They hugged again.

"Love you, too, Mom." Hearing herself say 'mom' aloud was cleansing. A recharge. A reboot.

Then her smile flatlined. "But there is something I need to know."

"Oh, sweet Rainn, what is it?" Belle beamed with motherly delight. "You've been gone for decades. I wasn't sure when, or if, you'd come back. I'm sure your life on Earth has been an experience like no other."

"Well, it's nothing like Enchanted Wood. But wait. What happened to me in the Wood?"

"Everything is happening as it's supposed to," Belle responded, sidestepping Rainn's question. "As I mentioned, your soul's residing in two bodies. I'm a spellfarmer, and we spellfarming witches call it 'splitting.'"

"Okay. And now I'm living as Rainn Moss on Earth, and I'm also Rainn Gaia, your elfin daughter, here in Enchanted Wood. Physically, I look the same as I do on Earth. But I feel different. So much more alive. I just hope all this news will be less of a shock to my brother.

"You see," Rainn went on to say, "I brought my Earth brother with me to Enchanted Wood, but we got separated. I had no recollection of my past life until I saw your photograph at Reese's place. That's when my mind began to connect the dots."

Belle put a hand on Rainn's cheek. "Everything is going to be fine, dear. Your brother will understand; even if he doesn't fully understand your lifeline here in Enchanted Wood, he will see it firsthand by being here. In this magic multiverse."

At the window, Rainn looked out at the branches filled with birds and flowers growing off tree limbs.

"Where do you think your brother is?"

"He's somewhere in the forest." Rainn's tone was cheerful and energized. "I don't know exactly, but I'm so excited to be here."

"You'll need to ascend higher," said Bell. "Think you'll remember the way or do you need me to tag along?"

"I'll be fine. I need to recharge. Love your cloud cottage, Mom! All the potted flowers and ivy and exotic colorful plants growing on the walls and ceilings—it feels like home."

Tree branches were growing from outside through holes in the wall and into the treehouse.

Rainn took a few slow, methodical breaths, quieting her mind, tuning in to the pathway of existence within her soul consciousness.

"Home," she said softly, eyes closed. "Home." "This
is home," Belle affirmed.

"Right, now about that bath?"

"Of course. Plus, since today's your birthday," Belle said, "your energy bath will be ten times as powerful." She gave her daughter a wink. "You always did find wonderful ways to do things growing up. That much hasn't changed. You found me on your birthday, you little loving devil you."

"Maybe my soul somehow planned that we'd meet on this day, Mom." Rainn shrugged. "I love you."

Rainn rubbed her hands together and made her way up a rope ladder hanging down from a branch twenty feet from Belle's balcony.

With arms outstretched, she tight-rope-walked along a wire-thin branch, flakes of redwood dust clouding the air around her feet. She glanced down; she could not even see the forest floor. With each successive step, the branch bowed under her weight and then wiggled back into place as she ventured further along the limb.

She took stock of the springy branch and decided to have a little fun. She flexed at the knees, lowering her center of gravity, leaned forward, and skated along the limb. At a knob in the branch, she caught some air, performing a pseudo-kick-flip. Reached a hand up, grasped a strand of ivy, and swung outward. She made her way higher into the canopy, disappearing into the overgrowth of green foliage.

"Almost too eco-central," Rainn said to the tree trunk. "It's like I never left. Been gone far too long and I remember how to treeze. I love, love, love my life. Both my lives!" she sang to the forest sky.

Rainn sat on a huge branch as wide as a sidewalk. Birds chirped. Other woodland critters made clicking sounds. Her sensitivity to sounds and scents intensified. The air was fragrant and clean. Yellow and purple flowers were growing upside-down from a limb. She leaned her nose into the silken bulb's cusp and inhaled the sticky sweet scents of mint and lime. Closing her eyes, she was connecting with the wilderness vibrations of all the floral life up here.

She pushed back tangled ivy and a massive leafy plant smacked her cheek; warm rays of sunlight poured through the canopy, creating a rainbow of kaleidoscopic light.

With legs folded, she sat on a quilt-sized leaf on the limb, settled in, took a few slow breaths, soaking in her energy bath. Peaceful. Soothing. Invigorating.

A small peep of a voice called out, "Is that all you really want—a sun buzz? I know the way to an eco-central carnival. You might earn a few extra gemstones for your theatrics at the carnival. They pay top-gold-coinage for on-stage performers."

Rainn was about to put on her game-face and challenge whoever had the gall to interrupt her energy bathing sauna in the sky. She looked through the deep webbing of branches; a blur of silver light began to take shape. A head. Legs. Arms. Torso.

What was it?

A gnome? A ghost? An after-life leprechaun?

There wasn't much about it that looked human; more details manifested: the wobbly outline of a little boy, etched in silvery blue highlights, transparent, dressed in blurry grey clothing: t-shirt, knickers, knee-high socks. His face was a mash of gray haze, glowing a dismal, dim shade of blue-gray.

"Hello there! You're a sprite, aren't you?" she said in a calm voice. "You can join me in my energy bath, if you'd like," Rainn offered.

"No, thanks. Join me in the carnival in the clouds."

She knew how to deal with haunts in her past life as an elf, and these old memories resurfaced; she was aware of this much: sprites, if that's what this creature was, loved to stir things up. She decided to play the alpha here.

She glared at him.

"You talking to me?" she spat with venom. "What do you want? I just returned home after being away longer than one might care to imagine. Don't you even think about taunting me with your illusory words and tricks. I know all about your kind. I can handle you."

Surprised to be speaking with such authority, Rainn continued in the same dark tempo: "You'll be knocked to ground zero before you can even yelp in terror, you worthless clump of energy." It blinked at her, but showed no emotion.

"A name. That'd be nice," it said. An aura of blue haloed its frame. Then it disappeared. Only to flicker back into view a few seconds later, hanging upside down from a branch above where Rainn sat on her leaf.

Rainn wasn't impressed or frightened. "What do you want, light bulb boy?" she asked in a huff.

"Your name would be nice, for starters," it repeated while glancing at its immaterial smoky gray hands.

Rainn paused, not wanting to be cornered into any conversations that might warrant the need for assistance. The spirits and undead, she recalled, loved to weave mental tricks that could trap others into agreeing to a haunting contract. Undead contracts could become month-long hauntings, or even years. Once an undead Being, especially a lonely one, found interest in you, well, they were difficult to shake.

"You're nothing but a lonely sprite," Rainn said mildly. "Just a child." She offered a staged smile. "I don't waste time with the dead. Plus, you're in the canopy. That takes virtually no energy at all. This is a space of rejuvenation for white-magic enthusiasts. It takes skill to get up here. The dead don't usually…" A question formed in her mind.

"Don't usually what?"

"How'd you get up here?"

"What do you know about ghosts? I'm just looking for a friend."

Rainn held up a finger, testing the wind. She began again, slowly, deliberately, "I'm entitled to a little peace in the sky. Leave me alone, you muddy illusion. You probably aren't even here."

The undead being dropped its head into his hands—literally popped its head off its shoulders, held it in its lap, and tossed it from hand to hand.

"Big deal. I'm not impressed." Rainn yawned. "You can't scare me with your illusions. Can you talk with your head in your hands? That'd be cool."

"I know you, elf girl. You're from Earth," the head said.

This caught Rainn off-guard. How did he know she was elfin and from Earth?

But she was charged up and mentally cleansed from her energy bath and remained calm.

"Having a nice time playing with your head in your hands?" she asked.

"My head sees in all directions of space and time. An enviable skill, yes?"

"Think what you like." Rainn dramatized a yawn.

"You're wrong about one thing, elf girl," the creature said.

Before she could respond, it took a little more shape, although still transparent. The blue-gray halo framing his gray body suddenly took on color, dressed regally: in a long black coat of silk. Gold etchings along shoulder pads and around the buttonholes emerged. It would have looked dapper if it weren't for the snorkel and diving mask resting on its forehead.

Tugging on the lapels of his suit jacket over a ruffled shirt with a silk scarf spun around his neck, he looked out of place.

Upon closer inspection, the coat was tattered at the elbows, and he wore dusty combat boots.

Rainn then recognized him. "Oh, god. You're, you're…. that ghost I saw back home." She thought for a moment.

He smiled. "And you don't remember my name? Hardy har-har-har," it laughed dryly. "You are an embarrassment to the sprite community."

She smirked. "Ah, so you are a sprite. Nice duds, dude." She remained as calm as the alpha elf she was in her past life.

She continued to size him up as he placed his head on his shoulders and tossed his snorkel and mask downward. "You litterer," Rainn spat. "Go clean up your mess." Two brilliant red eyes glowed in his stormy face.

This one might be more of a challenge, Rainn mused. She changed tactics.

"What is it I can help you with, sir?" she inquired. "You're looking rather dapper. Nice scarf. Goes well with your attire. Now, if you could just keep your head on your shoulders," she finished frostily.

The sprite, for the first time, revealed emotions. His eyes filled with tears. He pulled his head off his shoulders again, cradling it in his arms. Tried to hand it to Rainn.

"I don't want your head. Put it back where you found it."

Why was it crying?

"But, elf girl, I'm supposed to give it to you."

"Now is no time for head games." Rainn stood from her leafy energy bath and stretched.

He gave her a curious look. "You look like a lovely young elf. I was told you'd play with me."

"You'll have to excuse me," Rainn countered. "I'm taking a sun buzz. Have things to do. No time to play with the dead."

"Aren't you the least bit curious?"

"Pshaw!" She closed her eyes, raised her chin skyward, put her back to him, and returned to her energy bath, now standing, tugging on an overhead mossy branch, and giving it a squeeze, sending golden rays of light over her face and shoulders, taking an energy shower. Sans liquid. She washed under her armpits and scrubbed her back with a fern branch.

The sprite's voice suddenly crackled with rage: "You don't know who you're talking to, elf child! Give me your undivided attention. Now!" He simultaneously divided into two sprites.

"How do you like me now, elf?" the two sprites said. "I've twinned. Just like you and your evil brother." Then the two doubled into four sprites. Then the four melded back into one. The sprite, however, was no longer a boy. He was tall, aged in a wrinkled burnt candy-apple face topped with long white hair.

"I'm the all-knowing famed Doyle Alfred Grimes, owner of past and future lives. I am fame incarnate, a master illusionist, a weaver of dreams, a master thief, a king. The world worships me. And so shall you, you infinitesimal twit."

Rainn glanced past Doyle, as if she were more interested in how the tree leaves changed color in the fall than watching him tell his narcissistic story.

Rainn, riding the wave of her energy bath, feeling fearless, replied, "Forget to take your meds, Doyle? Leave me alone. Whatever world worshipped you, trust me, I'm not part of your little band of misfits."

"Oh, you're interested in me. Everyone is." Doyle scowled. "It's inevitable. I am the flowers you dream of in your hair. I am the wind in your sails. I am your beating heart. I am the breath that keeps you alive."

"Sounds like a boring sales pitch to me. Not interested." She crossed her arms and put her back to him.

She waited a moment and then turned to see the ghost, now a blur of energy, losing any semblance of shape and fading into mist. Gone.

Ah. Finally, she mused. *Alone again.*

Rainn was free again to bask in her energy bath. She sat down and drifted silently, allowing the solar-green forest to fill her up.

Numerous moments later, the sound of coins clinking stirred her from her meditation. Where Doyle had stood a moment ago sat four gold coins, dusted with age.

She heard a far-off whispering in her mind. A PMS solicitor.

Ha. You thought you were alone, called out a voice in her head. *Wrong, missy! Did you miss me? It's me. Doyle,* the voice said, speaking in her thoughts. *You see those coins? They are for you.*

She glanced around the canopy. No sign of the ghost anywhere, but she did see the coins on the branch.

Doyle whispered in her thoughts again: *Nice place you have here. Love what you've done with your mind. What little there is of it. Who's your interior decorator? Your mind is roomy enough for two. Splendid, my evil little elf. I fit right in with the décor. Thanks for the invitation.*

Rainn cringed and wrapped her hand around a tangle of ivy.

Blast! That nasty little ghost has slipped into my thoughts.

That's right. And I can hear what you're thinking, you silly twit. You gave me just enough time to slip my way inside you. Thank you for…oh, let's call it: posting bail. And now I'm here.

You weren't invited.

Rainn paused, doing her best to clear her thoughts. She knew it was best not to carry on conversations with a mind solicitor. She did her best not to think of him. But that was all she could do: think about this invasive ghost nosing around in her mind, the coins he left sitting on the branch, and Doyle's ability to create the illusion of twinning into multiple sprites. All of it was illusory magic.

Go on, continued Doyle. *Think up something good. Continue to dream of me. I'll be here, acting as your live-in guide. But I can't stay long. Let's consider this a simple contract. You've wasted enough of my time, so now you owe me a favor.*

I owe you nothing, she PMSed, sounding pissy.

Tell you what. I'll let you know when I need the favor. I'll surprise you. Consider it a birthday surprise. Happy birthday, little elf! Oh boy, have I got a surprise for you! A belated gift's coming. Count on it. Now, go count those coins.

Doyle chuckled in her thoughts.

She could feel an emptying going on in her head.

A vapor trail of mist snaked through the air in front of her.

The snaking mist took the shape of the youthful sprite again. Wearing wool shorts, knee-high socks, and a suit coat. He offered a slick bow. Then, in a blink, the sprite was gone.

Rainn began her descent to Belle's aerial canopy cottage. There, standing on a branch ten feet beneath her was the back of a young man; dirty-blonde hair, curly and disheveled. It had to be her brother. The young man turned and gazed around. A look of confusion stitched to his face. He didn't see her.

"Zane!" Rainn hollered excitedly. "Up here!"

She scampered down the tree, displaying her treezing skills, and stood before her wobbly brother.

"So happy to see you," she said. "How'd you get up here?"

Zane blinked. Said nothing. Just stared at her. He pushed aside ivy hanging in front of him, his deep blue eyes studying her. "I'm not sure," he said absently. "I'm at a bit at a loss. Were you talking to someone?"

"Zane. It's me. Rainn." She hugged him.

His arms remained at his side.

She leaned back and looked at his confused expression. "What's wrong? You okay?" He did not look well.

"I don't know….do I know you?" This was not what Rainn expected.

He gazed off a moment.

"I feel dizzy," Zane said. "And lost."

She could sense his epicenter of energy swirling out of him. A few leaves started to twitch. Rainn, too, was feeling a little dizzy.

Zane offered a crooked grin. "Where are we?" He looked past her to the green leafy canopy engulfing them.

"We're in the canopy. Let's get to my treehouse. You'll be safe there."

"Have you seen any ghosts? They're tricky little phantoms."

"We're safe now, Zane. Ghosts are gone." She placed a hand on his shoulder. His skin was clammy, cold.

"We should go," she said mildly, while her elfin antennae were on full alert for any more tree ghosts haunting the canopy.

"Been up here long?" Zane finally said, biting on his lower lip as he took stock of his height in the tree. "You're pretty agile for someone so young…and small."

She smiled sheepishly and flipped upside down, using her legs to crimp to the branch. With arms outstretched, she said, "I'm going to keep us safe, brother. I'm your sister." She released her leg grip, flipped upright in the air, and landed on her feet on the branch next to Zane. "Wanna race to my mom's, er, to the treehouse?"

"Not really," he said, void of emotion. "Not even sure how I got up here. Did you say you're…"

Zane's body began to quiver and shake. He tumbled out of the tree.

Rainn yelled out, "Zane!"

Zane disappeared through a tangle of ivy and branches. He fell, his scream slowly fading away.

THREE LIFETIMES AGO

Alfred, born under the namesake Doyle Alfred Grimes crafted his own profession: a mind thief. He did this before he learned to talk. This contractual occupation had been planted into the essence of his Being, where its roots twisted a stranglehold grip on him. His soul connection would soon be choked and lose its golden liquid hue.

From early on, as a baby, during his earliest conceivable moments of breathable life, while pinned to dragon-scaled diapers crafted on a loom by Grandmama Leocadia, Alfred could feel things in the air that others could not. These sensations soon took shape in his mind. He could hear what his parents were thinking; Mom and Dad's voices spoke their thoughts right between his ears.

Doyle Alfred Grimes didn't understand their language, not a first, but that didn't matter. One thing was certain to baby Grimes: Alfred was born a demon.

This might not be all that unusual except for one genealogical hiccup: his father was an ordinary demon of ordinary hellish stock, a farmer; his mom, also a demon, happened to be infertile due to a spellfarmer casting a spell that tied her tubes in a permanent fossilized knot.

Nonetheless, Alfred was here in Enchanted Wood.

At six weeks of age, a pair of tiny humps appeared on his little hairless head. Beneath those humps: about-to-sprout horn nubs, and his parents were overcome with joy.

His mother tucked him under the covers, a black candle burning on the window sill; she sang a demonic nursery rhyme, one of her favorites:

"Dragon fly, dragon fly, fruit bat die.
Ride me, ride me, under the sky.
Drop me in that great big hole.
Cover me, cover me, darken my soul.
Bury me, bury me, make me sigh.
Dragon fly, dragon fly, fruit bat die."

It turned out, unbeknownst to baby Doyle, along with his demonic potential that he was telepathic, a mind-thief in ways yet to be understood. The first of its kind.

He reached out his plump baby fingers and touched his mother's chin. A jolt of energy swept up his arm and he stole his mother's thoughts, making a few baby hairs on his head stand up.
His mother was left feeling confused.

"Oh, my. My memory's escaped me, love." She sang to baby Alfred.

"Poo. Poo," Alfred voiced.

Alfred began to hide his ability in his cribbed mind. Had to do it. A voice deep within him told him as much. He soon began to hoard these thoughts.

Alfred, one day soon, would learn to steer clear of redwoods. Two towering redwoods were healers in the community. Alfred had no interest in healing. Darkness fed his strangled muddied soul.

Alfred stood up in his crib, gripping the wooden bars and stared out the window. Redwood energy poked and prodded at his flabby baby skin.

He gurgled out another "Poo, poo."

He didn't understand it, not at first. Hell, he could not even feed himself! His main gift to the Universe was filling diapers with homespun chocolate poop that sparkled with starlit intensity.

His parents expected something different from him. They were Dark Art specialists. Gypsy farmers. They planned to lead their only child down the road of Darkness with them, but would soon discover that he didn't need any guidance. Not from them. Not from anyone.

Each morning the baby's diapers were filled with glittery goo poo. He was unable to manage and store all these stolen thoughts. Had to release it. Through his bowels. Little Alfred had an extra special dazzle to his talent. The glitter he left in his poo-poo diapers was merely the beginning. Yep, he was a magic-wetter, which was much more difficult to curb than bedwetting. Ask any demon.

From the age of three, the Dark Arts of magic, in no uncertain terms chose him. He lived in Village Vine, his hometown gypsy forest camp. Alfred, a toddler, grew bored of stealing Mom's and Dad's thoughts. He began to master the artful technique of harnessing energy with his mind and, in turn, stealing other villagers' thoughts.

His horns remained nubs hidden under his fiery orange hair.

"Such a cute little creature," said a neighboring farmer visiting from down the street. She hopped off her hay wagon, dropping off three bales of hay to the Grimes family in exchange for four jugs of goat's milk.

The farmer gave little Alfred's cheek a squeeze with her pudgy fingers.

ZAP!

She got shocked and pulled her hand away.

"Ouch!" The farmer frowned, and sucked on her burning finger.

Her throbbing fingertip had been scored with a blackened burn mark.

Alfred giggled and stared up at her, a long, slow, and somewhat creepy stare; she retreated a few paces as a flash of lightning sparkled in little Alfred's eyes.

He had sponged up her thoughts.

Farmer Lady stared off thinking, *Now, then. Why did I come here? Oh, my! I'm a bit lost.*

She leaned against her wagon as Alfred's mother gave her son a pat on the head and set the jugs of milk in her wagon.

Alfred's mother gave her a sideways glance. "Just bartering. Like we always do. You feeling okay?"

"Oh, yes," she lied, and climbed back into her dusty wagon and grabbed the black leather reins. "Could you tell me, er, oh my, where I need to be going?" She had forgotten where she lived.

Alfred continued to mold this mindful momentum as if it were wet clay, shaping and forming it with a simple twisted desire. Yes, he was thrilled by his ability and quickly learned that his mind-thieving feats were something others could not manage.

He grew into his namesake, as every youthful villager did. Doyle Alfred, called Little Al by his folks, found pleasure in toying with his secret mind-bending abilities. As a young lad, Little Al started to hang out with street vendors and Dark Arts performers older than him. He had a natural talent for impressing villagers. His onlookers grew, as did his confidence. Soon, he had an audience, and he had morphed into an adolescent village showman.

Al wasn't your ordinary street performer. For one, he was an eight-year-old mind sculptor while other street artists were much older: most in their thirties or forties or fifties, and a few vagabond veterans were into their hundreds. His youthful zest for chatting with strangers charmed them. Al would soon take advantage of his seemingly boyish grace and use it for personal satisfaction.

One night, his head throbbed in pain; his hidden humps on his scalp pulsated, like baby teeth coming in. He rolled over in pain and howled until he fell asleep.

He woke lying on a bloody pillow. A pair of tiny horns, each less than an inch long, had poked free from his fleshy scalp.

His feet hit solid ground, and he tumbled across the wood-planked flooring and shoulder-rolled into a wall, sending a potted bonsai tree crashing to the floor. He clenched his shoulder and looked up, stunned, and wincing in pain.

"A bit of a crash-landing there, eh, my boy," said Edge. "You blinked your way back. That was quite the theatrical entrance. You charge fees for entries like that?"

Zane sat up and shook out his arm. *The hell's going on?* he wondered. He was back in Edge Longstump's home.

Was I in the canopy? It's all a blur. My sister, she was there, he thought. The entire experience was weird.

Edge sat on the sofa. Cookie hopped into his lap. He stroked her a few times. "I've been in these woods a long time, and judging by what I saw, and didn't see," he grinned, showing off the gap in his teeth, "I'd say your epi riding is moving along nicely." Zane gave him a blank stare.

"You're going to be just fine." Edge rolled a toothpick around in his mouth. "Was this how you got to Enchanted Wood? An accidental epi ride?"

Zane gave this some thought, but all he could think of was seeing Rainn's shocked expression as he fell out of a tree, branches slapping him as he careened through the air, falling toward the earth. That was all he recalled.

He sided with telling the truth: "Long story. I'm worried about my sister. She saw me fall out of a tree. Did I…use my epi energy to get here? The whole thing seems like a dream."

Cookie jumped off Edge's lap and slunk along the floor, tail snapping. A bit of kindling fell off a stack of wood near the fireplace, and Cookie darted off after Lumpy, both disappearing down the hallway.

"That was no dream, my boy," remarked Edge. "Yes, you used your epi energy to travel. What? You in a hurry to get out of here? Don't like my company?" he asked with a frog-faced grin.

"You're the first person I've seen here who makes me feel comfortable." Zane stood up and spun his arm in little circles, testing his pain threshold. "If it wasn't a dream, did I…. Oh, hang on a second. I think I had a petit mal seizure. Not sure how I got to the canopy, though, but I saw my sister and then…I fell. Next thing I knew, I was here."

"Indeed. Epi travel. You wouldn't happen to be ADHD, would you?"

He nodded. "My memory's fogged over. How'd I get into the trees with my sister?" he said, as if asking himself.

"Your heart and soul want to find her. Sounds like you two are close."

Zane furrowed his brow. "Well, she's my twin. We are close, I guess. But she's a bit pushy." If anything, it was a forced closeness by relation.

"Is she an epi, too?" Edge asked.

Zane cast a glance out the window. "No. I mean, I don't think so, but she—she can do other things."

"Like what? Walk and talk? Sleep and dance? Sing and run?"

"Yeah. Sure. She can use her mind to talk to people. A telepath."

"You don't sound impressed."

"Oh, but I am. That's all that matters in her world, but I do need to find her."

"Give her a call," Edge said, stretching his thin stick legs onto a toad-shaped footstool.

"You get cell reception here? Can I use your phone? Mine's dead. That would be a huge help."

"We don't have any of those prehistoric human modes of conversing here."

"How am I going to call her, then?"

Edge pointed a finger to his temple. "Use your head. Mental communication, my boy."

Zane's face lightened; a lightbulb of recognition lit up his hollow brain. "Oh, you mean telepathic stuff, right?"

"Or you could seize your way back to her landscape."

Zane shook his head. "Nope. Nearly died the last time I did that. Fell out of a tree, and survived. How's that even possible? I should be dead." He gave his shoulder a rub.

"Practice makes the mind-body-spirit connection that much stronger. Like a rock, my boy."

"So does petrification. Doesn't mean I want that."

Zane stepped to the window, looking out at the tall green forest. "This place is beautiful. Maybe I should give her a psychic call."

"What a magnificent idea," Edge's voice dripped with scorn. "Why didn't I think of that?"

Edge, noticing Zane was still out of sorts, led him to his back porch. He instructed Zane to take a seat on a cushion surrounded by crystals. The crystals, each the size of a bowling ball, sat in a Himalayan glass bowl: amazonite, onyx, labradorite, selenite, amethyst.

"Relax," stated Edge smoothly. "Breathe. Breathe in the stone energy, and cue into your sister."

Zane followed his directions, getting comfortable surrounded by these planetary crystals orbiting him. His shoulders, within a meditative minute, began to sway back and forth. Images of Rainn colored his mind. Then, buried in his subconscious, a scene unfolded: he saw his sister, in full color, sitting in a cabin, speaking to a woman. A stranger. Chatting, but he could not make out what was said.

Rainn. This is Zane. You out there?

A few seconds later, a busy signal buzzed his brain.

Rainn? Rainn? This is Zane.

Who could she be talking to? After twenty minutes of sitting in silence, unable to correspond with her, he opened his eyes.

A light rain started to fall. He made his way back into Edge's cottage, wiping his moistened chin on his wet shirt.

"How'd it go?" Edge prodded.

"I could see her in my mind but didn't have any luck getting through."

"Luck has nothing to do with it."

"Yeah, but I got a busy signal. Never had that happen before."

"You're just not in tune. Keep at it. Go climb a tree."

Zane sat in the yard watching Cookie, panther-sized, prowl through the tall heather. Was Cookie a mystical mirage crafted by Edge. Maybe she wasn't a cat after all, but a spell.

The panther brushed past Zane; she looked, sounded, and smelled like a massive wild beast.

Deeper in the yard, Cookie got into a crouch, heather covering part of her massive frame. The tall, wispy grasses started to flutter. Then, she sprang out of the heather and took one bounding leap in Zane's direction, then two, then three. She went airborne a fourth time, her razor-sharp claws extended, readying to swipe at Zane.

Zane envisioned that claw slashing his face.

Everything shifted to slow motion: the panther opening its cave of a mouth, fangs glistening, breath clouding Zane's vision, claws slashing his face, Zane's head flinging up, body tossed upside down and then everything went dark….

Zane looked up, stunned, holding a hand over his face, wincing in pain. Crouching in a house. A man was standing over him, rust-red dreadlocks beaded in tropical crystals. He grinned and brushed a ropy dreadlock out of his face.

"Whoa, dude! Where'd you come from?" asked the dreadlocked stranger.

Zane, confused, looked around.

The panther was gone.

Edge was gone.

Cottage was gone.

In its place, was a different home. The house gently swayed back and forth.

Where was he? And who was this guy?

Oh, man, it happened again. I blacked out and woke up somewhere else, Zane thought.

"I, uh, I come from the forest," Zane said, unsure what else to say to the man. He sat upright, blinking, heart pounding, face aching.

"We're all from the forest, dude. Whoa is what I should be saying. That was one dramatic entrance into my pad. You okay?"

"Musta scraped my face against something? But I'll be okay."

"Sure about that? How 'bout some ice for your face?" "No. I'm good," he lied.

The man got down on bended knee, picked up a potted bonsai lying next to Zane, and started to scoop dirt back into the ceramic pot.

"Dude, you took quite a fall, from space or something. You a speller?"

"No man." He wasn't sure if he could tell him about his epi landing. "Oh, did I do that?" Zane asked, looking at the cracked ceramic pot.

"No worries. You okay?"

"Uh, I think so. I think I blacked out."

"And you landed here, in the canopy," remarked the man. "Welcome to my pad. Breathe it all in. Love it up here," he said, brimming with cheer. "Figured you were a novice witch when I saw you materialize in my aerial bungalow."

Aerial bungalow?

That was the same term Zane used as a name for his treehouse back home.

"Gnarly trick you just pulled off, brother. I'm Reese, by the way. Always a pleasure to meet a forest witch."

Zane sat up and leaned against the cedar wall, the baseboard was trimmed with faeries carved into the wooden edgings. "I'm not a witch. Witches are ladies, right?" he asked uncertainly.

"Nope," Reese replied. "A witch is a gender-neutral term. Both male and females can harness that power. Enchanted Wood is a special place."

Reese continued, "You know what else—I was just thinking about you? I don't know you, but I saw your face in my thoughts. And then you appeared here, crashing all over my nest. You tripped me out, dude. How cool is that?" He gave Zane a crooked grin.

Zane thought of taking a vow of silence but could not. "I'm not a witch. As far as I, er, you know." He then went ahead and told him: "I'm an epi traveler. Some call me the epi rider. Some call me the space cowboy. Some call me the gangster of love."

"Nice, dude. You make that up yourself?"

"Nope. Steve Miller Band."

"Never heard of it." Reese continued to yammer away: "There's always a lot of electricity flowing up here in the trees, but things are intensifying. Love it, love it, love it, mister witch-spelling maestro."

Zane investigated his hands. "So, I'm back in the canopy. Guess I never left." Zane's memory was fuzzy; he was confused.

"Yep. This is the canopy. My home. And that was a crazy-ass entrance."

"I'm looking for my sister. She might be freaking out. Saw me fall out of a tree."

"Does she know of your epi skills?"

"Sort of. But it's new to me. To both of us"

"What's her name?"

"Rainn. I'm Zane, by the way."

Reese smiled. "No way, dude. "What's her last name?"

"Moss."

He clapped his hands together. "Saw her yesterday. Flipped me out, dude. Yep, she was looking for you, man. This forest is a wild place for bringing like souls together. Talk about karmic flow."

Zane wiped his lip, smearing blood onto the back of his hand, tasting blood in his mouth. He stood up and at the open window spit. With care, he began swiveling his shoulder in small circles to get the blood flowing again.

"You're the first person to call me a witch, but I don't walk around with a pointy black hat, and I don't bathe in a cauldron of steaming oils. I'm an epi."

"Yeah, you told me that. Hey, it's all good. We're in the canopy. Safe up here, my brother. You sure you're okay? You're bleeding."

Zane gave an affirmative nod. "Just a few scrapes."

"You epis are a crazy lot. You can go places in a blink. But I've heard stories about crash-landings and whatnot."

"Yeah. It's a challenge," remarked Zane. "Sometimes I fly blind." He looked down at the spilled soil and broken pottery. "Sorry about the mess."

"I'm just glad you're okay. You've got a dangerous profession, brother."

Profession?

"What? Am I supposed to get paid? What's the going salary?"

"Bartering system mostly, but some earn gold coinage. Treezing's the coolest gig out there. Safer than epi travel, but to each his own." He gave Zane a nudge in the arm, fanning out his long, lean arms. "What do you think of my place?"

The treehouse's steep-pitched ceiling had dark-stained oaken crossbeams with living ivy wrapped around them. The interior was sectioned into smaller alcoves and a kitchen with a small round table and a pair of oak stools cushioned with pillows. A large bowl with soapy water sat on a table under a window. A slender redwood branch grew into the house through a narrow slot in the wall, used to hold washcloths and dish towels. Strands of ivy were hanging in through an open window.

"Take a seat," said Reese.

Zane sat on a colorful throw pillow.

"Nice place," Zane said while soaking in the peaceful wilderness vibe.

Something was scraping against the wall outside.

"What's that noise?" Zane suddenly stood up as if waiting for the treehouse to be attacked by Pterodactyls or an alien spaceship.

"The wind, dude. Branches claw at the walls. Just relax, man. Everything's good up here."

A fresh gust of wind shoved the trees this way and that, sending the entire house swaying and moaning.

"See what happens when we talk about the wind? Madge is listening. She can be quite the catalyst to keep the forest in constant motion. Keeps us all on our toes."

"Feel like I'm on a ship at sea. Just a little out-of-it. How far up are we?"

"We're in the clouds, dude," Reese proclaimed. "I still can't get over your entrance! You must love your dangerous talent."

"Don't know if I'd say I love it."

His eyes took stock of a set of cedar shelves filled with books, playing cards, and a band of pewter elfin miniature figurines, elves armed with weapons: sword, crossbow, wooden staff, dagger, and one playing a lute. Each shelf was carved in the shape of dancing nymphs and sirens.

"The whole place is vibrating."

Zane stood up and started to wobble. "Oh, man, are we having an earthquake," Zane asked.

"No, dude. Energetic vibrations. Probably aftershocks from your cannonball entrance." His tone remained neutral. "So, tell me: how long you been managing your energies? I hear it's not something for novices to toy around with, especially in the cosmic intensity of Enchanted Wood. You are a novice, yes?" The rumbling of the treehouse faded.

"I'm epileptic." Zane took a seat on the floor. "An epi, they call me." He found a sense of pride in his voice and placed a hand over his heart. "Yep, I'm getting pretty good at this epi travel stuff." That was a lie, and he knew it.

"Might want to invest in a helmet."

Zane, feeling dizzy, got down on one knee and put a hand on his head.

"You okay?"

"I guess. Just a little…"

"Out of sorts?" Reese said and reached out a large banana hand and hoisted Zane up and led him to a seat on a sofa. His hands were big as a bunch of bananas.

"I'm dizzy."

"Just lie back. Breathe. We're in Madge. Madge is the mother of all trees, the epicenter of electrical vibrations. Prime real estate, right here."

"We're in Madge? This tree's named Madge?"

"Yep."

Zane's head started to clear.

"Maybe we should head into town. You still dizzy?"

"Nope. Feel better. Need to find my sister."

"Need to get you grounded. I can take you to some shops and vendors in town. Place is straight-up dope. Maybe Rainn headed in that direction."

They stood in front of a city-block-sized building. Inside, a vaulted ceiling was supported by thick oaken crossbeams with rows of lanterns. The arched storefront window offered additional natural light. The place was abuzz with shoppers.

A green-skinned troll, about two feet tall, his body hidden behind a curtain of a beard, stood reading a newspaper at a magazine rack, his feet were dressed in pointy slippers. Zane felt a little out of place, like a misfit toy in a jewelry store.

Floppy hats and scarves sat in an open chest near the front door. Hooded robes lined a clothes rack, ranging in size from toddler to adult. There were robes of every color. A sign levitated over a clothes rack: *Ghost Fabric Sale. 25% Off. All Sales Finally Yours.*

Silver khaki slacks, denim shorts, cloaks, suspenders, shimmering sundresses, blouses, skirts. All the fabric glowed in varying shades from silver to a tinted blue.

Hand-carved bongos and wooden spools were stacked along the storefront window wall. Zane was about to ask Reese about the spools and bongos when he saw two young college-aged guys behind a glass counter wearing paint-splattered aprons. One rosy-cheeked, chubby guy was standing in front of a sign that read: *Clay Spinsters.* His co-worker was thin with brown equally thin hair. A handful of orphaned whiskers escaped his bald chin.

He started pumping a foot pedal while using his hands to mold clay on a wheel.

Zane and Reese continued deeper into the store and ventured into another room called *Book It!* Books and magazines, scrolls on rolled parchment, greeting cards, and posters. Several copies of *Magic Matters* and *Life of a Student Witch* were fanned out along the top shelf of a magazine rack. A stack of newspapers sat on the floor in front of a cash register.

"Look. A newspaper," Zane remarked and pointed a finger at it.

"You sound surprised," remarked Reese.

"Didn't realize you had a paper."

"What? A magical forest can't have a daily edition?"

"This isn't exactly New York City."

"Isn't that a polluted planet on Earth? Think I heard about that in my Universal History class in college."

Zane picked up a copy of *Redwood Strong Free Press*, thick as a Sunday edition, feathery light. The newsprint felt silky.

"Weird texture on this paper." Zane rubbed it between his thumb and forefinger.

"Our paper mills closed over three centuries ago," Reese told him. "Today's newspaper is made of renewable energy. A spell farmer developed a magical hybrid of beehive honeycombs and silkworms. Along with a little magical energy to bind the paper into what you are holding. Printing presses shut down at the same time. All because a young, brainy witch developed illusory ink that can be transmitted from the writer's thoughts straight onto this special paper stock. Mass newspaper production is now linked to our Thought Magic processor. The eyes have become electronic keystrokes."

Zane thought of his sister. "Reese? Is there any other way to contact Rainn? Can't PMS."

"Can't help you there, brother, but I know someone who can."

"Oh. Who's that?"

"She's a wise old elf. Belle Gaia. Lives in the canopy not too far from me."

Just then, a squawking sound came from deeper in the store. Zane, having an ADHD moment, gave Reese a look that said, 'We have to check that out.'

Reese led him up a wide staircase. The second level was lined with vendors in front of shops; a water fountain bubbled near a man selling cotton candy that crackled like firelight. "Red hot cotton candy! Get your red-hot cotton candy!" he called.

Amid more chirping sounds, they marched across the hardwood floor and turned down a narrow hallway that opened to a room with more shops and vendors.

Zane asked, "Is there a zoo back here?"

"More supernatural stuff. Come on."

Zane brushed past a clothing rack of cargo pants and then rounded a corner. A small glass house stood in the middle of the second floor, with shops lining both sides. Hundreds of metal bird cages hung inside the glass house. Some were mounted to poles. Others hovered in the air. A sign over the door said, AVIARIANS: RARE & EXOTIC!

A young man dressed in brown corduroys, a white shirt, and a green vest gave them a wave from inside the shop. He pushed open a glass door. Chirps and screeching sounds magnified.

Zane glanced at the employee's name tag: *Need Flight? Ask me. I'm Ned.* "If you need any mundane or enchanted assistance, just let me know." He wiped seeds from his hand onto his dirty smock, bounded up three steps, and began cleaning out an empty birdcage.

Tropical birds filled cages. Narrow-beaked flyers with colorful wings swung back and forth on wooden swings. Upon closer inspection, they looked reptilian, featherless with leathery wings. One bird flipped upside down on the swing. Zane thought it might be a bat. He remembered studying bats in biology class. Bats were furry and had a mouse-like look to them.

It flapped its wings and swung upright on the swing again. It was about the size of a hawk and puffed out its chest, showcasing purple and green checkered scales.

Reese stepped into the birdhouse behind Zane; Zane gazed back with questioning eyes.

"That's a dwarf dragon,"

"No way. Dragons? Colorful as rainbow sherbet. Straight fire!

Yep, That is dope!"

"Way, dude." Reese's eyes sparkled as he tried to speak the teen-earthling language. "All the kids want one in their crib."

The dragon squawked, fluffed out its scaly purple-green-checked plume, and craned its long neck. Its mane of orange hair made it look like the result of a lion pride gang-banging a pack of iguanas.

"I think it likes you, Zane. That dragon is dope. Hip as they come. So, are you ready to elevate out of here?"

"How big do they get?" Zane tapped a finger on the metal cage.

"It's full grown now. Hence the name: dwarf dragon. You think we want giant dragons sailing our skies?"

The tiny dragon bolted off the swing and clung to the cage with sharp talons. It nipped at Zane's finger before he could pull it away.

"Ouch." He glanced at his finger. "Hey…it drew blood."

"Don't tease caged animals."

"Wasn't teasing it. I was just—it's not going to give me rabies or anything, is it?" He sucked on his finger.

The dragon belched a cloud of purple smoke, hopped off the swing, and started pecking at brown pellets, dead bugs, and worms on the cage floor.

"Purple's my favorite color," said a small, tinny voice from inside the glass room. I'd love to go home with you. Magic is what you make of it."

Zane spun around. "Who said that?"

"I did," replied the same tinny voice.

No one else was inside the glass room except for Zane and Reese. Ned busied himself cleaning the cages.

Reese watched Zane for a moment and then said, "Dwarf dragons can talk, dude."

"Check me out," spouted the same tinny voice.

Zane's eyes widened with amazement. "Never had a pet dragon before." He stared at it. "Hi, I'm Zane. Polly want some crack?"

"Crack? Don't do drugs. Where's the Cracker Jacks, wise guy? Give it up. How 'bout a little peanut butter and cheese?" the dragon cocked its head sideways. "The name isn't Polly."

"They don't mimic like parrots," Reese told him. "You can carry on conversations."

I figured that one out on my own, bud, thought Zane.

"I like Zanes," another dwarf dragon trilled, tiny green eyes studying Zane. "If you live with magic, you believe in magic. If you believe in magic, you become magic. Let me live with you. I'll show you how to live."

"How much do you cost?" Zane asked the dragon eagerly. "I don't have any money, but I'd really like one." "Buy me," said the dragon.

"No. No. Me. Me. I'm the One. I'm the shit."

"No, buy me. I'm bilingual. Yo hablo espanol y ingles. Los dragones son diversion."

"What'd he say?"

"I said, 'I speak Spanish and English. Dragons are fun.' Comprende, Amigo?"

"Er…yeah."

"Any other questions, smart guy?"

"I like *him*," Zane said with a grin. "The bilingual dragon."

The bilingual dragon responded, "You picked the ultimate gemmy dragon in the Lot. Smart boy, yes you are."

The dragon extended its wings, showing off its scaly purple and yellow checkered chest, and started purring, then puffed out three rings of purple smoke. It opened its jowls, fangs glistening, Exhaling an arrow-thin flame right through the three rings.

"Show off," muttered another dragon.

"Dude, think you can front me the money?" Zane hollered to Reese. "I'll pay you back. Somehow."

Zane paced through the Aviary room. "Dude, come on," Zane pleaded. "I'll help you out around your garden. Do chores. Weed.

Whatever it takes. Please! We had a dog once, a beautiful chocolate lab. He died a few years ago. But a dragon? Oh, man!"

Reese grinned at Zane. "These dragons become attached to their owners, as they're honorable creatures. He'll be right on your shoulder, if you treat him right and providing you don't get a moody one."

"Even better. I'll be his pirate captain. I'll feed him and…do I take him for walks? Will he need a leash? A litter box?" He spilled out more questions for Reese, hoping to sell his desire to have one with an understanding of the responsibilities associated with having a pet.

Ned stepped up to them: "How can anyone say 'no' to a face like that?"

Reese retrieved a small satchel of silver coins from a pocket and walked up toward a cash register.

Zane's temples started to pulsate, and a voice entered his thoughts. "Someone's trying to reach me," he said to Reese. "I'll meet you at the front of the store."

Outside the shop, Zane cued into the PMS.

Hey kid. You there? This is Caesar. I'm here to pick you up.

Zane could see Caesar's bearded face in his mind. He replied: *Really? You're here? I didn't schedule a pickup. What's going on?*

Maybe Caesar had information on Rainn. This was turning out to be a potentially great day.

Zane half-jogged to the front of the store and peeked out the front door. He saw the Studebaker parked on the street. "We'll be right out, Caesar."

"Five minutes. If you're late, then you're on your own."

Zane met Reese at the counter and they walked out of *Aviary Speak Sleazy*, holding a metal cage with the dwarf dragon inside.

CHAPTER FOURTEEN
Rainn

Rainn returned to Belle's cottage in the clouds and explained the situation of seeing a ghost and then her brother's terrible accident of falling out of the canopy.

"Can you help me, Mom?" she pleaded with Belle. "I'm afraid he's fallen to his…oh god… I don't know what happened to him." She started to cry.

Belle consoled her daughter with yet another hug. "Just visualize him happy and smiling, walking and running, laughing and dancing."

Once Rainn calmed down, which didn't take long due to her energy bath and her elfin mother's words of encouragement, they traveled to the location of Zane's fall at ground zero. There was no sign of Zane or his body on the ground. She hoped he was okay.

Rainn had tried to reach him psychically, but he wasn't responding to her PMS.

While on a coach ride back to town, Belle explained to Rainn that she had cast an illusory spell on the exterior of her second home: the one on the earthen floor. "From the outside, it'll appear as a ramshackle old building," she said. "Keeps burglars from trying to enter my lovely abode while I spend time in the canopy."

They arrived to see a dark old building. More of a shack than a building or a home. Holes in the roof, patched with weather-beaten tarps. The yard, filled with wildflowers, bright and fragrant, and tall weedy bushes, was the only captivating piece of the property.

But once inside, her true home was revealed: a two-story Victorian with a winding staircase and a large fireplace. There was ornate furniture throughout. Walls shelved with books. Two hardbound books lay on a coffee table: *Canopy Recipes for Witches* and *Healing Gardens in the Sky*.

"I don't remember this place at all." Rainn's eyes lit up. "Lovely home, Mom. Did I live here, you know, long ago?"

"I bought it after you…departed." She looked down and sighed. "Anyway, I'm so glad you're back. Let's focus on Zane. But first, you need to eat. Protein'll provide the fuel to keep going."

Belle stood at her stone fireplace, mixing two scoops of stoneground planetary protein powder with chia and flax seeds with finely diced beet, carrot, and ginger.

Belle reached for two empty glass pints when a knock came to her front door. She blinked several times, and her blender slid across the counter and stopped next to a blue glass jar labeled *Canopy Cloud Seeds*. The pint glasses floated an inch off the counter, and then, with a nod, two coasters slid across the counter and propped up the pints.

Belle motioned for Rainn to remain quiet and peered through the eyehole at the front door. Nobody stood on the step, but just because there was nobody visible didn't mean someone was not there.

"Rainn, go upstairs, please. Stay out of sight," she said in a hushed tone.

Rainn disappeared upward to the second floor and paused at the railing.

Then, as expected, a figure materialized on the doorstep: a silver-haired crew-cut gentleman, although whether he was gentle remained to be seen—or unseen. In one hand, he held a leather shoulder bag, the other rested in his pocket.

Two more knocks sounded on her front door. Belle grinned inwardly, always up for a challenge among the less-than-living.

"Yes? Can I help you?" she began after opening the door.

"Awfully late to be selling Girl Scout cookies."

He bowed.

Belle sensed deep-seeded Darkness in this figure, and her elfin instincts were, often, spot-on.

"We're in a bit of a family situation here. Busy with life." Belle started to close the door, but he bowed again, and paused, not wanting to smack him in the skull.

He adjusted his grip on the leather satchel. Shiny silver hair complemented his dark, brooding eyes. A striking figure.

"Good evening, ma'am. Sorry to solicit you at your home residence like this. If you've got family problems, maybe I can be of assistance." He paused to clear his throat.

Oh, this should be good, Belle mused. Then aloud, she said, "I've no time for any witch pitches. I really must be—"

The man said, "You see, my dear lovely lass, I'm new to your neighborhood, an instructor at Enchanted Wood University, a Spelling specialist. I dabble in white and…" he leaned closer and whispered, "a little of the darker stuff, too. Students love to hear what's available on both sides of the podium." He winked. "Maybe I can assist you in your family issues."

Belle said nothing. Why would he come to her door with such an offer? It made no sense whatsoever.

He smiled a smile that did not reach his eyes.

"My mix of white and dark magic creates more opportunistic potential among the young spellers and treezers, if you know what I mean." He leaned a bit closer. "But don't get me wrong. I'm not here to sell any of my magic recipe books. Nothing like that. *You* come highly recommended. You are Belle Gaia, yes?" She said nothing.

"Heard of your witching talent." He peered past her shoulder, glancing into her lavish home. "I do like the blocking spell you've cast on your exterior."

"Oh, it's no spell," she lied, giving him a raised eyebrow. "As I said, I'm dealing with a family crisis."

"What's happened?"

You are not welcome here, and you certainly have no right to pry, she thought as she followed his gaze back into her home.

Something strange made her shudder: a lightning-laced cloud of energy camped out in the sky of her mind. This man had spun a spell on her.

Without giving it a second thought, she smiled as this electric storm in her mind controlled her facial expression, and gave him an affirmative nod.

"Maybe you *can* help me. Please, come in."

Seeing her shack from the outside and then looking inside to see a multi-storied home filled with tall, stained-glass windows, ornate furnishings, hardwood floors, tapestries on the walls was enough to turn anyone's head.

"This illusory magic inn here," the man said, "is, well, it's tugging at my heart. Love it."

Belle leaned on one hip and spun a finger through her thick, short-cropped red hair. "It's no illusion."

"Oh?" His wrinkled face remained blank. Obviously, he did not see.

"I'm getting off-track," he continued. "There's more to my story, and I'll just come right out and say it," for he knew his spell had taken hold of her. "I'm a mystic. Clairvoyant. Runs in the family. Hope to have a few minutes of your time. My name is Galvin Gable. Friends call me Gal," he finished with yet another bow, wiggling his fingers, and blinking at her sandaled feet. A swirl of silver sparkles flashed from his fingertips.

Belle wobbled a bit, feeling something press down on her feet; she retreated a few paces. "I'm Belle." She stared at her feet. They were tingling.

"'Course you are." His tone remained neutral.

With a spring in her step, she led him through her atrium and pointed to the sofa near the fireplace. "Take a seat. Care for a cup of tea?"

"Tea would be lovely. It's been a long trip. Won't take too much of your time." He studied the interior balconies decorated with gargoyles. "You truly have a lovely home. One of the reasons I'm here is to share my thrill of the mystic arts with young, hopeful telepaths and spellers of your magical forest."

"Well, Galvin—"

"Please, call me Gal." He took a seat on the couch, opened his leather bag, and pulled out a small wooden box with an engraving of a redwood tree decorating its lid.

Belle disappeared into the kitchen and appeared a moment later with two cups of tea on a silver tray.

"Hope you enjoy Chinese Bamboo Shoot tea."

He said nothing while eyeing a tapestry on the wall.

"Some of the art was done by some of my students," Belle informed him. "From several years back. At EWU." She placed the tea on a small end table next to the sofa.

"You teach Spelling at the university?" Gal asked.

"Years ago. I'm a certified spellfarmer, but I've moved on to other endeavors. After being forced to turn a few students into stone, just to quiet their energy, well, I had to shift gears. A quick and painless way to put the kibosh on disruptive classmates and set an example." She grinned. "Decided it was time to retire, having little patience for students who waste everyone's time with ego-driven spellcasting. Some of the students called me Miss Medusa."

Gal seemed to look right through her. "I like your style."

She smiled right back. "I'm not *that* kind of witch. I've never turned anyone to stone." *Not for longer than a minute or two.* "I would've had my license revoked." *But I was,* Belle mused, *tempted to have a few shipped off to a museum.*

He opened the wooden box. The interior was matted in red felt and divided into compartments. Each compartment held several shiny, smooth, polished stones.

"What do you have there?" Belle asked, eyeing his box. "You a jeweler?"

"No. Master illusionist. Also have a fancy for tracking magic, as you can see by my collection of stones." He pressed a hand to his chest, displaying jeweled fingers.

"Lovely rings. They're beautiful." Her eyes met his. "Simply beautiful," and she gave him a wink.

His shirt sleeve sparkled.

"Bought them from a wise old sorcerer eons ago," he said. "Rather attached to them." He fanned out his ringed fingers.

Gal explained a little more about why he was here: "My true calling," he began again, "is to share the power nesting in my stones, but, more importantly, I've been called on a mission of sorts. You, my dear, are part of my mission. You mentioned you're dealing with family issues."

"Yes, I'm looking for a missing child, a teenager."

"A missing teen? You don't say."

Rainn stepped to the railing to get a peek at what was going on downstairs.

She took one look at the man, meeting his glance. Listening, arms folded across her chest.

"Yes. It's truly unfortunate," Belle continued, as if she didn't notice Rainn at the staircase, and she didn't. "He's run away from home. The little bugger. A nephew of mine."

"Mom?" Rainn whined. "Why're you…"

Belle cast a disapproving glance up at her daughter.

Belle's witching senses would read through Gal's guise on a normal day. But the Mood Spell he sprinkled onto her feet had deadened her innate elfin abilities. Belle cast a sorrowful expression at Gal, placing her hand on his shoulder.

Although his features appeared solid, when she touched his shoulder, she knew otherwise. He felt like compressed air.

"How dreadful!" Gal cried out in dismay. "You must be simply beside yourself with worry."

Rainn, from atop the staircase, began tapping her foot, not buying his dramatics.

Gal paid no attention to her. He looked up, scanning the third-floor balcony. From the railing, a stone gargoyle riding an asp had its hands raised skyward; its haloed head wore a crooked grin. Gal then frowned as he noticed the gargoyle was wearing diapers.

Belle studied him intently, charmed by those black eyes and silver hair.

"My nephew…" he repeated and sighed heavily, "his name is Zane. Zane Moss. Been missing for several days. We're afraid some evil band of forest gypsies nabbed him."

"Your nephew?" Rainn spat. "That's a lie. He's my—"

"Your what, my dear sweet elf?" The man stood up, hands folded in front of him. "Go on, tell me."

"What do you know about him?" Rainn asked anxiously.

"Hello, my dear Miss Rainn. It's a pleasure."

"Do I know you?" she asked. Or did her mom tell this intruder her name?

"No. But I know *you.*" He offered a lopsided grin, but Rainn was not falling for his attempted charm.

"What about Zane? What do you know?" Rainn demanded.

"As I said, he's family."

"You lie!"

Gal remained stone-faced and continued in a somber tone: "I'm worried. I just hope he's not injured. That would be simply dreadful." His face, for a flicker of a second, curled up into an evil grin." I, too, have a family issue. My nephew's missing." "Is your wife helping out?" Belle asked.

"Mom!" Rainn said, sounding embarrassed.

"I'm not married, ma'am. Just an old incantation specialist, wedded to my work."

Belle leaned closer to Gal and batted her eyes at him. "I'd love to help. What can I do? Tell me a little about your nephew?"

"Mom, he's lying. What're you doing?" asked Rainn. "Do you have a picture? Maybe it's just someone with the same name."

Gal reached into his vest pocket, pulled out a pocket watch, and flipped it open, displaying a digital screen. His blinking eyes entered in a passcode, then he used his moving pupils to guide the cursor and opened a PHOTOS icon. He showed a picture of Zane Moss, a high school photograph, his senior Anklesteam High School snapshot.

"That's my brother," Rainn affirmed. "But he's not your nephew. You're lying."

He winked at her. "How long have you been staying here. Illegally, Miss Rainn?" She

said nothing.

"You and your brother are illicit energy travelers. There's a felony out on both of you."

Gal turned his attention to rotating ceiling fans.

Rainn decided it was time to PMS.

Mom. It's Rainn. What're you doing? This guys a fraud, a freak.

Belle's eyes remained on Gal as he walked past a potted six-foot-tall redwood sprout near a window.

Belle replied, sending a PMS*: I'm just playing along with this fool. Not buying his story, Rainn. Yes, he's evil. I smelled it on him the moment he arrived, but I need to keep him thinking he's got me under a spell. His illusory magic doesn't work. My spellfarmed plants in my home put a spelling firewall around me. He's nothing in the confines of my magically sealed home. Just need to play along. I'm just trying to get some information out of him.*

Belle, then, looked at Gal with a puppy-dog expression of her own. She purred, "Please, let's not worry about those felony charges. We need to focus on your nephew. Can I get you anything? Anything at all?" *What's the plan, Mom?*

Please, be patient. I need to talk to him.

Okay. Two canopy elves are better than one.

That's the spirit!

Just then, another PMS came in. Both Belle and Rainn could hear it: *Rainn. It's Zane. Can you hear me?*

Zane! You're alive! Yes! Yes, I can hear you! Rainn replied excitedly. *What happened to you?*

I'll explain later. I met a guy named Reese. Says he knows you. I just bought a…

Just then the PMS lost its connection.

Zane? Zane?

A few seconds ticked by.

We're in Caesar's Studebaker now. I'm new to PMS group chats. You hearing me okay? Zane went on to say to Rainn and Belle. *On our way back to—*

An automated voice got on the line: *I'm sorry, but your PMS has been disconnected. Please try your call again later. If you'd like to complete a brief survey, please think ONE.*

Gal called out, "Belle, something's come up, and I need to be going. Just got a call from a fellow professor."

This was a strange turn of events. "How can I reach you?" Belle asked.

"I'll find you."

He disappeared out the door.

"What do you think that was all about?" Rainn said while walking up to Belle.

Belle put a hand on her shoulder. "I was able to slip into his thoughts. Got a reading on his bio. He's a bad man. Undead. Gal is just an alias. Most know him as Doyle Alfred Grimes. Or Al."

"Doyle?" Rainn drew back a curtain in the window and examined the empty front yard. She was beyond relieved to hear from her brother. "Mom, when I was getting my energy bath, I bumped into a ghost. Said his name was Doyle. He was some sort of illusionist. He multiplied from one boyish ghost into more ghosts. He duplicated himself again and again. Then he shifted to become an old man. Creepy dude. But he looked nothing like this Gal character. He also made an appearance at my home on Earth. Both Zane and I saw him."

"Did he harm you?"

"Nope. He had more interest in talking about himself. Total fool!"

L ess than an hour later, the door creaked open then shut with a bang.

"The back door," Belle said and made her way to the kitchen.

She motioned for Rainn to go upstairs and remain out of sight.

Rainn, moving with elfin silence, disappeared up the stairs. Gone.

Belle stood in the kitchen. Gal was standing there with hands folded behind his back.

He gave Belle a twisted, forced grin.

"Decided to come back," he said. "Somehow, I feel you have information to share. Zane's the one I want. You've no use for him." His magnetic onyx-red eyes locked onto Belle's.

He was planning something. Belle could sense it.

Belle sent a PMS to Rainn: *Rainn, it's Doyle, but it's better if he's here in my house. He can't do too much damage to us with my protective energy fence set up. I'm surprised he got back in. Can you send a message to Zane? I can't reach him without his psychic access code.*

I'll try again, Mom, but what do we do about Gal?

Let me deal with him. Just keep your distance. He's a slippery one, and his illusory weave-work can be dangerous to you. But I can handle him.

"Mind if I look around?" Gal asked. "Thanks."

"You know I want to help, but you're wasting your time here. Zane's not here. I've never seen him. What sort of valuable spelling assistance did you expect from me, anyway? You never asked."

"Oh, I think this is precisely where I need to be." His tone darkened. He spun on the heels of his dusty black boots. "You see, miss, as I said earlier, I'm a master speller. My specialty is using stones as nests for my incantations. I really am quite a marvel to behold."

He turned to face the mirror and bowed to himself. "I can almost smell the protective fencing in your home. Nice work. Keeps nosey neighbors and trespassers off your property. But not me. Your spelling codes are not infused with the latest Forest Energy updates. I bypassed your codes with ease. Just waltzed right in." He flashed a smile at her.

Caesar's cab sped down Tanner, turned left on Flick Way, and cruised past three blocks of EWU student housing units: small log cabins and an entire block of green-and-white striped tents.

The Studebaker came to a stop at the corner, waiting for a young lady riding what Zane presumed to be a magic carpet. The carpet was made of a green and yellow silken weave. The girl on the carpet looked over her shoulder and shielded her eyes from the sun's glare off the cab's shiny chrome fender. She sat upright, cross-legged, with hands on knees. Pressed down on her left knee to steer the carpet left. She slowly floated across the street, picked up speed, and rode off. Zane, yet again, looked to Reese for an explanation.

This time the dwarf dragon Reese had purchased for Zane, spoke up: "She's a carpet rider. Too lazy to use her legs, I guess." "Never seen anything like it. Why haven't I seen more flying carpets?"

Caesar turned to the back seat and gave Zane a wink. He moved his eyes to the birdcage between Zane and Reese. He frowned. "Not a fan of talking lizards. There are lots of ways to travel in our forest village. Carpet riders are one of 'em. If you weren't epileptically charged, you wouldn't be in my cab." "What about my friend?" He pointed at Reese.

"Well, since he's with you, and you're in a bit of trouble, I make allowances for certain situations. Consider yourself lucky— both you and your hairy dreadlocked friend. Good thing I'm such an understanding guy." He scowled at the dragon. "And keep the scaly beast caged!"

Zane wrapped an arm around the cage protectively and whispered to the dragon, "Don't worry. You won't be caged for long. Guess what? I've come up with a name for you. I picked it out…because of you, Caesar."

"Me? Why go and do something like that?" Caesar said, crustily.

"He's got a checkered belly. See." Zane opened the cage, and the dragon flew out and sprang off Reese's head before perching on Zane's shoulder.

"So," began the dragon, "what *did* you decide to name me? Not Polly."

"Julius. I'm going to call you Julius."

Caesar smiled, showing his large teeth. He tipped his baseball cap at Zane and tucked his greasy, dark hair behind an ear. "I'm honored, kid. Just keep yourself out of trouble. Think you can do that?"

"I'll try…didn't know I was in trouble, aside from being lost." Caesar shifted his focus to Reese.

"Am I dropping you off with him? I can drop you off anywhere between here and Flick Street."

"Hang on a second," Zane interrupted. I'm getting a call from my sister. Can you park somewhere? I need to concentrate."

Caesar grumbled, "Already putting in overtime on you two." He pulled to a stop alongside a bakery. The place was crowded with college students.

Zane relayed all the information he received from Rainn's PMS to Caesar and Reese. "Can you take me to 2387 Canyon Ridge Way? That's Belle Gaia's place."

Gal leaned against the wall and raised his voice at Belle: "Where's Zane? You know where he is. Give the fool to me. Now! You've got a tracking stone in this house. I want it. Give it to me, or I'll have this place burnt to a pile of ash, and I'll go so far as to have the authorities pin arson on you." He jabbed an ethereal finger at her.

Belle remained calm. "Why are you shouting? I've never seen anyone named Zane. Don't know who you're talking about?" Belle said and retreated two steps. "If you so much as threaten me or my home again, you'll be sorry."

He offered a crooked grin. "What are you going to do: kill me?"

"They have laws to protect the living from ghosts and the less than-living. You know it. I know it. You'll be tossed into purgatory prison."

He waved a hand at her and chuckled.

"Enough with the games, woman. I know the kid's here. Somewhere. I can smell the twit's fear. You can't fool me. You're the kidnapper." He glared at her and began wiggling his fingers in the air, twin spiders on treadmills.

"Don't threaten me! There's the front door." She pointed. "Please leave."

A wind stirred the air, then a wavering gust hit her square in the shoulder, sending her head snapping back. The potted palm tipped over, and several paintings fell off the wall. A sofa slid back several feet, wooden legs scratching the floor.

Gal frowned.

"By the way," Belle said, "I know who you are…Doyle." He paused and gave her a brief study.

His ghostly face illuminated in anger. "Everyone knows me!" he roared. "You're just another notch in my belt loop."

He wiggled his fingers, spooling up an incantation with his mind. A fresh gust of wind sent a magazine and Doyle's box of stones tumbling off the coffee table and onto the floor. Normally, this wind spell would have sent Belle slamming into the wall. However, Doyle's energy currents, inside the protective barrier of her home, fizzled out.

His eyes locked onto her feet, volleyed to his own boots, then back at her legs. She buckled at the knees and then regained her balance. She could not move her legs. Her feet seemed glued to the floor. His energy-weave had cemented her feet in place.

Doyle started to whistle and walked up to Belle, who tried to bob and weave, but that was about all she could do. Her feet remained clamped to the floor, as if Doyle had cinched them into ski boots mounted to the floorboards. Doyle stepped up to her and placed a wraithlike fingertip to her face, sending tingles through her flushed cheeks. She jerked her head away from his feathery reach.

"Don't touch me," she snapped. "This is the last time I'm asking you. Leave my premises."

He spoke in a graveyard-quiet tone: "And then what? What are you going to do? Nothing. That's what. Now, if you'd be so kind. Where is the boy?" His mood shifted with the quickness of transient borderline personality disorder.

"What boy? Haven't seen any lost boys. This Zane person you're looking for must be in the forest. The redwoods. Go to the redwoods, you dark old ghoul! I'm sure you'll be welcome with Madge." Now, it was Belle's turn to laugh.

Belle PMSed Rainn: *Doyle's still here.*

No. Really? I never would've guessed.

Stop with the sarcasm. Stay nearby, but remain upstairs.

I've been listening, Mom. I'm ready to run down there and help.

"All that matters is that you're cemented in place, elf woman," Doyle said. "Hope you don't mind if I wander around. Won't be long. Ta ta."

He retrieved his wooden box off the floor and shoved it back into his shoulder bag.

"OK, now that you've got your belongings," she nodded toward a tall, leafy plant in her atrium, "there's the door. Don't trip on your way out."

Doyle grinned and floated an inch off the ground, hovering in his boots.

"Trying to impress me with more of your illusory magic, Doyle? Not working."

"How are your feet? Enjoying gravity? Care to dance?"

His boots smacked onto the floor, and he performed a little tap dance.

Belle tuned into her thought magic and sent a PMS to Rainn. *Have you reached Zane?*

I did, Rainn responded almost immediately. *He's catching a ride with Caesar.*

She got no response from Belle. Now was not the time to be put on hold. A moment later, Belle replied: *I'm in a bit of a situation here. Doyle cast a Cement Spell on me. Glued my feet to the floor. Not sure how long I'll be stuck.*

In your home? His energy-weave worked? I'll be right down, Mom. Time for plan B.

Plan B? We don't have a plan B.

We do now. Tell him Zane's on campus at the University. He's in the library. Maybe he'll leave to go search for him. Before Zane arrives at your place.

Doyle made his way to the base of the spiral staircase, took three steps up the stairs, and stopped. "Just consider yourself in timeout," Doyle said with a smirk. "You've been a naughty elf. I know Zane is close. I can feel it." He chuckled.

She said nothing.

He marched up the spiral stairs with purposeful intent, holding his shoulder bag like a purse. He stopped on the second-floor landing and walked down a hall.

A buzzing sound was coming from a room down the hall. He peered into the first room on the left. A bedroom with a king-sized bed and a mountain of pillows piled in front of a black oak headboard. A single silver vase with handles on the headboard shelf sat with a dim light spilling out of it. Doyle tossed his bag onto the yellow comforter. The vase started to jiggle. Doyle leaned a knee on the bed and grabbed the rattling vase, tipping it upside down. An alabaster stone flecked in black, yellow, and blue veins fell into his hand.

"Got it." He grumbled a few choice obscenities and pocketed the stone. It stopped vibrating once it was in his pocket. He stormed down the hallway into another room, his eyes sparkling with anger. Doyle loved the sensation of anger. It thrilled him to no end, giving him a sense of power and clarity.

He made his way downstairs, waved at Belle, and disappeared into her kitchen.

She said nothing. Anytime she struggled to escape, the dark, energetic vibrations weighed her down. Her legs were heavy.

He stepped out the back door and plucked the alabaster stone from his pocket, waving it in the air while walking along the side of the house. The stone made a clicking sound that quickened as he walked. The clicking sound slowed. He stopped and backpedaled until the stone clicked in rapid-fire succession and started to vibrate. He grinned and stared at a brick in the wall. As he moved the stone closer to the brick, the brick began to jiggle, and the tracking stone energetically pulled a single brick free from its slot in the wall and fell to the ground, revealing an opening; the tracking stone clung to the fallen brick with magnetic appeal, tracking stone flashing with neon brightness.

The exterior fake walls of Belle's dilapidated old cabin began to flicker. Doyle muttered a new incantation to power down what remained of Belle's illusory spell.

In a flash, her home's protective illusory spell dissolved: the haunting appearance of an old boarded-up cabin with faded gray slate walls misted over, and was gone; the divot-marred dirt path and weedy yard with sticky overgrown bushes also disappeared. Belle had designed this spell to keep prowlers, robbers, and cat burglars away from her property.

Belle Gaia's lavish three-story manor reappeared in the mist, bringing back its unique charm and luster: a beautiful sprawling estate with two acres of gardens in full bloom: purple pumpkins, lavender melons on thorny vines, ripening raspberry bushes, and countless other organic delights, all growing in tight, neat rows. Beyond the acreage leading up to her solitary estate, far off in the distance, stood a grove of gigantic redwoods.

Doyle snickered; being dead and ghosted, he had no appetite or desire to be entranced by the power of home-based organics. He had blocked those memories.

He spat at a yellow rose bush as tall as him and wandered around the side of the house.

Belle, crestfallen at seeing the illusory spell surrounding her property had been extinguished, muttered, "My protective spell! Oh, that beast!"

Time to PMS the professor.

Edge, you out there? It's Belle Gaia. This is urgent. Please respond.

No response.

An automated caller said, *your PMS network is experiencing higher than average call volume. Please hang up and try your call later.*

She sensed that Doyle may be planting viruses around her ability to communicate and protect her space.

She reminded herself to remain calm and breathe. *Stay focused,* she told herself, and was about to PMS again when her temple started to pulsate.

You there, Belle? Edge here. How are you, girl? What's the urgency?

She explained the situation to Edge about Doyle Alfred Grimes and her daughter's reappearance in Enchanted with her brother Zane.

I know Doyle is back at it, and I met this young lad, Zane, too. I sensed there was something more to that boy. His aural glow was humming when he stopped by my cottage earlier.

Have you seen him recently? Belle asked with a smidgen of hope.

Indeed. I'm sure Madge and her grove are aware of this newfound energetic Being in our midst. Zane stumbled onto my cottage a day ago. In a rainstorm. Camped out at my place, but disappeared on me, using his epi energy.

Did you scare him off?

Pshaw! Dear me, no. Nothing like that. He seemed impressed with my talents. Loved my lab, but he's a novice epi, a mere child when it comes to epileptic travel. He blinked away on me. Not sure where he went.

We need to find him. And I don't mean to put a fire under your redwood tree, but I really need your help on this, Edge. Doyle's on my property, nosing around. He's got me in a Cement Spell and blocked my illusory home incantation.

Oh, this is urgent. I want to help. Maybe I can get that hairy old cabbie, Caesar, to pick me up. He's always busy toting epis around. You've got connections with Rainn and Zane, yes?

Well, Rainn's my elfin daughter.

Oh.... I thought they were brother and sister.

They are. Rainn has time-jumped. She's my daughter from a past life.

Oh, this is interesting, Edge replied in a calm tone.

Without getting frazzled, even though her heart was beating a bit quicker, she asked, *Can you reach out to Caesar now?*

Will do. You at home?

Of course. Where else would I be?

Right. Right. You're spellbound by a cement virus.

Belle dialed up Rainn: *You okay upstairs?*

I'm fine. Is Doyle still in the house?

Contact Caesar, Rainn urged. *You may have better PMS connectivity. Doyle's messing with my telepathic network. Oh, and since you're twin siblings, and your internal neural networks are more similar, try to reach your brother again. But call Caesar, first. Tell him to go pick up Edge Longstump. He's a retired professor at EWU.* She gave her Edge's address.

Rainn quickly contacted Zane. *Brother, you there?*

Hey, what's up? Zane responded. *Everything okay with you? I was just thinking about you. I'm in that cab.*

With Caesar? Excellent. Tell Caesar to swing by and pick up Edge Longstump. Belle's in trouble. She's trapped, and so am I.

Things are way out of hand here. I just—

Suddenly, their PMS was disconnected.

As soon as Zane lost connection with Rainn's PMS, he felt Caesar's glowing eyes on him. Caesar stared at him through his rearview mirror.

"What is it you need?" Caesar asked.

"Think you can stop by and pick up a friend before we go to Belle's place? We need to hurry! There's a bit of drama going on at Belle's. Got a troll friend who is going to help us out. He's a professor."

"What's this about?

"Not sure. But it's urgent. I think they're under attack by haunted UFOs or something."

"You better not be messing with me, kid."

"What? About the UFOs? I am, but you never know. This place has more haunts than anything else. Hey, do they have graverobbers and tomb thieves here? My sister's freaking out." Zane shot a quick glance at Reese.

"I've got his address. It's—"

"Old Edge Longstump's still alive?" Caesar cut in and grabbed a fresh cigar, but didn't light it, instead, he rolled it around in his mouth. "Thought that green man had died. It's been years since I've heard from him."

"So, you'll pick him up?" Zane repeatedly thankfully.

"Just give me the address before I change my mind."

Edge stood outside playing catch with Cookie, his giant panther. He tossed a yellow Frisbee across the yard, and Cookie sprang out of the tall heather, snapped it up, and disappeared into the grasses. The heather moved about like an incoming wave.

Caesar's humming Studebaker steered onto Edge's driveway and parked in front of his hideaway home.

Cookie, aware of this potential solicitation, shapeshifted into a black housecat, scurried across the yard, and began giving itself a tongue shower.

Zane hopped out of the cab first and ran up to greet Edge; Julius flew out of the trees and glided in a big sweeping circle high overhead.

"Hey Edge, we need to go! My sister's in trouble," Zane said in exasperation.

"Just relax. You expressed the urgency of the situation, but getting all worked up will only deplete your energies. We'll get there. Breathe, my boy, breathe," Edge said.

Julius landed on Zane's shoulder.

"Oh, hey, buddy," Zane said to the dwarf dragon.

"Dragons can be dangerous or helpful, if you know how to train them." Caesar said.

"Hey," Zane said, "I just got him today. We should go!"

"Oh, I've had all the training I need, thank you very much," trilled Julius.

"I can see who's the queen of this duo," Edge replied dryly.

"I'm no queen," snapped back the dragon in spiked defense. "I'm a king, through and through."

Julius flew back toward Caesar's cab and sat on Studebaker's hood.

"Hey, get off my cab," Caesar shouted. "You'll scratch the paint!"

"I'm not scratching it, you grouchy old weed! Keep your roots in the dirt. I've got retractable claws. Your oh-so-precious paint job is fine. I'll sit where I want."

"You scratch it and I'll be making roasted dragon burgers out of your remains," Caesar dared. "Or, I've got a pair of dragon-hide sandals at home, and I'd love a second pair. Now, get in the cab. Now!"

Inside the cab, Zane's sweaty legs slid on the upholstery. Zane thought back to his first experience meeting Caesar and their initial cab ride: Caesar got a few dents on his rear quarter panel crashing into a boulder, but the Studebaker looked new again. In mint condition.

"Caesar, your cab looks great," said Zane, hoping to calm Caesar. "Take it to a body shop, did you? This is one fine ride."

"I've got incantation insurance for seizure-travel, but my policy doesn't include scratch repair for dragon claw marks." He glared at Julius. "I take pride in this magical hunk of metal. It's my lifeblood."

The dragon, seated on Zane's lap, stuck out its long, forked tongue at the back of Caesar's hairy head.

Edge pulled the safety shoulder-strap across his chest and clicked the buckle in place from the front seat.

"Well, Zane," remarked Caesar, "I think you've found a pet with a snippy attitude. You might want to get that dwarf in check."

"Can I ask you something?" Zane said to the dragon. "How old are you?"

Caesar swerved to steer around a cabin-sized boulder, and Zane's shoulder banged into the door.

Caesar veered back onto the weed-choked road.

"A hundred and six," said the dwarf dragon.

"Wow, you *are* old. How long do dragons live, on average?"

"Depends on diet and how much I smoke. Most of us can live for over two hundred years."

"Dragons smoke?"

"You've seen me breathe fire, right." Zane nodded.

"Breathing fire is rough on the lungs," said Ceasar. "Chain smokers don't live beyond a hundred. Takes patience to refrain from breathing fire every day, but it can be done. They have addiction clinics for us dragons."

"Can smoking give you cancer?"

"No, that's a disease on Earth, but too much smoking can collapse a lung. That'll kill a dragon. On the spot."

"Okay, kids," Caesar cut in, "you can share your soap operas some other time. We'll be there soon."

"Really?"

"Yep, within the hour, and I'm tired of hearing you talk."

A stone cabin capped with twin gables and redwood-tiled roofing was nestled amid a grove of Douglas fir. The sparkling midday sun painted shadows and light throughout the tree-lined stretch of landscape.

Along the perimeter of the cabin, in tight little toy-soldier rows, lay a stretch of Huckleberry shrubs and a row of sword ferns.

Rainn stared out the window. "Mom, something's happened to your spell in the front, too. Your beautiful gardens, I can see it all. It's lovely indeed."

"Funny how Doyle blocked my spell from unwanted solicitors," Belle replied, "but it is gorgeous, to be sure. My place'll be fine, just fine. But my feet, well…" She shrugged, unable to wiggle any life into her cement-spelled feet. "Would you be a dear and get me some healing salves from the kitchen pantry?" She told Rainn the names of three exotic flora blends.

In the kitchen, each herbal mix was shelved, alphabetically. Was her elfin mom OCD? Regardless, Rainn was pleased with the ease of locating what she needed. Belle had hundreds of spices and herbs and healing oils. Most, if not all, of her collective findings were harvested from the redwood canopy. Rainn recalled, in her life growing up with Belle a lifetime ago, that Belle preferred her assembly of bio-magic to be neat and tidy, so none of that had changed. Recipes for spellfarmers like Belle were essential in her line of work, and what she ingested through her personal recipes kept her alert, lively, happy, and energized with light and love.

Rainn turned a spinning spice rack and found the flora herbs, each labeled accordingly: elderberry bark, redwood firefly dust, yellow oasis flakes.

"You've got quite the variety, Mom," Rainn hollered.

Rainn heard a knock at the back door. She set down the spices, drew back a curtain, and peered through the kitchen window. No one was there. She opened the door and didn't see anyone, but her elfin intuition, as she reconnected with her Life Essence in Enchanted Wood, was rekindling her energies and her love for the forest. Memories were coming back into focus more and more readily, and she knew she wasn't alone. Being raised as a spellfarming enchantress by trade, her mother, Belle, many years ago had taught her many things. One of them: trust those little intuitive nudges.

"Ms. Gaia?" called out a tiny voice from outside her window.

Rainn spotted a little girl peeking from behind a tall, thorny peach rose bush.

"Hi, I'm Chloe," she said. "Is Ms. Gaia home?" The little elf girl marched up the path in her bare feet. She had slender legs that matched her equally slender waistline, and brushed a hand across her skirt. Her soft, dark hair was fashioned with bangs hanging over her right eye. She twisted her lower lip, then glanced back at the tree line off in the distance before returning her attention to Rainn. The girl bounced back and forth from heel to toe in her dusty bare feet and tucked the flop of bangs behind an ear. The little girl wore dangling earrings of silver lightning bolts that shimmered in the sunlight.

Rainn sensed the little girl was concerned—she wore it all over her cute little face and big bright eyes, as she dragged her toe across the grass, fidgeting with her hands, and sticking out her lip into a pouty face.

"Ms. Gaia's unavailable right now," said Rainn. "Are you okay?"

Belle hollered from the other room: "Rainn? Everything okay? Is there a little girl out there? Is that Chloe I hear?"

Rainn knew her mother's elfin hearing was exceptional.

Rainn and Chloe stepped into the living room. Belle spotted the unexpected guest: Chloe. She was dressed in a canary-yellow skirt and a spaghetti-string halter-top, and hopscotched across the living room and then darted behind a tall potted maple.

"Chloe," Belle hollered happily and waved. "I see you. No need to be shy. Come on out. Let me see your pretty little face!"

Chloe Shepherd, an elf girl, about as tall as a swan, poked her head out from behind the potted tree one more time. She batted her bright blue eyes and danced around Belle, grinned. She hooked her dark hair behind a pointy ear, mimicking Belle's act of pinning back her bangs.

"Hi Ms. Gaia," the elf girl said playfully. "I was just wondering," she glanced down to her bare feet and dragged her toes across the floor, "if you could take me to the canopy to play."

Belle smiled softly, "I'm sorry, sweetie. Busy now."

Chloe, with hands holstered to hips, pouted again, this time like a pro.

"You don't look busy. Busy with what?"

"How's tomorrow sound?"

The girl offered another elfin pout, re-engaging her lips and making her ears wiggle.

"Today's simply to a day to play in the vines," she countered. "Can't you play today? It's beautiful and warm and bright, like the constellation Orion's Belt. We could climb trees, dance on cloudy tree branches. Hide 'n seek in the canopy's always fun. I'm sure there's lots of little elves playing in the canopy sky-park."

"I've got a few projects to catch up on," said Belle. "I need a little time. Being an adult comes with responsibilities. We'll make time for the canopy park on another day."

"Children have responsibilities, too," Chloe dared, eyes narrowing with devilish desire.

Belle new Chloe had a mischievous vein in her and was all-too familiar with the little elf's dark-minded expression.

"Of course you do, my sweet little cherub, but there's work to be done. My gardens are calling." Belle gave Rainn a look.

"And who's this?" Chloe demanded, visibly deflated: arms folded across her chest, offering the best seven-year-old act of defiance that she could muster.

"Rainn, meet Chloe. Rainn's my daughter from a past life. She's come here from Earth to reconnect. Isn't that exciting?"

Chloe gave Rainn careful study as Rainn crouched down to her level and smiled. "You are such a cutie. I'd love to play with you sometime, but we have urgent family business to take care of."

Belle crouched down at Chloe's elf level, with her feet cemented to the floor. "I have family visiting. So maybe you can go ask your mommy, Chloe. See if she'll take you to the park. How's that sound?"

"Mommy's doing elf stuff. She's got to dis-enchant a bunch of cactuses taking over the backyard, or something like that." She shrugged and wiggled her ears.

Rainn felt a little spark of energy ping between her fingers. She shook out her hand, wonderingly, while Chloe's big, pretty eyes locked onto hers.

Belle smirked. "Well, then. I'm sure you understand. I have elf stuff to do, too. And please, darling, no wiggling energies with Rainn. I sense you're up to something already." She gave Rainn a consoling look.

"Oh, I'm fine," Rainn said, still shaking out her hand.

"Can't you wave one of your magic flowers in the air or something and make all your busy-time go away? The canopy park's so much fun. I love going there with you. You're the best at spellfarming tricks. You're the best elf in the Wood," she proclaimed. "Come on, let's go! Your friend can come, too."

"Thank you, my sweet little energetic elf. But I have to take care of a few things, and I haven't seen Rainn in a lifetime. She's my daughter. Didn't you hear me earlier?"

Chloe's wrinkled brow flattened, and she put her hands in a prayerful pose at her heart and then curtsied to Rainn.

"That's nice of you for understanding, Chloe."

"Oh, I suppose I can wait."

"Great! And isn't your mother at home working on the ornery cactus attack in her garden?"

"Yep." Chloe sighed. "She's stuck doing grown-up elf stuff. Like you."

Belle melted a little. "Tell you what. When my daughter and I finish our work, I'll call you." She tapped her temple. "Just have your PMS tuned in, okay, sweetheart?" Belle wagged a finger at her.

Chloe rubbed her hands together excitedly. "Okay. I'll tell Mommy." And off she went, skipping back through the kitchen. Rainn followed her to the kitchen and watched Chloe race outside and disappear into a mound of heather, sending butterflies dancing. Rainn grabbed the healing spices and gave them to Belle.

"How're your feet? You managed well, not letting on that you're stuck in the cement spell," said Rainn softly.

"Oh, I'll survive. Always do."

There was a knock on the front door.

"Oh, for the love of murky pond water!" Belle handed the vials back to Rainn. She paused in mid-thought, tapping into this *new* energy at the front door. "Let's hope that's Edge and Zane. It doesn't feel like an elfish visitor at the door. Go see who's out there ghosting my landscape?"

"Yes, Mom. I'm on it."

Then something pinged inside Rainn, and being of elfin heritage, she knew to pay attention when these intuitive pings ponged in her thoughts.

There, standing at the doorway, was Reese. In front of Reese was the egg-framed Edge with his long thin limbs.

"Hi, there," he exclaimed jovially. "Name's Edge Longstump. Got a call from Belle."

Reese sent his ropy tresses swirling about his head like woolen socks.

She studied his dreadlocked head half a moment, feeling entranced by his caring eyes. She had to stay focused on her mom's needs. "Come in! Come in!"

"All clear," Edge said over his shoulder.

Zane made his way out of the bushes and into the house. Zane looked worn out, as faded as an unearthed fossil, and dirty from toe to disheveled dusty mane.

Zane immediately gave his sister a hug and then, surprising to Rainn, he walked right up to Belle and gave her a hug, too.

"Oh, my. Thank you," she said to Zane. "So lovely to meet you."

Rainn and Belle were mother and daughter from a past life and Zane was not part of the family in that past life, so he did not know Belle Gaia.

Zane took a step back and studied her. "Something wrong?"

Rainn's mouth sagged open. How did her brother notice something was amiss with Belle?

"Oh, you are a wise youngster." Belle went on to say, "Give me another hug. Maybe it'll shake a little life into both of us. If you stick with white-magic purveyors, you'll be safe. Speaking of white-magic," she turned her eyes on Professor Longstump: "Edge, you old fool, get over here! Be a dear, reverse this cement spell."

She kept her hands on Zane's shoulders and cued into his energetic field: it told her volumes. "You're a buzz of electrical energies, mister Zane Moss. And I sense you're a good man. Just like this old troll who's going to help us out of our little predicament."

Zane's eyes, droopy with dark circles under them, suddenly widened as if he had just slammed an iced espresso; he straightened his posture and ran a hand through his disheveled, tangled 'work-zone-under-construction' hairdo.

Zane looked into her hypnotic eyes, feeling entranced.

Belle nodded, sensing that Zane was tapping into her healing hands. Many had been entranced by her glow. That was a given. But this was something more. "You're welcome here, my young traveler. Trust in the magic brewing within you, and it breeds within the Trees."

Edge began muttering incantations, pacing back and forth; he reached a hand into a vest pocket and sprinkled some blueish dust on Belle's cemented boots.

Within a minute, Belle slowly dragged a foot free, as if pulling it from thick muck, then the other.

She thanked Edge for extinguishing the spell.

"Nothing to it, old girl. Just try to stay out of trouble."

"It's good to be surrounded by positive souls like you all. You're lighting up my home. I love it and I love you all." Belle danced a little jig.

"Just be careful who you meet in the Wood."

Belle slowed her youthful jig and glanced at Rainn and then Zane. "Edge's right. There are many telepathing tree pirates; they want your threaded energies, and well, it's yours. Guard it with your life."

Reese spoke up, "Word around campus is: Belle's the best intuit in the Wood, and a seasoned spell farmer to boot. Nice to see you're in free boots again. Yep. She's the best at everything she does. She just knows things, I'm told."

Belle's cheeks curled up at the corners. "Thank you, Reese."
She cued into Reese's thought stream—since she didn't know
him—and saw a positive blue vibrant aura around his head, a sign
that Reese came from good stock and was telling the truth.

"I'm just a simple spell farmer," Belle replied with humility.
"Simplicity and sharing are key to leading a loving lifestyle. Keeps
me youthful and vibrant. "We need to get the Moss twins to Ick
and Madge," Belle said. "Time to clear our heads and get back to
the canopy. My true home."

"Who's Ick?" Zane asked.

"Ick's a redwood tree. A very powerful redwood that has been
teamed up with Madge for eons."

Rainn spoke up, "Maybe your little friend Chloe was right. Oh,
how she wanted to take you to the canopy, your palace of
restoration."

Zane gazed off, hands becoming clenched fists. A flash of déjà
vu cycled through him. He was unable to call out for help. The
scene around him became muted as he stared off emptily.

"You okay?" Rainn asked, concerned, seeing Zane's far-off
gaze.

"Zane? Zane! You okay?" Too
late.

Zane buckled at the knees and fell to the ground, body going
rigid and then gyrating with epileptic accuracy.

He blacked out, his head, arms, and legs flailing about; he
kicked the coffee table, shoving it across the floor.

"Stay clear of his eruptive energies," Edge ordered as he got
closer to Zane, and moved an end table away from his flailing
body.

An elfin voice from the open window shouted, "He's flipping on
his enchantment." It was Chloe. "Cool! I want to play with him.
He's straight fire!"

Belle grabbed a couch pillow and placed it under her brother's head. His body, a bomb of an epileptic energy, continued to seize in front of them. Rainn grabbed an afghan and put it next Zane to buffer his flailing arms and legs.

"Chloe," Belle called out over her shoulder, "I need you to go home. We're dealing with adult stuff. Go on now. We're handling this."

Chloe ducked out of sight.

"That elfin child doesn't need to see him epi out of here." Belle said, knowing Chloe to be a chatterbox, who would tell everyone she knew. The last thing they needed was gossip being spread across the psychic airwaves.

Chloe appeared at the window again, her little nose resting on the windowsill as she balanced atop a boulder surrounded by daisies.

"Oh drat," Chloe said, "he's not blinking away. I like it when they disappear." She snapped her fingers, "Gee-whizzing wizards. That's no fun. His epi energy won't turn over. He needs a jumpstart."

"Chloe, please go home," Belle called out, hearing Chloe's monologue. "I may need your help later. I told you I'd call you. Listen for a PMS from me. This is private. Please don't tell anyone what you've seen. It's our secret. I'll reward you with a gift later," she finished with a binding wink. Belle's spellcasting mind-energy nudged Chloe off her boulder stool, and she disappeared from the window.

"Oh goody!" And Chloe went off, skipping away with elfish delight.

Zane's bodily eruption subsided, and after a moment, they hoisted his unconscious body onto the sofa, his mouth clenched, a droplet of blood oozing from his lip.

Reese asked, "Is he okay?"

"Well, he's still here," Edge said, "but we have to watch out for another seismic burst."

"I think he'll be just fine," Belle said, checking his pulse and then putting a hand to his chest. "His fourth chakra, his heart chakra, is open. That's a good sign."

Rainn came in with a wet cloth and wiped the blood from his chin. "Must've bit his tongue or cheek. Is he still seizing?" She investigated his face.

"Yes," Belle said. "His body and mind are clamped shut. A petit mal." Belle hovered her palms over his mouth and closed her eyes to call in healing energy from the Redwoods, namely Madge.

Zane's jaw slackened, and the bleeding stopped. With one finger pointed a few inches above his chest, Belle traced a shape in the air, called Choku Rei, above his heart chakra, a common method used by Reiki practitioners to tap into energies of the spirit realm. She drew out a parallelogram and then sketched three tiny circles in three corners of the parallelogram. She closed her eyes, channeling energy from the White Light of Spirit. The fourth corner of the unseen parallelogram remained open, inviting healing spirits in.

"Reese!" Belle called out.

"Yeah?"

"I'm sensing some serious neurological overload. Can you tell me what you've been doing with Zane?"

"Nothing. I'm a student at E.W.U," Reese said flatly. "Found his sister wandering around in the woods."

Rainn nodded in agreement.

"She told me about Zane, that he was lost. Then Zane made a surprise epi appearance in my canopy home."

Belle nodded, then returned her attention to the unconscious Zane.

"What sort of healing are you doing on him?" Reese asked.

"I blend Reiki with my spellfarming redwood energy, a powerful healing combo. I'm tapping into the spirit realm of the Wood. I'm just a conduit, a channel. I call on the angelic energies and let them flow through me." She paused, closed her eyes, breathing and tuning in, listening from within. "I keep hearing the name Stanley. Stanley Moss."

"Mom, Zane and I are connected to Stanley. He's a great uncle of ours from Earth. He died long ago."

"Well, he's here," said Belle. "Helping. Do you know anything about this uncle?"

"Not really. Just what Zane told me. Said he moved to California long ago. Died when we were about two years old. I think, in California."

Zane's head began to quiver gently, as did his arms and legs. Belle gently placed her hand on his shoulder.

"Oh, this could be trouble!" Edge chimed in. "Keep a close eye on the lad."

Zane, then, disappeared from the sofa, leaving a halo of light framing where his body had been holding space.

"Oh, no! Not again!" hollered Rainn. "He's blinked out on us."

"Gone? Is he on another epi ride?" Reese asked, leaning back on his heels. "Whoa! This dude is a maze of energy. My arms are tingling. What a buzz, man! Intense!"

Edge piped up, "The boy did the same thing at my place. Let's hope he makes a safe landing."

"Rainn, what're you two running from?" Belle said.

"Nothing, Mom."

"Well, I think someone's following him."

Belle returned her gaze to the sofa, now vacant of Zane. Rainn looked out the window; Chloe was slipping across the yard, her legs a blur of momentum. Behind her, following along with long strides, was an exceptionally tall man dressed in a shiny silk suit of grayish-blue.

"Here comes Chloe," Rainn said. "Didn't you tell her to go home?"

Belle stepped to the window, a frown forming on her face as she saw the golem dressed in a suit. "Oh bother. This is sour timing. Looks like he's escaped."

"He? Escaped? Who?"

"The golem."

"Golem? What is it, a fugitive? An energy bandit or something?" Rainn asked.

Reese put up his hands defensively. "Just met the dude. I've got no allegiance to him."

"You know him?" Rainn looked at him questioningly.

"He's a clay creation," Belle said while sizing up the tall man in the silk suit following ten paces behind Chloe's racing feet. "Oh, when it storms!"

"Oh, golems. Right." Rainn looked beyond the approaching pair outside and rekindled memories from her past life here in Enchanted Wood. She remembered golems. "I haven't seen a golem since I was a little girl living here. That was eons ago."

"Some golems can be trouble. Depends on who mastered one," added Belle.

"By the looks of this one, I'd guess he's a bad guy, a very bad guy. Look at his squared-off head." He looked like a molded cousin to Frankenstein's monster.

"Some clay heads, when molded on the Wheel by a speller, well, they like to forge ahead and mask their creations a bit, but maybe I'm projecting racial profiling, or creature profiling, on this one. Let's see what he's got to say. Chloe's a smart one. She may've found an honorable golem."

Belle went to the door; Chloe, now hopping on a stone slab with all the vigor of an excited elf, looked up at Belle. Belle offered a stern glance and spoke with steely determination: "Excuse me, little girl, but I told you to go home. I'm busy."

Belle, keeping one eye on the approaching golem, continued to scold Chloe with a pointed finger. The golem stopped a good ten paces away, near the mailbox.

"Mommy had to go somewhere." Chloe turned on a heel and pointed at the golem. "Then he showed up." She spun in an excited circle, dancing to a silent tune. She was a bundle of happy elfin energy.

"And Mommy left you alone?" Belle shook her head.

"This man said he'd help." Chloe tapped on Belle's knee and whispered up at her, "I have to tell you something." Belle squatted down next to Chloe.

Chloe whispered, "I told you that tall man you had a guy flipping enchantment in your cabin, and he wanted to help. Right away.
Said he was a good helper."

Belle gave Chloe a consoling pat on her elfin head. "Oh, you saw someone flipping enchantments, did you?"

"Course I did! It was Zane. Saw him cruising down an alternate highway of existence. My eyes can see between the unseen. You know: I can see epis as they disappear during a seizing fit and get blasted like a rocket ship of energy to a new location. Lots of roads going into all sorts of places. He's got a lot of zig to his zag." Chloe grinned.

Belle was aware of some of Chloe's special elfin talents, but seeing invisible trans-dimensional maps was new. Belle's expression remained stoic, neutral; she stood between Chloe and the approaching towering golem. His head was higher than the sunflower garden he marched past. His hands rested in the pockets of his suit and he stopped. The scent of his wet clay cologne brushed her nostrils.

The towering chunk of clay put out a cordial hand and took her hand, giving it several hearty pumps.

"Greetings," he said. "I'm Coleman. Coleman Pick."

He removed his fedora and offered a gentlemanly bow. He was bald. His dome a greyish-blue shade. Bumpy scalp. He swept away beads of clay frothing on his lapel and looked around. "Nice place you have here. Heard you were helping a young man who was having trouble managing his epi energies. Got lost in the ether. Is he around? I want to help him get unlost, as it were."

I never told Chloe that Zane was lost, Belle thought. "Who're you looking for?" She asked with caution.

"He's a young fellow." Coleman nodded to Belle and then peered into her open doorway, seeing Reese. 'Bout the same age as this young man."

He pointed at Reese. "Goes by the name Moss. Zane Moss. Comes from special stock, and I'm just here to get him unlost. Yes. That's my duty."

"All by yourself?" Belle asked, wondering if this golem had the wherewithal to construct much more than directives from his Maker.

"He's just one lad, and I'm one golem. I always find the lost ones. It's what I do."

"Is he in some sort of trouble?" Belle said, acting as if she knew nothing of Zane.

"Not that I'm aware. But he may be one of the Enchanted Ones. As I said, we work with special stock—clients of noteworthy caliber."

"We?" Belle said.

"Yes. Me and my boss. Your little elf friend here said she saw him inside your house. Mind if I look around?"

Belle showed no emotion, save for flaring her nostrils. "I do mind. This is my home. Private property."

Chloe nudged into the conversation. "Hey, mister, you smell like a clay sandwich, you're not human, and you're certainly not an elf. Way too tall." She tilted her head back to take him all in. "You're as tall as the clouds. Must be chilly way up there." She put a finger to her cheek and then set her hands on her hips. "You don't have any hair. Not even up your big beak of a nose."

"Nice little girl," Coleman said, void of emotion. "What grand eyesight you have for such a pea of a nut."

"I'm not a pea and I'm not a nut. I'm an elf, you silly hunk of mud! My eyes are telescopic, so you'd better watch your step."

"You are just a child, little one."

Chloe looked to Belle and whispered, "Is he serious? I may look like I'm seven years old, but I'm…"

"Yes, sweetie," Belle cut in. "Seven to an elf is all grown up, energetically. But you *are* but a wee child."

Chloe returned her attention to the sky surrounding Coleman's head. "Wait. I know what you are." Chloe prodded at Coleman's shin with her finger. "You're one of those muddy creatures." Coleman stared at her unblinkingly.

Chloe spiked in, "A golem. That's what you are," she finished with smug satisfaction. "I'm smart," she proclaimed.

Coleman capped his scalp with his fedora and ran a finger along its brim. "I'd love to look at your home. You think I could step inside? Just to get out of the sun."

"I do mind," Belle snapped. "I'm in the middle of some private matters. Family matters. As I already said, this is my private home, so I suggest you kindly continue your search elsewhere."

"No Zane Moss here, then?" Coleman added, as if not hearing a word she said.

"You catch on quick," Belle said distantly. "Now, if you'll excuse us."

Coleman began backpedaling along the stone slabs.

"If the lad happens to show up, I'd appreciate it if you let me know," he said. "Oh, you'll need this." He walked back up to her, handed her his business card, tipped his hat, and wandered back into the woods.

Zane opened his eyes. Closed them. Opened them. A stiff breeze warred with his hair. He sat on a tree branch, perched like a partridge, thirty feet up the trunk.

He had done it again: seized to a new location. And, once again, he had epileptically slept through the whole journey.

"The hell. Again?" he cried in exasperation.

There he sat clinging to a branch, cheek pressed against the moist oak trunk, bark digging into this jaw, leaving indentation marks. He stared down at the landscape. Rows of tombstones, a gravesite, some with colorful floral arrangements: daisies and lilacs and roses and geraniums, others littered in crabgrasses and tall clumps of weeds. His eyes moved to a marble log cabin with a chimney stack. Deeper in his field of vision, on the other side of a metal fence, he could see rows of stone cottages. To the east, more tomb markers and huts and cottages. Tall elms and pines bordered the western hillside.

He leaned back, wiped drool from his chin, and lifted his head off the trunk, leaving tree bark indentations on his chin.

Weird, Zane mused. *I feel weird.* Then, his mind started to replay memories: He recalled being at Belle's cottage; his sister was there, Reese and Edge, too. But where was he now?

A breeze whipped through oak and pine; he swayed about on the flexible tree trunk and squeezed the branch into a chokehold. Peering down, hoping to gather his bearings, he looked to be a good fifteen feet up the tree.

He saw movement down below. Footsteps padded along the grassy floor.

A small figure, a forest gnome, a squat creature with thick legs and equally thick arms, pushed a kiddie wheelbarrow filled with dark soil. The gnome stopped at a pile of dirt and stared into an open pit: a vacant tomb. Using a pair of extendable, long-handled tongs, he reached into the open hole, pulled out an entire skeleton, and dropped it into the wheelbarrow, where it clanged noisily.

"Hey, what gives? You woke me up, you fat, ungrateful gnome," said the skeleton, stretching its arms.

"You are Mr. Fully Wells, yes?

"Indeed."

"You've been served. I'm just delivering the papers. I've copies of your eviction notices going back seven weeks. I'm the repo man, here to repossess your property. Just move along, would you." He glanced at a glowing wristwatch and read some text scrolling across its face.

The skeleton sat up in the wheelbarrow. He was dressed in silk yellow pajama bottoms and a nightcap with strawberries on it.

"You'll address me by my proper name: Fluffy."

"Be that as it may, you no longer own your grave plot. Graveyard Gardens owns its rights now. And it's being viewed today by a potential buyer. If you require further assistance, I will call on my support crew to escort you off the property. I'm here to give you a free ride out of the Graveyard Gardens."

Fluffy stared at him and would have blinked several times if he had eyes.

The gnome wiped his brow with a cloth and started pushing the skeleton in the wheelbarrow toward a small barn with a tall iron fence.

"But my ribs are showing," Fluffy said. "I'm topless. Need to pick up a few things. Can't have the neighbors seeing me like this." Fluffy covered his chest.

"Repo man will be here momentarily. All your possessions are now the property of Graveyard Garden Estates. I suggest you get a lawyer."

"You there, stop!" shouted a voice. A figure hopped off a moving coach as the driver tugged on the reins, bringing the four-horse team to a halt.

A man dressed in a creamsicle-orange silk suit took long, purposeful strides toward the gnome.

"Be a good little gardenia, mister gnome," began the tall, angular figure, "and put that bag of bones in my coach. I've a schedule to keep."

"Yessir, Mr. Doyle, sir. And what about the earthling?" asked the gnome, pointing to the treetops where Zane was currently nesting.

Zane squinted upon hearing the name 'Doyle.'

"Another skeleton failing to pay its rent, eh?" said Doyle. "Well, then, this is my lucky day. Just put those bones in my coach, and," Doyle paused and studied the skeleton, "Oh, you're not fully dead yet? Well, I'll fix that." He strode back to the coach, grabbed a sledgehammer, twirled it like a baton, and marched at Fluffy, high-kicking like a marching band drum major.

Doyle reared the hammer back and smashed the skeleton's ribcage, and then swiped at it again, knocking it off its skull clear off. What was left of the headless skeleton bounced out the wheelbarrow and danced about like an equally headless chicken.

The gnome tackled it and tossed it into Doyle's coach.

"He'll work great as components for a new psychic puppet," Doyle went on to say with cool, calculated calm. "And that Earthling is here, you say? In the Garden somewhere. He's close." He sniffed the air. "So close I can smell him. And he's filled with fear." He clapped his hands together. "Oh, what a glorious day to be dead!"

"Pardon me," called out the headless skeleton from the wheelbarrow. He went on in a pleading tone: "I've got enough gold coinage to pay my plot mortgage. Give me until tomorrow. I'll have it for you. You can't kick me out. I have rights."

Zane wondered how the skeleton was talking and then saw the cracked skull on the ground open its mouth and shout: "I want to speak to my attorney! I have rights."

Doyle glared at the skeleton, marched up to him, pulled out a miniature crossbow from his holster, took careful aim, then tossed his firearm to the gnome. "You take care of him. He's already dead. That's just remnants of his life-thread jabbering away."

The skeleton tumbled out of the coach, hit the ground, and went silent.

"There. That'll stop his bellyaching," Doyle muttered. "He's dead. Now, where was I? Oh yes. The human."

Doyle looked at his digital wristwatch, scrolling down the screen with his dead eyes, reading something on its face.

Doyle then glanced skyward and folded his hands in front of him, swaying from heel to toe. He grinned with evil intent. "Well, there you are! What're you doing in the tree, you twit? Knew I'd find you. You earthlings stick out in this landscape." Zane cringed and said nothing.

"Well?" Doyle said in an elevated, darker tone, "I'll gladly shoot you out of the tree. I don't play games. Nor do I have time for your dawdling."

Doyle started to flicker like a faulty lightbulb. His long dark hair, his Orangesicle-colored suit, his dark boots all started to glow and shift to transparency—a silvery-blue aura of energy hummed around his now-ghost frame.

"Come on, out of the tree, Zane. I'd like a word with you," Doyle demanded.

Oh, shit! He was going to tell Doyle, 'Sorry, dude, I'm not Zane,' but that was not going to work.

"I've got good news," continued Doyle. "Got a job for you, twit. You look strong and able-bodied, for a human. Now, if you'd be so kind. Get your slippery little ass out of the tree, and do as you're told." He took aim with a dagger-loaded hand-held crossbow.

Zane, unsure what to say, decided getting shot was not on his to-do list today.

"By the way," Doyle added, "have you checked the pockets in your mind. You should have received my letter."

Zane scampered down the tree and landed on the ground, his heart thumping. He stared up at the tall ghost.

"Go on. I'm waiting," Doyle said with arms crossed, sounding bothered.

"Letter? As in psychic letter?"

"The letter was sent via PMS and on paper."

"I didn't get any letter."

Doyle glared at him, his dark eyes going hot-white for a second, blinding Zane like the flash from a camera.

"Since you claim the pockets of your brain are empty, why don't you check your other pockets?"

He rifled through his pockets. "I must've left it in my—" Zane then reached into his front breast pocket and, to his surprise, pulled out a folded-up envelope. He looked at Doyle. The envelope felt brittle, creamy faded parchment sealed in red candlewax, and stamped with a Calligraphic capital D resembling a hydra.

"That's it,' snapped Doyle. "Now get in the coach."

Zane stared at him. Was he supposed to open the seal?

The coach's interior was of elaborate craftsmanship: solid oak, walls decorated with engravings of tombstones and lunar eclipses, blood-red curtains in front of windows. Cushioned benches. Several pocket watches hung off chains hooked to the walls. A small wooden box labeled DOLLS sat on the seat of a bench next to the headless, supposedly dead, skeleton.

Zane sat next to the skullless skeleton.

The skeleton, sitting upright, crossed its legs and shrugged. "You. You dirty human! Are you the one stealing my plot?" it demanded.

Zane just stared at him, wondering how this headless skeleton was talking.

"No." He had never met a skeleton named Fluffy before. Ain't all that many Fluffys around.

Boots clomped on the ground, and the driver, dressed in a black silk jacket over a lavender shirt, made his way to the horse, adjusted its leather halter, and gave the midnight-black horse a welcoming stroke. The horse nosed the driver's black fedora off his head, sending the white-banded hat falling dreamily to the forest floor. He recapped his bald head, looking just as dapper as Doyle.

There was something odd, a little off, about the driver. For one, if it was a 'he,' it had grayish-blue skin. Just a wisp of crow feet wrinkles around the eyes. He was square-faced and about as handsome as a blue brick. Didn't look all that human. Not to Zane. Zane figured it was some sort of fantasy creature, possibly a bulimic cousin to a Sasquatch trying to make its place in Hollywood's thin vein of success—meaning it was not easy to become famous if you looked too much like a cliched Bigfoot.

It brushed its long, thin-fingered hand across its suitcoat shoulder, sending a few flakes of blue into the air, then folded its hands at its waist.

"Oh, do stop being so quiet," muttered Doyle. "He's my resident golem. Coleman, let's get going, shall we?"

Zane knew a little about golems, mostly what he had read in fantasy novels. Golems, according to lore, were creatures created out of clay. Made in the likeness of a human, but they never looked all that human. Clay was clay, not flesh and blood. Beyond that, Zane knew nothing, aside from the fact that a golem was loyal, bound to follow and carry out the orders of its creator.

This golem, Coleman Pick, drove the coach deeper into the forested graveyard. This was the largest graveyard Zane had ever seen. He figured he was in store for more first-eyewitness accounts in this strange landscape.

Speaking of strange: *Where did one get the clay to make this thing?* Zane wondered evenly. Some sort of Claymation adaptation was all Zane could surmise. Was this special clay or something one could purchase at an art supply store?

The coach, after a ten-minute bumpy ride along a rutty path, came to a halt which, in turn, halted Zane's daydreaming at nighttime.

"Everyone out," Doyle ordered.

Doyle eyed the creamy parchment in Zane's hand and then, without looking at Zane, said, "That was supposed to be delivered years ago, when you were in Middle School on Earth." Doyle frowned. "How long have you been hoarding that letter?" Zane looked at him, astonished.

Zane glanced around at the grassy forest trying to come up with a response, the sound of crickets clicking away tuned up the airwaves of the treetops.

"Pardon?" was all Zane could think to say.

"The parchment, you twit!" Doyle sounded pissed off. But Doyle was always in a pissy mood.

Having forgotten he was still holding the paper, Zane replied, "I just found it now. I swear. Do you want me to open it?" His fingertips started to pulsate.

"No, I want you to use it as toilet paper to wipe your ass. Yes, open it!"

Zane nervously fidgeted with the wax seal, unable to peel it off.

"It was supposed to be delivered to you on your tenth birthday, but that never happened," muttered Doyle. "And it looks like you opening it is never going to happen. How did you even manage to find your way out of your mother's womb? And you actually made it here, to Enchanted Wood. Maybe dying's supposed to…oh never mind!"

Zane scratched at it the seal some more, sensing Doyle's comments were leading somewhere, but he wasn't sure what to make of all this.

"How old are you?" Doyle demanded.

"Eighteen."

"You remind me of Coleman. The old golem can be a blubbering fool," Doyle added in a crunchy tone. "I can't do everything all the time all at once by myself, but I do get dangerously close." He wagged an accusatory finger at Zane.

"You got a letter opener?" Zane asked, as if asking permission to handle a weapon at a crime scene.

"You're more moronic than clay brain. He's responsible for this."

Responsible for what? Zane wondered. Zane did not dare ask him what he was referring to.

The golem quickly added, "But you see, boss, time got away from me. Busy. Always busy. Interdimensional travel is a challenging occupation. I did find Earth, but I didn't find Zane. I tried, truly I did, but, well, I got called away on other matters. Matters you requested on my journey to Earth eight years back. It was going to be a birthday present?"

What was going to be a birthday present? This envelope?

Zane finally pulled back the fossil-hardened wax seal.

"Happy birthday," Coleman said and bowed. He looked as if he tried to muscle out a smile, but his clay head remained squared off and rigid. "You opened it. That'll be my gift to you. I'm here to service the Electrical Ones. Oh, wait! Isn't it customary, on your dismal planet, to have a birthday cake with candles? Tell you what: I don't have a cake, not here, but how's this?" He pulled a box of matches from inside the coach, struck a match, and lit all ten of his fingers.

"Make a wish," the golem advised, holding his hands up in front of Zane's face.

Zane offered a brief smile. Something about the golem settled Zane's nerves, but when he felt Doyle's gaze, his anxiety ballooned all over again.

Doyle swatted at the golem's hands, extinguishing the flaming fingers.

"The scroll, you twit! The scroll!" Doyle scowled. "Read it!"

Gee, what a grump, thought Zane, staring at the scroll in his hand; the scent of burnt clay in the air.

Doyle paced back and forth, darkening Zane's pseudo-birthday celebrant's offering by the golem. The air around Zane, once again, had a suffocating feel to it.

"Read it," demanded Doyle.

"And thank your lucky mothballs you're not dead," added the golem, attempting to offer a lopsided grin but failing.

"Oh, do shut up, clay brain," Doyle spat. "It's 'thank your luck stars'."

The creamy yellow parchment began to warm Zane's hand as he unrolled the scroll. It read:

Dear Moss Family,

Some of you may not remember me, but you've just forgotten. I'm dead. Feels great being dead. Don't worry. You'll get your chance to die in due time. I'm the leader of the Decidedly Dead Guys. Freshly recycled. I'm known by all as Doyle Alfred Grimes. I am famous, in numerous dimensions of space and time.

Oh, what's that I hear? Applause? You're applauding me. I understand. Thank you! I am all that and more. Used to tour your planet. Long ago. But I died close to two centuries ago. Just a blip in time, really. Consider my personalized letter a gift. And you're welcome!

Zane, we'll be meeting soon, in Enchanted Wood, for I
know you're here in Enchanted Wood, and my mark always
hits its intended target. My scrolls come with free home
delivery, placed directly in your hands. What could be
better?

But I can't take all the credit. Compliments are in order.
You can thank my trusty delivery man, although he's no
man at all. He's a golem. Goes by the name Coleman Pick.
An honorable and hard-working stiff. Most reliable
specialist you'll ever see, better than any online shopping
outfit on your planet.

We've much to discuss. You and I. Namely, your past
lives and, more importantly, your future successes. With
me. I will show you how to die. It'll be such fun.
And you're welcome!

Forever Deadly,
Doyle Al Grimes

With his mouth hanging open, Zane looked at Doyle and
thought, *Free home delivery? I'm not home.* "I don't want to die at
home," he muttered.

"That's only because you've forgotten how joyous it is to die.
And it says free home delivery. But, you see, you're here in the
Wood, and the Wood is, in fact, your home."

Doyle was sounding like an untrustworthy politician dancing
around the issue concerning Zane: his desire to stay alive.

"Trusty old Coleman here screwed things up, but that doesn't
matter," continued Doyle. "We're here now. That's what matters.
And you're going to do as I say. You'll be simply amazed once
you're dead. Getting screwed into the soil, six feet under, is the
only way to be."

Dead? Me? Screw that! Zane thought. He shifted his weight from left foot to right.

"Just know that I'm a gifted sorcerer," Doyle added, "a mind magician of the highest caliber. I'm getting the chills just hearing my own praise. How about you? Don't you feel the desire to bow to me?" He waited, showcasing shiny white teeth amid a '*hey, look at me'* grin.

Coleman climbed up to his seat atop the coach, "I don't get chilly sensations. No blood pumping in my clay, boss."

Although somewhat intrigued by this golem, Zane had bigger concerns: being murdered by one of these two crazy bedeviled troublemakers.

"Don't listen to the golem. Coleman has a tough time stomaching any thoughts of the ethereal, which I find intriguing, for he's crafted from one of my magical recipes. Birthed from my mind and these hands." He held them up as if they were dripping with wet gold.

Zane looked at the golem, swallowed his fear of being murdered, and returned his attention to Doyle. "But you're supernatural, Mr. Coleman, right? And you work for your maker?"

Doyle nodded. "His golem brain only stretches so far." He made a C-shape with his thumb and forefinger. "But he is loyal. Give him that much. Come now, back in the coach."

The skeleton then sat upright on the bench as Zane sat next to it. It appeared to be looking around, but it was difficult to tell. No skull.

Doyle crossed his legs and glanced at Zane, unfolded his legs, reached under the bench, and pulled out a creamy mahogany box. He flipped up the gold latch on the lid with etch marks from a wood-burning pen, upon which was written: 'Toy Heads.'

He rifled through the box of various skulls and femurs and wire-fastened fingers attached to trapezoid, hamate, and capitate bones. He retrieved a dented skull with scratches across both cheekbones.

"Hey, bag of bones, this ought to help, yes?"

The skeleton clicked the damaged skull onto its metal-plate-repaired spinal column, gave it a quick shift to set it with the ease of linking two Lego pieces together, tilted his chin this way and that, and yawned, as if waking from a nap.

The newly skulled Fuzzy Wells stared at the parchment in Zane's hand.

"Looks like you created this letter today," the skeleton said critically, bony digit rubbing the smooth parchment in Zane's lap. "Bought yourself some old paper, probably online, rolled it up, and added your own text. Nice try. Not impressed. And…the note says the guy's dead. How can he be writing this if he's dead?" Surprised by this skeleton's ability to carry on a conversation, Zane was even more amazed at its ability to read, and judging by its tone, it had a bit of attitude.

Doyle shook his head. "No one asked you to speak, Fuzzy! So shut the hell up or I'll have you cleaning out dumpsters in Graveyard Gardens with a toothpick and tweezers. You should be thanking me for putting a head on your shoulders. I must say, I've chosen a rather handsome skull to cap your frame." He glared at Fuzzy. "And you're welcome, you sniveling sack of bones."

Something about the letter tugged at Zane. He gave the signature a careful study. The artistic lettering and parchment left him wondering and feeling a bit wooden. Maybe it was the strange insignia at the bottom of the scroll; maybe it was Fuzzy and Coleman's human qualities; perhaps it was the fine penmanship of the parchment written with big sweeping letters. And then there was the single-initialed signature. A big letter D artfully complemented with an arcing swish of a dragon's tail: The signed D had been penned in blood-red ink. That D was a calligraphic work-of-art like none other. Zane was entranced.

The parchment fell from his grasp and rolled up into a scroll in his lap. He held it, without squeezing it, as if his life depended on it. The coach rumbled into motion. Doyle stared at him. Zane cringed, feeling empty inside. It felt as if Doyle was scavenging through his mind, rummaging around, the way a thief might comb through a bedroom chest of drawers for jewelry.

The coach steered along a rutted-out path, passing a heavily populated section of gravestones and crypts—acre upon acre of stone markers, more than Zane had ever seen. The coach made its way up over a hill and onto a dirt street lined with small stone cottages, rooftops hatted in metallic sheets. Mailboxes and small overgrown grassy yards with raised wooden flowerbeds and a variety of yard ornaments: stone gargoyles, marble lizards, dragons and snakes made from amber and tourmaline and other colorful crystals. The place was all aglow.

The coach stopped in front of a two-story stone dwelling with a tall water fountain of pure onyx: twin demon sculptures danced in a massive open clamshell pool; one spitting water out its mouth, the other peeing over the fountain, watering a mound of black-eyed Susans.

CHAPTER NINETEEN
Alfred

Little Al Grimes had a knack for looking at things from the other side of reason. It helped that he was raised by demon gypsies. Magic twittered in the family blood of gypsy folk, and he felt at home here.

Al grew into a corn stalk of a teen. Skinny. Red hair. Green eyes. Dimpled chin. A constellation of freckles from cheek to cheek.

Alfred felt…different from the other Dark Art enthusiasts.

Gypsy Central was where all the townsfolk had a flair for eccentric and all-out oddness, and Alfred fit right in; even faeries in this town were more peculiar than other faerie clans. Some fae would steal from the poor and enrich their own Hive.

Take Magdalena, a young starlet speller who lived with her father down the street from the Grimes family. Her mother was killed while attempting to climb a redwood when Magdalena was six years old.

Alfred and Magdalena liked to play street games together.

Magdalena would weave a spool of invisible Spelling Thread and Alfred and Magdalena, late at night strung a wire from a street sign post and attached it to a post on the opposite side of the street. Early in the morning, a street vendor at her flower stall was positioning her poison oak and spiky pricker bushes on a metal table. She marched around the table, tripped over the wire, and fell flat on her face, her chin landing squarely in a potted pricker bush.

Alfred and Magdalena, watched from inside a bagel shop. They high-fived and continued to eat breakfast.

Murder and madness were at the nucleus of most of their gaming and yet, they managed to remain anonymous when catastrophe struck.

Magdalena had moon-white hair, long and thick. A crystalline dagger nose stud. Dark eyebrows.

One afternoon, a pack of teens strutted down Mason Avenue. It was a gypsy girl gang dressed in ripped denim jeans, black leather boots, and spiked Goth choker collars. Their leader sported a pink Mohawk. The rest of the gang had clean-shaven heads decorated in tattoos This girl gang fed on the unusual and a love for spreading fear.

Magdalena whispered to Alfred, "Don't talk to them. They're bad news. Wanted criminals."

"Aren't we all? We're not exactly kids selling caramel-coated apples at the local carnival."

"See the one with the spiked hair. I killed her cat. An accidental spell. Anyway, we should go."

Mohawk Girl shouted, "Hey Mags, you owe me a cat, you bitch! Plus, burial expenses. Now!"

Alfred focused on her vibrant spiked hairdo and cued into her thought-stream. He had learned, some time ago, that by focusing on some physical attribute of a person—be it a honker of a nose, a bloody eye, tattoos, a scar—he could then cue into their internal mascara, the layered colors of their mind, and thieve their thoughts.

That's what he did to Mohawk Girl, leaving her speechless.

Mohawk Girl stared off and muttered something to her gang. Magdalena could not hear what was said, but Alfred was hearing her thoughts being played in his mind.

I need to get back to my Mustang. My horse, Mohawk Girl said in Alfred's mind. *Something's happened.*

Go. Get your horse. It'll die tonight if you don't go home. Now!

Alfred replied in her mind.

The girl gang, after a brief huddle, took off.

One day very soon Alfred would become the first-ever mind murdering magician.

Al Grimes had a plethora of stolen memories and thoughts, and he didn't know how to manage them.

He stared at his reflection in the mirror. "I need help," he said in sincerity, which was a difficult expressive tone to take for alpha demons. "Someone to manage my magic."

At first, he could juggle all these new thieved thoughts but they began to weigh him down, physically and emotionally. Alfred had become a memory addict. Yes, he wanted—needed—more!

When his mind was full and thoughts began to slop over the rim, he began to store them telekinetically in three of his grandmother's hampers that he had swiped from her cottage. His baby days of pooping them out no longer worked.

He hid the hampers, now packed with stolen thoughts, in his closet. His mom was a collector, too, and she had stored numerous hampers, many of them had remnants from his petrified dragon-scaled diaper poop. The hampers, crafted by Grandmama Leocadia, were safety deposit boxes. This was one of the few time Alfred Grimes smiled: stealing from family.

"Yes!" he proclaimed with devilish delight. "Now, I can burgle more thoughts, until I own everyone's memories."

"Who're you talking to?" his mother called out after knocking at the door telepathically.

"No one, Mom."

She pushed open the door with her mind.

"Oh, what're you doing with those? Are those *my* hampers?"

"Nope. Grandma Leo gave them to me. I'm busy, studying and packing."

"Packing for what?"

"It's for a project," he replied without looking at her. "I've got this. Please leave."

"Oh, for the theatre?"

"Yep," he lied. "I'll be taking supplies to the theatre later. I help with deliveries, stage prop material, that sort of thing." Another lie.

That night, he decided to hide the hampers under the floorboards of his closet. He didn't trust his mom. Using a crowbar and a shovel he tore out the flooring and dug a deep hole and placed bricks along the dirt walls to keep it dry and free from rodents and whatnot.

By the age of eighteen, Alfred's treasury of thieved thoughts had grown to fill half a dozen of Grandmama's homespun hampers. Alfred loved to steal from family. Hell, he would steal from himself if he could!

"I want it all," he whispered to Mags one evening. "I want to tap into that aerial storehouse of Redwood Energy."

"Easy Al," she replied. "Canopy's off-limits to Dark Art enthusiasts. Especially demons."

He waved her off. "It anyone's going to break the code and enter the canopy freely it's going to be me!" he howled.

Alfred's desire for more, however, began to wear on him.

"Magdalena," he boasted, "I love madness! I love pissing people off by reading their secret thoughts and desires"

He raised a fist at Magdalena, but she dodged his flying knuckles and kicked him in the kneecap, sending him to the ground screaming.

"The hell?" Alfred rolled over and moaned, clutching his knee.

"Don't mess with me, Al." She spat at him and stormed away.

"Screw you, too!" he muttered, eyes closed, his knee screaming in pain. "I'll just amuse myself. Got a thousand minds in my brain anyway!" he hollered. "I don't need you."

His mental health continued to deteriorate. Anger and moodiness grew on him like hair on a Sasquatch's ass. His flair for magical energies continued to grow stronger, manifesting, breeding within his very being.

Al, to his surprise—for he was the ultimate narcissist—took an interest in what other people thought about his on-stage performances. If they didn't like him in Village Vine, well, he would make their lives miserable. He stole from everyone: homeless ghosts, thieves, children, the elderly.

Mentally ill minds began to percolate within the cargo space of Alfred's consciousness as he now suffered from a borderline personality disorder. He experienced intense mood swings, depression, happy highs, sadness, anger, physical aggression, bouts of laughter. One minute he was wolf-rabid crazy, the next, kind and sensitive.

"More memories!" he muttered. "Must have more memories. I deserve to know what others are thinking. I am the king of this forest and everyone loves me and my craft. Everyone!"

Alfred, even while battling with anxiety and depression, continued to perform on the streets.

"You, yes you, the lady with the purple curly demon horns," he called out one day to a demon on the sidewalk. "I've got a surprise for you."

Alfred danced a little jig on the sidewalk, spun circles around her and stopped, his nose inches from her face. He took a step back and pulled a bouquet of yellow roses from behind her horned head.

"For you, my love."

He drew a long pointy fingernail along her temple.

She shuddered and gazed off.

"I know your name. Better yet, I know what you did last night."

She blushed and looked at the ground.

"Tell you what," he looked around at a handful of people and whispered in her ear. "You've been skipping demon school for weeks, but I won't tell anyone."

He gave her a peck on the cheek. "Off you go! Back to school."

She stared at him. Al hopped over to a three-foot-tall troll to try
and steal its thoughts.

His energetic mind, when he was on a manic high, took him to
new heights. But he'd always mentally crashed into depression.
The cycle was endless.

To ease his anxiety, he discovered an ability to telepathically
move the letters of one street sign and place them on another,
which caused quite a stir among locals and tourists. People got lost.

He caused a horse and buggy accident, by sneaking into the
buggy driver's minds. The driver lost focus and crashed his vehicle
into the bay window of a toy store. Children were injured. An
employee was killed. Parents were screaming. Alfred was happy!

CHAPTER TWENTY
Rainn

The plan was simple: go to Ablestone Acres. Belle had told Rainn to take a coach into Ablestone Acres, a village that butted up against Graveyard Gardens, where Doyle owned property, one of his numerous dwellings. Earlier in the day, Belle had received a psychic tip from a close elfin friend that a human was seen in town. That human, Zane Moss, had caused quite a ruckus in the area. To say Rainn was shocked was an understatement.

Rainn sat alone in a canvas-roofed coach led by a pair of sleek-bodied midnight quarter horses muscling its way up a hilly slope. The driver pulled the coach to a stop at the top of the hill. Rainn peered out a canvas flap, revealing to her a view of a town.

"Is this our destination?" Rainn asked, an unsettling feeling turning her stomach, worried about Zane's whereabouts and wondering if any of this news was factual.

The driver nodded and spit tobacco. "Yes, ma'am. Ablestone Acres proper is small, but all those huts and cottages spread out across the valley, and even those up there," he pointed a grubby finger toward the cliff-face of gray stone. "People live there, mostly for security away from wayward thieves in the area. Crime, both by haunts and able-bodied forest dwellers, is rampant in these parts. Not to put any scare into you, ma'am, but this is a dangerous segment of the Wood. I'm a bit surprised you're out here alone."
Yeah, you and me both, she mused.

"But they aren't all bad. This community also has its share of wealth and a variety of interesting folk. Lovely spot, isn't it." If he was trying to cheer her up, he must have failed Counseling 101.

Ablestone Acres, a two-street forest village spanning several miles, was sealed by rising cliffs and tall-treed spruce, oak, maple, and white birch. The driver snapped the whip, and off they rumbled down the hilly zig-zagging trail.

The horses clopped past several bamboo-framed shops hooded in thatch. These dwellings were built a mile from town. Deeper into the Green, they traversed, heading closer to the village, passing a still-water pond with two old gray barns marked off with wobbly wood fencing.

The quarter horses' silken coats gleamed in the patchy sunlight as they trotted onto the main thoroughfare and clopped past Tea Charmers Café, a weather-worn front deck occupied by two thin, ashen-faced men sitting on rocking chairs. A small gathering of patrons could be seen inside the café as a young woman drew back a snowy curtain laced in a rose-red sash to give the ambling coach a good long study. Further down the winding lane, they passed a collection of scattered homes, yards decorated in flower beds of blooming azaleas, colorful lilies, and pink-petaled poppies.

Rainn's temples pulsated. She blinked and cued into her PMS caller.

Rainn here. Who's this?

It's Esmeralda. I've got some important news. You sitting down?

The coach rumbled over a pothole, making Rainn bounce in her seat. Why did people always ask, 'Are you sitting down?' Had anyone ever passed out while getting unfortunate news? 'Oh, you'd better sit down for this one. I've got awful news.'

What's up? Rainn could sense tension in the fae's tone. *Everything okay?*

You want the bad news or the really bad news?

Just tell me.

I've been captured, caged in a bottle. My wings aren't working. Someone must've cast a paralysis spell on my wings. Help! I'm in a café or restaurant in this little town called Ablestone Acres.

Oh, this is good.

It is? Esmeralda sounded befuddled.

Not that you're caged. I'm in Ablestone Acres now.

Oh.

My mom told us to come here, but I'm trying to get news on my brother's disappearance. You think she knows about what happened to you?

Yeah. I spoke to her earlier. She then went on to say: *Did you get the news about your mom?*

Rainn, keeping herself calm, responded. *No. What's happened?*

She's suffered quite a setback.

I just spoke to her a few hours ago. She was in her usual elfin form. But Doyle was messing with her. Did that beast of a ghost do something to her? Where is she now?

Not that *mom. Your mom on Earth.*

Surprised, Rainn stared out the coach as it passed a cottage with a broken window and a two-by-four nailed across the door.

What happened?

She's in the hospital. Had a heart attack.

What?

Your mom and dad are in Paris, France. She'll be released today. They're cutting their business trip short. They need to stay in Paris for ten days before catching a flight back to the States.

Thanks for all the information. At least she's being discharged, so that's good news. I wish I could go see her.

That's not an option right now. Just focus on what's in front of you. Find Zane. I've got to go.

Okay. Keep me posted. I know you fae have your ways of staying on top of the news in various dimensions.

Ta ta.

Rainn glanced up the street, busy with shoppers and others sitting in a small park. Two female elves dressed in matching seashell-patterned skirts, holding hands, walked past her. They had matching long honey-blonde hair and sharp-tipped ears dotted with studded earrings.

If this neighborhood was filled with crime, Rainn wasn't seeing it. She leaned against the coach, listening to elves chat and point. A faerie-winged butterfly danced over a patch of marigolds, an empty stall with a sign in drippy paint that read *Digital Newsstand*. The elves kissed and continued to window-shop, holding hands.

Rainn breathed in some of that positive energy, gathered her senses, and focused on staying grounded.

"Find Zane and Esmeralda," she told herself aloud. "Oh brother, where are you?"

Oh, how she yearned to be back in the canopy. An energy bath would do her a world of good right now.

After dismounting from the carriage, she walked across the street and made her way back to Tea Charmer's Café.

The place was buzzing with activity as Rainn stepped down a hallway to use the bathroom, she heard something humming from behind a set of swinging doors. A sign over the door read: Employees Only. She pushed on the swinging door, peering into a storage room by the looks of it: a row of wooden kegs, stacked stools, an oak table missing one leg leaned upright with the aid of a keg. There was a laundry basket filled with clothing.

The humming got louder. Rainn looked back down the hallway. No one was paying attention to her, so she stepped into the room and followed the humming sound to another open doorway on the back wall, revealing a wooden crate covered in a red cloth. She glanced over her shoulder. No one was approaching. Feeling curious, she pulled back the cloth to find several six-packs of green glass bottles, each capped with a metal bottle cap. One of the bottles was vibrating and hummed. Something about the long-neck glass bottle had her undivided attention. Rainn pulled the bottle from its case and ran a finger along its sloping neckline. A fae was inside the bottle, celled, as it were. She pounded her tiny fist on the bottle and shouted, but Rainn could not hear a word she said. The bottle, however, vibrated in her hand.

"Esmeralda!" Rainn said in a wide-eyed hush. "There you are!"

Esmeralda seemed to be yelling for help, but Rainn heard not a peep. She just saw her lips moving, hands waving in frantic appeal. The fae was dressed in an asparagus-green sundress draped over her slender frame. Rainn twisted open the lid.

Esmeralda hopped up and down excitedly.

"Fly out! Rainn shouted. "It's open. Oh. Wait. You can't!"

"Right. I've been spelled by an undead fae. My wings are paralyzed. There's a hive of those faeries haunting these parts."

Footsteps padded from down the hallway; the swinging doors swooshed open. A woman poked her head in and frowned.

"'Scuse me,' the woman began. "Is there something I can help you with?" She was wearing a flour-dusted apron, her hair hidden in a bandana.

Rainn set the glass bottle down. "Oh, sorry. I heard some noises back here. I was looking for the bathroom."

"It's out there. Across the hall." She gave Rainn a disapproving look. "This room is for employees only."

"Right," Rainn said and grinned, using her elfin dexterity to hide the bottle at her hip.

Bad move.

The staff member tapped her foot insistently. "Get out from back there. What're you doing?" She pointed at Rainn with suspicious eyes.

More footsteps.

The woman turned her attention to someone coming in from down the hallway, and Rainn, without another word, side-stepped past the staff member and disappeared into the bathroom.

She shut and locked the bathroom door.

"That was close," she said, setting the bottle on the counter.

"Get me out of here!" Esmeralda demanded. "Remember, I told you: my wings've been spelled. Some sort of paralysis."

Rainn tipped the bottle upside down, unscrewed the lid, and Esmeralda squeezed through the narrow bottleneck and tumbled into Rainn's hand.

Esmeralda's hair looked different. The fae brushed a hand through her butter-yellow hip-length hair streaked in lime-green.

Rainn was going to mention the change in hair but was interrupted by Esmeralda.

"We need to get to the canopy," Esmeralda spat. "There's a lotus-leopard lily hybrid that grows in the canopy. If I can munch on some of that plant's root, it'll reverse this wingless spell."

They returned to the coach, and Rainn told her: "I need to find Zane. According to my mom, he may be in the redwood canopy. I'm talking about my elfin mom."

"I want nothing to do with that guy, Zane," Esmeralda huffed. "Although, since you just saved my ass, maybe I can show him what mischief is all about. Your brother's a troublemaker."

"What? What're you talking about?"

Rainn climbed back into the coach with Esmeralda on her shoulder, and the coach rumbled down a trail.

"How long have you been spelled?" Rainn asked, all the while wondering why Esmeralda said Zane was 'trouble.' She decided that a more careful tactic might be necessary since Esmeralda was a bit out of sorts, physically and mentally, and her spiritual currents had dimmed.

"About two days." Esmeralda sounded dejected. "Seems like a month. My brain's fried. Feel odd. I'm worried there's more to this spell than temporary wing loss. But those bottles are valuable. That green glass holds value beyond measure, girlfriend, but I need to get out of this hellish cell."

"Oh?" Rainn looked at the bottle again. Empty, although when she picked it up and tilted it, a glimmer of goldish blue haze filled half the bottle. Then the hazy cloud disappeared.

"They come from the Akashic Records Warehouse," Esmeralda said.

"Oh?" Rainn continued staring at the bottle. "Some sort of mystical stuffings, then, huh?"

"The place where past lives and remnants of soul energy is housed. That's what I'm talking about. It's the closest venue to Heaven that I know of. But it's not Heaven. And, yes, the bottles are all magicked-up. Jacked-up, if you ask me."

"Heaven?" Rainn said in astonishment. As she heard Esmeralda mention the words Akashic Records, chills rushed up and down her arms.

"That's right, and we need to keep your brother away from it." Rainn gave her a quizzical glance. "Keep him away from it? Why? What's he done?" Her brother was never one to be a troublemaker, so all of this was news to her.

"Heaven. Yes. Heaven. The space of divine wealth."

"What did my brother do to you?" Rainn asked, ignoring the fae's last remark

"Heaven is a vast space where soul energy resides at its highest level. There are, of course, suburbs of Heaven where evil little energy misers hang out. The suburbs of Heaven's Gate tend to attract a wily lot. One of those suburbs is Purgatory Heights. Akashic Records Warehouse Number Nine is located there." Esmeralda pointed to the bottle. "That bottle came from Warehouse number nine."

Rainn picked it up. On the bottom, etched in the glass, it read: Property of Akashic Records WH #9

Rainn tried to keep her tone positive. "You fae are the most resourceful bunch of flyers out there. But what's Heaven got to do with me, or Zane for that matter?"

"We can travel to the Warehouse, but Purgatory's a dangerous place."

Rainn nodded, but was confused as to why the fae was ignoring her questions about Zane. She went at it from a different angle: "How're your wings?"

"Might be permanent damage. There's something else. Might be worse."

"Speaking of what might be worse: Can you tell me what's going on with Zane?"

"My wings and possibly your brother have been spelled. Your brother was in the area when I got smacked in the cranium by a Dark Arts demon. It was just such a…" Esmeralda cast a glance at her folded-in dormant wings. Judging by her facial expression, she then uprooted finishing her sentence as quickly. "But, you're right. We must stay positive. Oh, for Hades' sake. I need my wing energy."

"What about Zane?"

The coach hit a bump in the trail, knocking Rainn's shoulder into the wall.

"Oh, right. Word on Fae Street is: he's been seen hanging out with the Decidedly Dead Dudes."

Rainn had no idea was that meant and told her as much.

"They're an underground gang led by Doyle Al Grimes. He's dead and has been causing problems in the Wood for as long as I care to remember. I think he wants to steal something from Zane. Not sure what."

Esmeralda sat down, arms wrapped around her knees, a look of frustration marring her usual cheery, faerie disposition. "Wanna hear what's worse? Explain this: how could I get captured and bottled by a demon speller? Oh, the fae back home at Flutterville will be poking fun at me. That much, I know. But, if we can get out of this mess, well, no one needs to know about my capture."

Rainn wondered if the fae was ADHD like her brother, constantly getting off-topic.

"So, tell me…. about these Decidedly Dead Dudes," she asked.

"They're a Dark Arts evil empire. A gang of ghosts and undead types. They're led by Doyle and have been, well, doing gang things: haunting people, stealing energy, kidnapping, ghostnapping, murdering, and various other ruthless activities. They've been on the Wanted List of undead felons, but no one seems to be able to capture them."

How could someone capture a ghost? Rainn wondered.

"But why would my brother be with them. Was he hypnotized or spelled?"

"Doyle can get into your head, literally, and start tinkering around."

"But there must be a way to help Zane." The thought of him being in a gang was giving her the heebee jeebies.

"If I can get my wings repaired and keep the gossipy fae from spreading rumors about me being bottled, I can try and help you out. But I do want to get back to Flutterville, my home village in the canopy."

Rainn thought being teased by fellow fae was the least of Esmeralda's concerns.

"I'm not going to tell anyone." Rainn offered a consoling grin. "I'm just glad I could be of assistance. Do you know who tried to capture you?"

"Your brother!" she spat.

Sunshine flickered in through the coach's window as the driver steered it over a crest in the trail, and downward they continued.

Rainn felt her belly flipflop. "What? That's not possible. Zane's nowhere near this part of the forest. In fact, we're trying to find him. He blinked out on us. He was on an epi ride. He wouldn't harm you. And why didn't you tell me that earlier?"

Esmeralda folded her arms across her chest, a defensive posture. "Good luck with that. He's an evil little demon. I saw him. He's planning something."

Rainn stared off, wondering how this could be possible. Zane would not do such a thing, would he?

"It's got to be some sort of mix-up. Not my brother."

Esmeralda shifted her attention to her shoulders, stuck out the tip of her tongue to concentrate and wiggled her nose. She moved one wing just a fraction, trying to flap it, but it barely moved from its folded-up position. The other wing slowly accordioned open and then closed with lifeless ambition.

"It's like trying to move a dead wing."

"Maybe we could add barbeque sauce and make Buffalo Wings." She shrugged. "Just trying to lighten the mood." Rainn tapped on the roof. "Driver! To the Eastern Rim. To Madge. I want to help this fae."

The driver shouted back, "Yes, ma'am," and snapped the whip. The coach slowly ambled down the dirt trail, taking them deeper into the Wood.

After a thirty-minute ride, the sound of hooves clomping in the distance revealed another coach rumbling into view from the opposite direction. Rainn's lanky driver pulled to a halt, as did the approaching coach. The horse-powered vehicles were in a face-off with fifteen paces of separation.

Once the dust settled, Rainn was staring at white-spoked wheel rims complementing a dark-themed, hardtop hansom, painted black. The coach was decorated with extravagance: gold and yellow trim. Big swooping, swirly lettering along the door: DAGWOOD

"Oh, for the love of darkness. I recognize him," Esmeralda said pointedly. "And the coach. That must be—"

"Doyle," Rainn finished for her. "How did he find us? He was at my mom's place."

"You saw Doyle?" Esmeralda responded in utter astonishment. A few seconds of silence ticked by. A horse whinnied. "Doyle's probably tracking you with dead-energy. That's how he's found us. Ghosts are a tricky lot. Haunting is in their bloodless veins."

The door to the coach opened. A tall man stepped out and ran a hand along his slick lavender jacket. It was Doyle Alfred Grimes. The door opposite Doyle opened, and out stepped Zane. Doyle pointed at the door. Zane returned inside the coach and closed the door.

Rainn, in severe shock, sat there staring out the little round wooden window. She wanted to holler out to Zane but something else tugged at her: Doyle's staring eyes, now glowing red, bore a hole in her head, mocking her.

Pleased to be free of the cement spell, Belle needed to reconnect with her daughter and Zane. She made her way into the woods and found a spot near a youthful hundred-foot redwood, just a baby, but a great spot for good PMS reception. Redwoods were great telepathic towers. She tried to reach Caesar, but even with her updated psychic coding system and the current PMS numbers of Enchanted Wood, he was not responding.

Something flew out of a nearby pine tree. A dwarf dragon.

It flew through a grouping of pines and landed on a branch, swaying under a limb, talons clamped tight.

Belle breathed in the scent of sticky, sweet sap and pointed at the dragon.

"I see you, little mister dragon."

The dragon remained motionless, slowing its tiny, racing heart from its long journey. It fanned out its wings, its red-scaled neck craning at the sun, like dwarf dragons are known to do.

"Hello there," Belle called a second time.

The dragon spread its wings and flew downward, spiraling and twirling upside-down as he got closer to Belle.

"Show-off," she muttered.

"Hello," said the dragon. "You look familiar. Aren't you that famous elf? Isn't your name Bell Bottom or Bells Broken? Something like that."

She gave him a wink. "You're close. It's Belle. Belle Gaia"

"Right, right. I'm glad you corrected me. I meet so many spellers in the Wood, it's tough to keep them all straight. I am looking for someone. He's a human. Zane Moss. Have you seen him?"

Belle stood up and dusted off her tush. "No, but we're looking for the same guy. Zane's my daughter's brother."

The dragon swished its tail thoughtfully and blew a smoke bubble out its nose. It inflated hovering in the air. He gently batted the air behind the smoke bubble; it popped, releasing a plume of purple smoke.

"Wait a second." His scaled brow furrowed in thought. "If Zane's your daughter's brother, doesn't that make them siblings?"

"Rainn's my daughter from a past life, and now she and her current brother," she added with air quotes, "are in Enchanted Wood. And you are?"

"Your worst nightmare."

She gazed at him unblinkingly.

"Kidding. I'm Julius." Julius stretched out one wing and then folded it back in.

"Listen," Belle said. "With your aerial flight and my spellfarming mind, we could make a great team. I need to find Caesar, too."

"Caesar?" Julius frowned. "I don't trust that moody thundercloud of a cabbie."

Julius, under contractual obligation to aid Zane, would follow through with helping Zane, although he didn't like the idea of being owned, like a pet. It left a bad taste in his mouth. But what charmed lizard wouldn't feel indebted to Zane, the young man who freed him of his caged existence at the infamous bazaar: *Dawning Fires*, an energy-crafting shop run by witches and apprentice spell farmers. Belle asked him one more time to work with her. He agreed.

After careful pruning of his scaly belly and wingtips, he shot off the branch, riding the breezes. Julius zoned in on his echolocation sensitivity and, while taking a sleigh ride on a thermal, spiraled upward into the sky, hoping to pinpoint one of two targets: Zane or Caesar. One would lead to the other, or so his dragon ingenuity presumed.

"Wait," hollered Belle. "Where you going? We need to stick together. I think they might both be near Ablestone Acres."

"That ghetto? You sure that's where he is? I doubt Caesar would be driving in that neighborhood." He spiraled downward and hovered in front of her.

"Yes, indeed, I'm sure that's where they are."

Julius tilted his head. "And why would he go there?"

"He's a novice epi. May've been an accidental epi ride or maybe Doyle Grimes has gotten a hold of him and taken him there. Doyle rules that neighborhood."

"Well, Ablestone Acres is near Purgatory Heights, and that is a place Doyle is known to frequent."

"That's what I just said." She shook her head. "Dragons!"

"Oh, don't start. You need me. Tell you what: that's far from here, as the dragon flies. Why don't I fly ahead ten or twelve miles, scope things out. My dragon senses are telling me a human may be in this segment of the Wood. I'll look for that mountainous beast Caesar, too. I'll probably smell his sour stench before my echolocation senses tune into that walking trash heap of a cabbie."

Belle sighed. "Fine. But do make it quick. I'll continue to try to reach Caesar."

"Sounds good. Let's meet back here in, say, two hours."

As Julius soared with lizard-tongued precision in search of lunch—he had to eat because a headache was brewing in his mind—he spotted a school of trout in a river, swimming upstream.

"Easy pickings," he said with a grin and dive-bombed the school. Snatched up a young trout from the silvery river water. Due to time constraints, he ate on the fly.

The late afternoon sun warmed his leathery wings. Julius buzzed treetop towers and circled into a more heavily populated area. To Julius. or anyone with good eyesight and a sense of smell, chimney smoke was a dead giveaway in locating populated valleys and ridges where woodsy villagers tended to congregate. Any novice air-sailor could spot a glowing fire pit a mile away.

Several families of trolls were camped around bonfires and pitched tents. Troll children wandered in an open grassy field, flying kites on invisible energy strands, and doing quite well for adolescents. With his echolocation humming, however, he sensed no blip on his radar that might be Zane or Caesar.

Julius soared onward, spotting several other camps, some housing trolls, while others were elfin campsites. Then he spotted a human clan; humans were the noisier and less cavalier of all woodland inhabitants. Humans trampled through the woods, boot crunching up branches and dead leaves while the elves moved like the wind.

Definitely not Treezers, Julius mused.

With wings wrapped around the breezes, Julius cruised into the afternoon, scouring the forest floor as he continued his pursuit. The sky, now clear of cloud cover, revealed a solitary star's glow: the sun. It gave light to the darkening forest floor thick with shadow. Julius had no trouble using echolocation to map his way through the dense forest.

With keen ears, watchful eyes, and an inherent memory of the forest, Julius finally spotted what he was looking for. There, in a clearing just outside an air-hanger, was a parked car. Next to that: Caesar. The hairy-faced man was bent over the hood of his Studebaker. A large fire roared nearby. Fireflies and pink-bellied lightning bugs along with dozens of nocturnal flashing-eyed critters lurked in the woods.

Torches lined a long, narrow, tire-marked path. From overhead, it looked like an airstrip. Julius zoomed in for a closer look, landing on a branch and peering into the hanger. Shiny cars. All cabs. Studebakers parked inside the hanger. A variety of models with the same checkered insignia door panel, reading: Epi Taxi, Serving Seizure Minds

Caesar splashed his hairy mitt into a bucket of soapy water and wrung out a sponge. He wiped down the windshield with lathery sweeps across the tinted glass. Bugs buzzed overhead. He stood bolt upright, dropping the sponge into the bucket. He cocked his head ever so slightly and lifted the brim of his worn baseball cap, his yellow serpentine eyes examining the sky. He spat over his shoulder and drew heartily on his cigar. Embers, a mix of fiery red and blackened ash, glowed under his nose. The evening sky, now salted with quiet starlight, colored the jeweled sky, bright and luminous, like angelic eyes. There was an underwater shimmer to the night air. Pure. Magnificent. Julius felt this vibrant pulse within the essence of his scaly Being.

The dwarf dragon flew low across the grass-carpeted hillside, banked over a mogul, and circled behind a small redwood on the opposite side of the hanger. He landed on a tree trunk, claws digging into the thick bark. Camouflaged.

He sensed only Caesar in the immediate vicinity and decided, after less than a moment's contemplation, to take flight and glide in silence, several inches off the green, his scale-encrusted tail clipping the dewy grasses beneath him. He loved the sensation of flying, be it high in the sky or low to the ground. Yes, flight had its advantages. To him, to be without wings for flight was to be without lungs for breathing.

He soared through an open window in the air hanger and hovered behind one of the cabs. From here, he scouted the hanger's innards with more assurance. Gently humming lanterns hung on ropes. A small glass-walled office in the front corner housed a table, two chairs, and a flat-screen monitor mounted to the wall.

Purple tarps blanketed several vehicles with white-fringed skirts revealing the bottom halves of white-walled tires. Other cabs, naked of a cover, appeared recently washed with that storeroom window-display-case sparkle.

He peered over the corner of the rear bumper and smiled admiringly at his reflection in the metal bumper. *You are a sexy dragon, aren't you, Julius?* The dragon grinned inwardly.

Footsteps crunched through the soil. Julius's ears flattened: a winged panther ready to pounce.

Here came Caesar, his booming strides; brawny frame filling in the sky around him with a smoky I-haven't-showered-in-days scent. Caesar, dressed in hiking boots, dirt-stained denim trousers, and a black-and-yellow-checkered flannel shirt, wore his familiar scowl while chewing on a cigar butt. A patch emblazed over his shirt pocket read: *Caesar's Energy T.*

"Out with you. I know you're in there," barked Caesar, his eyes scanning the lot in one long, methodical sweep. "This is my garage!" he boomed. "Out! Can't hide from me."

Julius, with wings buzzing, helicoptered over the top of the cab, grinned and very slowly spoke: "Hello, there, See Zar," he punctuated with phonetic flair. "Bet you're wondering why I'm here. Fair question."

Caesar, with hands on hips, water dripping down his soapy arms, stared at the dragon, face relaxing.

He drew on his cigar. "Oh, it's just you." He exhaled a plume of smoke. "Dragon. What do you want?" His tone softened. Thick smoke curtained his head. Black curly hair brushed his stiff shirt collar.

"Como estas, amigo?" Julius replied cheerily. "Glad you asked. I was—"

"Trespassing, you Spanish-speaking mongrel. That's what you're doing. Dragon thief."

"Thief? I'm no thief. Nothing of the sort." His metallic voice rose a bit. "I'm here with a purpose. And I think you know what it is." He batted his tail back and forth playfully, hoping to ease the facade Caesar was putting on.

"Don't care why you're here. Got things to do. Important things. Now get out of my shop," he grumbled, arms crossed defensively, cigar hanging out of his mouth.

Julius flew to Caesar's side and decided to get right to the point. "Seen Zane lately? He's on *my* list of things to do. Seems to be out of my radar range. Last time I saw him, he was with you, on one of your joy rides."

"How would you know who I've seen? You know nothing, lizard," he rumbled.

Julius glanced at the cab in the yard, soapy water streaming off the hood and down the front bumper. "Don't see any new dents in the magic fabric of your vehicle, so that's…encouraging," the dwarf dragon finished with a hopeful nod. "Hope I'm speaking slowly enough for your Neanderthal brain to keep pace."

"I don't give joy rides, mosquito breath. He's on my epileptic list. But you already know that. I'm just doing *my* job, which you're taking me away from."

"Well then, where, might I ask, *is* he?" Julius said, ignoring Caesar and whizzed across the hanger, landing up in the rafters, not wishing to be batted into the woods by one of Caesar's swinging arms.

With his talons clamped onto the wooden beam twenty feet overhead, he stretched out his wings and flapped, fanning the lingering cigar smoke that hung in the air. "Must you smoke, tobacco brain? It's stinking up my scales." Julius sneezed. "Nicotine shrinks brain cells. I'm allergic."

Caesar growled; his yellow serpentine eyes glowing as he studied Julius.

"But I'd like to add that you're looking rather…large and in charge," the dragon finished cheerily. He wasn't getting anywhere with this big-bearded man who, in the torchlight, looked like a werewolf in need of going on a low-carb, no-raw-meat diet.

From his perch in the rafters, Julius arched downward, zipped right between Caesar's legs, and landed on his shoulder.

"Hey! Get off." Caesar swatted at Julius with his baseball cap, sending Julius into flight. "Listen, mosquito, I've got things to do. No time for dragon playtime." He slapped his cap back on his head, messy hair curling out from under it.

"Oh, I can see you're *very* busy. How much do you charge for a car wash? I think you missed a spot on your cherished Studebaker." He pointed his tail at the cab with the soapy hood. "You polishing all these cars?" He swung the tip of his tail behind his ear and scratched it thoughtfully, eyeing one of the cabs dressed in a purple tarp.

Caesar glared at him.

"Since you're giving baths to cars, care to wash my wings?" He laughed and mimicked Caesar's cigar smoke by exhaling rings of smoke, au-natural dragon smoke.

"That's it! I've had it with you!" exclaimed Caesar. With a cigar dangling between forefinger and middle digit, he turned and strode off, heavy boots kicking up dust clouds.

In his office, Caesar clicked on the computer, the monitor light brightening his hairy face. He blinked at his flat-screen Goggle workstation, moved his eyes to the left, shifted to a new screen, and blinked several more times. A tiny white dot appeared in the center of the screen. A moment later, his screen revealed a psychedelic backdrop with a topless mint-green Studebaker, white-walled tires. Shiny chrome bumpers. Classy.

Julius watched the screen-display from the office window.

A flashing cursor appeared at the bottom of the screen: *Welcome to Enchanted Wood Thought-Magic Processor. Nice to see you,*

Caesar! Several small icons appeared. Instead of using a mouse, he guided the flashing cursor by making psychic eye-contact with the flashing cursor: a tiny Studebaker. He blinked, clicking on an icon entitled *Caesar's Cabby Mates.*

A new screen opened on his flat-screen monitor: a Supernatural chat room dialog box appeared, a ring of stars encircling a Third Eye on a forehead.

Caesar grumbled and tapped out his stubby cigar butt in a tree stump ashtray. He reached into his breast pocket and retrieved a fresh cigar, then held it under his nose and blinked, sending his thoughts onto the flatscreen email dialogue box.

Service Completed: Zane Moss, pre-epi traveler.
Destination: Ick.

Notations: Zane Moss blinked out of Caesar's cab. Zane left a handwritten message stating he was going to catch a ride with Doyle Al Grimes and travel to Purgatory Heights.

Julius hovered at the window, tail tapping on the glass. "Thanks buddy!" he called. "Looks like you screwed up this fare. Gotta fly. Zane's hanging with the wrong crowd while you're washing cars? The hell's wrong with you! Someone's got to save the human, and it's not gonna be you. Later, you hairy brainless fool!" And off Julius zoomed.

CHAPTER TWENTY-TWO
ZANE

Still feeling loopy after he had epi-blinked from Caesar's cab and then from Belle's home to Doyle's coach, Zane had no recollection of why his most recent epi-ride landed him in Doyle's presence. But something inside told him that joining Doyle Grimes would bring him what he, Zane, wanted: safety, success, happiness. All he had to do was follow through with one simple task, which, according to Doyle, was an easy feat. "It's a simple task," Doyle proclaimed in a soft, slippery tone.

What's he on about? Zane wondered and decided to play along, to hear him out. "Just one task?" Zane asked Doyle.

Doyle poked his head back into the coach. "Millions of people do it every day on your planet," Doyle told him. "And I've done it countless times. So've you. You've just forgotten, is all. Your past lives are littered in this activity."

"What activity?"

"Dying."

"Oh. Okay," Zane said in a confused monotone.

"You can come out now."

Zane stood outside the coach and placed his palms onto his lower back, leaned back to stretch, and yawned. Up the snaking trail, weaving in and out of white birch and pine, sat another coach.

"Is that Rainn?" he asked in a quiet tone and stepped closer to get a better look.

"Indeed. And she's trouble. You know she's only trying to steal your energy, you twit," Doyle muttered. "She's known about your potential since you were a wee boy, but she kept it hidden. She's an energy miser. A thief. But rest easy, you're with me now. You mustn't fear her. Just steer clear of her thoughts. She's going to try to get into your head. She's pure evil, Zane! Even though you're twins, she's nothing like you. She stands in your way. The only thing holding you back, in fact, is the dreadful Rainn Moss." Doyle forced out a shiver of his shoulders, "Oh, my, just saying her name makes me queasy, but fame and fortune await you! Just stick with me. The Dark Arts will bring you your just reward."

Zane, feeling dizzy, stumbled back a pace, and Doyle moved twenty yards in a second and helped Zane regain his balance; Doyle wiggled his ghost-fingers, sending some of his Dark energy into Zane.

Zane straightened up and clenched his fists at his side.

"Yes, I want that power!" Zane exclaimed.

"That's the spirit. Stay evil, and you'll stay on top of the universe," Doyle affirmed. "You've made a wonderful choice. Life here with the Undead will bring you fame. We are endless. We are eternal. We will rule Enchanted Wood. Your epi energy and my knowledge and all-out charisma will bring me such power. All forest dwellers will be following me as their leader.

Rainn stepped out of the coach and slowly approached, moving past a line of pines bordering the winding, hilly trail.

"Zane. Come over here," Rainn said. "It's important. I need to talk to you, brother. It's about Mom."

Zane turned his head and nearly lost his balance. "Whoa! Dizzy," he whispered and put a hand on Doyle but his hand passed right through him. Zane stumbled to one knee.

Suddenly, Rainn appeared and jogged toward them.

"Look what you've done, you witch!" Doyle barked at Rainn.

"Stop right there," ordered Doyle. "You've no right to be here.

This is my landscape. We are in Purgatory Heights' landscape now. This is my turf. Be gone, you wicked little wench!"

Sitting on Rainn's shoulder, Esmeralda shouted, "Do shut up, you foul-mouthed, lifeless ghost. Your words are hollower than your ghostliness. We're here for Zane. Zane, listen to me: I was at a wedding not too long ago. A fae wedding, and your mother came up in the conversation. I hear she's been traveling a lot with your dad on Earth. This wedding took place in Nyx Landing. It was a gala reception with dancing to drumming and fluting and luting music. Your parents are quite familiar with fae Beings. Bet you didn't know that. I also bet you didn't know that your mom is ill. Suffered heart complications, but she's alive. Unlike Doyle who only wants you as his boy toy"

"Wha…what happened to my mom?"

"She's okay. Being released from the hospital on Earth. Paris, France."

"What?" Zane said, his voice quivering, and looked to Rainn for affirmation.

Zane took a wobbly step forward, gazing at Rainn and Esmeralda. A look of confusion came over his face

"Zane," Rainn added. "Mom's okay. Got word she had a heart attack. Esmeralda's right. They're still in Paris on business."

"Oh, man. I wish we could see her."

Doyle stood in front of Zane and turned his back to Rainn and the fae. "Oh, do shut up!" boomed Doyle. "They're lying to you, Zane!"

"Let's just send mom Light," said Rainn. "Don't listen to that ghost. You've got a lot of power within you, brother. Send some of that positive lightning bolt energy her way."

"Rainn," Esmeralda said in a hush. "I can move my wings again. The muscles in my wingtips are working again."

She flew in front of Zane. "Zane, I feel your magnetism flowing through me. Thank you! You've healed my wing spell. I want to…" Instead of complicating the thought, she drifted off, head lolling to the side, shoulders tensing.

"Oh, shit, is she about to seize?" Zane called out and put a hand out as Esmeralda tumbled toward the ground.

Esmeralda crashed to the forest floor, shoulder rolled, got her wings humming in a furious blur of momentum and flew upward. She sailed in a wobbly zig-zag fashion then, gaining momentum, darted over a clump of yellow-petaled flowers and zoomed, arrow-straight, in the direction of Zane. She crash-landed into Zane's chest, ping-ponged off him, plunged into the flowerbed.

"Oh, shit!" Zane muttered, feeling his consciousness restoring as Doyle's spell began to lose traction.

Esmeralda zipped out of the flowers and landed on Zane's shoulder.

"Well, now," Esmeralda piped in and grinned. "What a rush! Is it Rush Week? I feel like a collegiate sophomore at EWU pledging to join a sorority house."

"Get away from him," barked Doyle. "He's mine. Both of you get back in your coach before I dig a grave and bury you alive." Zane swooped up Esmeralda into his hand and stumbled to Doyle's coach.

"What're you doing?" Esmeralda huffed as Zane held her captive, reached into a box under the seat in the coach, and stuffed her into a green-glass bottle. She slid down the bottleneck and landed with a thump. She looked out to see a matching bottle next to her, housing another fae, who was either sleeping or unconscious. She was, once again, trapped, the Akashic Records label etched in the glass bottom. She half-expected some sort of sleep-spell to haze her thinking and stun her into silence, but, instead, to her amazement, her mind remained clear, her thoughts sharp.

Zane shoved the six-pack under the seat, and slammed the coach door.

Esmerelda stood up and tapped on the glass with her knuckle, hoping to gain the attention of the fae in the adjacent bottle. The fae remained curled up on the bottom.

She tapped the glass again.

No reply.

She shouted, but her voice echoed off the glass, and she wondered if it was soundproof.

Now what?

Outside the coach, Zane half-walked, half-stumbled toward Doyle. Then he stopped and glanced back at Rainn. A look of confusion blended with sorrow marred his sister's face.

"You've kept secrets from me most of my life. Now, I realize my true potential," Zane barked. "I am meant to be here. A leader," Zane claimed. "And you're not going to take that away from me."

His vision began to blur. All he could see was a hazy shadow where Rainn stood. Zane buckled at the knees and fell to the ground, now on all fours. He sat back on his heels and gazed off with an empty expression. Then he shouted to his sister, "I need you to. Get. Out. Of. My. Life!"

Zane fell to the ground, body convulsing. And then he faded into mist, gone in an epileptic whirl.

At the same misty-eyed moment of epileptic disconnect, Rainn took off in a sprint, disappearing into the woods.

Back in Doyle's coach, Esmeralda, caged in a bottle, was unaware of Zane falling prey to another disappearing epi-ride. She pulled her long silky hair in front of her and started to braid it, an activity she frequently performed when nervous, weaving her hair into an artistic braid, which soothed her racing thoughts.

The fae in the bottle next to hers rolled over and stared at her, drool dripping down her chin. A flicker of excitement filled the fae's face as she fixed on Esmeralda's face. She sat up.

Esmeralda stretched out her wings with deliberate care. Pleased she had mobility, she fluffed out her wings and performed an exercise, sending her into brief three-second bursts of blurry wing action. "Oh, that's good!" she exclaimed.

Esmeralda glanced over her shoulder, smiling at her wings. "I can move them." Her wings became a blur of energy again, and this time, she hovered in the air. She flew at the capped bottletop overhead and her head smacked into it. She fell, rose up and tried several more times. The cap had been sealed by Zane. Why?

She was, nonetheless, pleased to be free of the toxins of the paralysis spell, but she was still caged in the bottle. Trapped.

She waved to the fae and pointed at the glass bottle's etchings. She mouthed the words 'Akashic Records' repeatedly and shrugged. DO YOU UNDERSTAND? she mouthed.

The fae's eyes widened as she watched Esmeralda floating inside the bottle. Esmeralda got down on a bended knee, pointed to the engraved label on the bottom of the bottle, and ran her fingers along the letter 'A' scored into the glass.

"Akashic Records," she repeated, re-underlining the scored lettering, her wingtips shivering excitedly at the mention of such a place.

The fae in the other bottle just stared off. Transfixed or something. But what?

Esmeralda knew, all too well, that the Akashic Records Warehouse contained a living library of past lives in biographical written form. This living Storehouse cataloged thoughts of individual soul-memories, too—all done through some sort of God-inspired transfer system; the soul energy of each tome, scroll, or leather-bound edition breathed with memories of soulful journeys. The library was, obviously, indexed, including videography footage of past lives. Esmeralda had yet to see any of this video footage, nor had she visited the Akashic Records Warehouse. Just the stories alone filled her fae colony with excitement and hope.

Right now, she needed help escaping the confines of this rare green-glass bottle made of a specialized hybrid of Aventurine, jade, and malachite. She did know this: the same material used to cage the fae was a by-product of the material used to store past-life records at Akashic Records Warehouse.

Someone climbed into the coach and sat down. She could see a pair of boots and pant legs. A whip snapped. The horses clopped down the path. The coach hit a rut that sent the bottles jiggling.

Esmeralda had been told that the Akashic Records Warehouse had to be policed because the rare glass used to make these storage vessels and encase these past lives was highly valuable, and thieves and Dark Artists began to steal these treasures and sell them on the Black Market.

This six-pack, if she were to wager a wing on it, was stolen property. The Warehouse, as far Esmeralda knew, was a private area. No visitors, whether they were tourists, ghosts, dead or undead, were allowed access. Admittance was set aside for Archangels and high-ranking soul workers.

So, how did Doyle and Zane get their slimy hands on these bottles? She wasn't sure who was seated in the coach, but she sensed it must be Doyle Alfred Grimes. Her fae intuition and all her fae friends in their Hive were aware that Doyle had had spies infiltrating the area around Akashic Records for eons. But there was no news of any of Doyle's Decidedly Dead Dudes getting inside the Warehouse. Her hatred for Doyle was a common feeling among locals. And this Zane character—what about him? A human with epi potential, now affiliated with Doyle. Not good.

She presumed Zane to be of the same evil caliber; she had witnessed Zane's actions first-hand.

She could not hear anything due to the sound-proof glass.

The thought of Doyle and Zane teaming up put the hairs on her antennae on high alert. The old ghost Doyle fit the stereotype of a thief, in creaking Hi-Fi resolution. It had never crossed her mind that Zane would do this. Not until she saw him in the act. Was Rainn in on it, too?

She stirred from her reverie as the coach rumbled to a slow stop. The coach door swung open. She recognized the back of a tall figure and his dark hair in a ponytail that reached his waist. Doyle.

Doyle opened the back gate, and a golem landed with a thump, jumping off the driver's seat atop the coach.

Ugh! Was Zane with them?

She could see Doyle and the golem rummaging through the back of the coach.

Then, like a slap in the face, a realization hit her. She knew there was something darkly familiar about the golem. Doyle had played a part in molding this clay creature into a living form. It had happened over a hundred years ago. Esmeralda, being a 365-yearold fae, had crossed paths with this golem. That memory, although fleeting, was restored and now etched within her. His name: Coleman Pick.

"Just wait in the coach," Doyle muttered while opening a small wooden crate and pocketing a handful of bright jeweled stones.

Esmeralda never liked Doyle. Not when he was flesh and bone three hundred years ago, living in Enchanted Wood, a famous magician and gifted user of illusory magic. And certainly not now, being dead and leading his underground gang of misfit demons.

But first, how was she going to escape this bottle? She sighed and pulled her knees up to her chin, leaning against the glass wall.

Doyle suddenly loomed into view, clouding her vision as his gloved hand grabbed the bottle and shoved it into the folds of his cloak.

"Hey, what're you doing?" Esmeralda shouted, but her voice was muted by the bottle.

"There's two fae in here," Doyle said.

"Yes. Six bottles and two fae. All accounted for," Coleman replied.

"Did you want me to bring you the other bottled fae?" Coleman called from the top of the coach, reins in hand.

"Don't worry about any of that," Doyle spat. "Just do as you're told."

Doyle placed open palms over the glass bottle housing Esmeralda, making slow, feathery motions with his hands until the bottle glowed, hovering. Esmeralda felt a wave of shivers flow through her. Doyle then set the bottle in the grass, walked away, and returned with a six-pack, which he set in the grass next to the bottled Esmeralda. He placed a handful of shiny red jewels from his pocket next to the six-pack and the bottle housing Esmeralda.

There was a thumping sound, followed by cursing.

Doyle looked up to see Zane reappear out of thin air, tumbling across the grasses.

"Oh, you're back!" he said. "Good timing! Come on, quit screwing around," Doyle sounded bothered. "You're wasting my time. I need you to watch these fae."

Zane sat up in the grass, shaking his head to refocus his attention.

Doyle strode back to the rear of the coach.

Zane stood up, dusted himself off, looked at the golem. "You, clay boy, what's your problem?" Zane spat. "I've been busy traveling about the Wood while you're just sitting there. Get busy!"

The golem stared at Zane, devoid of emotion.

"Just stay there," demanded Zane from the foot of the coach, a stormy look of impatience on his face and stomped off, taking heavy, thunderous strides.

Esmeralda's view was, yet again, shrouded in darkness by Zane's hand grasping her bottle in the grass. She was tossed back and forth, bumping into the glass wall. She looked over at them. The bottle was set in the grass again, next to a pile of jeweled stones. Doyle and Zane, standing near a tall pine, were conversing, but Esmeralda could not hear anything. Zane appeared to be doing most of the talking, pointing off in the distance.

Doyle said something to Zane. Zane turned his back on Doyle and walked in the direction of Esmeralda. He leaned toward her bottle, uncorked it, and, almost whispering, said to her, "Keep your voice down, and I'll explain everything soon. I need your help. And I'll reward you. I need to get away from old Alfred, but I'm going nowhere empty-handed. Just do as you're told, and I won't kill you. Just stay in the bottle, but I'm trusting you and leaving it unsealed. I'll be back."

"This is your last chance!" hollered Doyle in a rage. "You will join me! Oh, screw this!" He raced toward Zane, moving like the howling wind.

Zane stumbled backward, falling flat on his back. His body arms and legs and head started to shake. His convulsive feat continued for five seconds, and then Zane fizzled into mist. Gone.
Again.

Doyle scanned the forest, then marched in the direction of the bottles

Esmeralda saw movement in the branches. It was Zane standing on a tree limb about twenty feet off the ground.

Then, Zane disappeared from the branch and reappeared on the forest floor. Esmeralda did a double-take. Zane was still in the treetops, but she could have sworn she saw him epi-blink to the forest floor.

She spotted two Zanes; one on the ground and one in the tree. There were two Zanes!

The Zane on the ground marched up to Esmeralda. He started to flicker. She could see right through him. Transparent as all get-out. A halo of silvery light highlighted his frame. Zane seemed to be a full-fledged ghost.

Ghost-Zane stood in front of Esmeralda and placed a hand over his heart. His glowing haloed head pulsated like a beating heart. He had a halo leashed around his neck. He uncorked the bottle caging her.

"Hi, there," he began. "I'm Twane. Twane Moss. Zane's ghost twin. Scout's honor," he snickered. "I've been ghosting Purgatory Heights for two hundred years. I'm one of the good guys." He smiled and winked at Esmeralda. "Fae are cool, man. The coolest, hippest flyers out there."

"I'm not a man."

"Nope, but you are one cool chick. Fae chick."

A rash of thoughts itched at Esmeralda. She had heard of ghost twins but had never seen any. She had questions. Loads of questions, but now was not the time for any of that, and she was unsure whether she could trust him. But one thing was certain: he was a ghost! Was Twane also a shapeshifter, like Doyle? They could appear transparent or become solid flesh and blood, at will.

A rustling from the trees caused her eyes to follow the moving tree branches. Zane stood on a thin branch that bowed under his weight. He waved at her. He started to blur as his body vibrated with epileptic elegance; then he faded out of focus. Poof! Gone!

"Where'd he go?" Esmeralda asked Twane. "What's going on?"

"I'll explain later. Just trust me."

Twane appeared calm and peaceful as a sleepy poet.

"I must ask. Were you here when Zane was yelling at Doyle?"

He nodded. "Zane's gotten good at puffing out like an angry peacock, hasn't he? He is no longer afraid to act as if on stage; nor is he afraid of death. And certainly, he's no longer fearful of

Doyle. Or much of anything, for that matter. He can be a beast."

Zane? A beast? She wasn't so sure. About any of this.

Esmeralda, against her better judgment, decided to remain quiet for the time being, and see how things unfolded. Did she have another choice?

Doyle ordered the golem to retrieve a barrel from the coach and set it in the grass.

The golem followed instructions and removed a faded lime-green tarp from a barrel and hoisted it onto his shoulder.

He set it down with a THUMP near the six-pack.

Esmeralda gasped.

The barrel was labeled: *Angel Remains. Do not touch!*

Esmeralda wondered what sort of cockamamie plan she might be mixed up in. What in the world could they be transporting in this barrel? She had never heard of Angel Remains. She peered at Doyle who was busy wiggling his fingers.

Coleman called out, "Doyle, sir, should I bring the barrel?"

Doyle, with eyes closed, said, "Oh, do shut up, clay brain! I can't talk and telepath at the same time. How many times have I told you what an idiot you are?"

"Only every day, sir."

The scent of horse manure was strong; Esmeralda yearned for some perfumed flowers to rub in her hair, but she sensed something else. With one slender leg crossed over the other, she retrieved an ivory-handled brush from a satchel at her hip and drew the seashell brush through her long hair, easing her nerves. The act of combing her curtain of hair was just what she needed.

Doyle walked deeper into the woods zigging and zagging through a line of trees. He then walked right through a fat old oak tree and reappeared on the other side, dressed in flashy new attire. His ability to float through the tree was no surprise. His new attire, however, captured her attention.

He hiked toward Esmeralda dressed in a black-and-white pinstriped suit, his silent footfalls crunching through the grasses; he put his ethereal grip around the bottle housing her, and set it on top of the large oaken barrel labeled *Angel Remains.*

Doyle steepled his fingers in front of his nose and muttered an ancient incantation, speaking in tongues. Doyle had now shapeshifted entirely into a whirl of transparent energy. A cloud of silvery blue light tornadoed around him. The cloud then dissipated to reveal Doyle dressed in his pinstriped suit. His suitcoat fit with bright gold buttons. He wore a gray cape fringed in deep scarlet tied off at the neck. He seemed, according to Esmeralda's deduction, to have cast an illusory spell on himself. Some ghosts were much better at it than others. Esmeralda, tough to impress, noted his marvelous magic flair for cosmetic detail and choice of formal wear, as if dressed to dine with kings and queens of the forest, yet, she did not approve, concerned about his agenda.

Doyle ran a hand through his slicked back ponytail, then picked up the bottle, and stared at Esmeralda as if looking at a science project. The bottle started to glow. Doyle's expression appeared anxious.

"Put that down!" Zane ordered from the front of the coach. "I'll handle those bottles."

"This is my forest, you twit!" Doyle muttered with his back to Zane. "Don't tell me what to do."

Doyle then motioned toward the tree line, both hands holding the bottle. The green-glass bottle started to glow like inflamed algae, feeding off Doyle's overly excited ghost pulse.

"Oh goody," Esmeralda spouted, clapping her hands in ovation. She looked at Twane who appeared next to Zane; she had decided to play along, acting as if she wanted to help Doyle.

"That was amazing," Esmeralda said, beaming at Doyle. "Good show, Doyle, er, Mr. Grimes. Not too shabby for an old ghost. Now set me free! We'll help you get rid of that evil Zane."

He glared at her, shushing her with his finger to lips. His eyes went fiery red and then faded back to black. He began rearranging the bottles in the six-pack, moving them as quickly as a circus conjurer and his game of shells.

He pulled out a shiny gold-handled feather duster and began dusting the bottles, his hands moving in a blur. During his feather dusting, he removed Esmeralda and tucked her into the folds of his cape.

Half a breath later, Twane appeared next to Doyle. He, too, had changed his clothing.

"Everything ready?" Twane called. "It's showtime!"

Twane's head was hatted in a herringbone-feathered bowler's hat. Shiny yellow pantaloons striped in white. Big-buckled leather shoes.

What are these guys dressed up for, a Shakespearean tragedy? Esmeralda wondered.

"Yes," said Coleman with a bow and nodded to Doyle. "Shall I stow them away?"

"Don't touch the bottles," Doyle barked, with a sinister sneer.

Twane said nothing for the moment, carefully studying the glowing bottle. "Something's amiss here." He tapped his cleanshaven chin.

Esmeralda paced in the bottle and sighed. She could feel strained waves of energy pressing on her fae flesh. The glowing glass bottle began to heat up, causing her to perspire. What sort of incantation had Doyle used?

She sent her wings into a frenzy, trying to hover in the bottle but failed.

"Halt right there, missy!" shouted Twane. "You won't be escaping." He gave Esmeralda a wink.

Twane pulled off his bowler hat and flung it, discus-style. It swirled through the air in a big sweeping arch and landed next to the barrel. "Drat, I missed," Twane said, forcing out staged laughter. He glanced at Doyle and sighed dismally, raising his eyebrows.

"What happened to the six-pack? What's with the glowing green bottles?" Twane dared. "Don't tell me you've got plans.
Plans I'm not aware of." He pointed an accusatory finger at Doyle.

Doyle glared back at Twane. "My work is of no concern to you. Remember what I said the last time you tried to steal from me?"

Twane placed a hand over his heart. "Me? I never stole anything from you. Don't know what you're talking about. I'm here to work with you, you old ghost."

Doyle's eyes flickered red then back to black. "I'll take care of this barrel. Coleman. Move the barrel. You handle the fae. I've no use for her or you."

Twane took the bottle with Esmeralda in it.

Coleman hefted the barrel labeled *Angel Remains* out of the grass and set it into the back of the coach. Doyle and Coleman drove off.

THREE LIFETIMES AGO

By the time he was twenty-one, Alfred had manifested a stage presence and a bigger following. Rearranged his name, too, became known around the forest camp as Al G.

While other kids experimented with mundane acts of trickery among friends—filling a pal's pocket with mud, sticking worms down a little girl's dress, burning holes onto a sleeping spellfarmer's eyelid with a magnifying lens—Al was busy stealing, cataloging, and storing thoughts from unsuspecting minds.

His objective: create more magical accidents.

Then, the headaches started. Thunderboomers! They came out of nowhere, and nowhere was now here. Headaches graduated into full-blown *sledge-hammer-to-the-skull* migraines, bringing Alfred to his knees and under the covers of his bed.

"Magdalena," he'd say. "I need to have a lie-down. And it's going to get worse. Always does."

"One step ahead of you." She had just finished fluffing up his favorite pillows in his sleeping den. "Your four-poster canopy bed is ready and waiting with clean linen and there's some anti-insomnia licorice and chamomile tea next to the bed."

His small-horned head tilted to the left, adding strain to his neck. "My head must weigh a hundred pounds," he groaned.

"It's all those memories you're stealing. Maybe you should sleep in your coffin. That'll make you feel better. The mental weight must be getting to you, love."

"Bah!" He waved a dismissive hand at her. "I must bring about pain and destruction," he proclaimed through gritted teeth. But he had to stop talking. Even hearing his own voice intensified the agony in his throbbing head.

"There're some flowers that grow in the canopy," said Mags. "Might help. Little leaf grapes and epiphytes with a mixture of a few exotic roots. I stole a recipe from a spellfarmer," she added with a wicked smile. "But we can't get to those ingredients. Canopy's off limits."

Was she enjoying watching him go to war with a searing migraine? He went into his bedroom and got under the covers.

Epiphytes are plants that grow on other plants in the redwood canopy. All the other spellfarming ingredients were leaves and stems from a variety of canopy foliage.

She stood in the doorway. "If only I could get to the canopy. But it's not our place. Any demon who's tried has fallen out a redwood. Most were killed on impact. I can't have any of that."

Alfred closed his eyes, rolled over in bed, yearning for her to leave him alone.

"If only I could blend some yellow-petaled epiphytes with little leaf grapes and a bit of redwood root, oh, it'd be sure to cure your aching cranium."

Alfred wanted to bash her with words and claim she didn't know what she was talking about. He didn't trust spellfarmers.

Alfred had heard different stories: any leafy recipes from the canopy were poison to his demonic bloodline.

Several months later, after doing research, he wanted to set fire to the redwood canopy. He had gotten some tips from Grandmama Leocadio: Come harvest time, Eastern Rim spellfarmers and faeries would shuck, pit, chop, mash, and blend organic concoctions, and craft magical recipes with healing qualities. They congregated and shared their love for the forest and believed in healing themselves and others. They would jar organic recipes from Ick and Madge's canopy, blend milkshakes and grind out powders for healing recipes.

The whole story as told by Grandmama made Alfred sick and vengeful, oozing with hatred.

Years flowed by. Al kept performing in Village Vine. Fame found him.

Then, Alfred's relationship with Magdalena came to an abrupt halt. Did he end it or did she leave him? He didn't know. Nor did he care. One day, she was gone. Without a word.

Al slipped an ivy leaf tie around his neck, slid his thin arms into a red vest, and sparkly green coattail jacket. Yellow suspenders held up black wool knickers speckled in gold and green and red, matching colorfully striped socks.

He shuffled a deck of cards on stage. "I need someone to help," he shouted to the audience.

A sea of hands. Pleading shouts.

He fanned out cards in front of his face and asked a bald male participant with a dragon tattoo on the back of his head.

"Pick a card." Alfred then tapped into his consciousness, reading his mind, and scaring the life out of him.

"The three of clubs. Hmm." Alfred stared into the crowd with a theatrical wry smile. "This may be the start of the worst week of your short life, boy."

The young man frowned, shoulders sagging, mouth hanging open. "Short life?"

"I'm usually right. Nonono. Check that. I'm always right." He tapped his temple. "I'm hearing more. You've a girlfriend. Her name's Abby, yes? She has wavy blonde hair, and a nose bigger than her chin."

He nodded, dumbfounded.

"She wants out of the relationship. She just purchased a hatchet to chop off your…well, that's all I hear. There, there, you'll be fine. Off you go."

The tattooed man slumped forward at the shoulders, and his brow furrowed, face going red, either in anger or embarrassment, probably both.

Alfred loved to take the air out of a cheerful participant.

Forest college students continued to gravitate to his shows. They would holler:

"Al G. Al G. Al G. We love Al G."

"Al G, Al G love me! Al G."

"Read my mind, Mister Mindbender."

"Knowing you know my thoughts makes me want you. I love you, Al."

Al had no use for college. Didn't enroll. Learned all he needed in Demon School. Al expanded his knowledge-base by burglarizing the communal mind.

One night, after a show, Al stared into a dressing-room mirror and said: "I know it all. And everyone wants what I have. Well, they can't have it. The villagers bore me. Get on my nerves."

Al's elbows were great listeners but didn't provide any feedback, not that Al would listen to them.

Small crowds gathered around the wooden stage, clapping and chanting, waiting for the curtain to open: "We want Al! We want Al!" Drumming their feet on the ground and clapping hands, they roared: "AL G! AL G! AL G!"

As Al's fame grew, so did his battles with anger, jealousy, and all-out rage.

Bursts of anger sometimes appeared on stage. If Al was unable to read someone's mind during a performance, he would belittle them. Scream at them: "You useless twit! Your brain's empty. Get off my stage!"

His temper would rear its pimply head at a moment's notice. His parents tried to help, bringing in Dark Art sorcerers.

Al refused their help.

He boasted: "Dad, mom, I don't have anger-management issues. I'm perfect. Everyone else is the problem. You're all just jealous. Get bent! Get out!"

During one performance, a fat person in the first row shouted from his oaken seat, "Hey, Al, I heard you live in a swamp! How's life with the frogs? Al G. Al G. Pond scum! pond scum!"

Al, due to another headache beginning to pound on his skull, was unable to manage his psychic energies and mess with the fat guy in the first row. He, instead, had to end his show early.

Fame had its pitfalls. If his fans continued to show up and pay for tickets, he continued to perform.

"Okay, this is the last rider I'm picking up," Caesar said as Belle slid into the backseat next to Rainn. Belle wrapped Rainn in a hug. "So good to see you!"

"Thanks for bringing me along, too," trilled Julius, perched on Belle's shoulder. "How're things?" He looked at Rainn, her hair was wet, beads of sweat stood out on her face, her clothing was wet and stinky.

"Well, I was with Zane," Rainn said. "But things got good and crazy. Zane seized away, in a blur. Then, I took off running. Had to get away from Doyle. He's up to something bad."

"Sounds exciting." Julius's forked tongue darted in and out of his mouth and then windshield-wiped his eyes.

Caesar rested his hairy elbow on the seatback. "It's best if you just keep quiet, lizard breath. The more you talk, the more I think about you being here. Rainn's making her own decisions and she found me. She, unlike you, is a welcome passenger aboard my cab."

"Aye, aye, Captain Kindness!" Julius saluted the cabbie and crossed his eyes. Then flipped him the bird.

"I see you two are close," remarked Belle.

Caesar spat out the window. A tattoo on his forearm flickered from black and white pen and ink to four-color inked art: a 1963

Ferrari 250 GT racing car, silvery-blue frame with canary-yellow trim along the doors. The streamlined Ferrari tattoo moved up and down his arm.

"I've got a half tank of epi fuel. I'll need more." Caesar eyed Rainn in the backseat through the rearview mirror with his steely snake-slit golden-yellow pupils, then stared at his iClipboard and blinked. A list of names had appeared on the screen.

Under the heading, EPI QUEUE, three highlighted names captured her attention: Zane Moss, Rainn Moss, Twane Moss.

"I'm going to need to fill up." Caesar turned to look at Rainn. "My car tattoo moves up and down my arm when I dip below half a tank of epi fuel. You're Zane's twin. You've got epi energy in you. Think you can spare a few gallons, or are you an epi energy hoarder?"

"I, uh, I don't know what you're talking about," Rainn said. Where was he getting this information? "I'm not an epi. I'm psychic, though."

"Who isn't?" Caesar said, unimpressed and looked at his iClipboard again. "Oh, yes you are. You're in my database. You can flip a seizure and fill my tank now. Otherwise, we won't reach our destination."

She looked at Belle.

Belle said, "He's right. You can do this."

"But I'm an elf. I'm Rainn Gaia. I don't have…" She could feel Belle's feathery soft energy swirling through her heart-center, thumping away, reminding Rainn to remain calm and trusting of the situation.

"You've recently captured some of Zane's magical disability," Belle said. "It may've happened during your portal potty ride to this dimension, or," she placed a hand on Rainn's arm, "it may've happened during childbirth. Either way, you've carried some of Zane's DNA into this lifeline. But you'll always be my elfin daughter."

Rainn had never had a seizure. Not that she recalled. She glanced at the iClipboard in Caesar's lap again. "Who's that? Twane Moss? I don't know any Twane."

"He's a shapeshifter. A ghost," Caesar affirmed after blinking on an icon to reveal details on Twane Moss's background data. He blinked again, and his iClipboard went into sleep mode.

"Are we going sit here and rehash your family tree? I've got other souls on my queue," Caesar grumbled. "You aren't the only epi in the Wood." Caesar flipped a switch on his dashboard.

A digital screen appeared on the seatback in front of Rainn.

"If you need a little encouragement, just put your thumbprint on the bottom corner of the Touch Screen," Caesar said.

Rainn saw a photograph of her face appear on the screen. Beneath the photo: a thumbprint-sized divot. She placed her thumb on it. The screen illuminated. From her digital photograph, at her third-eye—a spot in the middle of her forehead that provides perception beyond ordinary sight—a bright stream of golden-liquid light shot out of the touch screen, and a laser pointer landed on Rainn's forehead, *her* third-eye.

A dizzying sensation rolled through Rainn. Her shoulders shuddered, followed by her entire torso quaking gently. Everything went black. Rainn blacked out....

The epi gauge on the dashboard went "BLIP." A half-illuminated lightning bolt on the dashboard began to fill up, revealing a full tank. Caesar sped off, kicking up dirt and rocks, fishtailing, straightening out his cab, and cruising through the woods.

Caesar followed alongside Beaver River with a mountainous cliff-face to the east where a village of huts and cottages were built into the jagged cliffs. He steered through a dark tunnel, flicked on his high beams, and drove through a cave for a half mile until he exited the cave and then traversed upward, climbing the mountainous path.

He came to a halt on the shoulder of the road with a wooden fence guardrail. They all climbed out of the cab and took in the sights: a hilltop view of a tangled assortment of cottages, huts, tents, and small buildings on the valley floor.

"Enough sightseeing," Caesar muttered.

They ventured onward, heading down the mountain, now on Pratchell Way. Ten miles later, he came to a stop near a brick building with boarded-up windows.

"Are we stopping here?" Julius trilled. "This place is a dump."

The cab doors swung open after Caesar pressed a button on the console.

"Everybody out!"

Rainn and Belle stepped out of the cab, with Julius flying into the air. The doors closed, and Caesar sped off.

Zane landed with a thud and rolled across the grass. He stood up and made his way over to Twane and Esmeralda.

Zane smiled, staring at Twane. Twane looked like Zane in every way except one: Twane was silvery blue and transparent. Twane told them he was a shapeshifting ghost and could appear as a ghost or, in Zane's likeness, as a human if he so desired. He had a wardrobe of fashionable attire in the closet of his ghost mind.

"Well, I've seen you change clothes first-hand, but what do we do about Doyle taking off with that barrel?" Esmeralda asked.

"Let's get into town," Twane said. "I can move like the wind. And, Zane, you can use your epi energy to blink your way to town, can't you? You've been seizing long enough."

Zane smiled. "I am getting pretty good at choosing destinations and then blinking my way to designated locations, for the most part. It does wear me out, though. I can bring Esmeralda with me. You just need to hold on tight."

"I'm not a clingy fae, but I will hold you."

"Where are we going?" Zane asked. "I need to connect with my sister." If he knew her location, he might be able to use his seizure energy to get there, but this forest was unfamiliar. A map app of Enchanted Wood would be helpful.

"Just steer clear of Doyle," Twane added: "He wants to steal your epi energy. Plans to turn you into a ghost."

"Yeah. Figured as much. Does that mean he needs to kill me first, or can he just, you know, wave his hands, and send psychic vibes into my brain, and then, poof, I'm a ghost?" Zane gave this some more thought. "Being a ghost could be fun, though."

Twane shook his head. "I like your attitude, but no. Doyle wants to coerce you, get you to join his side of darkness. Trust me. He's got spells that could make a mountain cry. You don't want any of that. There's *darkness,* and there's Criminally Insane Darkness. You don't want to mess with his band of evil. We call his band of misfit ghosts: CID."

"Sid?"

"Cid with a C. Criminally Insane Darkness."

Twane went on to explain that they would travel to Purgatory Heights and connect with Rainn.

"I'm a ghost. I can get there quicker than the wind. In fact, if it were a race, I'd have time for a cup of tea while the wind was still miles behind me. You, walking, will take two days, but if you use your epi energy, you'll arrive before me."

"Really? Thanks for the tip, Genius. Never would've figured that out." Zane rolled his eyes.

Dampness shrouded a large brick building. The sign read, Energy Bugger-Off Building, Purgatory Heights premier Dark Arts School of Murder and Madness.

There was not a lantern, torch, or anything resembling light in the predawn darkness save for a faint wavering orange glow coming from a triangular window on the third floor.

"Going for the haunted look, are they?" Zane asked. He stared at his hands. Turned them over, inspecting them as if he had borrowed them from someone else. Esmeralda flew out of his pocket and disappeared into a bush.

There was the sound of a squeaky wheel. A gust of wind. Someone coughed. Someone coughed again.

A figure appeared pushing a wheelbarrow along a cobbled path, wet with recent rains. The figure was dressed in torn, faded trousers and a hooded sweatshirt with holes in it; he moved with a limp and seemed to struggle to keep the slow-moving wheelbarrow in motion. He looked up at Zane. The man looked tired; eyes sunken into his saggy skull. A few hairs sprouted from his bald head. He was a zombie.

The zombie released his grip from the wheelbarrow, blew his nose into a cloth, and stuffed it into his back pocket. He tried to stand upright, but his bent spine and slumping shoulders had other ideas.

"You look lost!" The figure's voice was scratchy.

Zane looked around, hoping this crooked man was talking to someone else, but they appeared to be the only ones there.

"I just arrived," Zane began. "And was wondering if you could direct me to—"

The man coughed again. This time, with a sense of reckless abandon. His hacking echoed off the wet stone walls of the stone building.

"Good thing you found me," he said in a calm tone.

Yeah. Good thing.

"I'm the caretaker. You a student here?" He wiped his nose with the cloth.

"Yeah," Zane lied. "But I'm trying to get to Purgatory Heights."

"This is it, part of it, anyway. The many villages of Purgatory span hundreds of miles," he added with an echoey distance to his tone.

Zane looked at the quiet, dark building.

"Is the place even open? Seems empty."

"Beyond this physical emptiness, burrowed within the shadows, a carnival of silent vibrations padded the halls, the doorways, the staircases, and the boarding rooms." The man wiped his nose.

"Or maybe it's just a sleepy fortress."

"Sleepy fortress is a good thing." The zombie's eyes gleamed. Zane's eyesight adjusted to the dark.

The zombie reached into his back pocket and started another coughing fit. His right arm detached at the shoulder and hit the ground. He reached down and tossed it into the wheelbarrow. "Think you could follow me inside. Push my barrow to the gate. Need to mend my arm. It's just a popped seam, is all."

A small bit of blackish blood oozed from his shoulder.

"Oh, uh, sure, yeah." Zane's wrinkled brow expressed the shock he was hoping to hide. His left shoulder started to ache as he stared at the man holding his amputated limb.

"No worries. Happens every now and then," said the man. He dabbed the open wound of his armless shoulder with his nose-blowing hankie.

Esmeralda buzzed into view and landed on Zane's left shoulder. She whispered, "What're you doing talking to a zombie?"

Oh. A zombie. Now it all made sense to Zane. "Oh, hey Esmeralda. Just going to help this man to the gate. Seems he's injured."

"Welcome to the burbs of Purgatory Heights," the one-armed figure said to both of them.

The zombie carried his fallen limb out of the wheelbarrow and ambled into the dark house and down a hallway. "Thanks for the hand." He used his amputated limb like a pointer. "Take a seat anywhere," he pointed it at a large room and flicked on a light, illuminating a spacious chamber. It held a long couch of black oak with matching end-tables. Creamy blue upholstery, gold buttons riveted around the armrests, pillows with tasseled gold fringe.

The zombie disappeared into a room at the end of a long hallway.

Zane's temples started to buzz. Then his shoulders.

Hello? Zane? You there? called out the voice of Rainn.

Hi Rainn. I just arrived at a house. I'm in some old remote building in Purgatory Heights. Lots of weird stuff in here. I'm with Esmeralda and this zombie. I think he went to his inner sanctum to perform some sort of undead puppeteering surgery. He's lost a limb.

Oh.... Well...glad you're making friends. You doing, okay? Her tone remained neutral, surprising Zane.

I'm alive. So that's a bonus.

What village are you in?

Somewhere in Purgatory Heights. In the Energy Bugger-Off Building That's what this zombie said.

Zane, got to go. Meet us at Ablestone Acres. There's a big bazaar going on tomorrow. Lots of vendors.

Where in Ablestone Acres?

It's called Halos and Hand Grenades. Just ask a local for directions.

Oh...okay. You there now?

We're a few blocks away, staying at an Inn. Maybe Esmeralda knows the way. Got to... The PMS call went dead.

Wait. Rainn? Rainn?

Esmeralda spoke up: "What're you doing?"

"PMSing with Rainn. We need to get to a bazaar. It's called Halos and Hand Grenades."

"I know that place. It's an annual thing."

"Is it far?"

"Not if you can blink us there with your epi energy."

"But I don't know where it is. I need some link to it, some way to plant a seed in my mind to match its location."

"We're only about ten miles away. Since we're close, if you focus on the name Halos and Hand Grenades, and visualize the biggest farmer's market you can imagine, I'm sure your soul consciousness will guide you, er, us there."

Zane appeared as a misty cloud of energy on a busy street. No one seemed to notice his apparition-like appearance. He peered into a storefront window and watched his reflection: he had indeed morphed into Zane, a fleshy human, clothed in a moon-blue sweatshirt and khaki shorts. Hiking boots. Did this attire choose him during the epi ride?

The wide street, blocked off for six city blocks, had a grassy island running between the cobbled street, and was packed with shoppers and villagers out to explore this outdoor extravaganza. Vendors and artists were stationed at booths and tents selling crafts, food, drink, paintings and jewelry, sculptures, photography. A trio of children raced barefoot through the grassy island, chasing after a man on stilts. His shiny blue-sequined top hat was home to a bird nest with a mother finch and her babies.

He pushed his way through the crowd; Esmeralda poked her head out of the breast pocket of his shirt.

"Good show. You did it!" she exclaimed.

Zane whistled. "Wow. I just saw myself shapeshift from a phantom into…me." He bumped into a little girl at a food truck. "Oh, sorry," he said softly. She darted off.

"Jalapeño mango on a stick," shouted a dark-skinned woman. A turban decorated her tall mound of hair, curly stands hanging down her back. She met Zane's gaze. Her lovely black eyes tugged at him.

"Oh, fruit on a stick," he began, smiling at her beautiful beaming face.

Zane muttered to Esmeralda, "I'm hungry." He eyed a wooden cart housing mounds of apples, kiwi, bananas, and melons, all shimmering with earthen colors. "How much for the mango on a stick?" he asked the vendor.

Transaction complete. Zane took a bite. The mango's spicy sweetness exploded pleasurably in his mouth.

Esmeralda's eyebrows daggered down as she sensed danger with her fae sensitivity. She took flight, circling the fruit wagon.

"Uh oh!"

At a nearby stall, a heaping mound of figs sitting on a table twinkled in the sunshine. One of the figs glowed with jewel-like precision. With his free hand, he reached for it; his fingers went right through the fig and touched a bruised apple resting under it. Several other figs in the pile were also glowing milky blue and translucent.

"Please don't touch the ghost fruit," called out the vendor. "Unless you plan to make a purchase." The fruit vendor smiled a bright toothy grin. "Have any haunts at home, do you? Spirits and specters love my organic fruits. These're even tastier than that luscious mango, sir."

Zane spun around, feeling something buzzing by his ear. Esmeralda. There and gone in a flash. Slippery little electric eel, yes, she was. And she could disappear in these crowded streets.

She appeared in front of him, her blurry wings fanning his face. Then, she disappeared in a flit of an instant.

"Nice selection, yes indeed," called out another voice. "Appetizing, isn't it?"

"Oh my, you're…" Zane began.

"Hovering," said the dark-skinned vendor. "Ghosting is what I do. I'm one of the only ghost vendors at the Market."

Muffled silence caused Zane to shake his head. It was as if someone shoved wax in his ears, closing out the vibrations of sounds and chatter all around him. Then, his hearing was restored.

Strange.

The ghost went on to say, "How very observant of you, my young energy miser. You like what you see on my fruit cart?" The ghost vendor's turban glowed in luminous shades of purples, greens, and lightning golds. She was a sight to behold, a flickering bulb of colorful transparency.

Zane, mesmerized, wanted to flirt but had never flirted with a ghost before.

The ghost eyed him with a look of sweet sin, eyebrow curling up. For a few seconds, her luminousness became solid, taking on the full-color residency of an attractive, dark-skinned woman of African descent. The thick fabric of her shawl snaked around her shoulders as if it were alive. The beautiful tribal woman's face was now marred with wrinkles and age spots. Dark eyes peered out from beneath her turban. Back and forth, she jiggled between solidity and cellophane-thin transparency.

Zane stared in awe. Even though this wasn't his first ghost sighting, there was something odd and alluring about this ghost who flickered from a youthful beauty to an antique charmer. She was beauty personified with a rumbling hint of thunder to her glow. The wrinkled map of her face spanned centuries of timelessness. The more Zane stared, the more entranced he was by her odd charisma; she seemed to be tugging at Zane's thoughts.

She pulled off her turban. And, to Zane, it was as if she were undressing for him in front of the audience of onlookers; jet-black hair was woven into a towering weave ornamented in colorful wooden beads and jewels. Her steely gaze continued to hold Zane, making him feel miniscule, leashed to her vibrant energy; yet Zane couldn't take his eyes off this ghost. Those deep-set eyes, her frame, her smile pulled at his puppet strings.

Without another word, the ghost whirled around, the tail of her floor-length gown ruffling silently; she moved with a jeweled precision and turned her attention to another patron waiting to purchase a wicker basket of avocados.

"Excuse me!" Zane called out to the ghost vendor, "I'm looking for my sister and a well-know spellfarmer. You see anyone like that?"

The ghost collected dropped coins from her sale and placed them into her pocket. "What's that? Who're you looking for?"

"Belle. Belle Gaia. She's a well-to-do elfin speller in Enchanted Wood, ma'am. And my sister. My twin sister." He then looked around for Esmeralda. She was nowhere in sight.

A tall man raised a pair of avocados.

The vendor completed her sale.

"I believe she's here at this bazaar," Zane went on to say.

"Haven't seen anyone as handsome as you, kind sir. Good luck with that. There's more people here than I've seen in weeks. But I may be able to help."

"Oh? How so?" he inquired hopefully.

"Follow me," said the ghost beauty. "You'll want to see this."

With the snap of a finger, another ghost, a dreadlocked, heavily bearded man of even darker origins, appeared. He wore a Jamaican black-green-and-yellow-patterned gown and stepped in to watch over her fruit stand.

"Heard you're looking for a way home," she said as they wove through the crowd and onto the busy sidewalk and turned down a narrow alley between two tall stone buildings, their paired footfalls echoing off the walls. Wooden crates, garbage cans, boxes, and dented paint cans lined a wall.

Zane stopped in his tracks. How could she know anything about him? Where was she leading him? Where had Esmeralda gone?

Zane stopped in the alley. "Hang on, where're we going?" Zane asked, wondering if he was being conned. She looked at him over her shoulder, her dark eyes tugging at him with hypnotic appeal.

Oh, I can't miss out on this! He thought, easing his own doubt, and hurried to catch up with her as she opened a metal door fringed in rust at one corner at the end of the alley.

Zane followed her inside a shop, entering through a back door. The room was dim. No windows. The only light allowed entry happened to be a semi-parallelogram of daylight from the open alley door.

The ghost turned to him, a look of concern furrowing her brow.

"You're a visitor here, obviously not a local speller or spendthrift, this much I know," she fluted in song. "My keys will open any door. You want the key to the doorway home, yes?" She jiggled a ring of keys in her hand.

Keys?

"I just wanted to find my sister and Belle," he said mechanically, his mind fogged over in some sort of spell.

The ghost woman stopped at a table in the middle of the room and turned a knob on a hooded lantern, illuminating twin lantern sacks, and casting a soft, warm glow throughout the now shadow-infested chamber. Gemstones and books were scattered on the tabletop.

She wiggled her fingers, and Zane took a few steps into the room. She lit several candles on a mantle, accentuating darkness more than light. She held a single candle under her chin, pooled eyes of liquid black, smiling at him from across the room.

"Zane, is it?"

That got his attention. How did she know his name?

"Do I know you?" Zane asked, although this unfamiliar, unique ghost was not someone he would ever have forgotten. If he was ever to fall in love with a nightmarish savage beauty, she was it.

She chuckled and then became solid again, looking human. She tugged open a drawer and rifled through a handful of silken fabric. She wrapped another turban around her snake-charmer hairdo. "Oh, how easily you overlook the enchantments. Have you forgotten?"

Forgotten what? Zane wondered.

"My abilities are tinged with genius. A darkness so bright you can see into eternity." Her words echoed in his mind.

She wiggled her fingers, sending a vibrant spell at Zane. The gold fabric of her woven tasseled belt shimmered as if on fire. She wore flat-soled leather boots. One boot was missing a silver toe clip. She tapped a foot, expectantly.

"Well?" she asked. "If you want to see eternity, it comes at a price."

"Uh. What? What're you talking about?"

"Nice word choice, my young fool!" Her soft tone had now taken on a sharpness. "Did you think up that response all on your own? Quite an extensive vocabulary," she purred, or was that a tempered growl under her breath?

She continued with chiseled arrogance. "For someone with such electric potential, you don't carry yourself with the mien of a king."

Zane stared at her, confused. "But I'm not a king," Zane sputtered, unsure what else to say.

"You're going to need to pay me in full. Up front. No negotiations. This is no game."

"Pay you? For what?"

"Pay me with your electricity," she said.

"Do I know you?" Zane repeated evenly. "You look strikingly familiar."

The woman's facial features altered to that of an old man: Doyle Alfred Grimes.

"Not in this lifetime, fool! Now, you've already wasted enough of my time," Doyle said. "You ready to go home?"

"Doyle?" Zane said, feeling cornered. "I was planning to get back to you, but I got sidetracked."

"Now you're coming with me."

All the energy seemed to leak out of Zane. This beautiful woman was an illusion. But his brain, now muted by Doyle's spell, left him no other choice: he followed Doyle down a hallway and out a back door.

Doyle's black coach was parked outside, sunlight reflecting off its gold trim and scarlet sash curtains. The tall and lanky Coleman sat atop the coach.

Zane climbed into the coach and Doyle followed. The sound of bolts sliding into place, barred the door.

"Now, it's time for you to release your locked energies. Give them to me. It's in your DNA, as a human. You are merely feeding the energy to me, and then, in one telepathic circuit, I will cycle the energy back to you. Tenfold. You see, when you recall your past, your journeys, your pleasures, your pains, you will discover your true calling: to captivate audiences with me. We will make a remarkable team, Zane, captivating audiences, just as I did in a past life. You and I are more alike than you realize. The Dark Charm is within you. Yes, Zane, we are truly one and the same."

The coach rumbled Into motion, and Zane started to fade from wakefulness. His eyes gained weight and shuttered closed. He slid into a deep sleep.

Doyle chuckled.

Someone was approaching from down the hallway. Three footsteps. Then two. Then one.

Rainn looked at the closed door expectantly, as if it might burst open.

All was quiet. She waited. In the bathroom.

She reached out a hand. Click. The sturdy sound of a bolt sliding home. She was safe locked in here, she hoped, but something did not feel right. Must be the vibe here at Purgatory Heights. It messed with her mind somehow, like bootlaces tangled into an angry knot. After her energy bath a few days ago, she longed for the canopy's peaceful, rejuvenating energy. This venue, this space, this dreaded Purgatory locale was the opposite of that of Enchanted Wood's gentle flow.

She waited several more minutes. Listening. Just to be sure she was alone. Rainn unlatched the lock and opened the door. A quiet vacant hallway. She exhaled through her nostrils, but she sensed a presence in the air as dozens of tiny invisible needles pricked her arms, making the peach fuzz stand up. She closed and relatched the door, backpedaling, holding her breath, and stood atop the toilet seat lid, peered out the window onto a quiet streetlamp-lit alleyway. She started to crawl through, but the window was small. It would be a tight squeeze and a dizzying twenty-foot drop to street level.

A thumping came to the bathroom door. The door burst open, splinters and jagged bits of wood sailing. With her torso squeezed through the narrow window, a meaty hand grabbed at Rainn's booted foot. She kicked, landing repeated blows to its face and shoulder, and scurried out the window and dropped twenty feet into a dumpster half filled with wet cardboard boxes and trash bags.

She rolled over with a groan and took off in a limping sprint out of the alley and down two blocks before slowing her gait to a walk, she entered *Gladstone Penny's Glass-Blowing and Oddities* shop.

Heart thumping in her chest, she stood over a display case of tiny glass snakes and scorpions, and cats and dogs of varying breeds, each intricately rendered. She wiped her sweaty brow, transferring mud from dirty hand to forehead. She calmed her nervous system and gathered her thoughts, eyeing the storefront window for any signs of an interloper.

She never got a look at whomever had grabbed her foot. Why did someone burst through the door? She wondered.

Where did Belle run off to? The initial plan had been to stick together and connect with Zane at the Bazaar, but Belle had insisted that they should split up and search for Zane separately. Now she was here. Had anyone seen her escaping?

The glass-blowing shop, bustling with activity, was packed with shoppers. A mass of people had gathered on the sidewalk near the bay-front window huddled around someone working on something, but she could not see what was going on.

On another wall, shelves displayed miniature unicorns with twin devil horns, turtles with rainbow-sequined shells, faeries riding kites on invisible energy strands, and a large-bellied, twin-horned baby demon, naked except for a seashell diaper. The baby demon smiled a fangless grin. On the opposite wall, a dozen shelves housed puppets under a wooden sign reading: Psychic Puppets. NEW and ANTIQUE MINDS.

Then she saw what attracted everyone's attention outside: a life-sized clear-glass troll, sitting on a bench under the sidewalk's black awning. The troll had a lifelike quality to it; so much so that, at first blush, she thought it was a living troll or possibly a ghost. Several children prodded at it, tapping its arms and face.

She stepped outside and slipped through the crowd to get a closer look at the glass-blown troll. Painted with exquisite detail. Corn cob pipe in its mouth, greasy sharp fingernails, torn trousers, suspenders pulled over his bare chest and shoulders—all of it was fantastical, vibrant, seemingly full of evil intent.

The troll winked at her, or appeared to do so. Probably just a trick of the sun and shadows, she decided, plus, she had been through quite a dangerous experience. A female puppet appeared at the window inside the shop. Nobody was holding the puppet. It leaned its head against the window, dressed in overalls and a red-and-white striped shirt. The puppet leaned back and stuck out her lower lip in a theatrical pout. The craftsmanship and detailed carving gave it such life, breathing air in its woodenness, bosomy chest rising and falling.

Rainn, to her surprise, was transfixed by this puppet staring at her.

The fiery little puppet held up a sign that read: 'Hi, I'm Trixie! Buy my Mind!'

Someone shouted and laughed, returning Rainn's attention back to the crowd outside.

A child sat on a man's shoulders, waving excitedly at the four-foot-tall glass-blown troll. People laughed and hooted and whistled. The troll shifted in its seat. People gasped in wonder and excitement. A group of teenagers was clapping and pointing. The troll then reached up a glassy hand and struck a match off its thumbnail. The thumb caught fire and the troll held up the flaming digit to his pipe, puffing life into it. He exhaled a plume of smoke, which smelled like watermelon and grapefruit with a tinge of mint.

The troll suddenly returned to a frosty state of animation. Pipe in hand, resting on his knee, a crooked grin on his face. A frozen, glassy model.

Children giggled. Patrons clapped, shouting for more.

The passers-by all moved on to various other shops and outdoor vendors.

Rainn stepped up to the glass-blown troll. Something else caught her attention: a fae appeared on the troll's knee. The fae had purple skin and colorful hair, and wore a bright yellow sundress. Tangerine hair hung off her back in ringlets. A sour expression was on her face.

"Hi there," Rainn began. "You are a cutie."

"Oh, hello," the fae responded and sniffed, her tone suggesting melancholy.

"Why so glum?" Rainn asked. "This troll had everyone's attention, but now you have mine. Something bothering you?"
"That's nice," she said, devoid of interest.

The fae wore a belt made of rainbow-colored twine. She tore off a chunk of belt hanging limp and bit into it.

"You like sweets?" the fae asked, chewing. "This is strawberry licorice."

"Oh….no thanks. Nice belt, though," said Rainn.

"It's an energy-woven belt that is also edible." Stared downward and looked like she was about to cry.

Rainn, hoping to cheer her up, commented appreciatively, again, about her energy belt. "Never seen an energy belt before. You part of the show?"

"What show?"

"The troll. The glass-blown troll," she said with pointed interest. "The one that had everyone's attention." Rainn's eyes were now fixated on the fae's colorful belt. It glittered and shifted in its appearance: one second it was made of woven twine, thick and sturdy, and then it shifted to a soft metallic pewter color and then to what looked like candied material.

"I'm trapped here," said the fae, ignoring her question. "Lost a bet with a demon. Now I'm the troll's property."

Rainn gave this some thought, tapping her chin and dirtying up her cheek. She wiped at her cheek with her shirt. "But it's a sculpture. Magicked with something or other. How can it—?" "Tell that to Al!" she blurted.

"Al?"

"Doyle Al Grimes." The tiny fae hovered in front of the glass-blown sculpture and studied Rainn a moment. "You look human. And you know what? You look like him!"

Rainn tilted her head in curiosity. "Look like who? I'm not Doyle Alfred Grimes."

"Not *that* demon! I'm talking about the guy who sold me to the glassblowers. You look oddly similar." She sent her wings flapping and hovered close to Rainn's face. Rainn now noticed a thin chain linked to the fae's belt and attached to the glass-blown troll's ankle. "Yes, too similar!" She frowned and sat back on the troll's lap, and muttered a few choice obscenities and clenched her tiny fists in her lap.

"Who did this to you?"

"I don't know. I mean, I don't remember. But that evil ghost Doyle loves to mess with fae and he was working with someone. I got duped. Now I'm caged to this troll. Oh, wait! Now I remember his name, but he looks like you." The fae studied Rainn's face again. "Yep. Very much like you."

Rainn's expression flattened, and her stomach cramped. Oh no! Was she referring to her brother? "Was his name Zane?"

The fae stared at Rainn and said, "I think I heard Doyle call him that."

Rainn felt sorry for the fae. She looked lovely even with her current mood of despair marring her little face.

"He's caged other fae from our canopy village," the fae said. "Doyle traps 'em in bottles. Sells 'em on the Black market."

"I know about Doyle," Rainn said, choosing her words carefully. "And I think I know the guy he was with."

"You do?"

She looked out across the street at a street performer juggling snakes to roaring cheers.

"If it's Zane, then, well, he's my brother, but my brother's a good person. He wouldn't harm anyone. He's lost, and I'm trying to find him."

There had to be some sort of explanation for all this. Her logical mind tried to piece all this information together. Maybe, if this had in fact happened and Zane was in on it, Zane must've been spelled.

A feathery voice called out just loud enough for Rainn to hear: "Wondered when you were going to fess up." Rainn

looked around.

"No, down here," said a downy-soft voice. It was the puppet from the storefront window holding the 'Hi, I'm Trixie! Buy My Mind!'sign. "So glad you're here," continued the puppet.

"Huh?" Rainn looked at her, all two feet of her.

"I overheard you talking to that chained fae. About your brother. You want to see him?"

Belle stood in a crowd, watching a snake juggler. Rainn called out her name. Belle turned and waved. "Got something to tell you."

Rainn and Belle walked down the street to a less busy section of the Bazaar.

Rainn hoisted the puppet in her hand and shared all the information about the fae at the glass blower's shop and the puppet. She explained that this puppet in her hand was talking to her, but now it had gone limp. Nothing but dead wood decorated in clothing.

"How much did it cost?"

"The owner said I could take it with me. Free of charge." She shrugged.

"So, you went inside the glass-blowing shop?" Belle said, her eyes showing concern.

Rainn figured it was the puppet in her hand that worried Belle. "How was I to know the puppet was a problem? You didn't warn me."

"Not the puppet. I'm more concerned about you going into the glass-blowing shop."

"What?" Rainn replied defensively. "You told us to separate and look for Zane. How was I to know any of the dangers in this shop? You didn't tell me where to go or where not to go, and when I had to use the bathroom, that's when things got weird."

"Well, we're in Purgatory Heights. Weird happens a lot in this neck of forest. There are lots of Dark Artists in these parts. From here on out, we should just stick together. Have you tried to contact Zane?"

"I did. Twice. Can't get through. PMS isn't working. I even called the imp operator. She told me that his psychic line is no longer listed. But this puppet," she lifted Trixie in her hand, "it was talking to me. Told me it knew where Zane was."

Two streets north, from a second-floor balcony, Coleman Pick peered into the haze of shoppers peopling the street. "There she is," the golem claimed. "I see the Moss girl. Rainn."

Doyle materialized next to Coleman, phantasmal hands resting on the iron railing.

"Yes. I see her. It's time. Now we can gather Zane and Rainn and steal their energies until they are dead and gone." He paused, tapping his chin thoughtfully. "And I see she's got that meddlesome old elf with her. I need you to get back to the coach.

Have it ready at the corner of Eavesdrop Avenue and Ed Is Dead Lane." He laughed and floated through the closed screen door, tiny wisps of electric-blue haze clinging to the screened door, leaving threads of his aural glow hanging in the air, a misty, wet trail of energy.

Zane remained quiet in the back of the coach; Coleman steered the coach over a hill and parked in a small lot on Dead Ed Lane.

Zane's head was finally clearing. Doyle's cast spell must be wearing off; he was beginning to feel like himself again. Whatever that meant. Ever since arriving in Purgatory Heights and discovering his magical epileptic gift, Zane decided he would never be normal again, nor did he want to be normal, but he wanted to discover *what* he was. And more to the point: time to get the hell out of this coach.

Zane's mind began to churn out options. Maybe it was time to blink his way out of here. Another twenty minutes passed and his head cleared up more, having recovered from whatever hypnotic energy Doyle had cast.

Zane cued into his epi energy and visualized Madge in all her grace and splendor. If anyone was going to help Zane, he'd go with his gut instinct: Madge.

He pictured her tall, eternal tree trunk. Glowing. Her energetic epicenter of pure, divine White Light. Her ability to share her energies with fellow forest healers. Zane wanted in on this. He then pictured himself standing high in Madge's canopy, the breezes dancing through the treetops, the trees swaying. Zane swaying. Zane feeling safe and secure a hundred and fifty feet off the ground. A small smile curled on his face. Déjà vu came whirling in from the distance of a long-forgotten dream; distant thunder echoing through the Woods of Zane's mind. Zane accepted this stormy jolt as positive vibrant energy, just what Doctor Midnight ordered.

Doctor Midnight? A voice asked in Zane's mind.

Doctor Midnight Madge.

It's just Madge.

Okay.

Zane refocused and encouraged déjà vu to flow through him.

Blink, he mumbled silently. *Blink to Madge. Bind me to my epi energies. Take me to Madge.*

A dizzying fit rolled through him. His hands started to tremble; he clasped the window sill, and then faded into a misty silvery cloud.

Coleman looked over his shoulder. Zane waved at him and flipped him off, then Zane faded away. Gone.

Zane's body felt light and airy, as did his thoughts, as if he were inflated with helium and nitrous oxide. If this was freedom, he was loving it. His mind drifted toward his core, just below the navel: his Dan Tien, as the ancient Taiji Sifus called it. His epileptic energy-center.

This chi, blended with his epileptic propellants, created a storehouse of pure travel-shifting energy. Like a shapeshifting werewolf, Zane was a travel-shifting epileptic.

He blinked, and, just like that his shoulders disappeared, followed by his hands and arms fading into silvery dewy mist.

Everything went dark.

He blinked again. An illuminated dashboard appeared in front of him: a detailed topographical map of Enchanted Wood. He scrolled through various maps, swiping left and right, as if swiping for a female dinner date on the Tinder app. He saw Purgatory Heights, and quickly swiped left a few more times, reverting to the map of Enchanted Wood.

The redwood canopy was a detailed aerial and ground-zero map detailing trailheads, riverboat access points, canopy trails, and villages in the redwood sky. Zane was on overload with information.

A tiny icon appeared in front of him: crisscrossed lightning bolts flashing. Using his mind, he dragged the icon over a Redwood Forest map labeled *Eastern Rim*.

He blinked, clicking on *Eastern Rim* and the redwood canopy lit up revealing a map in his mind. Then Zane realized that he was moving. His shoulder slammed hard into something prickly, and, just prior to losing consciousness, he whispered, "Fucked up again. Now what?"

His vision cleared. He stood in a tree, hands clasping an overhead branch. He caught the scent of tree sap, the sounds of birds chirping, wind blowing through his hair. He looked down, but could not see the ground, had to be a hundred feet up the tree, maybe higher. He was surrounded by tree limbs, thick ivy, leafy plants, and flowers growing off branches in full blooming color. The floral canopy life looked Kaleidoscopic. Euphoric.

Something blurred past him, scooting through a threaded tangle of ivy. A bird?

It then reappeared, perched on a limb. A dwarf dragon. The dragon belched a cloud of smoke.

"Julius!" Zane called out. "Boy, am I glad to see you."

The dragon squawked excitedly and belched again, this time exhaling a tiny stream of flame. "Hola amigo! Que paso?" *Hi, friend. What's up?*

Zane wasn't fluent in Spanish, but after three years of Spanish class in high school, he did a quick mental translation.

"Bien. Muy bien." Then he shifted back to English. "There's a lot going on. Just got here. Where are we?"

His heart rate slowed and he found himself filled with peace. The joyous rush of being away from Doyle's clutches was a relief he would not soon forget.

"En Espanol, por favor." *In Spanish, please,* said Julius.

"Mas informacion, amigo," Zane offered.

"Close enough," Julius said and buzzed in, landing on his shoulder. "You been hanging up here long?"

"No, dude. Just got here. Get this," he added, grinning. "I escaped Doyle. Feels good to be up here." He went on to explain his encounter with Doyle and Coleman, and his epi-ride away from Purgatory Heights. "I've been looking for you. Got stuck in Purgatory Heights a few hours ago, but my intuition and echolocation senses told me to return to Madge. I was just—"

"So, we're on Madge then?" Zane's eyes lit up. "Oh, this is good." His face beamed with excitement. "I did it!"

"Well, we ain't done yet, partner."

"Indeed!" He looked out into the thick green foliage and inhaled the canopy air. "Smells so good, so natural, so clean up here."

"If you could just learn to manage your energies, amigo," said the dragon.

Now that Julius and Zane were side by side, Julius used its echolocation abilities to view Zane's recent travels. "Looks like you've been busy blinking from one spot to the next. What's your plan? Do you even have a plan?"

"Look, man," said Zane. "I just got away from Doyle. I consider that a victory."

"According to your travels, you've done a lot of epi flying. You do that too much, you're going to wear yourself thinner than a ghost's panties."

"I do feel tired."

"Well, you're on the run from the law and Doyle. Might need to rest."

"The law? Not sure about that. I just got away from Doyle." He paused to focus on Julius nipping at his leathery wings. "But I'm trying to manage all these electrical impulses. I am getting better, but my epi tank feels empty."

"Probably running on epi fumes. That'll only last so long. Figure out how to tune your vibrations to a controllable frequency. Then you'll be able to manage flight patterns and simultaneously refuel your tank. You are an epi. If you get good at it, you'll be able to use your mind-energy like a road map. You'll be flying like me, mapping out destinations."

"You know what? I just figured out how to view a visual map in my mind. Is that cool or what? I think that's what got me here," Zane added, sounding relieved. "I'm my own personalized GPS navigator."

"Whatever works. It's your psychic mapping system."

"Oh, like PMS, a psychic messaging system. Only different."

"Right, Captain Obvious. But remember this: You don't have wings, so when you do go on an epi flight, be prepared, have a destination set up, and a landing spot. Too many crashes are bad

Zane, then, to his amazement, saw a fuel tank appear in his mind. The tank was half-full. "I feel good. Really good right now. I think being in Madge's canopy is filling up my epi tank. I need to find Rainn, though."

"And she's been looking for you. I was with her not too long ago. I think she's still in Purgatory Heights."

"Oh, man! Really?" Zane leaned his nose over a white lily growing off a tree branch and inhaled. "You think we should go back to Purgatory Heights?" That was the last place he wanted to go, but if his sister was there, well, was there any other option?

"Why don't you try to call her?"

"Oh, about that. Something's wrong with my PMS. I can't seem to make any calls."

"Bet you've got a virus or something," said Julius. "Maybe Doyle wove a spell. That would be my guess. What did you do with Doyle?"

"Doyle was messing with my mind." He recalled being in his coach, but beyond that, everything was blurry. "It's all foggy. I just remember being in Purgatory Heights, and now I'm here. The rest is a soupy bowl of broth."

"You need to get down on the ground," said Julius. "Head west. Just follow the sun. You'll find a stream. That will guide you."

"Wait! Zane said. "Aren't you coming with me?"

Wordlessly, the dragon took flight and was gone in a blur.

Zane, feeling exhausted, did not think he had the energy to climb down the tree. If any time was epi-time, this was it. He visualized the forest floor, double-checked the epi fuel gauge on his odometer, and blinked.

Branches and leaves smacked his arms, legs, and face. He cringed and smashed into something hard and wooden. He lay there breathing, opening his mouth as if to howl in pain, but nothing came out. Everything went dark. The sound of a creaky door slowly banged closed and open against a metal latch that would not click closed. Zane opened his eyes. He felt exhausted, closing his eyes. A beam of sunshine streamed in through a sashed window. He stopped fighting to stay alert and drifted off to sleep.

Edge marched through the woods, backpack bouncing off his shoulders, walking staff in hand. He stared at an old weather-battered coach near a bubbling brook. The open back gate shuddered open and closed in the wind.

He stomped closer, the brook splashed against the rocky embankment trumping any other sound in the forest. Edge leaned his pack against a tall stand of grasses growing near the orphaned coach. Plants had taken up residency on its exterior: flowering daisies and spiky weeds sprouted from the walls and on the rooftop, with mosses growing on the wooden wheel spokes. The coach had been here for many stormy seasons.

All appeared quiet until he heard a tiny rumbling: someone was snoring in the coach.

Edge got on his tippy toes in hopes of peering in through a broken window, but due to his diminutive troll height, he could not see over the tall heather growing along the coach's wall. His feet then left the ground, and he hovered a few inches higher. Just enough to get a peek inside.

The interior was small, but far from shabby. In fact, it was the opposite of the coach's exterior, which was being taken over by a horticultural attack.

Edge saw a lacquered marble end-table on clawfoot legs: Mother-of-Pearl lacquered tabletop with dragon etchings on it. A teapot and two upturned tea cups were shelved on hand-carved redwood trays. There was a short, cushioned bench. On it, with feet sticking out from under a blanket, lay the snorer: Zane Moss.

Edge opened the door on rusty hinges. The hinges creaked and broke. The door splintered and hung crookedly on one remaining hinge.

"Come on, my boy! Time to wake up," Edge ordered with one foot on the coach's step.

Zane continued to snore. Edge prodded at him with his walking staff.

Zane rolled over. "Ohhhh, my head!" he moaned.

When he saw Edge, a crescent smile took shape. He sat up. "Where, where am I...? Wait. Don't tell me." He peered out the back of the coach and watched tall, feathery heather flow this way and that. "I remember being high in the canopy. I was with Julius. After that, everything's a blank."

"Time to get back into the clouds!" said Edge.

Zane got to his feet and stood up, wobbling He sat back down. "My head is pounding."

"Come out of there. I've got something to soothe your aches."

Edge pulled a small satchel from his backpack and revealed a vial of goldish-blue liquid. His hands moved quickly, and within a few seconds, he had mixed a few pinches of herbs in a stone bowl, ground them up with a stone mortar and pestle, added a few drops of an oily liquid from an eyedropper, and told Zane to sit down in the grass.

Edge rubbed the salve onto Zane's forehead, where a bump and bruise had formed. Within less than a minute, Zane's pounding headache subsided. He thanked Edge.

"Now," began Edge in an urgent tone, "we need to ground our energies with the Wood. Come with me."

Edge sat cross-legged, meditatively, near the brook, eyes closed.

Zane stared at him for a moment, but remained quiet, not wanting to disturb him. Then, he positioned himself next to Edge.

Edge spoke in a hush. "It's okay, my boy. Tell me something good." His eyes closed, with sunlight reflecting off his balding green scalp. "I need you to sit in meditative silence with me. Group meditation is empowering. We'll feed off each other's soulfulness."

A slow-moving flood of energy filtered through Zane, soothing him.

Oh, wow! He wondered if the salve was responsible for making him feel so calm. "I'm remembering my epi ride. I remember portaling down the tree, like I was in a tube of energy. Pretty cool, huh?"

Edge opened his eyes, hands on knobby knees. "Yes, you did well, but then you smacked your skull on the landing. Not sure how you managed to find that old abandoned coach, but you're back. These are things you need to continue to work on. We'll now be going to Purgatory Heights. I've got a plan." *Purgatory Heights? Again?*

They meditated for thirty minutes. Then Edge explained his plan to Zane.

The puppet stirred and tried to struggle out of Rainn's grasp. "Ouch! Let go. You're cutting off my circulation," grunted the puppet.

"Look. Mom! It's alive! Told you." Rainn raised the puppet by its wrist, where it continued to punch the air.

"'Course, I'm alive, you infinitesimal fleshy viral infection!'"

"Hey, I'm an upstanding individual," Rainn retorted. "How dare you?"

Belle jogged up to her, after stopping to chat with a local on the sidewalk. "Oh, my, that is a nasty one." Belle smirked. "Don't let her words get to you, daughter!'"

Rainn gave Belle a quizzical look. "You know about these things."

"Look, girly," spat the puppet. "I'm not a *thing*! I've got a name."

"Oh, right!" Rainn held the puppet in the crook of her arm. "You look almost real. What is your name?"

"Trixie." Trixie sighed and rolled her lifeless black eyes. "Are we done with introductions? I've got a schedule to keep. I know about Zane."

"What?" Rainn responded with mixed relief and concern. "What do you know? We're looking for him. Tell me, or I'll squeeze the oxygen out of you."

"Don't need oxygen. I'm Supernatural, unlike you." Trixie cackled.

A couple holding hands approached through the park, nodded at the puppet, then glared at Rainn, and continued their merry way.

Belle motioned for Rainn to follow her away from the crowded street. They weaved through the crowd and crossed a cobbled pathway with trees forming a tunnel of overlapping branches. They sat in the shade.

Belle eyed the puppet critically. "What can you tell us about Zane? This is no time to joke. I'll have your strings spelled."

She spat on Rainn's sneaker. "Oh, I'll tell you," she said to Belle. "For one, he's lost his psychic line. Can't call out or receive psychic messages."

"That makes sense," Rainn said. "I haven't been able to reach him, although he is new to PMS."

"Are you done interrupting me?" continued the puppet. "He's not here. Not in this bazaar. He's been burning through the skies, wasting epi fuel. Humans are known to waste what they have."

"And how do you know that?" Belle asked.

"I'm a doll of possession. Haunts live in me, for a price. It's how I make a living, for lack of better words. I was in contact with a ghost, a new Spirit in the ghosting community. You know a guy named Great Uncle Stanley?"

Rainn's eyes shone bright. "Yes." She clapped her hands.

"Claims he's your uncle or some such nonsense."

"Right. He's my dead great uncle. Have you seen him?"

"Not face-to-face, but I did speak to him. He embodied my woodenness and shared some information. Apparently, Stanley is working with Zane. His messenger if you will. Well, Stanley, while inside me, shared details about Zane. Stanley knew of Zane's PMS line of communication being blocked and asked me to connect with you."

"Blocked? By whom?"

"Don't know. I'm just passing on information. He's headed back to Madge. I recommend you go there."

"Did Zane travel to Madge alone?" Belle said.

The puppet shrugged. "Heard, through my gossipy puppet friends, that Zane's working with Doyle."

"Oh, that can't be true!" Rainn said in disbelief.

"Madge? Doyle wouldn't be going near Madge. We were just in her canopy," Belle added. "Didn't see him. Didn't sense his energy there. That's odd."

"Well, you might want to try again. Zane's odd, too. I'll go with you, since I do have a vested interest in the human epi. Oh, one more thing. I like to be up-front. Zane might die, and if he does, I want to be there. Puppets get jazzed when a virgin ghost comes wandering into our sphere of existence. I'd love to have him entertain me with his fresh, unfettered soulfulness."

"That's one way to entertain you, isn't it?" Zane said with a glimmer of hope. He looked down at his skinned knee, beads of foam forming around the scraped flesh as Edge patted it with a healing salve. Zane had, once again, performed the same sort of crash landing.

"At least we made it through. Another epi landing in the books," Zane said, pleased with himself.

Edge dusted off his shoulder after tumbling with Zane through a bramble of bushes and rolling to a halt in a thorny bush.

"Well, my boy, we have landed on ground zero near an oh, so familiar redwood, but I need to check a few things and make sure I didn't break any bones."

Edge tugged off a strand of thorns and prickly ivy clinging to his shirt.

The heathery valley, the old coach Zane had slept in, the bubbling brook—all of it was gone.

"But we made it somewhere new," Zane said and offered a crooked grin. "Hey, what's wrong, Professor? I feel like I let you down."

"Oh, you let me down, all right. Hard on the ground." Edge's tone remained even, but Zane sensed the troll's displeasure.

"I swear, I just performed a stellar epi ride earlier. It was like I was in an elevator, going down, and then I was napping in that coach you found me in."

"So, you're saving all your crash-landings for when you bring along a guest? I see how it is. Well, all my bones are intact. You good?"

Zane stared up Madge's massive trunk, feeling like a mosquito to this gargantuan creation of life. He pressed a finger onto the trunk and then rested his palm on it. Then his arm started to pulsate. Birds soaring high overhead chirped. He knew at that instant whom he had reached.

"Hello, Madge," he whispered. "Oh, how I've missed you!" Leaning forward, he bowed at her charismatic wilderness charm, then peppered her trunk with kisses.

"See, Edge? We did it. We made it to Madge," he said pointedly. "That was the goal, right? If only I could stand right here, rooted next to her, for infinity.

"The goal, my novice epi, was to land up in the canopy, not down here," replied Edge. "I'm no treezer, but I've done my share of tree-scaling. But you—?" He shook his head. "It'll be better and safer if you create a ladder. I don't like the idea of taking another epi ride with you into the canopy. We might end up in a pine tree on the northern slopes of the Wood. That's enough bruising for one day, thank you very much!" He stepped out of the shade and into the sunlight, and took a slow, gentle breath of air.

"You'll have to envision a ladder woven of tangled vine-like tendrils of electricity," Edge continued. "You can weave them into a ropy thread. Then, you can climb that ladder of epileptic energy. It'll be like scaling up a rope bridge growing out of the trunk. A living bridge, but proceed with caution. Once you get the hang of it, it'll feel like walking on the moon, but don't allow your ego to make you think you're invincible. You are not."

Zane gazed up and up and up Madge's trunk; the first 100 feet were bare of any branches, then the basement canopy started to sprout branches. Zane felt an innate bell go off in his belly, stirring up his neurosensory map of natural energies.

"I know I'm not invincible, Professor, but I'd like to give the epi rope a shot. Sounds like fun. Let's do it."

Without another word, Edge stood at the base of Madge and, suddenly, started to scale up the trunk, hands and feet finding notches in the thick tree bark. Edge climbed fifteen feet up in a blur, moving with the grace and ease of a lizard.

Zane's mouth hung open, and his eyes brightened. "You never fail to amaze me. Must have dragon blood in you. Thought you were going to wait for me to weave the rope bridge. I didn't know you were so nifty with tree-climbing."

"Nifty?" Edge retorted dismissively, and grunted. He was now upside-down on the trunk, hands and feet clamped onto chunks of bark. He spider-walked another twenty feet up in a matter of seconds.

"Wait for me!" Zane hollered.

Edge did not wait. He continued up the trunk until he then disappeared into the canopy. *Guess he's not waiting.* Zane decided to change tactics; it was time to use his epi energy and navigate up the trunk *his* way.

I've got half a tank of fuel in my Dan Tien. Might as well use it, he marveled. *Can't waste any more time. I've already lost sight of Edge.* "Based on Edge's plan, we're going to need to stick together," he muttered. "Maybe this is some sort of teachable moment."

Zane focused on his most recent vision of Edge scaling up the trunk, virtually defying gravity.

Something hit him on the top of his head. He looked up. There, dangling from the tree trunk, was a long, thick rope made of what looked like silvery-white clouds all coiled into thick, ropy strands of thick mist. The rope had knots in it every few feet.

He grinned inwardly and wrapped his hands around the coiled, cloudy rope. It was sturdy, like thick twine, but soft in his grip. He made his way up the rope. After climbing and breaking a sweat, he looked down to see how much ground he had covered. He sighed. "Looks like only about twelve feet. I've got miles to go."

Beneath him, the rope he had climbed was blurring into a vapor trail. No turning back now. He clamped his hand around another knot and continued skyward. Madge's trunk was so massive in diameter that he could not see around it.

He reached the basement canopy: smaller branches shooting out from the trunk, but not thick enough to support his weight. Onward and upward, he scaled. Now, half hidden in all the branches and flowers and ivy growing off Madge, he sat on a limb to catch his breath.

Suddenly the silver-clouded rope was gone. The forest floor below seemed a mile away. He felt as if Madge were wrapping him up in a bear hug seated on a branch and protected by the basement canopy.

A tiny voice whispered to him, "You're on your way, my love! Keep going. Stay the course."

He inhaled slow and deep; the sticky sweet scent of tree bark and honey and fragrant flowers filled his lungs, his nostrils engulfed in heaven.

He looked up. "Madge? Is that you? Thank you, Madge," Zane said. "I love you!" A puckering sound moistened his cheek. A kiss from heaven.

He found his footing on a sturdy branch that bowed under his weight and took two shuffling steps along the limb, reaching up to grab a curtain of ivy hanging down from overhead. The ivy seemed to hold his hands, and he swung off the vine in a big sweeping arc and landed, with a plop, on a branch higher up the trunk.

He regained his equilibrium, sweat beading his brow, salty perspiration stinging his eyes. He climbed higher into the canopy with ease, grabbing branches and notching his feet onto sturdy limbs. His confidence to climb grew, as if he had mastered this artform—probably in a past life.

"This is where I was born to be!" he shouted to the green sky. "I am home!"

"You made it, my boy," said the voice of Edge. Zane looked around. "No, no. over here!"

There, on a nearby limb, a good ten feet further out on the branch, sat Edge.

"Join me," he said. "I think I'm onto something."

"Me too!" Zane grinned. "This canopy is so…welcoming. I feel light as air up here."

Zane, to his own personal satisfaction, took another long, slow, methodical inhale; a burst of electricity jolted him with even more confidence. "Oh, thank you, Madge! Thank you, thank you, thank you!" he shouted.

He grabbed a length of ropy ivy, gave it a tug, decided it would support him, and swung outward in a long sweeping arc and landed on the branch next to Edge.

Edge gave Zane a wink and skated along the branch, getting some distance between them. He hopped further out on the long, thin branch, bowing ever so slightly under his troll weight, and sprang onto a lower limb; this one thick as a sidewalk, blanketed in purple-gold-green moss.

"Found another opening," Edge said. "Come on, stick with me now." He squatted on the wide branch and felt around with his hand.

Zane watched Edge's entire arm disappear and reappear in the colorful moss. Edge sticking out his tongue to enhance his concentration.

"What are you doing?"

"Got it!" Edge's left arm remained buried in the moss. He knuckle-tapped the spongy moss until he found a hatch, and opened an organic hatch that had grown into the tree branch, beneath all the moss.

"There she is," he muttered. His arm reappeared, and then he reached into the hatch opening. "Come look. It's hollowed out in here. Madge is a wonderful seamstress when it comes to crafting living hidden closets."

Edge opened the hatch, a round porthole doorway and disappeared inside. After a moment of clanging and banging, Edge poked his head out the open hatch and began setting tree-climbing gear onto the sidewalk-sized branch; a sack filled with rappelling ropes, carabiners, zip lines, grappling hooks, and various spools of wire and thread. He underhanded a coil of rope to Zane.

Zane caught it one-handed. "Ah, this feels right as rain. What else is in that sack?"

"This is all we need. We're going to need this gear. It'll make our canopy journey that much more efficient. And, hopefully, you won't fall to your death. That would be no fun."

This brought Zane back to reality, reminding him to move with care up here.

"But I can use my epi energy," he claimed. "That'd be easier… wouldn't it?"

"Really? How much fuel is left in your tank?"

Zane blinked three times to engage the digitized PMS dashboard in his mind.

"Oh. I see. Less than a quarter tank. Almost on empty. But how did I lose so much…oh, from the rope climbing, right, Edge?"

"Nice deduction, my boy. Hence the reason Madge stowed this gear up here. She knew you'd be here."

"She did?"

"She's all-knowing; surely you understand."

Zane nodded excitedly. "Indeed! She's a god."

"And now, you've got god-grown gear to navigate your journey. Just don't screw things up. Remember, you still have that human body and mind to carry along with you on this electric journey. You'll do just fine, going to meet up with someone, and I think you'll flip when you meet her."

Zane spun round excitedly, slipped on the mossy branch, screamed, and tumbled off the edge, falling head-first through the canopy.

Rainn removed a towel from her backpack to create additional space; Trixie climbed in, kneaded up a small nesting space, and sat cross-legged.

"As long as I can stick my head out, I'll be fine," she said. "Just need room to breathe."

Rainn opened her mouth, as if to speak about the puppet's recent claim of air-free living, paused, then said it anyway: "You're a wooden carving. You don't breathe?"

"Trees breathe," Trixie replied. "And I'm made from a tree."

"Oh. Right." That made no sense whatsoever. 'Deadwood' is what she wanted to mention. She wanted to tell the puppet she was nothing but a voodoo-dolling tool, but she kept this thought to herself; no sense in ruffling her rigid persona.

They arrived in Madge's grove on the Eastern Rim of Enchanted Wood.

"Oh, can you feel it?" said Belle. "The air, the energy, the vibe here is so much more enriching than P.H."

"P.H.…? Oh, right. Purgatory Heights. Yeah, pretty much anything is better than Downstate's caverns."

Trixie tsked. "You two done coloring the air with your cosmetic words? I want nothing to do with going Downstate. We've got business to take care of. And being grounded is not one of them. You're wasting time. Wasting *my* valuable time," she boomed.

"You're just lucky I'm here. I'm the carving incarnate of all carvings. You're jealous of me. Don't think I don't know. You want what I've got."

"What's Downstate?" Rainn asked.

"In a word: Hell," spat Trixie.

Rainn looked to Belle for confirmation.

"She's correct," said Belle. "It's a haven for Satan's spawns and cities of demons." Belle then paused, making sure the puppet was finished with her self-proclamations. "Listen, Lady Trix, let's not discuss Downstate."

"Enough, elf woman!" sneered Trixie. "Onward and upward! If my readings are correct, and they have yet to be incorrect, then Zane's up there now. So, I suggest we get up there and find him." Trixie blinked several times, and her head gently vibrated.

She went on to say, "By the way, Zane's made a few changes. Changes you'll surely notice."

"Oh," said Rainn, wondering if these were hopeful changes or unfortunate circumstances. "How can you be so sure he's even up there? What changes?"

"I perform readings. I'm a psychic puppet. Your empty, dented paint can of a brain will never reach what I can touch with my thoughts. Haven't you been paying attention?"

"Course I'm paying attention. You're somewhat of a clairvoyant. Your head is twelve sizes too big for your own good. Am I supposed to be impressed?"

"That goes without saying."

Trixie went on to explain a bit about her background as a psychic puppet: Spirits were drawn to her essence, like a match to a gas-greased bit of timber. A spirit enters her woodenness and gives her, Trixie, the life, memories, and skills of said spirit. Often, Trixie psychically channels the spirit and all its knowledge base from Enchanted Wood or Downstate, or any nooks and valleys and mountaintops in between.

"So, who's inside you now?" Rainn asked.

"Your mom."

Rainn gasped. "What? That can't be right." Tears pooled in her vision. "I don't believe you. You're just messing with me!" Her words, however, came out less than accusatory. Oh, how she yearned, with redwood-clarity, to speak to her Earth mother, Rose Moss.

Trixie smirked and then bubbled out a dramatized tinkling of giggles. "Just wanted to see what sort of love you as a human-elf hybrid have for your Earth mother."

"I'm not a hybrid. I'm a full-blooded elf, but I have all the memories of my alternate life on Earth. Don't say things about my mom like that! Very uncool. I want to—" Unable to refrain, she started to cry. "I got, uh, news that my mom had a heart attack in Paris." She paused to regain her composure. "But I was told she was discharged. Surely, she's okay and hasn't, you know, drifted off into the ether."

"You mean: is she dead?" Trixie fired back, her voice devoid of emotion. "Are you even listening?"

Rainn wiped her moistened cheek. "Who then? Who am I talking to? Who's inside you?"

"Me. You're talking to Trixie."

Rainn exchanged a glance with Belle.

"Don't play games with me about my Earth mother. If you know where Zane is, I just figured the spirit within you must also know him." She paused and then offered another idea. "I got it. Stanley—you're channeling Great Uncle Stanley."

"Not even close."

"Rainn, it's not worth the effort," Belle said. "You're getting yourself all worked up. Trixie's just playing games. She wants to drag you through emotional puddles. Stay strong."

"But Mom, I'd like to know who's possessing her. We don't even know if we can trust this thing. This puppet."

"Hey Rainn," said Trixie, her tone suddenly changing. "Remember when we were messing with that portal in the barn back home. Back home on Earth. We ditched school. Had to steer clear of your uncle? I had a seizure in your bedroom. Then, the following day, we found the porta potty in the barn. That's when the whole thing started."

Rainn's vision blurred; a new wave of tears fell. "Zane?"

"That's right, sister. You know it's me," said Trixie. "I'm here, in this puppet. I'm Zane. Had a bit of an accident. It's cool being able to see you through Trixie's eyes."

Rainn's eyes watered. "No. This can't be happening. Zane? Is that really you? What happened?"

Trixie climbed out of the backpack, adjusted the shoulder strap of her spaghetti-string blouse, and bent down to wipe at a grass stain on her knee.

"Life is much simpler this way! I'm a bit, oh, how shall I put it? Hollow," Trixie said. "Tell you what. Maybe this'll help you believe that I'm possessing Zane."

She pulled out a folded-up piece of paper from a pocket, and opened it: "Zane told me to write this down. Said it was a text message he sent you back on Earth the day you both portaled to Enchanted Wood. He said your Uncle Bob agreed to check in on you two while your parents were in Europe. You sent him a text about skipping school, and he responded. Here's the text correspondence: LET ME DRIVE US TO SCHOOL TODAY. IT'S AN EMERGENCY. EXPLAIN LATER.

Zane had texted her back: SURE. I DON'T WANT TO HANG AROUND IN THIS HAUNTED HOME ANYWAY.

"Sound familiar, Rainn?"

In the upper Heights of Madge's living green rooftop layer, a shard of sunlight pierced through a gap in the dense, thick-branched canopy; Zane followed Edge's lead, watching him move with a liquidity that rivalled dancing river water. Zane did his best to keep pace and discovered, rather quickly, that he had an innate ability to maintain balance while climbing through the trees, too; the more he strode through the canopy, the smoother his footfalls and hand-grasping holds.

Zane wiped the sweat from his brow as Edge grabbed a branch and stopped at an opening in the canopy: A rope bridge spanned a forty-foot blue-sky gap in the canopy. On the other side of the bridge stood a familiar figure: Reese.

Reese waved and dove off the bridge, fell six feet, clasped onto a tree branch, spun upside down like a monkey, and crimped his legs around the sagging limb, long rust-red dreadlocks hanging down. "Take the bridge over here. Let's go!" he shouted joyously. "So good to see you two up here in the clouds."

Zane and Edge crossed the bridge and looked down at Reese, hanging upside down six feet below them. Reese gently swayed back and forth, his arms hanging down, saying, "Take hold of my arms, and I'll swing you to the other tree."

"Really?" Zane said in a tone of doubt. "Dude, I love it up here, but that's straight-up crazy. This bridge is sturdy enough. Can't we just venture deeper into the canopy?"

"Trust me. Now jump, grab my hands while you sail toward me. I'll catch you. We need to move to the next redwood."

Zane exchanged a glance with Edge. "Is that what we're doing? Sounds like a dare. Not liking it. At all." Edge
shrugged. He said nothing.

"What? You're crazy," Zane complained. "Everything's so tight in here. So green. So lush. All I see is one big mash of green splashed with colorful flowers." He continued to search through the dense canopy. Why not go through the canopy and climb down?"

"This is how we do it, Zane," Reese called out. "Come on, brother. Trust the jump. Take the leap."

"That's a long way down," said Zane. "And the drop to the forest floor is…deadly."

"Give me your hands, ADHD boy; I'll swing you over to the rest of my treezing mates."

"No way. You're not tossing me. That's nuts!"

"You need to trust me. Have I ever steered you wrong? This is my playground in the clouds. Being up here jolts me to the core, and makes me feel invincible. Don't you?"

"Sure. I can see you're managing just fine. But how're you going to throw me into the green mash of madness and expect me to land safely? I don't know," Zane muttered. "I'm not some sideshow circus performer."

Something blurred through the trees and landed on the rope bridge: Julius.

"Oh, dude, you're here, too?" Zane asked, pleased that his whole Good Vibe gang had gathered here in the sky.

Julius landed on a branch, nibbling at his shoulder, then went airborne again and hovered in front of Zane.

"Is this really my next step?" Zane called out to Edge a second time."

"You can do it, my boy! I've got faith in you."

"It's best if you follow the old fossil's advice," Julius added. "That old troll knows the canopy and we're on a bit of a schedule. He knows the shortcuts. There's more going on than meets the eye."

"How'd you find us?" Zane asked.

"Echolocation." Julius twilled. "Now stay focused and make the leap!"

Zane heard a crackle of branches and spotted another flash of color between the green-layered canopy. A woman dressed in a checkered pink-lemonade and lime tank top skated down a branch, arms outstretched, long caramel-colored hair flowing behind her. She seemed to be surfing the branch, barefoot.

Two more men, also barefoot, were scaling up the tree sinewy muscled arms and legs moving about. Treezers.

Another treezer, bare-chested, had a pack over his shoulders. He was linking carabiners to rope lines, eyeing an overhead limb.

"Look," Zane said pointedly. "What's going on? Who are all these Treezers? Friends of yours?"

"Another one!" Zane pointed to the woman with long purple hair, skating on a branch, silky hair whipping behind, arms outstretched. She came to a screeching halt, now sitting on a limb that stretched over the rope bridge.

"This place is crawling with treezers. You are all treezers, right?" Zane asked.

A circus of tree-loving people was popping up everywhere. Was he being followed?

Purple-Hair woman, perched above him, sprang off a branch, sending bark flakes falling as she somersaulted through the air and stuck her landing on the rope bridge, sending a vibration through the planked flooring.

Zane's mouth gaped open. Impressive. Before he could even respond, a burst of silvery energy tingled through his bones, tickling his senses. His eyes remained locked onto this acrobatic purple-haired woman. Was she planning another aerial maneuver?

She then made eye contact with him, a small smile curving her lips upward, and she skipped across the rope bridge, twirling and dancing, waving her hips and finding a groove.

Nice, thought Zane. *Here she comes. Hope there's not too much dirt on my face. When's the last time I showered?* Zane wondered and wiped his brow, adding to the smudge mark already on his cheek.

"That was really cool," Zane eventually said. "You're amazing! Graceful. Crazy good. And oh, so lovely on the eyes."

She stood facing him, nose to nose, about the same height as Zane, or maybe an inch taller. Her eyebrows arched upward as she reached out a dirty hand in greeting. Zane shook it; his vision remaining glued to her sea-green eyes.

"Hi there!" she said, her voice like silk. "Friends with Edge, are ya? I think Reese wants you to make the leap!"

"I can blink my way there, epi-style."

Edge hollered. "Not enough fuel in your tank!"

Zane, not wanting to come across as a wimp in front of all these treezers, especially Purple Hair woman, said, "I'm Zane." His eyes roved over the slender line of her face. She continued smiling gently while Zane was doing his best not to stare.

"What's your last name?" she inquired.

A pair of birds squawked loudly from the branches.

"Moss," Zane said over the singing birds.

"Moss, did you say? Hmm."

"Is there a problem?"

She said nothing. Her long purple hair framed her angular face.

Zane, now thoroughly enamored by her minty scent and silken voice, tried to play it cool, but his heart was spinning like a top over her wilderness beauty.

All that came to a screeching halt as she stepped past Zane on the bridge. At the other end of the bridge was a familiar face: Reese. He had removed himself from his upside-down position on the branch.

She jogged up to him, wrapped her slender, muscled arms around Reese, gave him a tender kiss on the lips, and whispered something in his ear.

"Hi sweetie! the woman said with enough allure to bring in a new gust of wind.

"Hey, baby!" Reese purred, dreadlocks bouncing silently in the wind. He wrapped an arm around her waist and pulled her in for a hug. Reese glanced over her shoulder at Zane. "What do you think? Isn't she the best? This is Jade Berry, my girl. She happens to be the best female treezer this side of the stars. She moves with effortless precision."

Jade offered a modest smile and rested her head on Reese's shoulder.

Zane, feeling embarrassed for ogling over Jade, wanted to melt into the floorboards and hide.

Jade said, "I do my best to stay above ground. The canopy is our ultimate palace in the clouds. We love it up here. Surfing the trees. Bet you do, too."

Zane opened his mouth as if to speak.

Jade gave Reese another hug and studied Zane for a moment. "You a treezer?"

"Me? No. I'm new to all this Treezing, but the energy up here is amazing. Intense. Can't seem to get enough. And I love being so close to Madge."

"She's everyone's mother," Jade said. "The Mother of all mothers."

"I'm a firm believer that Madge played a part in bringing us all together," Reese chimed in, "and we've been looking for you, Zane. As you can see, I brought a few friends to help. My search party, if you will. Glad we found you. Now, we need to connect with Rainn and Belle. We can chat more once we get to base camp."

Jade said, "I knew there was a reason why I sensed so much electricity flowing out of you, Zane! It's spilling out of your ears, dude. You are the electric circuit I've been hearing about."

Zane offered a sheepish grin and shrugged. He had no idea he, Zane, had become the talk of these local treezers. It filled him with a zip of pride and a whole lot of astonishment.

"Don't look so distraught," Jade added. "We've something in common."

Zane wondered what it could be, and hoped she would tell him.

Jade said, "I'm a treezer and a spell-farming epileptic."

Zane's arm hairs bristled to attention, and a wave of shivers skirted up and down his spine. He had not expected this.

"That's right," Reese added. "She's the trifecta of energy all spun into one eternal soul."

"I'm friends with Belle, too," Jade said. "She's told me about you. She's been worried."

"Wow!" was all Zane could say. *Finally! Someone else with epilepsy. If only she wasn't with Reese. Oh, well. Now was no time to be thinking about that sort of stuff…or was it?*

"We should get back to base camp," Reese said, "and help Zane ground his energies and reconnect with Madge's root vibrancy as he tunes into her energetic groove of the grove."

"Great idea!" Jade beamed. "Keep it simple. Staying tuned into Madge keeps you connected to a charmed existence. The redwood canopy is straight fire."

Julius landed on Zane's shoulder. Zane's body reacted by softening at the shoulders. He closed his eyes, inhaling.

"That's it," Jade said. "Release! Let it go. Trust in Madge and know that you have everything you need right here." She pointed to his heart. "It begins with faith in your connection to the vibrant pulse that is Madge. Yes, Madge is the heartbeat of this forest. Trust your inner electricity, Zane. Even though your heart energy's a bit frayed, you just need to recharge. What better place than here in the arms of Madge."

"Your words are warming my shoulder, and I can feel them down to my toes."

"That's my fiery talons, you fool," muttered Julius.

Zane ignored Julius. "Now it's in my arms, my hands, my face. It's…" He gazed off into the canopy.

"Go on," Jade replied.

"I feel something in my chest and my head, like a pair of brass gongs just clanged together."

"That's it. Let the energy of Madge soothe you. Reconnect with your true spirit."

Another gust of wind sent Zane's bangs blowing across his cheek, covering his eyes. He gazed to the end of the bridge. "Who's that?"

They all spun around.

"Hello, you living scoundrels of the forest!" called out a ghost, his voice crackling like burning kindling. "I couldn't help overhearing your plans. Thanks for the invite."

"What're you doing haunting the canopy? Go back to your cellar, you old ghost!" barked Jade. "You're not welcome here!"

"Ahh, yes! Nice to be well-known. I am difficult to forget." He bowed. "So, when're we gathering at base camp? Sounds like a party to me," Doyle rumbled in a baritone voice.

"You're not invited, you sick old ghost!" spat Reese.

"The name's Doyle. Doyle Alfred Grimes, thank you very much. Call me Al." He smiled softly, a wispy strand of mist frothed under his nose, forming a handlebar mustache of silky energy.

Zane stared, mesmerized, eyes growing larger with intrigue.

Doyle floated a few paces closer on the bridge. A silvery wisp of electricity haloed his head and long dark hair, crackling and buzzing like a Bug Zapper. He tapped his fingers in front of him, as if typing on a keyboard. He then faded from transparency to four-color solidity. His cloak, thick and woolly, moved about his frame, as if alive.

Zane felt mentally drawn to Doyle, entranced by his gloom. Somehow, his thoughts of Doyle hit nerves like his thoughts of Jade. Weird.

"You're the ghost I'm looking for," Zane said in monotone. "Hi. Name's Zane. Zane Moss. What can I do to support your cause?"

"Don't let Doyle's energy seep into your thoughts," Jade warned. "He's a troubled old-man ghost." Too late.

Doyle dialed a PMS. But Doyle's thought-magic message ping-ponged back to him. Madge's energy protected Zane, at least for now.

Doyle muttered something incomprehensible, then said, for all to hear: "Tell you what I'm going to do, you half-conscious twit. I'll share my energy with you. Teach you how to fly, how to dematerialize, how to reintegrate your energy and how to bring wealth and love into your life. You'll soon have a harem of women sharing space with you. How's that sound?"

"Yes, sir. I'd like that," Zane replied. "I do want to learn how to dematerialize….and become a ghost, one of the undead."

Doyle wiggled his fingers and floated to within a few feet of Zane.

He tried to send another PMS to Zane, but it, too, was blocked.

"I can teach you to walk through walls, through hearts, through egos, through all that attempt to overtake you," Doyle purred.

Zane was curious.

"Ha! Yes! Stick with me, you twit, and I'll go grave shopping with you," Al continued. "Find your future plot. Your home. Hell, you could have an entire block of crypts if you so choose. Together, we'll parade our energies all over this forest. The life after is one big party, and what party isn't complete without adding some of my theatrics? I'll even offer you a discount."

Zane felt a hand on his shoulder. It was Reese's. "You okay, dude? You're spacing out on us. Don't let that ghost trick you. Is he still here?"

Zane gave Reese a curious glance. "He's standing right here." Zane pointed to Doyle with his eyes.

"I don't see him," Reese said. "C'mon, man! Let's go."

Zane seemed to snap out of it, but his eyes remained on Doyle.

Doyle, decked out in a woolen cloak over a pinstriped suit, vibrated with electric-blue transparency. He spun his top hat on the tip of his fork-tongued cane, and performed a little silent tap dance on the bridge, ending it by coming to a sliding stop on one knee. "Ta da." He bowed. To utter silence.

Zane, confused, said nothing. He yearned to go with Reese and Jade, but something about Doyle's energy had him reconsidering.

"Tough crowd," Doyle said. "Only you can see me, you twit. Only you have the vision." He grinned evilly and winked at Zane.

"Zane, my young apprentice, this must be your lucky day. I just got done speaking with a friend of yours."

"Oh?"

"Belle."

"Nice. Lovely elf," Zane said in a monochrome, grayish tone. "I was at her house. Seems like a week ago. I'm feeling a bit foggy."

"I know lots of people in the woods, but I really want to get to know you, and you want to know me—to be like me, yes? Right. Right. We'll make quite a duo on stage, you and I. Think about it. You'll be famous. I'll pave your way to stardom."

Edge appeared from an overhead tree branch. "Go back to your haunting grounds," the troll spat to Doyle. "This is not your turf."

Doyle looked up and grinned. "Ah, another overly ambitious troll with sights on my Dark Arts. You're nothing but a croaking frog."

Edge jumped off the branch and landed on the rope bridge with a solid dismount.

"Get out of here. Now!" Edge said and began wiggling his fingers.

Doyle's expression flattened. His dark, ghoulish eyes glistened like firelight.

"We don't have time for ghosts," added Jade and then whispered to Reese: "Are you seeing Doyle? I don't."

Zane looked at Jade's lovely face. "Doyle is the coolest, right?"

"I don't see him," Jade said, "But I know him. He's ruthless, evil, and an all-out demon. Don't listen to him. Come on. Like Reese said, we need to get back to the forest floor."

Reese added. "He's trying to trick you. Don't be rubbing elbows with that crazy ghost. Come on, stick with us," he pleaded.

"Silence!" Doyle boomed. "Don't listen to them, Zane. You can feel the true essence of my power, I know you do. That little starlet named Jade and that grumpy old troll, they're liars! They know nothing. They're only spreading false rumors. Listening to them will only lessen your fortune. Come with me, be a part of the future. My future! My steadfast posse of possessed Decidedly Dead Dudes know the Way. This is my forest, and I want you to be part of my wooded kingdom."

Edge chimed in, "Zane, my boy, this ghost is a negative vibe, a creepy haunt here to criminalize the Wood and destroy anything in its way. He thrives in graveyards and war and chaos. Stay here in the canopy of Light. That old ghost cannot survive here for long."
"Enough!" screamed Doyle, having lost his patience.

Edge continued to move his hands in a rapid haze of energy.

Doyle then blurred into transparency, then morphed to a misty cloud, and was gone.

Jade said, "That ghost has a few screws loose. I couldn't see him, but I could hear him."

"Yep. Impulse control issues," added Reese. "May be bipolar. Great work, Edge!"

Zane said, "A bipolar ghost? No way."

"Way, dude," said Reese. "Doyle's a cracked nut."

"Ghosts don't last long in the canopy. Too much Goodness, as it were, up here. The vibrant pulse of Madge was getting to him. He had to bail. Madge's vitality simply wears out black-magic purveyors."

"Is he really a mentally ill ghost?" Zane repeated. "That's crazy! Never heard of such a thing." He was feeling charged up again, catching his third wind, or maybe his fourth. Much of this, he realized, had to do with Doyle's departure.

Zane's attentive eye returned to staring at Jade, a beaming wild beauty.

"My boy," Edge said to Zane. "You're feeling the pulse of Madge. She's filling us all up. Allow it. Breathe it in. Focus on her, the greatest of all redwoods."

Zane wanted to get to know Jade better. That's what he wanted.

Even with sweat beading Jade's brow and her shapely perspiring torso, she smelled like warm wildflowers, honey, and mint. If pure love had a scent, it was Jade. Or was that Madge and her elegant fragrance, a tree as tall as the sky?

"Just have faith," Jade added. "Believe you can protect yourself. You're an epi, after all. How cool is that? We're like cosmic twins. We've both got epi energy flowing through our veins."

Zane, feeling as if struck by Cupid's Zen-laced arrow, remained awestruck—now by her voice; her mysterious tone had his attention, sending him into a dream-like whimsy.

Edge snapped his fingers in front of Zane. Zane's shoulders shuddered and he pulled himself free from staring at Jade.

"Let's talk about all this when we get back to camp," Reese added, and placing two fingers to his lips, he whistled musical trios of notes that sounded like a chant. Zane was told by Edge that Reese was informing the other treezers to end the Zane search party.

They all gathered on the rope bridge, winds kicking into gear making the bridge wobble. Zane spoke to Jade: "I'm amazed that you and I are epis. Do you know how to navigate epi rides to specific locations? I'm having trouble with that. I tend to…crash land a lot, oftentimes flat on my back and in unexpected areas."

"We'll talk shop later," said Jade, "but I agree with Reese. We should get to base camp soon. Storm clouds are rolling in with the wind. We don't want to get stuck up here in a lightning storm."

A flash in the sky reflected off her green eyes. "Storm's already here!"

"Oh, that's not good, but if we can avoid Doyle, then I think we can steer clear of this storm's thrashing, yes?"

Reese said, "Let's put some muscle in the hustle."

Edge disappeared up a tree and returned half a moment later with a backpack.

"Zane, you'll use this gear to get you down to the forest floor." Edge ordered.

Zane sat on the rope bridge and untangled the rappelling gear. Edge began linking hooks to rappelling ropes, testing the pulley system.

A stiff breeze sent a coil of rope sliding along the planks that bumped into a pile of grappling hooks, sending a loose hook tumbled off the bridge. Zane reached down to grab at the rope, saving that one, but several more hooks disappeared into the chasm.

He stood up, holding the rope railing. Then something shoved at Zane, some sort of invisible presence. Maybe it was the wind. But he felt a distinct shove at his chest, and he tumbled backward and fell over the side of the rope railing.

"Nooooo!" Zane screamed and disappeared through a mash of thick foliage. Five seconds later: THUMP!

"Zane! Oh Zane!" Edge muttered with pain in his voice.

Jade, Reese, and Edge scaled down the tree, moving with deft athleticism. There, on the ground, lay Zane's body, one leg bent at an odd ankle. Zane looked broken. Lifeless. Edge got down on bended knee as Zane had blurred into transparency. Edge could see right through him.

"So, this is it?" Zane said softly, his eyes looking around anxiously. Zane then faded into a cloudy vapor, and then he was gone.

THREE LIFETIMES AGO

Doyle Alfred Grimes learned to manage his anger on stage, for the most part. His curly red hair grew into a hilly mane, frizzy dreadlocks that looked like rust-red sea foam. He hid these massive tentacles in a crocheted tam hat.

By his twenty-fifth birthday, his curls had grown halfway down his back into wiry, bushy dreadlocks. His fans loved his look. Hordes of groupie chicks followed him. He was a stunner, an oddity, charismatic: a Dark Star.

Half his act was stage presence: big hair, suitcoat and tails, glittery red vest under green sequined jacket. His mind-thieving skills left them, literally, speechless and lost. But then illness arrived: physically and mental instability. He met with local witch doctors and sorcerers complaining of memory loss, chest pains, weight loss.

His father, one afternoon, while they were sitting on the back porch in July, told him, "Why not help us out. You're earning money." Al felt there was something more than magical about all this, and he did want to support his family. Well, sort of. Maybe just a little. Well, maybe not at all. He had never told them how much money he had earned. He hoarded it, and stowed it in underground hampers.

He wanted to look good or look unique. Al chose the latter. His eccentric behavior of talking to his elbows soon graduated to other audiences. He started talking to trees, ordering them to "Hurry up! Grow!"

Locals enjoyed his odd persona. Every now and again, while on stage, he was caught muttering to his joints. "This is the last time I'm gonna tell you," he shouted at his bent elbow. "Straighten up or get out!"

Well beyond his teen acne-years, his face became scarred, pockmarked. Zit city. Was it all these stolen memories oiling up his complexion? He didn't care. His steely, cold green eyes and mass of hair kept him in the limelight. He hid his face behind his curtained dreadlocks.

After all these years of impressing the forest locals, he grew bored of the hoopla. Something was nagging at him, voices. Constant chatter in his mind began to wear on him.

Al, although a recluse, was never alone. His addiction to stealing thoughts was more real than he realized. Unexplained deaths in the community continued to rise. Was Al to blame?

Even as his interest in performing waned, he drank up his mysterious cultish attention. Many followers grieving over deceased family members would go to an *Al G show* to blow out the pipes and recharge themselves.

His act began as a cousin to clairvoyance. But he was no cousin, he was King. Just ask him. He then discovered something else: after years of practice, his artful gift of mind-murdering energies came with consequences. To go along with his on-again, off-again bouts of depression and anxiety and mania, his migraines continued to ruin him, sometimes for weeks at a time.

Nevertheless, if bedridden, he'd reschedule and continue to perform.

Audiences raved.

"Tell me how you do it?"

"You're amazing! You are my full moon! A lunar delight!"

"Your freak is straight fire!"

"Come freak with me!"

Al just stared them down in icy silence. *How dare you try to understand me and my private magic? You're nothing but a primate*

Over the next several months, his anger intensified, as did his lack of sleep. He was losing a bit of his dark charisma, too. Despite this, his shows continued to sell out.

The Al G Show reached a new level of stardom. He needed an assistant or an agent or a manager, someone to help organize and plan his schedule and his life. He thought of reaching out to Magdalena but could not locate her, figuring she was dead.

He met a young starlet named Miss Rigby Leek at one of his performances, and, as usual, read her thoughts. A day or two later, between gigs, he connected with her again. He was, quite simply, enchanted by her beauty and charm. Dark curls hung off her shoulders. Boxy hips and squared-off shoulders, but petite everywhere else. Deep, dark eyes.

He refused to let on about his desires for her. Her eyes, however, grabbed ahold of him, clung to him, and would not let go. Rigby, it seemed, showed up just in time for Al. She became a temporary distraction from his downward mental spiral.

He hired her as his assistant. Her rugged charisma complemented Al's wild 'I've been living under a trestle' look. They soon grew close and a relationship kindled. Yet that relationship alone was not enough for Al. He needed something more. But what?

The more minds he stole, read, and stowed away, the more energized he became. At the same time, his energy was leaving chinks in his armor. Insomnia had set in; rusty-riveted wakefulness hammered into his head when he was trying to sleep. Then, new waves of energized memories flowed through him, almost to the

point of mentally drowning him. But Al would surface again,
treading water with Life.

Off he'd go, as if waltzing on water, just him and his magic
mind. His magic-dosed life was a wobbly roller coaster. "Must find
a way to harness it," he would profess to his elbow. "Just leave me
alone already!" Often, his elbow yelled back at him.

Lack of self-control surfaced, too. He would bark at Rigby if
she was late or wasn't there to catch him if he tripped on stage. His
coordination began to falter which soon led to smaller crowds.
High attendance and sold-out shows became a thing of the past. He
was becoming a has-been.

He made claims to his reflection in a tall cracked mirror: "I will
attract big crowds again. And until we do," he paused, glancing at
each elbow, "I won't be happy. Simple as that. So, let's get it
together. Quit screwing around!"

Rigby took offense, assuming he was yelling at her, not his
elbows. It was no secret that he got off on seeing his actions set her
anger afire. She was losing her patience with him.

At least his elbows never walked out on him. Never talked back,
Always listened. They'd bend, but not break.

Soon, even his mind-reading abilities were fraught with
questions. Some people didn't believe him. He was, after all, a
Dark Art specialist, but kept his demon identity private. Using
magic for pure selfish desires had its drawbacks. Dark Magic was a
double-edged sword: chaotic and empowering with grueling
consequences. A successful Dark Magic enthusiast yearned to
sequester the mind-numbing consequences of evil-minded
performances by linking them to a past or future life. Alfred knew
nothing of this. But Rigby did and she wasn't about to share any of
this with him.

The forest troll police had questioned him about an incident
during a performance where an audience member was injured and
became an amputee, having lost his left hand which was sliced off

at the wrist. This incident added another knot to the fabric twisting up his already-endangered relationship with Rigby.

Al needed to get away, but everywhere he went, so, too, did his stowed thoughts.

One night, well past midnight Al made plans for a solo night hike: a dip in chilly Lake Ox and then climb the dunes. He needed a jolt, something to recharge his spirit. His emotional battery was dying. Then, to add to his misery, another big thorny wave of depression crashed into the shores of his mind. Al hoped the silent solace of wandering up the dark forest's sand dunes would set him at ease. Just Al and his elbows, and twelve thousand village voices vying for positioning in the crowded subway of his brain.

Oh shit, am I losing control here? he thought. This can't be happening. This is no time be a screwed-up idiot like everyone else in this forest." His scolding just echoed off all the other voices in his head. He was too warped by his own narcissistic nature to see the truth: too many minds in his head barking orders at him.

Al ascended the cold dunes, bare feet sinking into the sand, guided by the moon's silvery glow. He wandered to a cliff. Sat down to star-gaze. He felt safe here. Alone. In the dark. Peaceful as a freshly unearthed tomb. The wind whipped through the sands, smacking him in the face.

All remained quiet until…

Someone or *some thing* was humming.

He glanced over his shoulder, studying the shadowy darkness.

More humming.

"You are rude!" scoffed Alfred.

Something emerged from the bushes.

A small shadow of a person stepped into the moonlit clearing. A child? A dwarf? A troll? The shadowy figure placed hands on hips and stared at him. Al, ready to scream at him for invading his private hike, remained quiet waiting to see what all this 'barging-in-on-his-time' was all about.

Why would a child disturb him? "Who are you?" asked the shadowy figure.

It didn't sound like the voice of a child. Too much baritone gruffness.

"What're *you* doing here?" Al squinted into the moonlight.

The figure, cloaked in darkness, hovered closer. Al could not make out any facial features.

Suddenly, the tiny figure's face and hands began to glow, as if crafted of fleshy florescence. The creature floated a few inches off the ground.

"Boo!" It launched into a series of giggles.

Al stood up, sand caked to his hands and trousers.

"You're a simple haunt. Are you lost or something? I know all about you weak little ghosts. The fuck's your problem?"

"You like nightmares?" asked the figure with a glimmer of satisfaction. "Enjoy juggling those voices in your head? I know you do. We all know *you* do," it enunciated with crisp clarity.

Al took an apprehensive step back. "Do you know who I am? I'm a star. My fanbase is known across the Wood," he boasted. But for the first time he sounded curious as to how this ghost or whatever it was claimed to know him.

"A star? Really? You sure about that, Alfred Grimes?" continued the little creature. "Why don't you soar. Into the stars. Hide in the sky. That's what you want, isn't it? You want to leave."

The haunting figure fluttered closer. Al was uncertain whether it was wearing any clothing or if it was just a clump of undead energy. The figure was a blurry mash of energy.

Its glow brightened. Now it took on shape and substance, age unknown, wearing white-framed sunglasses with dark lenses, and a plum-purple gown. The figure drew up its hood and interlocked its little fingers in front of its twine belt. Twiddled its thumbs, generating sparks of white-hot lightning between its fingers.

"You're a troubled soul, Mister Alfred Grimes. I've seen it festering in you, many moons ago, but I thought, even hoped, you'd find a flicker of wisdom in your egocentric tyranny, and educate yourself on the finer elements of forest energy. Your energetic temple is a wide-open circuit, and you've had easy access to this power, but, as often happens, you want too much, and now you don't know what to do."

Al just stared at the purple-robed being whose lightning-enhanced hands glowed so bright that he had to look away.

"I hoped it wouldn't come to this," it said.

"Come to what?" Al asked and squinted, trying to get a better look at it. "You must be a child ghost. You don't know what you're talking about. I'm wise beyond my years."

"You have much to learn, demon child," Al said. "So much." His eyebrows arched at being challenged before he stumbled back a pace in the sand, one knee buckling; he recaptured his balance and leaned into a pine tree branch.

"You are a demon fool playing with a fire you can no longer contain," said the small figure. "Time is consuming you and you're coming to…."

"Coming to what?" Alfred demanded.

"You really do need an education. Word on the street is…" The figure paused again and crossed its arms. "Enchanted Wood University will be accepting enrollment for ghosts this fall."

Al said nothing.

"Storing thoughts," continued the figure, "is a dangerous game, especially for the living. You'd be better off as a ghost. Aren't you tired of being sad? Depression is a heavy wheel to turn. This metal wheel is taller than you are. It squashes happiness in exchange for greed and pain. Surely, you know pain. Darkness is your wheel. Your wheel of momentum is now controlling you. Come with me. I've got the perfect solution to all your depressive thoughts and anger, you full-blooded demon. You can, quite simply, die, and join us. Get a degree in ghosting. Make a real living."

"I'm not depressed," Al lied. "I've got everything I want. And more. So, take your psycho-babble elsewhere."

"Okay. So, you're depressed and in denial. A common reactive tendency."

Who was this guy? An undead therapist?

"I know all I need to know!" Al fired back. "Mountains of knowledge are stored within me."

A moment of silence was greeted by a fresh slap of wind, scoring Al's face with sand-blasting, and blinding him

Al screamed and squeezed his eyes shut. The wind subsided as quickly as it hit.

"I know everything, and then some," Alfred moaned, blinking away the sand from his eyes. "I'm a star. The Dark Star. I don't need you meddling in my affairs. I've got things to do. People need me!"

"So, you say," the figure said, speaking in a tone of indifference. "But you don't know *me*, now, do you? You don't even know my name. You don't know where I live. So, obviously, you don't know everything. You only know what you think you know."

Al pursed his lips. The glowing figure lifted his sunglasses and grinned.

Al stepped toward the figure; his anger festering. Thoughts boiling. Al, unsure what else to do, ran at the creature, stumbled in the darkness, and tripped over his own feet.

"Whoops!" shouted the figure as Alfred passed right through him and tumbled headfirst off the cliff and tumbling twenty feet. He screamed and fell another fifteen feet.

Thud! He landed on his head, and snapped his neck. Dead.

"I hear your final scream echoing in my ear. Isn't that nice?" the creature said. "You'll be much better off." The figure snickered from the edge of the cliff. "The forest will be a better place now that you're gone."

CHAPTER THIRTY-TWO
RAINN

Rainn struggled to keep backbone-strong, but she had the spinal rigidity of a Slinky. Thoughts of Zane and their mom on Earth worried her. She didn't want to think the worst, but she worried upon hearing news that her mom on Earth had a heart attack. She told herself, "Everything's going to be fine." Yet, she doubted this.

All this time spent in this strange magical forest had her on edge. Tears ran down her cheek; she needed to get back into the comforting folds of Madge.

Belle put her arm around Rainn and spoke softly, "Listen, daughter. You are going to get through this. Until we know what's really going on, we must remain focused on finding your brother. Think with your heart, telepath that loving energy into the forest. Allow it to come back to you tenfold. Together, we will discover what has happened to Zane. Please don't dwell on that which you don't know. Think positive."

Rainn sighed. "You're right, mom. I'll try and PMS him again. I did speak to him, though, so I know he's alive."

"That's the spirit, dear heart!" Belle began to hum a soft, joyous melody that reminded Rainn of her childhood, a happy, playful time in her life.

Rainn's teary vision cleared, and she reminded herself: *I'm happy to be here with Belle in Enchanted Wood; my forgotten past-life has returned to me. I am in a sacred healing space.* She allowed these intrinsic motivators to seed her thoughts with joy, prosperity, abundance, and health.

She told Belle she was going to take a brief hike in the woods and try to contact Zane. She wanted to be alone.

Rainn walked alongside Beaver River, a winding waterway close to a quarter mile wide. She sat on a boulder, listening to the river at work, splish-splashing against the rocky embankment. She dialed into her PMS network and tried to telepath Zane.

A busy signal BUZZED in her mind. Did that mean Zane's PMS line was working again? He had to be alive; he just had to!

A voice then entered her mind, a gruff, demanding voice. A psychic solicitor?

It said: Rainn, *if you must steal it from some unintelligent lifeless sap, so be it. How long might it take you? You're wasting time! Have you even been listening to me? Do you know how valuable I am?*

What? Who is this? Rainn asked, not recognizing the caller.

The line went quiet, but she sensed someone was there, listening, trespassing on her thoughts. She could feel tiny feet walking around inside her brain. She shook her head, heaved out a sigh, and took a slow breath before speaking.

Who is this? she demanded, this time with a little more oomph. *I don't take kindly to unsolicited PMSers.*

You have no choice. Zane is finished. Kaput. Lost a battle with gravity. The voice chuckled. *He shouldn't have been wandering in the canopy. But all that is done. Now, you, my dear sweet telepath, you must follow my teachings! You have no other choice. Become one with Zane and bridge a whole new existence. Yes, your future is about to change. For you and me, your twin energy with Zane has extinguished, but work with me, and you can become whole again. However, if you continue along as you currently are, well, your life will be a tangled mess of uncertainty. You're a mess, human! An emotional trainwreck. This much I know.*

Liar! I just spoke to my brother…Hello? Hello? Who is this?
No reply. CLICK. The psychic line went dead.

Half a breath later, her temples pulsated with an incoming PMS.

Who is this? What do you want! She spat in a venomous tone, her heart rate quickening. *I won't be treated this way! Why're you calling me? I've got friends in high places. You've no right to berate me like this. Tell me your name!*

Rainn Moss, the caller responded with soft, deliberate care, *This is Edge Longstump. Professor Longstump.*

Rainn went quiet for a moment, heart continuing to knock in her chest. She ran a hand through her partially shaved scalp and then began twirling a long strand of bangs between her fingers.

I sense your distress, my young lady, said Edge. *You do remember me, yes?*

Of course.

Good. Good. Rest easy. I come with important news. Just breathe.

Oh…hi, said Rainn. *It's nice to hear your pleasant voice. Just got off the line with a solicitor, and whoever it was, had me rattled.* She stared out at the turbulent waters of Beaver River, then got the courage to ask: *Have you seen Zane? I'm worried about him. Haven't been able to track him down.*

That's why I'm calling. I was with him in the canopy a short time ago. There was a ghosting incident.

Rainn's heart sank. Fresh, salty tears welled in her eyes. *What happened? Is he okay? I spoke to him not too long ago, but, well, I'm worried. Something's not right.*

I'm just going to tell it to you straight. I was with Zane, and he fell or was psychically pushed off a rope bridge. He plummeted to the ground. He…well, he suffered grave injury, but there is a way you can help. He needs you. We need you here!

Ghosting incident? What did that mean?

This was not the news she wanted to hear. A fresh puddle of tears blurred her vision.

But…is he alive?

Edge continued: *Our utmost sympathies from our troll community are with you. But you, my dear sweet one, you can help your brother. Your twin energy is linked to that of your brother. That's why you sensed something was amiss. Please hold on to the redwood energy within you. Allow it to fuel you with strength and courage. You are needed, Rainn. Your brother needs you.*

Oh…. okay. Edge's soothing tone removed some of her tension. *Is Zane okay, then?*

He did not survive the fall.

Rainn started to sob. For the love of all redwood canopies, this could not be happening.

He's transitioning, Rainn, explained Edge, *but you might be able to realign his lifeline, so to speak. If you enter his body, you can keep his spirit alive.*

But…is he dead?

Yes.

She stared into the river at her watery reflection. *But you said I could communicate with him. How could I do that if he's…. gone?*

You and Zane, as twins, are connected in so many intricate layers. You can help the transition.

I'll do anything! she said while sobbing.

You, dear Rainn, will tap into your brother's soulfulness. I'll explain more soon. We need to meet in person and discuss this privately. Never can tell who might be listening in on our telepathic conversations. Please join us at Madge at your earliest convenience. Namely pronto! Now!

Tears cascaded down Rainn's cheeks. *Is he there? His…. body?*

Not in my line of sight. He blinked out on us. I think it was an epileptic outburst. You can possess Zane's body, once we find it. More later. Meet me at Madge.

Rainn refused to disconnect: *But, but, you think he's...does that mean he's in the area?*

My troll instinct says he has not departed this plane of existence yet. He had grown fond of Madge. I believe he is still here. Just don't see him. He's got to be somewhere in the forest, but he blinked out on us. On a positive note, your brother had become enamored over another epi-rider. I think the word is: smitten. He just met this girl. Her name's Jade Berry. She's Reese's girlfriend.

Rainn wiped away more tears.

Meet me at Madge the voice said. *Edge out.*

Rainn returned to Belle's home and explained the situation.

"I've tried, again and again to try to reach him on the telepathing PMS phone line. Even if he is…oh, I can't say it. He's just got to be okay." Just thinking the word 'dead' gutted her. "But he's not gone," she professed, counseling herself. Did that mean he might be a ghost?

She had to believe that Zane was going to be okay, whatever form he might be in. "I believe what Edge told me about Zane, and we need to meet him." She felt a silvery sensation spiral up and down her spinal column. "Even if he's…. gone, I still should be able to connect with him via PMS."

"Follow your intuition, dear heart," said Belle in a willowy soft tone. "Trust in the forest. Trust in Madge. Trust in the power of your heart!"

Rainn, in her haste, decided now was a prime opportunity to test out her epi energy and attempt to travel to Madge's grove, something she had yet to explore on her own. Maybe she could connect with Zane, if she was in fact an epi. She explained this to Belle.

"Just follow your intuition, daughter."

She stared off. "I'm still a little confused on the 'I-should-possess-Zane's-body' thing. That's what Edge told me. Can I really do that, Mom?"

Belle informed her that, if Zane did, in fact, die, then she had a small window where she could entertain the idea of possessing his body.

"And Edge said, 'Zane ghosted on them.' Does that mean Zane's…a ghost, as in no longer with us?"

Zane woke up from what he presumed was another convulsive episode. He felt mushy, a fleshy sack of jelly. He lay in a field of heather, tumbling, swishy, tall heather combed his skin. A lily padded pond with three tall, thick oaks growing at the opposite end of the pond umbrellaed it in shade. A single-track trail bordered by tall heather meandered toward a redwood grove.

"Redwoods. Yes, mostly redwoods," Zane muttered, staring out into the distant horizon of a redwood grove. He knew this pond looked familiar. He'd been at the pond once before and knew this redwood grove had to be Madge's. He stood up and looked at his hands, turning them over, studying them as if seeing them for the first time. He could see right through them. His hands and arms were transparent, silvery-blue hue.

Oh, shit. Am I dead? A ghost. The hell happened?

His entire body was a silvery-blue. He thought of his Great Uncle Stanley.

A stiff breeze sent the heather and Zane's hair into a cyclone fit; blueish winds seemed to pass right through him, but he was pushed backward a few paces and hovered a few inches off the ground.

"I can float." He was happily stunned. "Whoa, crazy cool!"

If he was dead, he had no recollection of dying. He didn't feel dead, whatever that meant. He padded across the grasses, and then, with attentive focus, he hovered a few inches above the grassy turf and skated toward the pond. He envisioned gliding across the air in a pair of hockey skates. With each successive foot-plant and push off, his air-skating confidence grew. Soon enough, with hands folded behind his back, he skated toward the pond and then, to his ghosting amazement, skated across the still-water pond, darting in and out of lily pads. He skidded to a halt on the pond water, carving his feet into a hockey stop, sending out a sparkly splash of water.

He felt a tapping at his head, and his temples pulsated in rapid-fire succession.

A voice spoke in his mind: *Zane? Hello? Zane? This is Rainn. You there, brother?*

Something splashed in the pond. A swan landed, causing a rippling wake; it twitched its tailfeathers, shaking off excess water.

Hi Rainn. Where are you at?

Oh my, it's you! Oh Zane, I thought, uh…I just, it's just that…

Are you crying?

No. I'm not that dramatic, she lied. *Brother, I was worried. Thought something terrible had happened.*

Well, now that you mention it, he said with a sly grin. His phantasmal fingers wiggled like a choreographed team of finger-sized tornadoes. *Something* has *happened.*

What? Oh, brother! Just tell me!

I'm not sure what happened. I'm about a mile from Madge's grove, at a pond. He gave his recent incident some thought. Thinking back to his most recent forest memory. *Well, I do remember being in the canopy with Edge and this cute girl. A treezer. She was really…. beautiful.* He paused. *But she's with Reese.*

Brother, focus. Stop ADHDing! What happened to you, Zane?

You ready? You're the first to hear this. I think I'm a ghost. Not sure. But I'm talking to you, so maybe I'm, you know, alive…. or maybe I'm undead or some shit like that. But I feel good, though.

Something about that girl. Her name's Jade. Something about Madge, too. Oh, look, there goes a butterfly dancing around a swan. The grass is tall here. I just feel good, sis.

Rainn smiled and wiped at her drying eyes. *You still sound like the same old ADHD brother of mine.*

He grinned, watching the swan in the pond float toward another swan with her family of baby cygnets following behind her like doting school children.

I may sound the same, but I look different. Rainn. Like I said, I think I'm a ghost.

Edge told me what happened. And he *mentioned something else. About me possessing you, but I think he thought you were dead, so, well, I don't know what to do. Can you even possess a ghost? Sounds kind of creepy.*

Zane shrugged and said, *You think you know how to do that? Possess me? Will it bring me back to flesh and blood?* He sounded so calm, and Rainn thought Zane would be freaking out.

Zane, I'm willing to give it a shot.

Well, I don't know.

What do you mean, you don't know?

Return to what? Flesh and blood? I'm not so sure I want to carry all that weight—emotional and physical and psychological nonsense. That's such heavy stuff. I feel light as the wind. He glanced at his feet hovering off the ground.

Zane, what are you saying? Rainn began to cry.

Oh, Rainn, don't start with the waterworks. I'm the one in this situation. Maybe we should meet up. You know, in person.

We don't have much time! Edge told me you were transitioning. And Belle confirmed all this. In a matter of time, you might ascend, or descend, or transition to a haunting community. That's what Belle told me. For all you know, you might end up haunting someone's basement. Or living in a graveyard. And there's also Hell. You might even end up in Hades.

Whoa! Whoa! Whoa! Okay, back up, sister. When you put it that way, I'd rather stay here in the redwoods and haunt the trees. Maybe I need to think this through a little more. This all just happened, so let me think this through.

We don't have time. I need to meet up with Edge, and, well, find you. He says he can help. I'll bring Mom, too.

Mom?

Oh, I mean Belle. My other mom. My elf mom.

Got it. I'm near Madge's grove. I can see Madge from here, but it looks about, oh, half a mile away.

Zane stood under the shade of the oak and waved at a swan family lounging in the pond. He sat down in the tall heather, waiting. The gentle squawk of a swan heightened his senses. The sound reverberated in his ear; the fluffy white and grey-feathered baby cygnets swam around lily pads, following their mother.

The sound of an engine approaching had Zane stand up. Caesar was behind the wheel of his red Studebaker. The epi cabbie killed the engine.

Caesar, Rainn, Edge, and Belle all greeted Zane with smiles, but Zane could sense the lack of authenticity in the smiles, especially from Rainn.

"I'll start," Zane began. He looked at each of them. "I feel good. So, tell me: am I a ghost?"

"A rather charismatic ghost, if I do say so my damn self," Edge responded.

"So, then, I take I've been damned." Zane nudged Edge in the shoulder, but his hand passed through.

Caesar chuckled. "You look about the same. Maybe a little thinner."

"Right, right. So, Rainn told me something about a bodily possession," Zane added. "As much fun as it's been over the last hour or so of being a ghost, well, I think I'd prefer a little more solidity in my life."

Edge went over the process of Rainn possessing Zane as a ghost. It sounded complicated, but Rainn was all for it, and Zane agreed.

Zane stretched out, on his back on the grass under the shady oak.

"Just close your eyes, my boy," Edge prodded. "Relax. Let us do the work. Since you two are twins, your sister is going to possess your ghost aura and pull you back into that of a human, if that's what you really want."

"I do. I mean…is there anything that could go wrong?"

"The only downside is: you may return with some injuries suffered from the fall out of the canopy, but we'll deal with all that. Belle is a master spellfarmer, and I've got plenty of sorcery and healing energies to help, too. Don't you worry: this ain't our first trip to Rodeo Drive."

Zane opened his eyes and stared into the blue sky. "That's rodeo. Not 'row day oh.'"

"Right. Got it. I don't have all the Earth-based lingo down."

TWENTY MINUTES LATER

Rainn had completed her entry into Zane's ghost shell, possessing him. It was dark inside Zane. She couldn't see a thing, but Rainn's consciousness was in fact now possessing Zane's body.

"Oh, shit. Something's wrong! Edge! Help! I feel weird," Zane said, but it was Rainn's mind speaking from within Zane's ghost shell.

A jolt of electricity shocked Rainn. She peered through Zane's eyes. Zane, still in his ghostly ethereal state, sneezed and sent Rainn sailing out of his body. Rainn tumbled across the grass, rolled to a stop, and stared up at the blue sky in a panic. She was out of breath, huffing for air. She glanced across the grass to see

Zane near the pond. He was transparent—a ghost. His ghostly silvery-blue frame blurred into mist and faded away, gone.

Rainn sat up on her knees. "What happened? What did I do? Was I just in Zane's ghost body?" She shivered at the thought.

Edge and Caesar approached her.

Zane felt woozy. Light-headed.

Do ghosts get dizzy? he wondered.

He was sitting cross-legged but felt different. He was solid again, in a human body. He smiled and raised a fist in the air.

"Yes! I'm back! I'm not a ghost." He swallowed as Caesar and Edge walked up to him. Zane then realized his voice sounded different. Like a girl's voice. That wasn't his own voice. He inspected his body and saw something new: his chest.

Yep. He had boobs. This was a first.

"The hell's going on?" he said aloud, but he sounded like Rainn. "What happened?"

He ran his hand over his partially shaved scalp—Rainn's scalp. He had long bangs—Rainn's bangs.

He felt his face, and then ran a hand over his boobs a second time. He then realized that he, Zane, was a she. Zane was in his sister's body. Somehow, he was now possessing Rainn's body.

"Rainn. What the hell did you do to me?"

How did he wind up her body? This was not what he envisioned as part of the whole I'll-possess-you-and-free-you-from-being-a-ghost plan.

"Edge? The hells' going on?"

"Come with us. We'll get this figured out!" was all Edge said.

Zane, in Rainn's body, followed Edge and Caesar through the woods until they reached a small cottage, looking vacant with the front yard overgrown with weeds.

Rainn walked to the window as Caesar jiggled the front door. Locked.

Rainn peered through the window seeing a table and chairs, and a small kitchen. A bed in the corner. Caesar knocked on the door. No one was there. Edge stepped around the back and opened the back door. Rainn followed Edge into the cottage, stepped through the kitchen, and into the bathroom, staring at his mirror reflection. Oh man, really? No flipping way! Zane stared at his reflection: his sister's face stared back at him. He was possessing Rainn's body, and his conscious mind had taken over Rainn's thoughts, too. Zane stuck his tongue and turned his head left and right. He, or rather 'she' was in fact Rainn Moss.

Rainn stared into the sink as the strange sensation of déjà vu swept through her mind; every image, every thought, every sound was an exact replica of events that had just transpired seconds ago, and was happening again, right now. Déjà vu. The way her palms gripped the sink, the sound of Caesar saying something from down the hall, the bathtub faucet dripping water—all of it had happened seconds ago, and was happening again, right now. All the stress of possessing his sister's body had Zane on edge. The body of Rainn tumbled out the bathroom doorway, her shoulder smacking on the hallway floor, and she blacked out, body erupted into a full-blown seizure.

As Edge raced up to the seizing body, Rainn faded to mist. Gone.

Rainn sank onto the earthen floor and lay down on the grassy slope. She turned onto her side and opened her eyes. Blades of grass and weeds tickled her cheek. She shuttered her eyes open and closed; a warm, minty scent in her nose. She lay there beneath the canopy of a large oak. Her memory had gone south on her, or hopefully north by northeast; anything south reminded her of Downstate. She wanted nothing to do with Downstate. Her mental compass twirled as if attacked by a brigade of fridge magnets. Something dug into her shoulder: a thick tree root. She had just enough energy to roll onto her back.

Her jaw ached. She spit out a bit of pinkish saliva. Had she bitten her tongue? Or maybe it was her cheek. Difficult to tell. Her back ached, but not as much as her tongue.

She felt as if she had been trampled by a pack of buffalo.

She lay there attempting to piece together the last several minutes: she remembered PMSing Zane, and that she spoke with Edge. There was something else, though. Then she recalled the plan Edge had choreographed: since Zane had plummeted out of the tree and fell to his death, and was now a ghost, she was instructed, by Edge Longstump, how to take possession of Zane's ghost. Once she possessed Zane, she had hoped to free Zane from his current ghost life and return him to flesh and blood.

How did the possession go? She was drawing a blank.

She stared out at the blinding sunshine and then dropped her arm over her eyes, thinking. She was tired.

Boots crunched through the woods, fading away. Someone was walking away from her, disappearing into the shadows of a line of trees at the forest's edge.

A flickering bit of light glowed from the shady forest.

Something buzzed by her head.

"You, there! Sir. You okay?" called out a spritely little voice amid a welcoming chill breeze.

She sat up on one elbow, leaning it in the grass; her elbow was about the only thing that didn't ache. Her mud-stained trouser leg, torn from the thigh to knee revealed something new: she had hairy legs, more muscular than she remembered.

A fae stood on her shoulder, plum-purple hair extending all the way to her knees. The fae wiggled her hips, making her dress shake, and grinned wickedly, baring shiny fangs. "Hey there, bud. What's shaking?" it said.

Bud?

"Hi, I'm Rainn?" said Rainn, but her voice sounded strange to her. She sounded like a guy—sounded like Zane.

Oh shit, what happened? She swept a finger down her cheek. A bit of stubble on her chin. "Feel a little woozy," she said out loud.

"You'll be fine," said the purple-haired fae.

Rainn would beg to differ; not only was her head throbbing, but she was in a different body.

"What's…where am I?" Her voice—did not sound like hers.

A handful of bright bulbs of light buzzed overhead: more faeries.

"Young human. What're you doing here? You okay?" said a fae with hair the color of fire that crackled and popped. "What's your name?"

"I'm…Rainn, but, well…maybe I'm, I don't know." *But why do I sound like a guy?*

Boots crunched through the forest.

"Oh, there you are? I've been looking for you."

Rainn looked up to see another Rainn approaching her.

The hell's going on? She stared at her exact twin.

Sure enough, Rainn was in Zane's body and vice versa. They had switched bodies.

"I thought you were going to help unghost me, Rainn. This is worse," said Zane, now possessing Rainn's body. "And you look…well, you look like me—the real me, the Zane me." Zane huffed. "You mentioned I might be stuck living in a graveyard with a tomb in an apartment complex in some hellish resort town of Downstate. What the hell did you do? Maybe you should just go to hell. And you know what else: It's like I'm yelling at myself. I'm staring at you, and I see me. You're in my body. And I'm trapped in yours. I was fine when I was a ghost. I don't even remember dying. It's like I didn't die. But now I'm living in, oh, well, I've never been in girl's body. Why did it have to be your body?"

She wanted to scream back but spoke quietly: "And you think *I'm* happy? Think again. I don't want to be a dude." She took a breath and added, "Let's just breathe. See if we can figure this out. We've been in worse situations."

"We have?"

"Well…whatever. Just think. Relax and think."

"Oh, that's another thing: when I was a ghost for less than two hours, I didn't have to breathe. Now I'm stuck inside you, sister. Just what did you think you'd accomplish?"

Very good question. Rainn didn't have the foggiest idea.

"Have you seen Edge or Caesar?"

"Oh, that's another thing., Rainn. I think I blacked out or something. I was in a cabin in a bathroom. Edge and Caesar were there. Then, well, a strange sensation of déjà vu enveloped me. Then, well, it's all a blur. The next thing I recall is being in the woods and saw you…or me? So…here we are."

They both returned to examining the body they currently inhabited. In Rainn's body, Zane was dressed in his sister's skinny jeans and combat boots. Long bangs, shaved around the side of her head. Slim waist.

"What's with the combat boots?"

"I don't know. Must've happened when we switched bodies. A magical accident. The boots look good on you."

"Whatever."

Rainn, in Zane's body, was dressed in torn trousers, a T-shirt, and sneakers.

A hive-sized cloud of fae buzzed overhead. A blur of greenish gold energy shot out of the hive huddle and landed on Rainn's shoulder.

"Hi, there," sang the voice of a familiar fae: Esmeralda. "We heard you needed some help. You two look alive and well to me. What's the problem?"

"Oh, Esmeralda, you don't know the half of it. We've switched bodies. It was my first possession attempt, and, well, something went sideways," said Rainn from inside Zane's body.

"Well, considering you are twins, that's not such a change," said Esmeralda.

"Yes. It. Is!" Zane and Rainn chorused.

"Don't even get me started! I was much happier being a ghost," the consciousness of Zane spoke through the body of Rainn. "Dead's not such a bad deal, thank you very much. But this?" the Zane inside Rainn pointed to her perky boobs. She then looked at Zane. "And what's with that gash on my neck. What did you do to me…. uh, to us?" the mind of Zane huffed from within Rainn. "You take my body for, what, ten minutes and make a royal mess of things. You've flipped us!"

Zane took a seat on the grass, his finger covering the seeping wound at his neck. His finger disappeared into a gaping gash, which felt like warm gelatin but wasn't leaking any blood.

"Wait a sec! This doesn't feel like blood. It's all gooey. Am I infected with some funky bacteria?" Zane peered up at Rainn, who stood hovering over him. "Maybe I'm, I mean you, maybe you're dead, and this is some sort of undead funk in your bloodstream." More questions filled the Moss twins' minds.

"Not sure what question needed to be answered first," the mind of Rainn said through Zane's body. "Am I possessing and maneuvering a dead body? And, am I going to be a man now, permanently? I'm flesh and blood, but that gash at my neck isn't bleeding red blood."

The huddling mass of airborne fae snickered.

"What was your first clue?" asked a fae with fire for hair. "You humans and your body possessions. You're a funny breed." The Moss twins shook their head at the fae.

"And I'm stuck in Zane's body," said Rainn. "I've got balls, for God's sack!" What a conundrum. That sounded wrong on so many levels.

"That you do," said Zane. "Take care of my balls, would you. Oh, and I died a guy and was happy being a ghost. Now I'm neither."

"You're cute," said the fire-haired fae. "If it weren't for the oozing wound."

The mind of Zane, now possessing Rainn's body, began to sense her sisterly feminine flair. Rainn, when taking a step, moved with purposeful grace, sturdy with gentle flexibility at the hip. This was a whole new sensation: Being a woman.

"Have fun, girly! Always have fun. That's our motto," said the fire-haired fae.

Rainn, from Zane's body, spoke up: "We need to go to the Bleu Beagle. It's a pub not too far from here. Belle's there. She messaged me just prior to our transformation. Something's happened to Jade and Reese."

The mind of Zane, living through the eyes, and body, of Rainn, sat down at a table and tried to get comfortable, but her hair and clothing were drenched after walking through a heavy rain shower. Her immediate, albeit far from her most pressing concerns, however, was getting comfortable having boobs inside a wet shirt. She sank in her seat in the booth, legs and back squeaking against the burgundy vinyl. Rainn's mind, in her brother's body, excused herself to the bathroom.

The Bleu Bugle, a tall-roofed cabin, was a popular hybrid business model: restaurant-grocery market welcoming spellfarmers, hitchhikers, vagabonds, undead and even haunts. The place was packed. Plus, Zane, now a 'she' was still adjusting to life from this feminine perspective; he walked and talked like Rainn, while his mind remained Zane Moss.

Zane was pleased, nonetheless, to be out of the wet night air; for the last thirty minutes of their hike had been spent in a steady downpour while listening to howling wolves and barks and hoots and screeching sounds from various woodland creatures.

Rainn came out of the bathroom and sat down. "Well, that was a first."

"What?"

"Taking a—how do men phrase it—a leak into a urinal. Peeing standing up is easy," she said with smiling eyes.

"Let's just keep a look out for Belle," Rainn said, squeezing out water from the bottom of her T-shirt. "Said she'd be here."

Zane dabbed the wound on his throat with a napkin. "And what about this gaping gash? It's not bleeding, but it's all gray and mushy. What's going on with this body?"

She shrugged and said: "Not sure. Maybe a ghost wound?"

The mind of Zane stared at his own body seated across from him. Saying nothing.

"Hopefully Belle will have a solution," Rainn added. "And that we can get this figured out."

The restaurant had an artistic flair: honey-yellow glazed wood walls filled with murals, sketches, written phrases scored with a wood-burning pen. Much of the art was akin to boxcar graffiti one might find on Earth.

"Nice art in here. I like the vibe," Rainn said.

"All crafted by local artists," said a gum-chewing waitress. "Be right with you." And off she went, disappearing into the kitchen.

The front door opened. Belle and Edge entered quickly. Belle put her water-soaked cap on a hat rack shaped like a bowling pin. They moved past a bartender standing behind a crowded bar filling a pint with ale from a tap; they all took a seat in a booth.

The small waitress approached and pulled a feathered quill out of her checkered apron. She handed out menus.

"Get you anything to drink?" Her eyes, big and round, got even wider. "Oh, my! Hope I'm not being too personal. Looks like you've had a rough day, sir." She stared at Zane's face. Was that because Zane had been staring at her unique features?

The waitress continued, "Nice scratch you got there. Been battling reincarnated trans-dimensional two-thousand-pound dragons? How 'bout a bag of ice for that?"

"Sure. Thanks," Zane stared at the menu, deciding doing that was better than staring at her.

The waitress, all three feet of her, was the first female troll Zane
had encountered, dressed in combat boots, and striped candy-cane
stockings under a green skirt and a revealing tank top. A mop of
greenish-gold hair spun into a snaky bun to match her frog-green
skin. A roadmap of tattoos covered her arms. One tattoo, a lizard,
swished its tail, then scurried up her arm and disappeared under her
hairy armpit.

"Think I could get a Coke?" Rainn asked.

"No Coke. Pepsi."

The Moss twins stared at each other with smiling eyes. They
recalled seeing the *Saturday Night Live* skit on a YouTube clip.

"How 'bout an avocado, zucchini, and bean sandwich? Or," he
added quickly, "do you only have cheeseburger, cheeseburger,
cheeseburger?"

Belle looked over her menu at Zane.

Rainn said, "Inside Earth joke."

A single candle sat in a saucer on the table. The flickering
candlelight cast shadows on the waitress's squashed nose.

"This your first time at the Bleu Bugle?"

Zane nodded. "Yep. And we're thirsty. Bring us water and
something with a little pick-me-up."

"Strawberry-honey seltzer's popular."

Rainn would've smiled, but the thought of smiling made the
pained muscles in his neck move. The consciousness of Rainn, in
Zane's body, remained stone-faced so as not to inflame the pain
and touched his cheek one more time and made her way to the
Women's bathroom, and then remembered she, the consciousness
of Rainn, was walking around in Zane's body.

The consciousness of Rainn entered the men's bathroom, tilted
her head, and stared into the vanity over the sink. She stared at the
face of Zane in the mirror; his left eye, ringed in a purply bruise,
and looked more painful than it felt. Where did that come from?

Did he get punched? Must have happened when he fell out of the canopy. Zane returned to the table.

The front door swung open. A man in a dark poncho stepped in, water dripping off a wide-brimmed hat. He took long strides past the island bar, moving with smooth precision, a panther's gait. Even though he was exceedingly tall, his hat almost brushing the ceiling fans, no one paid him any notice. He sat in the booth next to Zane's table, his body somehow folding into the seat accordion style.

The figure spoke over his shoulder, eyes boring holes into Zane's head. "Have you brought what we discussed?"

Zane said nothing, assuming the wide-brim-hatted figure was talking to someone else.

Belle turned in her seat, met his gaze, and chimed in, "This is a private gathering, if you please!" She turned and whispered to Zane and Rainn. "Don't engage. I sense something off about him."

The figure removed his hat and set it on the seat next to him. His face was carved in wrinkles. Skin the shade of a peeled plum. The whites of his eyes stood out in stark contrast to his flesh. Dark hair fringed in silver touched his shoulders. Bright eyes shone like twin candles.

This guy must be a demon, Zane thought from the body of Rainn.

"Is he still looking at us?" Rainn whispered to Belle. "I can feel eyes boring into my skull."

Belle stood up and flagged down the waitress.

"Yes?" said the troll waitress. "Can I help you?"

"Could we get another table?" Belle said, pointing with her eyes at the plum-faced patron and then pulling the waitress up to the bar. "He's making us feel uncomfortable."

She rested a hand on her narrow hip. "It'll be about, oh, fifteen minutes." The waitress waved an arm at the packed pub. "We're busy, as you can see."

"All I see is a demon in our midst."

The troll cast a glance at the tall figure. "Oh, he's a regular," said the waitress while chewing gum. "Harmless demon."

The demon stood up and tipped his hat. "Oh, I'll be leaving." He offered a modest bow, showing off twin tiny horns curling out from his head.

Speaking through Rainn's body, Zane said to the demon in a calm, curious tone: "Do I know you? I think I do."

The demon looked past their table as if he didn't even hear what Zane said and strode toward the bar. Zane was about to turn to look at what had this demon's attention when the demon turned and spoke in a clear, elevated tone: "And I'll have you beheaded if you cross me again, boy! You understand?" He pointed a razor-sharpened talon at Zane. "You owe me, and I need you and your twin to meet me outside. Now!"

Zane looked down and fidgeted his fingers in his lap. "The hell's that all about?"

The demon's eyes flickered: a flaming shade of neon yellow.

Zane looked around, feeling half the bar staring at them. "Pardon, but I, uh, never met you before. I don't even know who I am. So, if you know something I don't, please share." Where did he get the balls to make such a statement. Maybe Rainn, possessing his body, was feeling overly confident.

The demon growled and took three thunderous steps toward their table. "I've got Jade and Reese with me. Caged. In a safe place. And I'll be ending their existence unless you follow me. You hearing me, you infinitesimal human?"

The rest of the bar returned to their personal conversations, losing interest in the scene.

"Zane! That's enough," Belle said in a soft, yet steely tone.

Zane said, "But I think we should listen to him."

"You know it's part of the deal," the demon ordered, hovering over them, smiling crookedly, showcasing blackened teeth.

Rainn, uncertain what to do or say, decided she had to respond; she came at it from another angle. She flirted out a slippery little smile. The demon just stared at her, stone-faced.

"Things've gotten a little weird with my portal flush," he said. "I see that you match the photo I received via PMS."

Just then, a group-PMS chat came spinning into both Zane and Rainn's minds simultaneously.

It'd be so much better if you just dropped dead, said the voice of this demon in Zane and Rainn's minds. *You Moss twins are destined to die a youthful death unless you heed my wishes. Now please, meet me outside.*

A smile snaked across Rainn's features as the mind of Zane within her recalled his all too brief experience being a ghost. He wanted that feeling again. To be a ghost. And to be out of his sister's body.

"Me, dead? Is that what you'd like?" Rainn said softly. "Let's do it, then."

Belle, in shock over what she was hearing, assumed some sort of energy spell had been cast by the demon.

The waitress arrived with the manager. The manager was a tall, thin man. Narrow face, puffy cheeks with a few thin veins. "You'll need to leave now," the manager demanded. "We run a peaceful establishment here."

"Gladly," responded Belle.

The demon slid away from the table, floating a few inches off the ground for a few seconds, his taloned hands shining in the light. Rainn stared at the table; the demon's black hat with a lavender band was now transparent. Silvery-blue. Rainn could see right through it.

The Moss twins started to make their way out of the Bleu Bugle, and a skillset from a past life memory, at least for Rainn, surfaced: she was a young, smart, dexterous elf trained by Belle, and over the years, she had learned the mind-magic power of installing barbed-wire fences around her mind, to ward off demon solicitors. Her psychic fence was labeled with little wooden signs:

DANGER! KEEP OUT!
ELECTRICUTION AWAITS SOLICITORS!

Rainn crafted such a protective incantation now.

Outside, Belle told Zane and Rainn that she discovered they had *possession-flipped,* as she called it, one taking on the body of the other. It was a rare spelling glitch, but not unheard of.

"You both managed yourselves well in the face of that undead demon. Consider it a learning experience." She licked her finger and stroked the air. "Chalk a victory up for the Moss twins."

"Enough with the cheerleading," grumbled Edge from the middle of the street. "Everyone needs to remain on alert. Stay mindful of what you think. Think before you speak or act."

A black coach parked across the street sat under the hooded light of a street lamp.

The demon was gone. The rain had ceased, leaving moonlit puddles in the dirt road. A woman stepped out of the coach: Jade Berry.

Zane's spirit lifted upon meeting Jade's gaze and he marched over to her, "Jade, great to see you. Thought you were in a spot of trouble and we're dealing with a mess now."

Jade gave the body of Rainn a quizzical glance. "Do I know you?" She disappeared back into the coach and closed the door.

Zane, then, remembered that he was in Rainn's body. "Oh, right. Let me explain," Rainn called out.

The mind of Zane in Rainn's body then noticed Reese also seated in the coach. He gave Reese a wave, but Reese only stared, saying nothing.

"Hey Reese!" Rainn called out, then turned, and waved, urging Belle and Edge to follow her.

They all stopped a few feet from the coach and stared at the occupants.

"I can explain everything," Rainn offered to the riders in the coach.

"Your timing is spot-on. You see, there was a bit of a psychic snafu," Rainn started to say, but then she was nudged by Belle to refrain from sharing too much information.

Reese and Jade remained in the coach. Neither of them speaking or even glancing in their direction.

The ghost demon then appeared in front of the two-horse team. He moved like the wind and appeared at the coach door. Placed one clawed hand on the brass-ringed doorknob, turned, glared at Rainn, and then spat at Zane.

The demon spoke: "I died in a past life, when I was young and famous. You two are nothing but twigs, splinters embedded in my flesh. Lifeless humans. Bah." He leaned in close to Zane, breathing on him. "You see, I was murdered. Murdered with a capital M. Happened over three hundred years ago, but it seems like yesterday." The demon exhaled a sigh. "I feel much better now. Thanks for asking, you twit."

Zane and Rainn turned to look at Belle and Edge. Neither of them was in sight. Where did they go?

Chatter and laughter spilled from the Bleu Bugle, but all the other shops on the street were deathly quiet, shuttered, and closed.

A bright blur of blue light lit up the street. The demon, now haloed in silvery-blue flame, smiled under the spotlight showcasing his tall lean frame.

The mind of Zane, inside Rainn, continued to find courage that he didn't fathom was in him. Rainn took two strides closer to the demon, folded hands behind her back.

"I'm here on business," Rainn claimed. "And I know who you are, demon. Why are you hiding your true persona with this silly lightshow? Something must be scaring you. You're hiding from someone or something."

"I fear nothing," spat the demon. "You know nothing."

Rainn offered a big smile, eyes sparkling. "You, demon, are hiding behind a mask. I can see through your Halloween getup. I know who you are. Doyle. Doyle Alfred Grimes. You've died many times. I know all about your historical wicked ways."

The demon didn't flinch, didn't blink. "You don't know who I am."

The mind of Rainn, in Zane's body, joined the conversation. "That's right. I can see you, too," Zane said. "You think we didn't know it was you? My sister and I know all about you."

Rainn chimed in, ordering the demon to listen while jabbing a finger at him: "I've no interest in what you *think* you know about me. About us. But we are the Moss twins, and we are here to protect the forest. You are done wreaking havoc in the Wood!"

The demon grinned and twirled on his toes, his long frame moving with ballerina-like precision and grace. Once he stopped his little dance: "Be that as it may, Zane and Rainn, you have completed your end of the contract, yes?"

Zane looked to Rainn, seeking validation of what the demon was talking about. They were both confused. "What contract? I've agreed to nothing," Rainn countered.

"That's right. My sister and I have nothing to do with you," said Zane. "Must be something you made up in that narcissistic head of yours, but don't you worry your little demon brain! You are a demonic ghost who soon will vanish from our lives. For good." The demon growled at Zane, a began wiggling his fingers in the air.

"Get out of the way!" shouted Belle.

The demon's talons shivered back and forth in violent spasms as if mocking Zane's convulsive potential. A spiderweb of electricity shot out of the talons. Rainn ducked and the spray of electricity hit

Zane in the shoulder; his whole body jolted and its force shoved him into the front window of *Auntie Nellie's Motel*, shattering the glass and sending Zane toppling to the ground inside the motel.

A neon sign, now hanging sideways on the broken pane of glass, flashed, CLOSED ON HOLIDAY

Zane lay there, face down, unconscious.

Rainn's brow furrowed in anger; she glared at the demon.

The demon then dove at Rainn, tackling her to the ground and rolling on top of her, pinning her shoulders to the ground with one massive, scaly arm.

"I've no use for you," the demon whispered in her ear. "It's your brother I want." The tip of his reddish-gold snout had a chunk of it chewed off, leaving an ashen-pink scar where the tip of its nose once resided. The demon brushed Rainn's forehead with its snout.

"Give me one reason I shouldn't just gnaw off your head and spit it on your brother?" A long string of drool stretched from its moistened jowl and splashed on Rainn's neck. She flinched, holding her breath; the stench was foul as spoiled milk.

"How 'bout brushing your teeth?" she said in a husky tone, hoping to convey menace.

She shook her head slowly and stared at him. "It's me, you fool, Zane. I'm possessing Rainn's body right now, demon! I'm Zane. Z.A.N.E. Zane. There was a mix-up. Anyway, get off me! You stink! You hired me to do a job, and I'm trying to do it, but it's going to take a little longer." The body of Rainn, with Zane's consciousness still inside her body, struggled, trying to free her arms from his demonic grip to no avail.

The demon laughed. Craning its reddish-gold scaled neck back, its lifeless black eyes rolled back in its head like a shark swallowing fresh kill. "I don't believe you," the demon said. "You humans are fools!" It slapped Rainn across the jaw, then punched her in the head, knocking her unconscious.

The demon then turned its attention to the body of Zane lying in a heap with broken glass everywhere, and stormed off.

ONE HOUR LATER

"It was supposed to be done, already. We never should have given Zane the opportunity to join us," the demon said.

Doyle, seated at his large oak table rested his hands on the table and stared through the demon, as if it was not standing at his desk. He leaned back in his chair showing no emotion, a stately expression of dead calm. Several more seconds drifted by.

The demon shifted from right foot to left, appearing anxious. Doyle tapped his long, thick fingernails on his large oaken desk. A stack of parchment sat in the corner with an onyx-handled dagger letter-opener on top of the heap.

Doyle rose out of his cushioned plum-purple black oak chair riveted in gold buttons; each button etched with a court jester. He raised a finger, waved it in front of the demon and weaved out a finger-spell. The demon began gasping for air, clutching talons around its throat, pleading for Doyle to stop.

"So, you're telling me you had the Moss twins together and left them on a street?" Doyle replied in a monotone, and shook his head in dismay. Doyle's left eye began to twitch—it did that when he was concocting a ruthless retaliation plan.

"The Moss twins are worthless humans, your Lordship," replied the demon, now on his knees, gasping for breath. "I think they're dead."

"You think? You think? I didn't hire you to think, you slobbering fool! And don't call me 'Lordship.'" He waved off the incantation with the snap of his finger; the demon sat back on its heels, filling its lungs with air.

"Go get them!" Doyle ordered. "Do not return without them! Bring them both to me. I need his epileptic body. Both those twins are mine."

"Got it. What do you want me to do with the two treezers locked up in my coach."

"Reese and that woman?"

"Yes. Reese and Jade. But they're still ensnared in your spell. Dazed, as it were."

"Keep 'em locked up in one of my tomb cellars in Graveyard Gardens."

Belle and Edge helped Zane sit up against the wall of *Auntie Nellie's Motel*, then assisted Rainn. Both were groggy and out of sorts.

"Here. Drink this." Belle lifted a cup to Rainn's lips.

Rainn swallowed, her face pinched up, eyes closing. "Tastes awful. What is it?"

"Canopy-bred healing elixir. It'll help ward off any viral spells that demon might've cast."

She gave Zane a cup of the elixir.

A red Studebaker pulled to a stop at the curb. Caesar rolled down the window.

"Let's go. I've got a schedule to keep. You aren't the only ones in need of a lift. Oh, I see you've got Zane and Rainn together. This is good."

He stepped out of his cab.

"I don't feel well," Zane said and looked at Rainn, who was finishing her drink.

Caesar's big boots clomped across the dusty road, sending up clouds in his path.

"Let's go, kids! Time's wasting and it's going to take both you to pool your epi energies to transport us back Downstate. You sure that's where you need to go? My epi spool meter shows it's gonna take about half a gigawatt, round trip."

Zane stood up and said, "Feel a little better now."

"Good," Caesar replied. "You look tired. Sure, you got a half gigawatt of epi energy in you?"

"How much is that?"

"1.21 gigawatts was what powered the DeLorean to travel through time in Spielberg's *Back to the Future*."

"No idea if I've got that much in me." Zane looked to Caesar for an answer.

He nodded. "Between you and your sister, it should be enough, but it's gonna wipe you out."

A silver, convertible Cadillac came speeding around the corner, fishtailing, and narrowly avoided a collision with Caesar's cab; the dust cloud settled and then the driver then floored it and spun out a 360-degree revolution three times in the street. It came to a stop, nose to nose with the Studebaker. The convertible idled and the drive killed the engine, the motor making clicking sounds as the engine settled.

The demon that attacked Zane and Rainn outside the Bleu Bugle stepped out of the car, and approached Zane.

"You! In my car! Now! You, too, girly!" he barked at Rainn.

"They're not going anywhere with you," Caesar cut in.

"Oh, I think they will," said a dark voice from across the street.

Doyle was standing on the sidewalk outside The Blue Bugle. "I've got your mother with me."

"No, you don't. She's right here!" Rainn shouted and turned to look at Belle. Belle was nowhere in sight.

"I'm sorry, my love," Belle murmured from the Cadillac's open backseat window.

The demon moved in a blur of speed, opened the car door, and pulled Belle out, a large Bowie knife held to Belle's throat.

"Get in. Now!" ordered Doyle.

Rainn and Zane got into the Cadillac.

Inside, a ten-by-ten square room was empty of furnishings save for a small oak barrel where a fat candle burned, wet wax dripping down its side and pooling around a cracked dish; Zane and Rainn sat on the floor, side by side, leaning against the cold stone wall.

"Ah, I see you're enjoying your free room and board," Doyle said in a soft voice. "Nice and quiet up here, yes? You've had plenty of time to rest and restore."

Doyle's muddy red pupils had a faint glow, just enough to cast light and shadow around his nose; he moved across the room as quickly as a vampire after a feeding. He placed a long-fingered hand on Rainn's shoulder and met her gaze. His red pupils' glow brightened for a second, then dimmed.

"It's time to release your spooled epi energy, both of you! I've got Belle in another chamber." He looked to his watchless wrist. "She's scheduled for a hanging," he said. "Haven't had a good hanging in months."

Zane and Rainn returned their attention to the floor, shoulders slumped. "What's with the grim mood, my twin twits? Or, I know: you'd rather have a much less painless finale: the guillotine, yes?" Doyle clapped his hands together. He pulled a pewter coffee mug from a pocket. "Release your epi vitality into the mug. Then seal it with this." He held up a lid. "Zane, you're first."

Zane hung his head between his knees, said to the stone floor,

"Oops. Must've left it in my other body," spoke Rainn from inside Zane's body. "We've done a lot of possessions lately and, well, surely you understand. I don't have it on me. Sorry, Alfredo," Zane jeered. "I'll have to get to you another time."

"It's Alfred."

"Whatever you say, Alfredo."

Doyle's expression remained emotionless until the corners of his lips curled, smiling like Evil incarnate: his fleshy facial features altering to a gray-boned skeleton. Bits of mold grew on a crack in his skull. Doyle pocketed the mug and retrieved something else from a jacket pocket.

He began twirling a crystal-clear cube that hovered over his palm. Each side of the cube held a different photograph of the Moss family. One was a group shot with various images of Zane and Rainn when they were nine years old.

Zane and Rainn recognized the picture cube. Zane had kept it in his bedroom at home. "Where'd you get that?" he demanded. "It's mine."

"Oh, got your interest now. This cube is not really here. Sleight of hand, sleight of mind, my psychic energy is psilocybin that is slaying your fragile little brains, you twits. You are not really seeing the cube of family photos because your family is dead. Gone. But fear not, you will be dead with them soon enough!"

"That's mine!" Zane's mind blurted out from the mouth of Rainn.

Doyle spoke in a casual, even tone: "My golem found it in your bedroom. If you didn't want it found, you should have locked it away somewhere, but it's useful. The Moss family is extinct. You're not really seeing this cube."

"Whatever," replied the consciousness of Rainn from inside Zane's body. "Don't even know what you're talking about. Don't care. I see you're quick with your hands, dead man. Not impressed." Rainn swallowed and Zane's Adam's apple bobbed like a leaky helium balloon.

"You're young. Just a boy, or just a girl," Doyle remarked, but your energy potential is rare, Zane, and you need me to navigate your explosive power." Doyle looked from Zane to Rainn and back again.

"I'm not a boy, and I'm eighteen. Going on eight-hundred. I've lived and died," Rainn said from Zane's body, with a sharp edge to her tone. "I've seen darkness. I've seen light. I've felt pain. I felt sorrow. I was an elf in a past life. And I'm alive today. But I just got these new threads, you see. My brother and I—we're interchangeable." Rainn drew a hand up and down the length of her torso, like a game show model advertising her clothing.

Even as the mind of Rainn said this through Zane's mouth, she wondered if Zane had talked to Doyle about their body swapping. Did Zane have private conversations with Al? Did it matter? Rainn decided to go along with Zane.

"Traveling through that theatrical portal," Rainn added, "allowed me time to stop at the Akashic Records Warehouse and pick up a loaner body, but they didn't have one in my size," she lied. "So, Zane and I swapped. Cool, huh? Still working out the kinks, but we've learned to alter our appearance. Just like you, Alfredo."

"In more ways than you know," Zane said. "In fact, how can you know which one is Zane and which one is Rainn?" He laughed, uncertain how Doyle would take this.

Doyle's eyes widened with staged curiosity. Was he impressed, or concerned? The twins didn't know.

Zane was about to boast further when Doyle said, "Don't try to mesmerize me with your silly games. If you're residing in another body, you'll be stuck there for some time. Now, on to more pressing matters. What about the murder?"

The murder? What murder? Zane wondered from the body of Rainn.

"All taken care of," Zane responded with assurance. Rainn's eyes stared at the photo cube on the table. She needed that cube.

Doyle smirked. "There's more going on here than either of you realize." He folded his arms across his chest. "Everything that is happening to you right now, is only happening because you believe it is."

The twins studied Doyle's wrinkled jawline. His skull was slowly being taken over by flesh. A slow worm of skin crawled over his cracked, graying skull; his face soon transformed to human skin, aged by too much sun, wrinkled beyond time.

Doing her best to ignore Doyle's metamorphosis, but it was still a little upsetting, she asked, "What's that supposed to mean?"

"Ahhhh, glad you asked." Doyle raised a single fleshy digit and flipped them off. "Whatever you think it means."

Doyle then began twirling the photo cube on the tip of his middle finger, where it spun faster and faster, a blur of sparkly colors and shadows.

Zane returned his gaze to Doyle's magnetic stare.

"You're really no help to me," Zane's mind said through Rainn's mouth. "We had a deal. Murder's complete. I did it. I, Zane, did it!" Zane's mind claimed through Rainn's mouth, "and you said you'd set us free."

The mind of Rainn wondered: *Murder? You murdered someone, Zane?*

"But I'm not here." Doyle grinned, revealing cracked teeth. "Surely you understand that: What I believe is happening right now is not what you two envision. These lives you think you're living is a façade, an act of my unbridled thieving magic. I've done all this to you." He snatched the spinning cube off his finger and pocketed it. "I've done it for you, two. Call me: the Kind Thief." Confused and caught off-guard, Rainn wondered if her brother had been spelled. Did he really murder someone? If so, now she was trapped in the body of a murderer. Not good. Not good at all.

"Oh, this can't be happening," Zane voiced through the mouth of Rainn.

"I'm only here talking to you because you both think I'm here. Do you even know where you are?" Doyle laughed.

Rainn and Zane looked at one another. As far as they knew, they were in some suburb of Purgatory Heights, near Downstate. Rainn removed her eyes from Doyle and responded, "I'm in Enchanted Wood with my brother. But since I'm in Rainn's body, you need to remember that Zane," Rainn's hand pointed at Zane, "yes, Zane is completing a contract. We will return to our true bodies in time."

"Are you going to return to your original bodies, though?" Doyle laughed again.

Rainn, in Zane's body, overcome by stress, felt that fuzzy déjà vu sensation cripple her thoughts. It was a precursor to an epileptic convulsion. A seizure was about to arrive. She dove at her brother, tackling him to the ground.

Then both twins simultaneously were overrun by an epileptic convulsion. Everything went dark…

The door of a tall log cabin swung open. A pool of warm, welcoming yellow light spilled across the dark forest, illuminating a long rectangle of the yard.

"Hello out there!" hollered a friendly voice.

Zane and Rainn lay tangled atop one another in some strange wrestling pose. Zane removed his arm-bar chokehold, and rolled off his sister.

"Damn it all!" muttered the mind of Zane through Rainn's mouth, "I'm still possessing you."

Zane sat up on his knees, hands on thighs, breathing heavily. "I'm not liking it any more than you, but we must keep our possessed identities secret. No more blathering on about psychic body swapping."

They looked around. No sight of Doyle.

"I agree. Mum's the word."

A lovely young elf, close to five feet tall, stood in the doorway of a cabin, rocking back and forth on her heels. Her silky hair was not quite blonde and not quite white; it was more the color of muted honey. Locks of hair hung down her back in ringlets. She wore a mint gown stitched with an assortment of tiny snowy moons.

She smiled, revealing shiny white teeth. "Hello, you must be the duo I've been awaiting. Do come out of the dewy night air." "Who is it?" called a familiar voice from inside the cabin.

Trixie the puppet poked her head out the doorway leaning a hand against the door frame, one little foot crossed over the other.

Zane and Rainn, trying to come to grips with what had just transpired, both assumed they had just taken another epi ride. Zane nodded to the elf. "Be right there." He whispered to Rainn, "Sister, did you just seize us away from Doyle's clutches, or did I?"

"It was me, brother," she replied in a hush. "It was all adrenaline and reflexes, but I'm still getting used to possessing your body. You must've come with me on the epi ride, since we were holding each other when it happened. Not sure if it was me having a seizure since I'm possessing your body or if it was your body that seized." She shrugged. "But I felt its electric darkness flow through me. Seizure energy has a mind all its own, isn't it funny…? And, don't say anything to Trixie. I'm not sure I trust her, "Rainn added. "She's possessed, too."

"I mean, we're possessing each other, and now we both have this epileptic gift, right," Zane said from the mouth of Rainn.

"Yeah, it's hilarious," replied Rainn dryly.

"Please, come in," repeated the elf. "Got someone inside who's dying to see you," she hollered over her shoulder and disappeared inside.

Zane and Rainn, both still reeling from their rapid-fire electric exit, all cast by Rainn, looked at one another questioningly. Neither of them liked the elf's word choice: 'dying to see you.' "What do you think?" Rainn asked her brother.

"Don't think we have a choice. Let's check it out. I'm starving."

The elf returned to the door. "Please, we're friends here, and it's best you get indoors. It's dangerous out there at night. Wolf packs have been prowling my neighborhood the past few weeks."

A toddler elf, maybe three years old, stood in the doorway dressed in bright blue knickers, barefoot. It disappeared into the house only to come rocketing between the legs of the tall elf, somersaulting across the grass, all the while being guided by a leashed dwarf dragon tugging the toddler elf deeper into the yard.

The elf, with her back to Zane and Rainn, stood in the yard, cucumber calm, as the dwarf dragon paced back and forth, sniffing the ground, and lifting its colorfully spiked tail, relieved itself.

"Just taking care of business, eh," Zane said by way of greeting. "What's your name?"

"Friends call me 'Honey,'" said the toddler elf.

"Hi Honey, I'm…Zane, and this is my sister, Rainn."

The elf named Honey jabbed a finger at the dragon. The dwarf dragon took flight and returned into the cabin with Honey holding the lengthy leash one-handed. Like a water-skier, Honey slalomed through the yard, bunny hopped the three front steps, and disappeared inside.

A loud CRASH was followed by "Whoops!" from the tiny elf.

Zane and Rainn stood in the foyer watching Honey with a 'Who, me?' expression staring at the shattered vase and a half dozen daisies spread across the puddled floor.

Zane's attentive eyes on the destroyed vase suddenly flipped upright. He grinned from ear to ear; Belle Gaia appeared from the kitchen.

She wrapped Rainn and then Zane in a big hug.

"Oh, it's lovely to see you got clear from Doyle's clutches," she said. "He's always in such a dreadful mood. Hey, Holly, I see she's had another incident," Belle shouted over her shoulder.

The tall elf stepped in behind Belle. "Oh, Tank. you'll be fixing that table, my dear little miscreant."

Zane looked at Rainn and said, "Tank?"

"Yep," said the elf named Holly. "My daughter's named Tank, and now you understand why. She's a wise one filled with wonderful magical attributes. She's just a bit…. destructive."

Rainn smiled and crouched to the little elf's level. "Hi, Tank," she said. "Thought you said your name was Honey."

"No. It's Tank, but I don't tell my name to strangers."

"Oh, these are not strangers," Belle added with a lovely ring to her tone. "Rainn is my daughter from a past life and this is her brother, Zane, from her current Earth life. They're interdimensional travelers."

"Oh, joy," Tank replied in a flat tone. "Yippie." She rolled her eyes and began to sweep up her mess with a whisk broom.

"Zane, Rainn, meet Holly, my sister from the same Mister. She's a spellfarmer, like me. Maybe the only Speller this side of the forest that can help remove possession viruses."

"Oh, that's about the best news I've heard!" Rainn said, and grinned. Zane nodded in agreement.

Belle continued: "I heard what was going on with you two back at the Bleu Bugle, but I couldn't get my spelling recipes to clear the virus. Strange hex. A code I couldn't crack, plus, the intrusion of dear old Doyle Alfred didn't help the situation."

She placed an arm around Holly's waist. "We're here to help. You can trust Holly. Oh, I've got something else to share, but I'd rather Holly get to work on you two and see if she can de-possess the hex spell. Just remember, Holly, Zane is a pure-blooded Earthling. Rainn's got elfin in her, and Rainn's running two lifelines simultaneously: her past life with me and her current life thread on Earth."

"Busy girl. Busy, busy, busy." Holly smiled a soft pillow grin at Rainn.

Tank appeared at the doorway with her leashed pet dragon. The dragon padded over to Zane, gave him a sniff, and glanced at him through snake-slit golden-green pupils. Its shiny scales glistened in an overhead oil lamplight, a checkerboard blend of dusty gold and burnt orange.

Bird songs chirped away, sounding like the birds were singing inside the cabin where a fire crackled in hearth. The singing had

Zane's ears in telescope-mode, tuning in to the chatter. "Something feels a little off here," he said. "Anyone else feel it?"

Belle leaned in and whispered to Zane. "Holly's already spooling up her spell. Both of you take a seat. Relax" Zane and Rainn sat on a pillow in front of the fire.

"Just play nice," Tank said to her dragon. Puhleeze! I want to stay and watch Holly in action."

The dwarf dragon looked at her. "You're the clumsy one."

She stroked the dragon's long, sleek neck. "No acting out, okay," Tank added as if not hearing the dragon. "Give 'er a chance to weave out a spell."

The checkered dragon exhaled a strand of purple smoke rings from one nostril.

Boots clomped across the kitchen floor. Edge appeared in the doorway, one foot flopped over the other, munching on a piece of carrot cake. He swallowed the rest of the cake, and wiped his fingers on a cloth.

"Everything's good on my end, Holly. Your recipe spell has me vibrating. Tasty cake, too."

Edge ruffled Tank's hair. "Greetings, my fair princess! Haven't heard any crashing and banging in the last five minutes. Nice going. Keep it up," he said in a jolly voice and sat down on a floor pillow, closing his eyes.

Tank feigned bashfulness, batting her eyes playfully. "Oh, I'm not a princess. I'm—"

"Talking about your dragon," Edge cut in dryly with eyes shut.

"Oh, of course you are!" Tank pivoted away from Edge, offered a playful curtsey, and led her dragon into the kitchen. Zane opened his eyes, surprised that Edge was in such a jovial mood, considering the circumstances, then closed them and was pulled back into his meditative vibe.

Edge leaned in for a closer look at the dragon, pulled a monocle from a chain in his breast pocket, and placed a wooden tongue depressor on the dragon's forked tongue. "Say, ahh!"

The dragon's head remained steady; its long tail coiling around Edge's leg.

"Oh, she'll be fine. I'll give her a chunk of ginger root to eat. The heat from the ginger warms up her fiery belly and wards off illness." Tank grinned a toothy grin. "You've got enough flaming bubbles in you, don't ya, girl?

The dragon blinked.

"She's really a lovable dragon," affirmed Tank, and raised her arms. Everyone else, seated in silence on cushions, waiting for a moment to venture into the halls of meditative silence, gazed at her as Tank proclaimed to everyone, as if they were concerned with her *little-me* universe: "My dragon's feeling a little under the weather, is all. Unable to spark much flame. May be swollen lymph nodes. Not sure. I received a referral from a fellow speller."

Belle, with hands resting on knees, quietly said, "I think proper introductions are in order before we meditate. Zane, Rainn, meet Dr. Anna Tank, an Enchanted Wood certified speller. She's one of us. She likes to go incognito."

Zane and Rainn stared at the toddler elf with wonder and surprise.

"Oh, this is good. So good!" Zane and Rainn chorused.

"I had no idea," Zane added.

Belle spoke up: "I was going to save her introduction for later, but just know that we've gathered a strong team of healers here for both of you. We need you two to return to your own bodies, so please continue to soak it all in. Allow your thoughts, your pulse, and your soul to reconnect with the séance. Just breathe with us, accept us as healers, and trust in the process."

The mind of Zane in Rainn's body, quite suddenly wondered where he was.

"Can I ask something before we continue?" Rainn asked. "I feel welcome here in Holly's home. And safe. But where are we? It'll set my mind and heart at ease and help me connect with the séance vibe we're about to tune into."

"Enchanted Wood, Eastern Rim," replied Belle. "A small camp about twenty miles from Enchanted Wood proper. Only a few miles from a portal to Purgatory Heights. That was your epi entry point—the portal hole bringing you out of Purgatory Heights. I'm just glad you were able to follow my psychic nudging."

Rainn and Zane nodded and returned to their quiet, meditations.

Dr. Tank then stood behind Zane and Edge and placed one hand on each of their heads. The tiny elfin doctor closed her eyes, joining in the séance.

The dragon smacked its plated tail excitedly on the hardwood floor, tail unrolling to a full ten feet.

"Very flexible dragon," Edge said in a calm voice, appearing not the slightest bit surprised as the dragon then uncoiled its neck, extending it like a snake.

Holly, with eyes closed, sang out in a soft tone: "Everything's lining up." She displayed a toothy grin of approval, radiant eyes open to the multiverse, her dark, savage eyebrows contrasting with her honey hair. She continued, "Stay here, in our séance Center. Your sphere of existence is everyone's center, your nucleus of inner calm. Relax the mind. All of us are fused as One."

A moment of silence took up all the space in the air. It was almost suffocating.

Dr. Tank's eyes sparkled, as did her fingers; she waved her dancing digits over Zane and Rainn's head. Trails of lime-green electric mist fizzled from her fingertips.

Dr. Tank called out: "Bridge a path of travel for Zane and Rainn Moss, our two lost souls. Return them, Lunar Witches, to the home of their proper flesh-born body, the space where they reside."

She muttered other incantations and blew a kiss at the dragon.

Some unseen force jolted the now thickening cabin air.

Zane and Rainn both shuddered. Dr. Tank's eyes focused on the twins. "Use my ooze, my salve of reanimation of soul."

Zane blinked. Said, "I feel…safe." Rainn nodded in affirmation, but the jury was still out on the dragon.

The dragon then blew a chain of flaming bubbles from its mouth. The bubbly chain hovered over Zane and Rainn. The dwarf dragon moved with asp-like dexterity and quickness. The tip of its spiked tail lashed at the bubbles, popped them, one at a time, in rapid-fire succession. The flaming vapory mist from the broken bubbles showered Rainn and Zane's head. Twin bodies began to quake gently, and both faded into mist. Gone.

Zane and Rainn woke up lying on a blanket of spongy redwood needles on the forest floor.

Zane yawned and looked around. "Whoa! Must've drifted off…. oh, man. This is good!" He sat up and looked at his hands. "I'm back. Back in my body. We did it. Dr. Tank did it! We did it!" He looked at a redwood, and turned his head, as if waiting for the tree to say something. "Where the hell are we?" he asked the tree.

Rainn smiled and studied her arm. "Oh, I missed me!" She peppered her arm in kisses. "You can keep your masculine vibes and your body, brother. It's all you."

"Did we seize our way here? If so, we did it without a portal," said Zane. Rainn and Zane each felt a tingling buzz at their temples. "Just a sec," Zane said in a hush. "Someone's trying to reach me."

"Me, too."

They both heard the familiar voice in their heads, a voice they now realized how much they missed hearing: Dayne Moss, their father.

Their dad, via a PMS Group call, began speaking in their mind with telepathic clarity: *Hey, you two. It's Dad. Hope you are well. Can you hear me?*

Zane and Rainn, both shocked to hear their dad using PMS, stared at each other.

Dad? Rainn said, *It's amazing to hear from you, but how'd you… how'd you get—I mean, wow, you're communicating psychically. Are you a telepath, too?*

Zane added, *Dad, I missed you! This is crazy cool. I had no idea*, he said excitedly and then, in a neutral tone, asked: *What's going on with Mom?*

I'll get to all that, Dayne said. *Heard about some of your travels. Gotten into a few mix-ups, have you?* He burbled out a laugh. *I'm catching a flight back to the States. I know you're far from home, but tell me, how are you?*

The twins remained quiet.

Dayne said, *Oh, this is my first time hosting a group psychic chat, and you are two of the most important beings in my life. Are you in Enchanted Wood?*

Zane opened his mouth. Rainn shook her head in curious disbelief. How did he know this? What, exactly, did their dad know?

We're in a forest, Rainn said. *We think we're still in Enchanted Wood. Lots to share, Dad. Lots.*

Excellent. Glad you two are alive and, by the sound of it, you are both well, yes?

All things considered, yeah, I guess, Zane said and gave Rainn a nudge.

Zane and Rainn both sensed a stress-free tone in their dad, and they hoped that there was good news regarding their mom.

What's going on with Mom? Zane asked again.

I'll give you details soon. Please get to Old Atlantis Bay. You'll be able to catch a ride back to Earth.

What? Atlantis Bay? Where's that? A ride with who? A portal? Where are you, Dad?

CLICK. Telepathic line went dead.

An automated voice came on the line: *Your telepath has been disrupted. Line terminated. Please try your call again later. To return to the previous menu, please say, 'One, two, buckle my psychic shoe.'*

Rainn and Zane stood outside on the crest of a hill, breezes swirling up tiny tornados in the grasses and wildflowers— wildflowers looking like a colorful-hatted crowd of people dancing. The early morning sun rising over the watery horizon filled the Bay with an orange rippling glow.

They followed a single-track trail down a steep slope that led to a natural stone staircase of shale stairs bordered by tall squarish bushes.

Zane pointed to a stubby wooden sign. The paint-peeled white sign read: Old Atlantis Bay. Telepaths only. Dangerous mind currents. Beware of psychic tide!

"Looks like we made it." Rainn said to her brother "I'm excited to see Dad."

"Me too. There, you see that big ship?"

"Yeah. So?"

A large ship anchored in the middle of the bay was facing a windblown beach lined with cabins and shops.

"We're here, but Dad didn't tell us what to do. What do you think he knows about Old Atlantis Bay?" Rainn asked.

A car horn honked. There, driving along the summit they just descended, a red Studebaker was cruising northbound, leaving a dust cloud in its wake. The cab stopped. Caesar stepped, studying the beach.

"Caesar!" Zane hollered and waved.

Caesar's thunderous voice called out, "Come on, kids! Time's a wasting." He climbed back into the cab, hairy arm hanging out the window, smoke curling out his mouth as he tapped his cigar against the side-view mirror.

The twins made their way back up the shale staircase, wind sending Rainn's long bangs snapping in front of her face.

"Hi, Caesar!" Rainn said with Zane followed close behind. "Surprised to see you here."

Caesar reached for something on the seat and underhanded it to her: a bag of granola. "I've got some peanut butter protein sticks and water, too. Come on, get in."

Caesar handed each of them a strip of jerky.

"Oh, thanks," Zane said, biting into the jerky. "Tastes like honey and peanuts and, oh, is that lime?"

"High protein. Meatless stuff. Figured you humans would like it. Need to keep your body fueled up."

Rainn, while munching on honey-glazed granola, said, "The Bay. That's a big body of water. Does it channel to a bigger body of water?"

"Yep. That's what bays do. Old Atlantis Bay leads to a shipping port a few miles west. That's where we're headed. He tossed a canteen to Rainn. "Thought I had water, but this Gunpowder Green tea will have to do."

The twins shared sips of the cold, refreshing drink.

Caesar drove along the summit at a snail's pace and ventured into a heavily wooded section where the road snaked back and forth. Down, down, down they traversed.

"What is this place? Our dad told us to come here." Rainn then began to explain their surprise to hear their dad contacting them via PMS, and that he knew about Enchanted Wood.

"Oh, I got word from Belle, too," Caesar said. "she said to be careful and look out for Doyle. Also, I spoke to Dayne Moss." Zane and Rainn stopped chewing.

"You spoke to our dad?"

"Your father's a good man."

"You know him?"

He nodded. "He helped me coordinate this meeting here at the Bay. You're going back to Earth. Just need to get you on a portal ship home."

"Great news…but I'm still confused." Zane gave Rainn a look, seeking validation. He bit off another chunk of jerky. "Yep. Your dad was just checking in on the two of you." "Did he say anything about our mom?" Rainn asked.

"Nope. Left me a message, though. It was brief. Not many unsolicited calls get through to my business line." Caesar, now driving down at sea level on a dirt road, came to a clearing in the woods. The beach. Homes were stacked along the cliff face of this coastal village.

"Is this Old Atlantis Bay?" Zane asked, sounding amazed.

"Yep. It's a portal village. Ships here can travel to interdimensional locations."

"Ah! That's why Dad said to catch a ride here."

"So, tell me, Rainn," Caesar asked, "how long have you been an epi? The reason I ask is: my queue shows your brother has the epi gift, but it didn't display your magical disability on my chart."

"Not sure. I'm new to this stuff. But it works, I kid you not." She didn't want to bring up their possession glitch. Not yet. She was not sure if possessing Zane had anything to do with her gaining access to this epi energy.

"Oh, you don't need to tell me."

But Rainn went ahead and told him anyway: "Up until a short time ago, all I knew how to do was speak to fae telepathically. Esmeralda was my main contact with inhabitants of Enchanted Wood. I believe in magic and other weird stuff, but I didn't realize I had this epi gift until recently."

The cabbie drove past a row of small huts with clay rooftops that butted up to a steep cliff.

"I must say, Enchanted Wood is cool," Rainn continued. "I prefer the straight-fire stuff. Just saying. Esmeralda told me about

Zane's magical disability, but I didn't believe it, not at first. Never saw him black out or convulse or anything like that. Now, I've got the bug, the same bug he has." She jabbed a thumb at Zane. "Man, I feel energized!"

"You sure are talkative," Zane shook his head.

"I'm still trying to figure out what's going on. With Dad and Mom, and everything." Rainn took a second to exhale.

"We're both epis," Zane said.

"Thanks, Captain Obvious," grumbled Caesar. "I recommend you two steer clear of too many more crash landings. I don't want to have to keep changing my schedule to pick you up and guide you to your destination. But I owed your Pops a favor."

"What favor?" Zane asked, wondering, like his sister, how involved Dayne Moss was in all this.

Caesar pulled to a stop in a small parking lot, vacant save for two pickup trucks loaded with lumber. The cabbie reached into his shirt pocket. "You'll need these." He handed each of them a ticket labeled Old Atlantis Bay Boarding Pass. Ship Flight 711.

"So, this boat'll take us back to Earth?"

Caesar nodded. "That's the plan."

He parked in a lot overlooking a pier and the Bay, and pointed a meaty finger at a seemingly endless row of ships docked at the harbor. Shops and restaurants lined the harbor. Lots of shoppers and travelers were filling the harbor.

"Which boat do we take?" Zane asked while marveling at all the artists and musicians out adding colorful, charismatic life to this active beach scene

A young man standing atop an oak barrel was performing to a crowd of onlookers. He marionetting two puppets, one in each hand. Children giggled and pointed at the lifelike puppets.

Two pretty ladies danced on the beach to music coming from musicians: two trolls playing the flute, a tattooed elf with a

Mohawk banging away at a bongo, and a young man, possibly human, strummed away at his Spanish guitar—a bouncy acoustic vibe.

The dancers wore white and black face-paint and hula skirts. They were twirling and shaking their hips to the cheering crowd.

"So, where are we going?" Rainn asked Caesar.

"I really think we should give Dad a call." Zane took another pull from his canteen of gunpowder green tea.

Something PINGED in Rainn's pocket. She had all but forgotten about her cell phone. "Oh, my god, it's working. I mean, the battery's been dead since we arrived. Not sure what activated it." She pressed the screen of her phone, but it remained dark; none of the buttons worked.

She waved her cell phone uselessly in the air. "No reception here, but I'm sure a message came through. I heard it. What's that thing you're waving around?" Caesar said.

She told him.

"You Earthlings have odd contraptions."

She tried to restart the cellphone, but it would not respond.

Eventually, Caesar, appearing bored, asked "Have you PMSed?"

"With my dad?" Rainn asked while fiddling with her phone. "Not yet. Figured he couldn't, well…"

"Oh, he's able," Caesar said. "He called *you*." He looked at her in disbelief. "Rainn, why don't you sit in that bucket of sunshine over there and give it a whirl. Reception should be good here at the Bay. But don't waste too much time. You need to get on that ship."

"Good cell reception?"

Caesar stared at her unblinkingly. "PMS."

She sensed his distaste at her statement and explained that she and her brother had possessed each other, leaving her confused.

"Never heard of such confusion over a body-swapping psychic incident. You sure it's not just you being human?"

"The reason I didn't try to PMS my dad is I didn't think he could accept my calls."

Caesar said nothing, clicking a button on his dashboard and the taxi's back doors opened.

They thanked Caesar for the food and tickets.

"Just get on that ship. Pronto!" Caesar commanded. "This is a water port. Portal village. You can telepath to various locations in a variety of dimensions, and don't get lost on the ship." He laughed.

Zane and Rainn were uncertain what was funny. "Which ship is ours?"

"It is the largest ship in the harbor," Caesar pointed. "That big blue and white one. See the tall mast and sails with dragon wings?"

They walked slowly toward the shoreline. Caesar stepped out of his cab, drew on his unlit cigar, and followed them toward the pier.

Rainn turned to face Caesar. "Wait. Let me try and contact Dad before we get on that ship."

"Good idea, but make it quick."

"When does the ship…take off?"

"In about an hour and a half," Caesar confirmed.

Two fishermen walked past them, each carrying a short, stubby fishing pole and a net of glowing fabric.

Rainn drifted away from the busy pier and toward the cliffside, and walked in little circles around matted-down grasses, like a cat mapping out its sleeping den, and sat cross-legged.

"This is a great spot. Looks like it's been used a lot." She waved at Caesar.

"Dragons mate here."

Caesar and Zane stopped ten paces from her.

"Oh…. Kay. How about unicorns?" Rainn asked.

"No solo-horned horses, but plenty of flying lizards. Dragonelles, faeries, and whatnot." Caesar took a long, slow inhale of the salty air.

Now he was singing her song, and she wanted to hear more.

"Bring it!" she said with a smile. "You serious about dragons mating?"

"Haven't dated any, if that's what you mean." He bit off the tip of his cigar. "Focus, my young ones. Focus!" Caesar urged. "Tap into dear old dad."

"Are you going to leave us again?" Rainn asked. "You know, until now, I thought you were just a big grumpy old hoot of a man, but now, well, thanks for everything!" Rainn, feeling mesmerized by the energy of this port, allowed her mind to clear and created a dance floor for her PMS to channel up, as it were.

"You're feeling the phantasmal energy in the air here. Old Atlantis Bay is a telepather's dream. Just focus, girl. Are you as ADHD as your brother?"

"Hey," Zane said with a grin. "No one's as ADHD as me. I own that. Is that vendor over there selling licorice jumping rope? What's everyone fishing for?" He pointed to a beach peopled with fishermen.

"Not fish. They're fishing for old souls. Trying to reconnect with old mates," Caesar said in a hush and then put a finger to his lips, requesting silence for Rainn to focus.

With eyes closed, seated cross-legged, she spooled her mind to the magnetic telepathic pull of Old Atlantis Bay; it drew her deeper into her subconscious arena, wrapping her thought-thread around her mental spool and drawing her closer to Universal Mother Energy. The port air grounded her and made her feel safe, and floaty.

She opened her eyes and then her mouth, as if to speak, but Caesar had already returned to his cab. Zane was watching fishermen cast energy lines into the water. Two young elves darted toward a tree near Caesar's cab. They marched and laughed through the grass and climbed a thick, wide-bellied oak, scaling it with ease, bare feet finding nooks and knobs, and disappeared into the thick leafy treetop.

Rainn sat in silence for a length of time, trying but unable to send out a PMS to her dad. She got to her feet, unsure how much time had passed, but then plopped her butt onto the grass again and closed her eyes.

A gentle tapping came at her Third Eye. She remained quiet, listening with her meditative mind.

A little voice in her head whispered, "Let go. Let it grow. Believe."

She inhaled slow and deep, a crescent smile curving her lips.

The whispering voice spoke louder: *Rainn? You there? Rainn?*

The PMS caller did not sound familiar to Rainn.

A silvery sensation drifted across her scalp, welcoming her in. She sank deeper into silken silence. A vision took shape in her mind: a woman dressed in moon-colored silk walked along a beach, then turned, and stared at Rainn from the shoreline of Old Atlantis Bay. It was her mom.

Yes! Rainn cried delightedly. *Hi, Mom! I love you*! Mom!

Her mom was here in her heart, in the very essence of her being; skirt billowing outward, a cloud of energy illuminated by torches burning on cabin porches, windowsills filled with potted orange hibiscus ringed in yellow daisies and daffodils.

Rainn? Rainn?

Yes? she replied in her meditative slumber. *I see you, mom! I hear you!*

Her mom crept closer, her gown's moon fabric billowing in the breezes. She waved at Rainn and then disappeared inside a tavern.

Rainn's vision of the beachside tavern faded. Bummer! She was having a beautiful experience: a psychic story had played out for her, but was it merely a telepathic hallucination? She didn't think so.

A new tapping came to her temple.

Hello? Rainn said.

Remember to focus on your brother.

What? Who's this? The voice was masculine. *If you please, allow me to channel back into that lovely beach. I want to talk to Mom.*

The psychic solicitor said nothing.

I'd like to connect with my mom, she repeated. *Who is this? Why're you interrupting?*

Is this our first fight? said the psychic caller.

She now recognized the soft, honeyed voice.

Reese? she called out.

My sensory perception cued into your wanderings. How are you, my sweet little morning flower of sunshine? Now, get on that ship.

A clicking sound in her head was followed by the sound of a bird chirping.

She kept her eyes closed; shivers rolled through the hills and valleys of her flesh and splashed across her face. She wondered why Reese called her 'my sweet little morning flower of sunshine.' She liked it but wanted to return to the ethereal beach scene and find her mom.

"Focus, Rainn. Focus," she whispered to herself. The grasses tickled her legs. She tapped her temple and called out: *Mom? Mom? You there? It's your daughter. It's me, Rainn.*

No reply.

"Rainn! Rainn!" hollered Zane.

She opened her eyes and spotted him standing on the ship's dock.

"Come on!" Zane shouted. "Time to go."

She walked with Zane past the Old Atlantis Tavern and stepped onto the pier. Alternating black oak and teak floorboards warmed her sneakered feet and the floorboards began to hum, buzzing with energy. Ropes anchoring other boats to their slip pulsated, slithering like live snakes.

Rainn stared out into the pier's endlessness, disappearing into the watery horizon. Ships on both sides of the pier filled every slip.

A tall black transport with white sails captured her attention. A husky voice called out, "Hey, you! Beauty queen! Can I offer you dinner?"

She looked around the ship, but didn't see anyone.

"No. Up here."

There, high in a crow's nest, a bearded bald man was scaling down the rope ladder. Soft leather boots hit the floor with a gentle thud. He studied her and scratched his chin, hand disappearing into the bushel of his beard.

She spotted Zane ten yards ahead of her, motioning toward their boat.

"Meet me inside," shouted the man now on the ship's deck. "We offer a variety of food and drink to all visitors. Surely you need to eat before you travel, yes?" He dusted off his worn trousers and disappeared through swinging wooden doors.

Rainn was curious about this bearded man had to share, and she climbed onto his vessel. She inhaled the sugary scent of hibiscus, honeydew, and lemon coming from inside the swinging doors. "Rainn? Rainn? "she heard her brother calling out for her.

Rainn brushed him off, mesmerized. *I've got time to check this out.*

She made her way onto the ship and down a flight of stairs and below deck. A barkeep was wiping a mug and humming, towel draped over his shoulder. More humming echoed off the walls of this small one-room tavern. She spotted a familiar faerie sitting atop a pyramid of neatly stacked upside-down shot glasses.

"Hey!" Rainn said excitedly. "Esmeralda! What're you doing here?"

Esmeralda whispered something to a tree fae sitting in a shot glass. The tree fae was dressed in clothing made of flower petals and ferns stitched with clouds and sunshine, and a rope belt with a silvery dewdrop belt buckle cinched around her waist.

A voice entertained Rainn's mind: *Hi, Rainn. Esmeralda here. Let's telepath. Safer that way. Lots of unseen ears and minds might be listening to us here at the Old Atlantis Bay Portal.*

Rainn responded with ease: *Sure. Who's the fae you're with? Some guy told me you had food in here, but I need to catch a different boat with Zane.*

He's further up the pier. You'd best be going. Remember Madge and Ick? Those twin redwoods are magic.

Hearing those words made her beam with delight. *Right. I'm off.*

Rainn heard a clicking sound, and another voice entered the PMS conversation. *You're no fae. What're you doing on this PMS channel? This ship is are not for wingless.*

I've got a boarding pass. I'm going with my brother.

Not on this ship.

Oh, sorry. You're right. Stepped aboard the wrong ship. I'm out of here.

What're the travelers' names?

Why was this PMS caller continuing the conversation? She needed to go.

Zane Moss and Rainn Moss, Rainn told her.

Zane Moss? The voice of the fae shouted. *That human's trouble! He's an epi, yes? Heard everything about him. Half the forest knows about him.*

What? Now, it was Rainn's turn to be shocked.

His name's been plastered all over the psychic airways, continued the tree fae.

But he's not *trouble!* Rainn said in her brother's defense. *We've got a portal flight out of here in about fifteen minutes. We're going home.*

Esmeralda spoke up on the three-way call, *"Rainn's a good soul. Friend of mine from Earth.*

I'm sure she is, but have you told her? Said the tree fae.

Told me what? Rainn interjected.

"There's been an incident with her brother. You'll need—"

What incident, Rainn cut in. *What's going on? He's on the pier.*

There's been a killing. That brother of yours, Zane, is part of some unsettling news, continued the tree fae.

Rainn's heart sank. "Oh, my God!" she blurted out loud. Her eyes welled up and she rejoined the PMS: *What…what happened?*

His name's Zane Moss, yes? The fae repeated as if seeking confirmation. *Just want to make sure we're talking about the same criminal. He's a wanted felon.*

Rainn shook her head. No, this could not be happening. *That's a lie! He's with me.*

The PMS lost its connectivity.

Hello? Hello? Rainn shouted. *Hello? You there?*

Rainn closed her eyes. Something was buzzing at her ear. She opened her eyes to see Esmeralda perched on her shoulder.

"Oh, Esmeralda! Zane hasn't done anything wrong. There must be a mix-up, and I need to go. We need to board a portal ship. Zane's out there."

"You need to tell me everything you know about your brother," Esmeralda told her.

Rainn looked at Esmeralda. Esmeralda nodded and raised her eyebrows encouragingly.

Rainn took a mental pause, focusing on her elfin calm to steady herself.

"There's not much time! And I need to go. We both arrived in Enchanted Wood and then 383ravelled Downstate and escaped all sorts of trouble. We got boarding passes for a ship to portal us out of here. Zane's no criminal. I was just with him."

"He's wanted for murder," Esmeralda told her.

Zane stared at the tall ship with dragon sails, its topmast disappearing into the clouds. He was getting anxious to board. He looked around. Where did Rainn run off to?

A tugboat steered in front of the tall ship, flickered from three-dimensional solidity to grayish-silver transparency: a ghost ship. It disappeared into the mist

"Nice ship," Zane muttered, impressed. He then shouted, "Rainn!"

A blurry shape of red and gold spiraled high overhead, zigging, and zagging through the jammed pier. A dwarf dragon. The dragon buzzed in close to Zane and twirled around and around his head, a red tornado of energy, and then, in a snap, landed on his shoulder.

Zane recognized the dragon's signature landing. "Hey, Julius. Man, am I glad to see you," he said. "Talk about good timing. Can you help me find—"

"Where's Rainn?" Julius cut in. "You need to get on that ship."

"Right! I know. She was with me and then just disappeared."

"You twins are scheduled to depart. Best if you get on board. You cannot miss the journey! I'll go look for Rainn." Zane sighed and nodded in agreement.

At the entry point, he handed his ticket to a Longshoreman dressed in a red vest over a blue shirt. The gate agent punched his ticket with a control nipper. Zane made his way across the plank, and hopped onto the deck. A group of shipmates was busy hoisting a sail, receiving directions from a bushy-bearded man in the crow's nest.

"Starboard side. Starboard side. Just a bit more," shouted the man in the nest.

"Zane! Zane! Wait for me," shouted Rainn, appearing on the pier.

Zane turned to see Rainn running up the pier, veering around two barefoot children skipping invisible energy-rope. With a full head of steam, she bounded onto the plank bridge, but was stopped by the gate agent. Esmeralda poked her head out of Rainn's shirt pocket and then disappeared into the pocket again as Rainn's ticket was punched.

"We need to get below deck," said a panting Rainn. "Now!"

Zane, unsure where she got her information, wanted to ask why below deck, but said, "Good thing you made it. What happened to you?" he asked, sounding miffed.

"Quickly, mates! All hands and energy mates on deck!" Esmeralda called with a seafaring, swashbuckling accent.

"You two! Hold it right there," barked a gruff voice.

They turned to see a fat-cheeked man, about as wide as he was tall, glaring at them. He had sweat stains on a yellow bandana covering his bald head.

"I'll need to see your tickets." He patted his plump belly and then jabbed a fat thumb at Zane. "Come on! Ship's about to set sail. I'm the Gate Supervisor. Your boarding passes. Let's see 'em!"

They handed him their tickets.

The man had an eye patch covering the middle of his forehead: his Third Eye patch. He plopped a monocle over the patch, and scanned the barcode on the back of each ticket. The barcode, Zane now noticed, was a line of sheet music. The barcode glowed, and Beethoven's Fifth Symphony chimed to life. He tore their tickets in half, ending the symphonic tune, and handed them each half of their tickets.

"Enjoy your journey, psychic mates," he said. "Just needed to verify your tickets. We've been dealing with psychic stowaways."

Rainn and Zane, along with the pocketed Esmeralda, made their way below deck and found their tickets included access to a small compartment, small being the operative word. A single barrel sat in one corner, two hammocks were patched to the wall, a set of nylon straps, a coil of rope, rappelling gear, and two life jackets.

Zane stared at the wall. "Wonder what all that's for?"

"Hand grips, in case things get dicey while we transport out of here," Esmeralda told her. "Safety tools in case of epi turbulence or unexpected psychic tidal wave energy. You will be traveling back to the Third dimension."

"Aren't you coming?" Rainn asked, a look of concern in her eye.

"No."

Zane took a seat on a hammock, swaying gently, and then lay back in the sturdy nylon netting.

"I need both of you to listen carefully," Esmeralda went on to say, "I know you're aware of your ability to travel with your epi energy. But this ship, paired with your epi energy, allows travel into the past and even, if you become adept at your magical disability, venturing into the future dimensions and lifetimes, but please, use caution!"

"Oh, we will! We made it this far." Rainn replied.

"If you think getting lost in Enchanted Wood was easy to do, this is a whole new realm of possibilities. Mostly positive possibilities. But watch out for demons and psychic thieves. They are everywhere. That's why that gate agent double-checked your boarding passes."

She buzzed into the narrow hallway, her humming wings getting quieter, then louder as she flew back into their cabin.

"Could one of you close the door? Thank you."

Esmeralda landed on Zane's shoulder. "Both of you listen. Especially you, Zane." Zane nodded.

"I don't know if you've seen the headlines in the psychic news or any of a variety of telepathing networks, but I figured it's best if you hear it from me and your sister."

He looked from the fae to Rainn and back again. "I don't like the sound of that. What's up?"

Esmeralda told him, plain and simple: "You're wanted for murder. Did you kill anyone, recently?"

Zane's mouth hung open. "What? No way. I didn't kill anyone! What're you talking about?" he demanded and gazed out the small porthole window at the Bay. Crestfallen, he went on to say, "Not that I recall…but Alfred Grimes had me cornered and, well, I was supposed to complete a job for Alfredo. He had me sign a contract, but I didn't murder anyone, not that I recall anyway. A lot of shit has gone down. But murder? No!"

"Zane," Rainn said in a consoling tone, "I was told the same thing by a few treezers in the canopy. What really happened? I'm your sister. Just be straight with me."

His glance narrowed. "Are you serious? You think I killed someone. No way. I haven't done anything. Alfredo set me up!" He looked at Rainn with a scowl.

Esmeralda waved a finger at him. "Please! Let me finish. You haven't murdered anyone. Not yet. But it is going to happen. I spoke to Belle, and she can see into your future. The psychic press can foretell future events with near-perfect accuracy in hopes of curtailing future violence."

Zane got out of the hammock, feeling anxious. He began clasping and unclasping his hands. "That's got to be a mistake. I don't plan on murdering anyone."

"Be that as it may," Esmeralda said softly, "Here, in this realm, you are a fugitive. I recommend you take this ship back home to

Earth. You'll be safer there, for a time anyway, but eventually the authorities will hunt you down. They can travel across dimensions of space and time, just as you can." A knock came to the door.

Esmeralda put a finger to her little luscious lips and whispered to them, "Don't reveal your identity. No matter what they say." A second knock.

"Yes?" said Rainn.

"Rainn. It's your mother."

Rainn looked at Zane expectantly. She opened the door, anticipating a hug from Belle.

Rainn stopped, dead, in her tracks, staring at someone she least expected to see. Shock and concern gripped her.

The twins stared at their Earth mother, Rose Moss, standing in the hallway.

"Mom!" Rainn and Zane chorused.

"Oh, my dear sweet children," Rose crooned softly. "I'm here to let you know that I am, as you can see, alive. For the most part."

Zane and Rainn could see right through her, transparent and glowing, silvery-blue aural light surrounding her. Was she a ghost?

"But all is not well," Rose went on to say, her tone shifting to a chillier tone: "I come with a message. But first, Zane." She stared into his eyes, head tilted, looking confused. "No matter what you've done or will do, I love you. Always will."

"Mom. Oh Mom, how'd you, how'd you get here?" A hundred questions filtered through Zane.

Rose glanced down the empty corridor. "Oh, lordy me. Gotta go! My children." She took off down the hallway, high-stepping with deft athleticism, moving at a blurring speed.

Zane and Rainn watched Rose disappear before reaching the compartment door, leaving silvery-blue footprints on the floor.

"The hell?" Zane whispered.

The sound of metal chains clinked against the ship, as anchors raised and the ship set sail.

The view of the coastal village of Old Atlantis Bay had faded into the distance long ago; the high-powered psychic ship sailed over choppy surf as it headed in the direction of storm clouds on the endless horizon. Onward they sailed for 25 nautical miles, continuing at the steady clip of thirty knots.

Zane drew back a short red curtain revealing a small round porthole, his mind a blur of curiosity, frustration, angst, and worry. How did his mom show up like that? And why did she run off? Did she die and transition to the life of a phantom? Was she running from someone? He and Rainn went over the scene several times but were both at a loss.

Esmeralda spoke from the perch of Rainn's shoulder: "I know seeing your mom in that state of existence was a shock to the gonads, but you must remember this: Old Atlantis Bay is filled with spectral energies. Lots of vibrations and phantom images funnel through her twenty-four-seven. What you see can be intensified, especially to the simple human mind. No offense!"

"But I saw her," Rainn said in a hush. "She was standing right here, and then, poof, she was gone, a ghost cloud!" Rainn sighed. "Our mom—she never showed any signs of believing in phantoms and whatnot and now it looks as those she's become something she never believed in.

"She did believe in spirits," Zane offered.

"What? No."

"She liked her wine. Those spirits."

"Sure. Try to make a joke, brother, but you know it and I know it: she was purely connected to a physical, earth-based *only-things-you-touch* are real sort of existence. Seeing her like that was like watching a worm tap dance on stage. Is she really…. a ghost?"

"I've got to go now!" said the fae. "My fae hive needs me. Safe travels, you two." Esmeralda buzzed out the door. Gone.

Zane and Rainn spent the next ten minutes recalling their last conversations with their mom, then the flooring of the ship began to sway violently. The twins tumbled across the floor and smacked into the wall, the door banging open and closed, its latch not connecting. The ship, after a few minutes of this upheaval, righted itself.

 Zane shouted, "Holy guacamole! Look at that," he said and pointed out the porthole window.

The sea out the window was getting further and further away; the boat was rising, curtains of seawater dripping off the sides of this now airborne ship.

Higher and higher, the vessel climbed the sky, moving through clouds, and into a pure blue sky.

"Grab those hand straps and take a seat," Zane ordered. "We're about to depart, epi style."

Zane gripped the straps, one in each hand. He closed his eyes and tuned the channels of his epileptic mind to a déjà vu frequency. He had learned, after all his epi rides, that when he sensed déjà vu messing with his thoughts, instead of simply being overtaken by a convulsion, he could channel that déjà vu energy and use it as fuel for traveling through space. Everything around him, every sound, every object in his line of sight, every smell, was an exact replica of events that had transpired seconds ago, and was happening again. Right now!

The airborne ship was quiet, having morphed into something like a blimp. Yet, waves of epi energy surged through Zane's mind and body, rolling over him, splashing and smacking him in the mental surf, in a spiraling washing-machine cycle controlled by the convulsive undertow and riptide.

A warming sensation then rolled through him, like a blanket of warm midnight. Everything went quite quiet, calm, still. Darkness enveloped him. He blacked out....

He opened his eyes; he was lying in a bed, an unfamiliar bed. The sound of a machine said: BEEP BEEP BEEP, sunlight came streaming through a slit in a tall, curtained window. Voices could be heard from the other side of a closed door. His room was in semi-darkness. An IV was plugged into his arm. He was in a hospital.

He lay there, breathing, thinking for countless minutes, exhausted and unaware. Time was difficult to track in Zane's bruised consciousness.

The first words out of his mouth were, "Oh shit, I'm back on Earth."

He recalled being on that airborne ship with Rainn and Esmeralda. He recalled PMSing with his dad, seeing his phantom mom, living in Enchanted Wood, in purgatory, and meeting Professor Edge. His entire Enchanted Wood experience remained etched, with clarity in his memory.

Sometime later, a nurse entered and smiled. "Well, hello there. How are you doing, Zane?"

He said nothing. "Can

you hear me?" Zane

blinked.

"Okay, I'll take that as a yes." The nurse smiled.

She checked his pulse and blood pressure and disappeared down the hallway.

An hour later, his dad, Dayne Moss stepped into the room with a smile on his face. "Oh, Zane. It's so good to see you are up! How are you?"

"Fine," was all he could manage after several seconds of confusion. Zane wanted to say more, but he wasn't even sure where to begin. What about Rainn? What about his mom and her phantasmal departure from the ship? What about Enchanted Wood? He didn't know the answer to any of these questions, but he did know one thing with unbridled certainty: he wanted to get the hell out of Earth. He wanted to go back to Enchanted Wood.

Earth, he decided, at this foggy moment of existence, was a very messy planet. Messy and charred by human societies across the globe.

His dad stood at his bedside and explained that he, Zane, had been in a car collision and suffered a head injury called a traumatic brain injury or TBI. Comatose for a week. The driver of the other vehicle, according to police reports, crossed the center-divide of Highway One, a winding coasting highway, linking San Francisco to Pacifica to Monterey and down into Southern California. The two cars impacted head-on at fifty miles per hour in Pacifica.

Everything, including his life, according to his team of doctors, had come to a screeching halt.

Oh, how little *they* knew, Zane thought.

That afternoon, he and Rainn stared at each other for a moment. Zane slowly said. "You remember, don't you?" He wanted to say more, but he couldn't form the words due to his brain-injured mind.

She nodded yes, and whispered, "We must be careful what we talk about here. But yes, brother, I remember Enchanted Wood. The telepathic lifestyle. All of it. It is more real than Earth, but for now, I'm glad you are safe in this hospital. And I'm here with you."

"Can we…go?"

"Go where?"

"Doesn't feel right being here. I don't feel safe here. Earth's…. scary and wrong. Backwards."

Rainn glanced over her shoulder to make sure they were alone. "We must stay here, for now. You need to recover from your head injury. I just wasn't sure what sort of shape you'd be in. You know, with you just getting out of a coma."

"Everything's foggy. But I remember The Wood. The canopy. The elves. Trolls…hey, you're an elf, right? An elf from a past life. Don't you want to go back?" He looked at her pleadingly.

The door swung inward, and a male nurse stepped in. He was tall and offered a pleasant, cordial smile as he pushed a cart with lunch on a tray. "How's our trooper doing on this glorious morning. Hungry? Thirsty? It'd be great if you could try to eat something."

Zane nodded and absently reached for a carton of orange juice.

"Anything else I can get you?" the nurse asked.

"No. Thanks. I'm good."

"Your doctor will be in to check on you later today. Ring if you need anything." He pushed open the door and turned, the nurse studying him. "You sure there's nothing else you need?" The male nurse had Zane's attention. He seemed to grow another six inches in height as Zane read his name badge. It read, *Al Grimes, RN.*

The nurse turned, as if to leave, then returned into Zane's room, the door closed behind him. "Oh, one more thing. In case you've forgotten, you're a fugitive wanted for murder you are about to commit in the very near future. It's inevitable." He rushed up to the bed, moving like the wind, and leaned over, getting close to Zane's pillowed head. Rainn stepped back a pace as Al shot her a tectonic-shifting scowl, detaching her ability to help the situation with any of her remaining psychic energies.

"Get out!" the nurse shouted. "Now!"

Rainn stood there a second. The nurse wiggled his fingers at her. She turned, pushed open the door, and disappeared into the hallway.

"Good," said Al. "Now we've got some privacy, you twit! Now listen to me, you epileptic fool, I've already alerted the authorities in my Home dimension. You'll be tried as a felon, convicted, you murderer." He grinned as he left Zane's room, winked, and said, "I'll be seeing you Downstate. In Hell!"

Later that night, at 3:04 a.m., a knock came to the door. Zane, for the last hour, had been lying in bed, wide awake, as if he just drank a Red Bull and three shots of espresso. He stared wide-eyed at an all-too-familiar figure: Twane Moss.

Twane, dressed in moon-blue trousers and a bright yellow shirt with a smiling moon on it, nodded. "Well, I guess this is it. You've decided to stay here? Really, Zane? On Earth? What a waste of an opportunity."

Zane sat up in bed. Staring at his doppelganger. But there was something off-putting about Twane. A tension wove through the air, setting Zane's nerves into a tangled blur.

"I didn't think I'd see you again. Especially here," Zane said, "and I didn't plan on returning to Earth. It just happened." "Well, Earth's not high on my list of vacation planets," said Twane, "but let's get right down to it: you know why I'm here. And it's killing me."

Zane bit his lower lip, confused. "What're you talking about?"

"Really?" Twane went on to say. "That's all you've got? childish lip-biting curiosity? Is that why you stole my soul? You're a runaway, Zane. A future fugitive. I'm virtually useless since you took off on all of us. When you left Enchanted Wood, you stole a portion of my soul," Twane added angrily.

Zane just stared at him. Eventually, he asked, "What? I didn't steal your soul. I don't even know how to do that."

"You're an epi telepath, a witch with a magical disability. That makes for quite a dangerous combo, if used correctly. I've been keeping tabs on you since you entered Enchanted Wood. I even have a psychic print-out of some recent Akashic records—your records. Listing your illicit energy travels to Purgatory Heights. And about your looming murder? What the hell are you thinking?" Twane became transparent, a wafer-thin ghost. Zane could see right through him.

"I wasn't always a ghost, you know," Twane went on to say. "In fact, if you were really in tune, you'd be able to channel into your past life thread and see everything I've done for you."

Twane's tone grew louder, "but you know what? You're worthless! A piece of energetic slime, you shitbag! Enough is enough. I'm going to put a stop to all this. Even if it means ending your life thread and my own"

Zane pressed a button near the bed to alert hospital staff. But what could they do with a haunt in the room? The door swung open. It was, in fact, a nurse. The *wrong* nurse.

Al Grimes stepped in, dressed in nursing attire: scrubs and a light-blue smock with cartoon mice eating cheese. The door closed behind him.

"Oh, for the love of the canopy," said Zane in a hush. "What do *you* want?"

"Ah, I see you two are getting reacquainted, yes?" Doyle said in a chilly tone, walking right through Twane as if he were a sheet of fog. Twane's body stretched out, becoming a thinning trail of mist, and then blurred back to Twane.

Al ran a thumb across his dewy name tag and then wiped his moistened brow, having absorbed some of Twane's phantom energies. He smiled and pulled a gleaming 12-inch dagger with a twisted blade from his pocket.

He tossed the weapon from left hand to right. The dagger flickered in varying shades of electric blue and black-iron steel. He stepped up to Zane and raised the dagger. The cold blade glistened as Doyle plunged it at Zane's head; Zane moved suddenly and the blade pierced the mattress near his throat.

"Oops." Grimes chuckled. "I missed. Sorry 'bout that."

The dagger's finely carved handle and the blade itself became transparent.

"Oh, would you look at that?" Al tsked. "Wrong weapon. This is a phantom dagger. Great for killing ghosts, but not much use for you in your three-dimensional body." He leaned closer to Zane, inches from his face. "Did you miss me?"

The phantom dagger shifted back and forth, embedded in the mattress.

Zane winced at Al's dragon breath, reached for the dagger, and pulled it out of the mattress. The hilt felt cold in his grip, weightless, yet with substance; its elemental hardness made his arm vibrate.

Grimes leaned back, a crooked smile on his face. He then, ever so slowly, placed his cold, lifeless hands around Zane's throat, and began strangling him. Zane stabbed at Doyle twice, missing him. Then Twane jumped in between them.

Zane swiped aimlessly again, missing Al a third time, and swiped the blade at Al wildly again and again. Doyle dodged each flailed attempt.

The blade then plunged deep into Twane's neck. Twane gasped and clutched at the impaled blade. Silvery-blue fluid trickled down Twane's neck.

He tumbled to the ground, moaning, and disappeared.

"You murderer!" spat Doyle. He winked at Zane after getting off the bed. "Now you've gone and done it. You killed him. You killed a ghost."

The door swung open. Zane, sweating and panting, stared at two nurses. One flicked on the light. They saw the room holding Zane, and Zane alone.

"Are you okay?" the nurse asked.

Zane looked to the floor. Twane was gone. Grimes was gone.

"I think so," he said. "Must've had a nightmare or something."

Three weeks later, Zane, having transitioned out of the hospital, was now at the Neurocare rehabilitation facility, a center for individuals suffering traumatic brain injuries. He was not enjoying his stay at the treatment center. He wanted to get out of here. Go home. Being trapped at this facility was dismal enough, but even worse was the fact that he was trapped on Earth.

Rainn took an Uber to the Embarcadero BART station in San

Francisco, en route to visiting Zane at Neurocare in Walnut Creek. She sat with him in his room. "How you doing?"

"Okay, but this place is a drag. I know I'm not a hundred percent, but I miss Enchanted Wood. Can't stop thinking about it. It's crazy how much I miss the forest!"

"Me, too." She grinned. "I've got some good news."

"Good news?"

"Yep. Just got a PMS from my elfin mom."

"Oh. How's Belle?"

Rainn asked, "You want to make a run for it?"

"A run for…what?"

"Back to Enchanted Wood. We can go." She smiled. "In fact, we're needed there."

Zane thought about this for all of three seconds, glancing out the window at a garbage truck rumbling by.

"When? How?"

"Today. As in now."

Zane wasn't sure whether to believe her. "C'mon, Rainn, don't mess with me. How're we going to get there? I'm still a bit out of it. I'm back in my Earth body, and with it comes my Earth brain, a closed-head injury. But I'm fine. I'm good," he lied.

She gave him a hug. "I understand. But if we go back, Belle and Edge can heal your injuries way faster than anything here on Earth. This planet is eons behind the times. You know it. I know it. And we'll learn to heal others. In the canopy."

Zane leaned back thoughtfully. "Sounds great, but, well…" Zane went on to tell Rainn about his encounter with Doyle and Twane in his hospital bed.

Instead of showing concern, Rainn offered a consoling smile. "All the more reason to return to Enchanted Wood. We need to be with our People."

Zane stared off. A whimsical smile on his face, liking what he was hearing.

"Got another surprise for you," said Rainn, pointing to the window.

Outside, pulling to a stop at the curb, was a shiny red Studebaker with a very hairy driver sitting behind the wheel, cigar in his mouth.

The cab's back door swung open and their dad, Dayne, stepped out followed by their mom dressed in moon-colored silk. Both of their parents waved to them, smiling with a glimmer of excitement on their faces.

"Mom!" Rainn shouted from the window. She tugged at Zane's arm and they raced outside.

"Oh, I missed you, Mom!" Rainn exclaimed. "I thought something terrible happened. Worried you were…a ghost. Are you—are you alive?"

Rose opened her arms readying to embrace her children, and said, "Oh, your father and I have so much to share with you."

~~END~~